Chaos in the Caravan

(Book II of The Osten Chronicles)

Author: Daniel Thorman

ISBN: 978-1-963913-30-9

Imprint: Native Publishers, The

The Osten Chronicles

Dedicated to:

The Curfiss Family

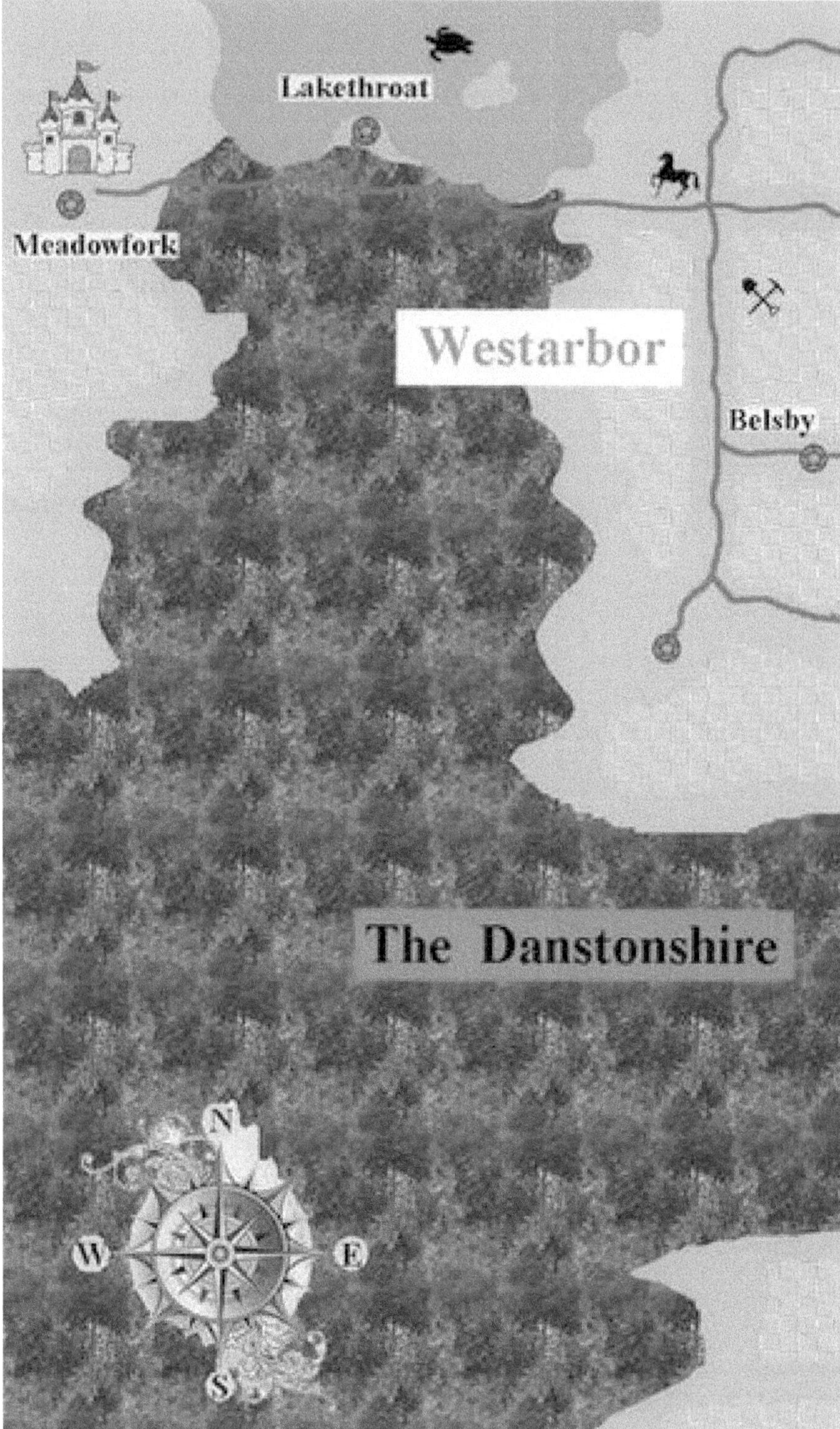

Meadowfork
Lakethroat
Westarbor
Belsby
The Danstonshire
N
W
E
S

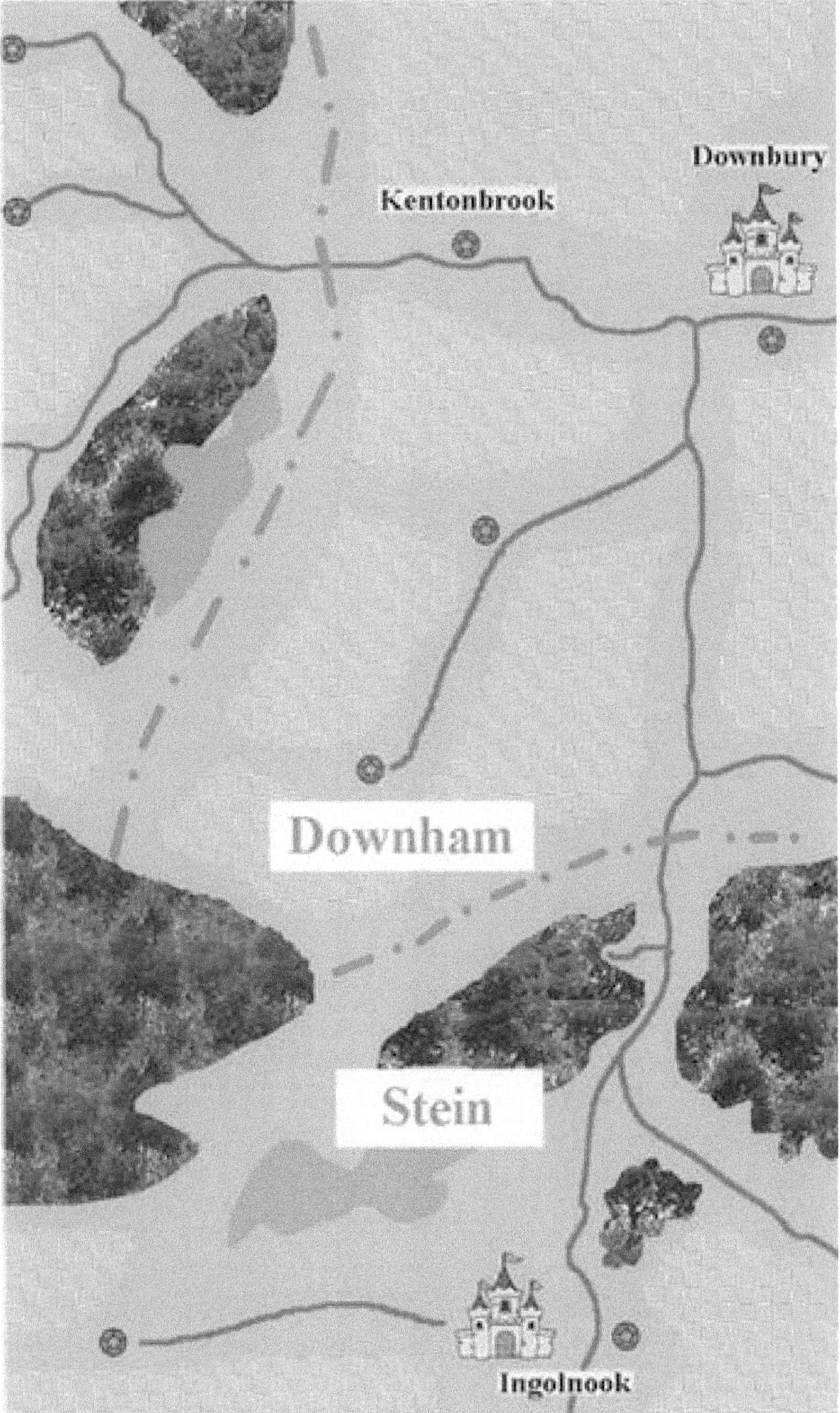

Downbury
Kentonbrook
Downham
Stein
Ingolnook

PART I

A Caravan's Tail

(All That Glitters)

CHAPTER ONE

The Fool

"The noblest art is that of making others happy."

~ P.T. Barnum ~

"You down there!" came a familiar voice from high up above.

As I straightened to cast a glance upward, I nearly lost my footing on the slick mud of the slope. From atop the curtain wall and leaning out between its crenels stood the knight.

"Remember, it's to be green side up," he began to lecture with a palms-up gesture.

Was that a joke? Could it be he'd finally forgiven my earlier transgressions? I wanted to laugh and make some snarky reply, but as we were in the public eye, I doubted such a response would be fitting.

"I shall try to remember it, Sir Trenton," I said instead, assuming a suitably humbled mien.

The outer ward still bore scars from the battle with the goblins. Indeed, the entire surrounding town of Meadowfork had suffered much abuse from the cretinous little invaders just four short months ago. All in our community had to pitch in to set things back to right before the full onset of winter. The rough

1

ditch before the keeps walls had been drained, and men were even now applying clay and smoothing its sides to form it into a proper moat.

My cousin had been called upon to do some heavy lifting over by the mill. Lacking his abundant magical strength, it was deemed that my gifts would be better employed assisting our keep's gardener in laying out sod. Zak had gathered it into great rolls from farmer Green's pasture and was even now lining them up and rolling them out on the slim stretch of ground that separated the moat from the outer walls. I, meanwhile, had been assigned to utilize my magic to cause the newly laid grass to stitch together with the adjacent strips and to establish firmer roots in the muddy ground which lay beneath. It was a task for which I was uniquely well suited. 'Green side up,' indeed.

I bent back to my task with a lightened heart and continued to encourage the little shoots to send out their rootlets. As it was late autumn, it was a bit beyond the ideal time to transplant sod. But nurtured by my gift, the new growth should thrive and form a befitting greensward of which the baron could be rightly proud. Although it was true that working with plants taxed me far less than it would another mage, I was nonetheless beginning to tire. I had been at this all morning, and my inner garden was showing signs of its displeasure, growing lackluster and slow to respond. Still, the baron was determined to show the keep in its best light to our special visitors tomorrow. So I wasn't too keen on letting up. The newly installed drawbridge was almost ready to be tested, and we men of Meadowfork all scurried about to complete the cosmetic work prior to day's end.

When once again I was considering taking a break, a harker mounted the battlement and drew all eyes upward by striking the bell atop the keep's gatehouse. As the ringing subsided, the man drew in a deep breath and proclaimed:

"His lordship would have it be known that time for the final test is nigh. All are to gather your things and clear the area. Stand well back, and you may observe Westarbor's latest wonder!"

We all hurried to comply. After crossing its dry bed, Zak and I scrambled up the moat's sloping far side to find purchase upon the freshly laid cobblestones beyond. We then hustled across the outer courtyard and up to the mill's tail race where my father and Javier Lewis stood beside their contrivance. The two had installed a secondary sluice gate with which to regulate the flow of water into the keep's moat.

The men were in deep discussion so I decided to forego the greeting and merely stood nearby. I saw Royland approaching from the direction of the mill where he had been assisting with clearing the last of the rubble. We waited as the baron himself strode forth along with several of his knights to stand imposingly on the battlement above the gates.

"Are you ready, Master Harper?" the baron called down.

"Yes, your lordship. Master Lewis and I are prepared for your order," returned my father.

The harker struck the bell once more, and my father began turning open the sluice gates. Water from the race began to trickle then to pour more vigorously into the erstwhile dry channel which conducted it smoothly down to the slowly filling moat. It was almost anticlimactic when one recalled the cascading torrent which had originally filled the jagged trench Master Chadwick had so violently wrought during the last battle here. The gathered townsfolk, nonetheless, cheered and politely applauded.

It was then that a trio of harkers atop the east tower hoisted great trumpets skyward and blew out a harmonic set of notes. As their dulcet tones resounded about the keep and began to trail off, the jangling of heavy chains could be heard as the great drawbridge embarked upon its maiden descent. The sturdy oaken planks bound with iron bands slowly separated from the stone walls of the newly extended gatehouse. They descended at a measured pace, at last coming to rest on the pavers of the main thoroughfare with a hollow, reverberating rumble.

It was a sight which we would eventually come to see as commonplace. Today, however, it sparked a sense of pride within all who had taken part in the project. Furthermore, those in attendance could well appreciate the added protection, having recently been forced to seek safety behind these very walls. The clamorous cheering dwarfed the prior acclamation and rose to echo merrily above the keep and across the hills of Meadowfork beyond.

***

After some further afternoon exertions, the keep was finally deemed fit enough. Though salty sweat streaked my hair and stained my garments, I had at least escaped most of the mud that now caked my confederates. Some were quite put out over it, questioning the diligence of my labors with laughing hints that I must be a shirker. The castle's staff had assembled a cleansing station by the well in the inner ward. We all lined up to be repeatedly doused by buckets of water as we roughly sloughed off the filth before trudging home for a more thorough scrub.

Royland and I were once again being hosted by the baron in the lavish mage's quarters in the keep's rear wing. This was chiefly due to the mill's partial collapse when the witch had worked her wicked spell. All the beds in the mill's remaining livable space were taken up by my father, Uncle Robert, Aunt Winnie, and Gregor, who had returned and was now properly my father's apprentice.

Nonetheless, it was toward the mill that my cousin and I now trod. My toes squished together uncomfortably within my soggy boots. I had been trying not to think on it for several weeks now, but we would soon be leaving this place. Having been found to possess the gift of magic and upon completion of our apprenticeships, the king's law commanded that we promptly place ourselves at the service of the mage's guild. Master Chadwick had declared us journeyman aspirants over two months ago now, and yet we had found reasons to linger. With the imminent arrival of the caravan tomorrow, the last of these justifications was removed, and his majesty's mandate could no longer be safely ignored.

I considered my cousin as we ambled up the hill. He was a walking contradiction. Though at nearly six feet he towered well above my more modest height, I doubt that he weighed over six stone sopping wet (which, at present, he most definitely was). Though work at the ranch had begun to fill him out somewhat, and his old slouch had given way to a more erect posture of

4

late, he still fell well short of what one would consider a heroic frame. As if sensing my thoughts (which, for him, was entirely possible) Roy glanced over at me with a sly smile.

"There'll be a surprise guest for dinner, Lucas," he said with an enigmatic air.

Today's efforts must have truly worn him out, for Royland rarely spoke much. The constant droning of my cousin's gift ordinarily rendered him all but mute. This forced him to focus his amazing mind inward until he had expended a considerable amount of magic and the buzzing receded.

Departing the main thoroughfare just past the mill's wreckage, we slogged toward the barn to change into dry outfits and make ourselves more presentable. Upon entering, some of the secrecy promptly fell from Royland's mysterious announcement. Munching on a mouthful of fresh hay, Mr. Strongback stood in the first stall. He bawled his bovine greeting as I walked over to scratch his forehead between his wide-set eyes, a grin of pleasure tugging at my cheeks. Had my master come to see us off? Royland shook his head, his own grin broadening.

At the still functioning back door to the mill, we were greeted by Gregor Cain. He bowed his head and squinted downward for a moment then looked back up with a lob-sided smile saying, "You may enter - seeing as there's no mud on your boots. We'd get a proper scolding were it otherwise. There're two old gray mares running the place presently."

He clapped me on the shoulder and considered doing the same as Royland stepped in. Reconsidering, he hastily amended the gesture to a simple wave.

"Hey Roy," Gregor said. "It was plumb amazing watching you heft those stones out of the race with your mind."

My cousin smiled and nodded at Gregor in pleasant greeting. We just might make a respectable socialite of him yet. Gregor then conducted us back to the kitchen's small dining area from which appetizing aromas drifted to awaken the empty pit that served me as a stomach.

Our fathers were there and already seated at the table with Aunt Winnie fussing over them. Seated beside them was Tilda, proudly regaling them with a list of ingredients for some dish she favored. She turned at our approach.

"*There* you two are," she happily exclaimed. "*Now* we can begin."

I greeted her with a hug. Royland came around to stare her in the eye - as close to a hug as he ever bestowed.

"Hello, Tilda," he said. "How's our master?"

Tilda shrugged and launched into a full report.

"Elizar sends his regrets about missing your send-off," she began with a cautious air and then continued on in a conspiratorial tone. "He's been rather moody of late. He refuses to use his cane and only *picks* at his dinner. I swear - the old goat wouldn't fare *half* as well without someone as patient as I to look after him. He hides his limp rather well, but I've noticed him using his shepherd's crook more than he was usually wont to do. He and that shaggy *mutt* of his prowl about the meadows at all hours until even the *sheep* have become annoyed at their presence..."

While she nattered on about my master's infirmities and predilections, I felt a sharp stab of guilt. I was still haunted by memories of the witch. Although I had been forgiven for the pain we had inflicted, and the horror had faded somewhat, recalling what we had done and especially how it had made me feel still caused me to cringe. How could a person be so uncaring of the well-being of others? Grandma Abbey had, in fact, delighted in everyone's suffering, and I had been made to fully share in this revolting revelry. The harm I had caused while under her control still gnawed at my very heart. Not the least of this harm had been striking down my old master up on that battlement.

Keeping busy helped. So I had thrown myself into my studies and any task that came my way with zeal. Uncle Robert said I shouldn't 'stew on it' and that I was 'being maudlin.' Just give it some time and look at it again from a distance, he had advised.

It was worse late at night.

As Tilda seemed to be winding down, I struggled to regain the thread of the conversation. Aunt Winnie was setting a small roast before my father who was preparing to carve it up. Uncle Robert was having a quiet word with Gregor while Royland had seated himself and was staring distractedly at a fly batting against the window. The fly suddenly ceased its futile flapping and arrowed straight up to and out of a gap in the thatched roof above. Although this back part of the mill had escaped much of the damage caused by its collapse, it was not entirely unscathed. Another sin to mar my sullied soul.

Tilda was looking at me expectantly.

"... I said, is there anything you need for your journey, Lucas?" she repeated. "If so, I can keep a watchful eye out at the faire tomorrow. I'm staying with Karina at the bakery, but your father was kind enough to let me rest my cart in his barn much nearer to the event. That way, it'll be no trouble at all to gather all my purchases..."

The journey. Though I'd been trying not to think about it, it struck home once again just how soon I'd be leaving this place and all of its familiar and soothing associations. A sense of excitement and adventure once again failed to arouse my spirits and instead evoked only feelings of ennui tinged with a dollop of dread. I'd heard of homesickness, but I hadn't known that one could experience it prior to actually leaving a place.

Dinner proceeded apace as all settled in for a cordial meal and comforting conversation. My bleak mood slowly dissolved as we shared tales of past triumphs and our plans for the upcoming days. I determined to enjoy this remaining time with my family and friends under the imperfect roof of my carefree youth.

***

I sat up in my bed.

I knew not what had awoken me. Through the cottage's thin walls, I heard only the howl of winter gusting through the treetops. Then I heard them. Booted footfalls upon the groaning planks of the front stoop. A low muttering arose from beyond my door as a sharp pounding shook its frame accompanied by the clatter and rasp of metal striking metal.

"Open up," commanded a voice from just behind the door.

I quailed. No one of good intent would disturb a poor girl at this late an hour. My heartbeat quickened and worry furrowed my brow as my awakening mind strove to make sense of the situation. I hoped for a less than sinister reason for the intrusion. Mayhap, someone was injured or otherwise in dire need and merely seeking shelter from the night's chill? Arising and pulling my nightgown close about me, I sought to respond, but my throat was constricted, locked in the throes of dread.

"Break it down!" shouted a gruff voice a moment later.

My straining eyes attempted to pierce the gloom of the unlit room, seeking some weapon with which to defend myself. I took a stumbling step toward the small hearth that yet shed some scant glow from its dying embers. I reached for the cast-iron poker.

Suddenly, and with a great splintering crunch, the door gave way. At once, I was wrapped in the frigid, night air which burst in from outside along with a group of angry men in heavy mail. I backed toward the far wall whilst brandishing the poker before me like a talisman.

"Careful men," said one near the back. "Restrain her quickly lest she cast some dire charm upon us!"

"Please, sir," said I, my protesting voice atremble, "what would you have of me?"

"Be still *witch*. And make no sound or we shall have out your tongue," said he with spittle ejecting from his down-turned mouth.

In a trice, I was surrounded, disarmed, and struck soundly across my face by the back of a mailed gauntlet. I tasted blood. The sharp pain receded only to be replaced by a swelling ache on the entire right side of my face which extended all the way down to my teeth. I felt their rough hands upon me, and hot tears streaked my cheeks as a foul rag was pressed firmly into my mouth and bound therein.

I struggled helplessly. After being hooded and having my arms tied behind me by stout, hempen ropes, I was hauled none too gently out into the cold. The wind pierced my thin garment, and I felt a groping hand upon my buttocks as one man laughingly remarked: "She'll fetch a fine fee; I'll wager."

Soon I was bouncing along in the hard, flat bed of an open wagon attended by my pitiless captors. As I shivered there, I tried to minimize the battering of my head into the boards upon encountering each rut in the road.

They had finally caught me out. It was the boy. Surely, it was he who had betrayed me. Who else? No one knew of my secret but he. And he was like me. Had I not explained to him the dangers should others find us out? A cold pit of anger began seething in my stomach, and my eyes narrowed beneath my hood. Trust in any man, I thought, and it will earn you naught but a broken heart!

. . . *A broken heart . . . The ground shifted and quaked beneath our feet. I felt a shattering of my consciousness and a sharp, stabbing pain in the center of my chest, A blackness descended on my soul. Had I failed? . . .*

I sat up in my bed.

My sweat-drenched sheets had somehow gotten tangled about my legs, and I felt my heart beating against my aching chest as I struggled to free them. The chamber maids doubtless believed me a bed wetter by now as this had not been my first such episode. I fervently hoped it might prove to be my last. But as Uncle Robert would say: 'If wishes were fishes, we would all have full bellies.'

As I slowly got my breathing under control, I lifted unsteady legs over the edge of my mattress to alight upon the luxuriant rug of the mages' quarters. I had no idea of the hour. I only knew that I was still tired right down to my bones. I invoked 'manent vigilate,' my shepherd's spell of wakefulness. This magic often proved useful, but in recent days I had found it a poor substitute for a restful night's sleep.

My straining eyes attempted to pierce the gloom of the unlit room. Upon emerging into the common room of our suite, I took a stumbling step toward the small hearth that yet shed some scant glow from its dying embers. I reached for the cast iron poker, remnants of the nightmare echoing through my mind.

Laying on a fresh log from our meager supply and prodding the fire into a livelier state, I considered my troubled dreams. They were always about Abigale. Unlike my more ordinary nocturnal visions, these didn't soon fade after awakening. Instead, they remained crisp and clear with each sight, sound, smell and thought coincident with vivid emotions. I had written Master Chadwick about them. His shrewdest guess was this was some lingering effect from my mind having been joined with hers at the moment of her traumatic, final death. In shattering the witch's heart, had I been infused with the wretched remnants of her life story?

Keeping busy helped.

I padded over to the shelf and retrieved several fresh candles. I suddenly realized that it was quiet. Shouldn't there be snoring from my cousin's adjoining bed chamber? Perhaps my night terrors had disturbed his slumber in a curious reversal of the normal order of our evenings. I nestled a candle into its holder and lit it from the fire in our hearth.

This brought Sebastian back to mind. The old chandler had been disconsolate when 'his lady' had been exorcised from me. For three days following the Day of Remembrance, he refused to leave the grave where her bones had been put to rest. He muttered incessantly to her marker and would accept no meals. Taking pity, the baron had ordered he be sent to Tomlinton Abbey on the Tillman fief. There he would live out the remainder of his days in the care of its monks and abbot. To lure him from the graveside and at Megan's suggestion, I spoke harshly to him in the manner of the witch and handed him the golden chain from which the witch's heart had hung. After further belittling the man, I commanded he guard it. Though deceitful, we thought it a mercy to give the old lunatic a renewed sense of purpose. The keep had a new chandler now.

I knew better than to return to my bed. I hung our small kettle over the fire to heat some water. Agatha Grimbley had given me a jar of tea leaves which she claimed contained a mild soporific said to soothe one to sleep. I hadn't found it very effective, but it gave me something to do.

Over dinner with my family, I had received several parting

gifts. My father had presented me with the sword he had carried in the Battle of Arborvale during the First Goblin Wars. I didn't properly know how to handle a sword. I imagined the pointy end went into one's opponent. Father had pointed out that merely wearing one would garner respect in certain quarters, but that I should most certainly seek some basic instruction. Tilda had given both Roy and I sewing kits, claiming that if we were to be traveling, we must soon learn to look after our own garments. I laughed when Gregor revealed his gift - an old tin cowbell. 'You just never know when one might come in useful,' he had cheerfully chortled. I resolved to better situate these items.

I had finally taken stock of the sturdy backpack I had received from the Cains. It contained a rather eclectic assortment of items and had proven its worth repeatedly during the siege and in the intervening months since. The Cains called it a 'bugger out bag' and always kept one near to hand. Therefore, I had christened mine 'Bob' and did likewise.

When confronted by a strange situation, I needed only to root through Bob's contents to strike upon an idea. I had personalized my Bob by the addition of several items like the small tools I used for gardening. But I was mindful not to displace too many of Bob's standard offerings. I still had no idea why I might need a small roll of cheesecloth, but I remained well assured that one day it would come in handy. Though 'planning for the unexpected' seemed to run counter to logic, I was beginning to grasp how it might be accomplished. At least I knew I had a reliable partner in this endeavor in Bob.

The sword wouldn't fit within Bob, but I noted my Bob already had a whetting stone and several other dojiggers with which to care for and sharpen such implements. I spent the next hour reviewing and shifting Bob's contents until I was convinced I could readily retrieve whatever was needful. I half-dozed there before the fire as the candles burned low and Royland's raucous rumblings recommenced.

As I worked, I notice something else that was passing strange. I began to feel a presence deep below the ground. It seemed somewhat akin to my inner garden from which I worked my magic yet different somehow. It was a writhing river of twisting angry energy just at the corner of my inner vision. When I sought it directly with my mind's eye, it withdrew. Perhaps it was my tired mind playing tricks, but it seemed just like the ley line that the witch had used for her devilment. But that made no sense. Apart from when I was in the witch's thrall, I had never felt it before.

The morning found me stiff and muzzy headed when the watchmen rang the bell at dawn. My teacup lay toppled on its side. With the use of my wakefulness spell, I became marginally more human once again. I dressed and headed for the dining hall to break my fast. It was the day for which we had prepared. Roy and I would finally meet those who would be our traveling companions over the next several months.

***

It was mid-afternoon when I headed out from the keep. Word had come yesterday evening that the caravan was pulling up stakes at the Powell fief about a day's journey east. Not an hour ago, the harkers had announced its imminent arrival at Meadowfork, so the townsfolk were all turned out and eager for the first glimpse of the newcomers.

Although Westarbor had played host to caravans in prior times, there had been a strange dearth of such over the last twelvemonth. Sitting at the kingdom's most westerly expanse, Westarbor shared a border with but one other barony through which all such traffic must flow. It was our misfortune that it was Downham Barony. Some suspected that for some inexplicable reason Lord Downham, had had a hand in sundering the trade that was our lifeblood.

Our liege was therefore most pleased to welcome the 'Trans-Osten Mule Caravan And Trade Spectacular' to his gates. The 'Tomcats' was one of the largest and most prestigious troupes to regularly ply the king's highways. Our worthy baron had likely called in many favors for our inclusion in their route. A feast was planned for after the ceremony of welcoming. And as I was now the Lady Megan's protector, it would be my first time seated at the high table. At present, however, I sought a less prominent perch from which to observe the upcoming festivities.

My decision was made final when the drawbridge was ratcheted closed making the keep inaccessible to any who didn't fancy an afternoon swim. Guardsmen were clearing the outer courtyard. I hustled up the main thoroughfare while searching through the faces in the crowd.

My attention was soon drawn to the rubble about the mill. In clearing the debris, Royland had shown the foresight to stack it in tidy rows which rose ever higher towards the back. The good people of Meadowfork were pleased to discover my cousin's makeshift benches formed a well-nigh ideal grandstand from which to oversee the event. I wish I knew how he so constantly conceived such clever ideas. After all, he had been instructed to *clear* the rubble, not to construct his own amphitheater. And yet there it stood.

Having doubtless arrived a bit early, Kevin and Evan, two journeyman bakers of my close acquaintance, had claimed premier seats up toward the front. It was almost a set of stone thrones upon which they sat. They beckoned me over toward a third such that they were jealously guarding between them. But then I saw Zak. The strapping man was sitting alone at the remote end of a bench about midway up. In both his appearance and his caustic manner, the gardener was a bit off-putting to others. Once one got to know him, however, it became clear that he was a gentle soul who was only being rightly (if a bit preemptively) defensive over the mockery he had often endured. I waved and smiled at the twins, shook my head in negation, and proceeded up to Zak's more outlying roost.

Zak chuckled at my ungainly climb up the ramshackle pile of stones and pointed over toward the greensward we had laid beyond the moat.

"G-g-good job, Lucas. It's all g-g-green side up."

He raised his other hand palm upward and chortled once again. Evidently, Zak approved of Trenton's defamation of my intellect - that or he just thought it a good jest.

"Yep, and brown side down, my friend," said I, slapping Zak's upturned palm with my own.

The surrounding townsfolk seemed bewildered by the strange greeting, but their attentions soon returned to their former pursuits. As I sat beside Zak and asked about his next project, his lazy eye stared straight at me. I could tell his attention was elsewhere, however, because his right eye began tracking something else. Turning around, I spied Mollie Green below peering purposefully about.

"Up here, Mollie!" I shouted, flailing my arms.

No sooner had the girl completed the treacherous ascent when we began hearing faint music in the distance. I moved over so that Mollie could take her seat between Zak and me. With a grin, I noted that she sat fractionally closer to my large friend and subtly leaned in that direction. I saw in her sweet smile a likely end to my friend's isolation. As the music swelled, people craned their necks to glimpse the source, and then a few stood up. I hated that. Soon all were forced to stand as well lest our view be obstructed by the person before us. We could all be sitting in perfect comfort were it not for the greedy actions of a few. Ah, well.

My grudge against the greedy dissolved the moment the first wagons came into view. They were hauled by teams of mules. These were like our knight's horses if somewhat smaller, but their ears stuck up almost like those of a rabbit. Although most bore a blackish color on their forequarters, their hindquarters were stark white and covered in spots. I was to learn later that such mules were the byproduct of breeding a stallion of a similar coloration to a female donkey. Their glossy coats shone in the late afternoon sun, and each had bright ribbons woven into their manes leading up to a great plume that protruded up from the forelock. Their hooves clattered on the cobbles seeming to keep time with the music.

Stranger still were the occupants of the wagons. In the lead position was a colorful wagon with a heavyset, mustachioed man standing in its bed waving at the crowd. He sported a wide, floppy hat. This was followed by a wagon where a trio of musicians sat effecting their strident melody. There were some jugglers walking alongside while keeping colorful clubs aloft in cascading arcs. These jugglers and jongleurs were followed by several dozen heavily laden merchant wagons bearing the exotic wares for which we hungered. It was a rousing display as the wagons circled about the outer courtyard in seemingly effortless yet meticulous arcs. Some swirled inward and the whole came to rest at last in a double row that circumscribed the square leaving open a wide lane down its center.

As the wagons stilled, the harkers up on the battlement again blew out their triumphant fanfare and the drawbridge began to descend. Large garlands which had heretofore rested atop each merlon were flipped down to hang facing outward. Into them was woven an array of bright blooms each to form a letter. They spelled out 'WELCOME TOMCATS;' (this was Megan's contribution). Again the harkers hoisted up their horns and a second blast heralded a new commotion. As the drawbridge at last touched down flat and even, the baron and his six knights in residence paraded forth upon their steeds. These were followed by their squires.

The gentry of Westarbor keep was a splendid sight to behold all bedecked in their armor and finery and with their heraldry on full display. It gave my heart a jolt and for the moment banished all my worries and weariness. I was now quite glad to be up on my feet. The picture lacked only Sir Declan's presence. For upon Trenton's promotion, the man had promptly retired to take up a fiefdom in Arborvale, and the seven had become six once more. The new fief was to include the Fowler, Turner, and Tillerson ranches, and men were already lining up to request farming tenancies and household positions.

The knights kept a tight and disciplined formation. When their procession achieved the courtyard's center, the mounted baron confronted the heavyset man who I would later learn was Cameron Ross, the caravan's master. My liege made a brief utterance which I couldn't quite discern but felt certain was some kind of ceremonial greeting. In response, Master Ross elegantly doffed his broad hat and made a deep bow made only slightly awkward by the man's fulsome girth. I could tell the man was unaccustomed to a posture of subservience.

The baron then turned to address all and in a ringing voice proclaimed: "Let the faire commence!"

At this, dozens of white doves were released from atop the east tower. These were joined by a gaggle more emerging from the dovecote's holes to take chipper wing above brimming wagons and noble knights alike. A great cheer arose from the gathered crowd to spur them on their way. I think even the merry members of the trans-Osten troupe may have learnt a lesson in showmanship from our good liege's welcome.

***

The crowd began to disperse (or at least to separate). The wagons and their tempting wares were now fair game, and many of the onlookers rushed forth to secure the first glimpse of the wonders they might contain. Shrewder heads were making their way back to their houses to rest and return better prepared. It would take some time for the merchants to get properly set up, and many of the people of Meadowfork needed to retrieve their own wares with which to trade.

To be sure, there was at present no lack of coin among the common folk due to the baron's recent renovations. Much to his chancellor's dismay, our good liege had been generous in paying his laborers promptly for their work on the new drawbridge and moat. As a result, his people could afford to splurge on a few rare items of comfort. The benefits thus derived were two-fold: the traders were more apt to return, and the baron himself would enjoy the people's goodwill. Therefore, I suspected this was an intentional move on his lordship's part.

I picked my way down my cousins ramshackle but sturdy pile of rubble. Shouldering my way through the throng that milled about its base, I made for the keep along with the many others eagerly pressing their way forward into its courtyard. As I ambled along, I watched the merchants of the caravan locking their wheels in place with loose stones and unharnessing their strange beasts to be led away toward our stables. Men were untying and peeling back the dingy, gray canvas tarps from atop the wagons' beds. These were flipped to hang over the wheels and skirt each cart nearly to the level of the ground. The exposed underside of each tarpaulin had been painted gaily in vibrant colors with symbols and icons depicting the wares to be had. Skirted thus, the wagons were readily transformed into merchant stalls, and their tempting treasures were revealed.

The newcomers stood in stark contrast to our more plainly dressed people who shuffled forth to mix among them. Not only were the 'Tomcats' more gaily clad but also they lacked the amazed look of wonderment that adorned my people's faces. Many stopped to gawk at various sights, and the crowd thinned around me as I strode purposefully on toward my destination. I slowed only as I neared the drawbridge that now lay open before the keep's gatehouse. To either side of it stood the jugglers.

They bracketed the bridge and kept a steady stream of clubs flashing in a high arc above it. Both were slender of build like Royland. But whereas my cousin could be rightly described as 'gangly,' these two were more 'lithe' or 'lissome.' I think the difference was the graceful economy of their movements; their athleticism was artful. I considered passing between them underneath their archway of brightly whirling batons when I noticed that the one on my right was a young woman.

"*Benalavioshi, rothuchi ioshi!*" she cried as she tossed all of her clubs at once to her confederate and stepped toward me.

With casual precision, the young man deftly handled this sudden barrage. He plucked each oncoming club from the air to stack neatly at his feet and then approached me as well.

"You are one of the mages going to Conclave. Are you not?" she said, sidling up to stand uncomfortably near. Her long saffron tresses had so much curl that they actually bounced upon her advance.

"Yes. I am Lucas Harper," I replied.

"You do me honor with the gift of your name," said she. "You may call me Tulip, and this is my brother, Benalav. We hail from Lorédon."

Her speech was strangely accented and her melodious voice had a lilting rhythm that fell pleasingly on my ear. The bright colors of her immodest attire and that of her brother were well suited to entertainers. The skin-tight outfits probably afforded them the freedom of motion required to ply their craft. It was, however, a bit overstimulating up close.

"Are you elves, then?" I asked.

"We are indeed of the first people," she said, flashing a bright smile. "but we take no offense at your quaint term for our folk.

I had read of the elves, but I had never before seen one. Examining her face, I noted her high cheekbones and almond-shaped eyes. She had thick, pouty lips resting atop a narrow chin. My eyes began to travel downward to her figure as young men's eyes were wont to do.

"Go ahead and have a good look, then," she suddenly said.

She struck a brazen posture, turned her head to one side, and brushed back the long golden locks which draped well past her shoulders.

"You humans always seem so fascinated with our ears upon first meeting one of us."

Her...ears?

This snapped my attention back up to where it more properly belonged. Her ear was indeed strange, sweeping up to a delicate point the tip of which bent slightly outward. Behind her, her brother grinned at me knowingly.

"Ah ... your *ears* ... are lovely," said I with a sudden loss of eloquence. "You call yourselves the first people?"

"Yes," she replied, "or the *nuvapua watheesh* in my native tongue."

"Well, I'm most honored to meet you as well, but I mustn't tarry. I have an appointment with the baron to keep."

"Then by all means keep it. We will have much time to talk upon the open road, Lucas of Meadowfork."

And so it was that I was accosted by a pair of elves on my way to meet his lordship. That it made me a bit late mattered not a whit. For when I was announced and let into his council chamber, I found him deeply submerged in matters of state with Gerard Keaton, his chamberlain. I strode down the long aisle adorned with its heraldic shields and tapestries. The two briefly resurfaced to acknowledge my approach.

"Your lordship," I intoned, bowing low.

"Ah, Lucas," said the baron distractedly. "Have a seat and bide a bit. We shan't be but a moment."

I stepped up onto the raised platform and took my seat at the table while the two older men returned once more to their discourse.

"The treasury is tapped out, sire," said Gerard.

"You always say that, and yet we manage to find a way to meet expenses," returned the baron.

"This time I mean it," said the chancellor, running a hand through the thinning hair of his balding scalp. "The recent renovations are one thing, my lord, but I fear this latest payment to the merchants guild may have taken the last of the wind from our sails."

"One has to spend some to make some, my friend, as you well know. We need to reopen the trade routes. And how better than to hire the most prominent trade caravan in the land to showcase our barony's wares. Downham's devilry may have dealt us a severe blow this past season, but all is not lost. We have, withal, an overabundance of copper ingots stacking up at the mine. We shall be well recompensed upon their safe delivery to Eagleskeep."

"But I fear such a risk, sire. It disregards both of two inviolate accounting principles taught to me by my father. Firstly, don't count your chickens until they're hatched. And secondly, don't place all of your eggs in one basket."

"Your father was a poultry farmer, Gerard, not a proper accountant. I refuse to 'chicken out' of this venture. No, we must proceed in it or else *become* the backwater barony that Downham intends. We shall meet again tomorrow eve to review the expenses in detail. Bring your ledgers, and we shall see precisely how much 'wind' yet remains to sail our ship of state. For tonight, we feast."

I was coming to realize it was our lieges vision that drove the barony's success. Although a fine administrator, Gerard lacked foresight. Though penny wise, he was pound poor. As the worthy chancellor trudged wearily toward the chamber's far end, Lord Westarbor turned to regard me where I sat.

"So, what did you make of the welcoming ceremony, Lucas? Was it favorably regarded?"

He was merely asking to be polite. The baron was a savvy man well attuned to the mood of his people. Moreover, both he and his daughter shared a wild magical talent that enabled them to suss out the emotions of others at a glance. I nonetheless gave him an answer.

"It was stunning, your lordship, a most magnificent spectacle. The fairgrounds are even now being established and the people are all eager for the events to follow."

"Good," he said as he reached to a stack of missives before him. From it, he retrieved two thick envelopes each bearing an elaborate, waxen seal. From the seals, I caught the glint of magic. I was not lacking for talents of my own.

"I'm sure you recognize the enchantments on these. Needless to say, they must not be opened until they are delivered into the hand for which they were intended. They are letters of introduction to the mage's academy at Conclave. Your former master drafted them, and they were only this morning delivered by Goody Fowler to my chamberlain. I shall entrust them to your care."

"Yes, your lordship," I said as I received the letters.

"As your sponsor to the academy, I must remind you that your actions and comportment reflect upon the barony. There haven't been any new mages from Westarbor in well over a decade. See to it that you and your cousin conduct yourselves with honor in service to the king and do nothing to tarnish our reputation.

"Yes, your lordship," I repeated.

"Very well, then. Carry on," he said. "I'll see you at the feast."

At this, the baron returned to his pile of missives and began to sort through them. As I arose to depart, it occurred to me that I scarcely ever saw his lordship at his leisure. The man was constantly engaged in activities to make life better for us all.

"...and your lordship?" I began with some hesitation.

The man looked up, and his blue eyes bore into mine.

"Thank you," I said.

The man beamed.

***

My father's sword hung uncomfortably from my waist. Derrick Lester had helped me to dress and belt it on. He had also instructed me in how to secure it in its scabbard with a leather lanyard. This 'peace knot' was a requirement at the feast. There would be a lot of drinking, and men's tempers were known to flare up at such events. Therefore, to enforce the baron's peace, such a knot was customary. Nor could one simply leave the sword behind as it was as much a symbol of status as it was a weapon. I didn't mind either way. It was not as if my poor skill with the blade would threaten anyone. The sword made it awkward to walk as well. Its weight dragged you to one side, and it had a tendency to bang into or catch upon low objects at the most inopportune of moments.

I stood in the receiving line exchanging pleasantries with the arriving guests while I awaited my own turn to enter the dining hall. Among the nobility in attendance, to which I was reluctantly considered arisen, even the order of arrival was a matter of importance. High station dictated others must await your pleasure. Because of this, the baron would arrive and be seated last. It seemed the reverse of what one would expect. Having gotten here early, shouldn't I even now be seated in comfort? But it was the exact opposite. As I was to escort Lady Megan, only the baron and his wife and son would come after.

The dining hall had been decorated all in a hunting theme. I hardly recognized the place when I had briefly glimpsed within. Evergreen boughs hung from every lintel with stag horns and the like protruding in between. I silently applauded the efforts of his lordship's servants for the admirable way they had 'spruced it up.' Trenton's stuffed gryphon had pride of place up at the left side of the high table. It stared outward across the hall to greet each newcomer with wicked delight. Evidently, the gryphon had been forgiven its recent role as the spy in our midst. It was too fine an exhibit to languish long in the exile of the trophy room.

Its enchantment had been purged, and it stood again among us as the proud symbol of accomplishment it was meant to be.

Indeed, all the hunting trophies had been liberated and now graced the walls surrounding our feast. Just inside and to either side of the entryway stood the runners up. To the left was an entire tree. Upon Its deadwood branches squatted the eerie forms of owls. These ranged from little screech owls and common barn owls all the way up to a great horned eagle owl with wings outspread. Its like was rarely seen in our lands. To the right was a huge brown forest bear. He was reared up with his paws before him, their claws fully extended. From his gaping mouth one could practically *hear* his ursine roar of challenge.

The clothing worn by our nobles was breathtaking. Shimmering silks, ermine collars and all manner of expensive and fine raiment were commonplace. I myself was garbed in a fashionable green tunic. It was my best outfit and had been presented to me by the good ladies of Arbordale on the occasion of my fifteenth birthday. Although made of wool it had a fine sheen and the embroidery upon it had earned me more than one envious glance.

The newcomers wore a diverse assortment of garments. Among the practical shirts, breeches and cloaks of the merchants was a riotous array of hues and patterns sported by the entertainers among them. The clashing colors put me in mind of Chief Ravenbald, the goblin who had sought to overrun us. Was it only this past summer?

One gaudily clad man approached who stood out even from among his fellows. His skin-tight leotard was of two hues: his right leg being the bright red of a carnation and his left a vivid yellow. This pattern was reversed on his doublet, the right being yellow and the left being red. It was then inverted once more upon his outlandish hat which arose in two curling points to end in silver bells. The jingling bells were matched by a set affixed to his outrageously upturned boots. His face bore the pasty white grease paint of a jester complete with a painted-on smile.

This jester was an enigma. Although he had a smile painted onto his face, underneath, he wore a somber expression. This caused one's eyes to flicker back and forth between the two when one attempted divining the man's true mood. The effect was most unsettling and many seemed wary of him as he moved down the receiving line exchanging pleasantries. He stepped closer to be greeted by Sir James Webb, one of our knights in residence. Sir James then turned to introduce his lady wife, Lady Eleanor Webb née Wood.

Before he could do so, the jester with an ostentatious bow proclaimed: "Wait a moment; let me guess. I can tell by your manner and the way you dress. You must be a lady of the knight."

Sir James at first looked astonished. Then his brow descended in ire. From the way his hand twitched, I suspected the jester might owe his continued good health only to the baron's peace.

"Blackguard! How dare you give affront to a woman so? Would you care to step outside and repeat that insult?"

The jester seemed taken aback, hastily saying: "Your pardon, good sir. I meant no offense. A poor fool am I, of no consequence."

And with a small shrug, he turned and jangled his way toward the dining hall.

Not long after the commotion had settled down, there arose another. It began when I spotted Miss Tulip and her brother approaching. As she was dressed in attire more appropriate to the occasion, I expected that her 'talents' were not to be on display here. I smiled and caught her eye as she passed by and into the hall.

Suddenly, there was a shriek, and I saw the maiden dive to one side. She came up in a crouch, her eyes wild. From somewhere on which I ought not to speculate, she had produced a long, slender knife that looked as deadly as her intent.

"*Najhema siqua!*" she cried waving the dagger before her menacingly.

Startled guardsmen soon began rushing forth to enforce the baron's peace, but Benalav leaped quickly forward to interpose himself.

"Please," he shouted above the rising buzz of confusion, "my sister means no harm. She was badly frightened as a child by three bears!"

As guardsmen circled about the pair, Sir Nolan swiftly stepped forth and into the fray.

"Stand down," he commanded.

Turning to the young Elven maiden, his voice took on a gentler tone.

"It's all right, miss. That bear's been dead a long time. 'Twas this very blade that did the deed back when the barony was young. I'd gladly share the tale over a tankard. Allow me to escort you and your brother to a table. I would hear more of your own encounter with such creatures."

At this, the gentle old knight offered his arm while the young woman bashfully looked about the hall with chagrin. Finally, she took it. As they walked off, Benelav launched into the story in his thickly accented speech.

"She en-coun-tered them when seeking shelter in a cave back in our homeland. It was only a mother and her cub at first. All was well until the papa bear arrived to find an unwelcome intruder in his den..."

"I am here, Lucas," said Megan, only just arrived. "You may commence making suitably impressed noises about my gown and hair style. Did I miss something?"

It was shaping up to be a very lively evening. I thanked the stars above for peace knots.

***

It was finally our time to enter the hall. I gladly made the required noises of praise for Megan's preparations. My lady's hair really *was* most impressive. Her raven tresses had been braided into an elaborate coiffure atop her head with animated ringlets to either side. I suspected Lynette's artful hand in creating such an effect. The gown was elegant and (of course) blue. Its sleeves began to broaden at the elbows until at her wrists they hung down well past her knees. I still hadn't become completely used to the nobles' fashions. It struck me that Megan could almost take flight were she only able to flap those arms with enough vigor.

"You are amused at my expense and I like it not one bit," she said folding her wings before her.

I had learned that it was of no use trying to hide my feelings from Megan. She always saw straight through any bluff or polite misdirection I attempted. She valued honesty, so I gave her the truth.

"I am still getting accustomed to courtly styles, my lady. I was imagining the difficulty of any number of tasks with sleeves that draped so deeply."

"You are forgiven then," she said, "for I too find them appalling. Just try to eat soup without dipping them in. Still, the daughter of the baron must dress to meet decorum. Speaking of which, it is time for our entrance."

So I offered my arm and we entered.

"Lady Megan, daughter of Westarbor," called out the stentorian voice of the harker, "escorted by Journeyman Aspirant Lucas Harper."

I ushered the lady up toward our seats. They were just to the left of those of her parents. Servants drew back the heavy chairs and one stood behind each of us. I hoped that my sword wouldn't catch in her sleeve as we claimed our seats and Megan shot me another offended glance. What? That was a legitimate concern. I wasn't making fun; I thought back at her.

'Sir Trenton Arenson, First Heir of Westarbor' was announced next and took his place to the right of his parents' seats. And finally, 'Vincent Arenson Lord Westarbor escorting the Lady Westarbor.'

I expected some long-winded speech was to follow, but I was mistaken. The baron was brief. Once seated he lifted a goblet and said simply: "Welcome honored guests. Please enjoy the hospitality of Westarbor."

When our liege had drunk from the vessel and set it back upon the table, a low murmur of conversation arose and servitors rushed forth to set before us a plenitude of platters. The boards of the high table well-nigh groaned under the steaming weight of the freshly prepared delicacies.

Contrary to my usual desire to eat two of anything offered, I had found in recent days my appetite had fled. I think it was the sleepless nights or perhaps my adolescence had peaked and this is how adults always felt. It was true that in my youth I had never been so pampered as to satisfy my hunger whenever I wanted. Several months of living in privilege at the castle may have jaded my palate. Whatever the cause, I only sampled reasonable portions of this and that.

I noted that Royland had also won a seat at the high table. Unlike me, however, he was seated at the far end near its foot. As a mage, he rated somewhere just below the petty nobility but still well above the artisans and craftsmen. He too was making only a token effort at eating. I overheard a servant ask him whether there was some specific dish he desired. His quiet reply was overwhelmed by other discussions nearby, but the man rushed off saying: 'I think we can scrape some of that up, but I can't guarantee its freshness.'

"Well, it's a glum companion I've chosen for this feast," interjected Megan.

"I was just thinking, my lady, that I must be leaving soon."

"It's more than just that, Lucas. I would have you speak of it. Is ought amiss with your magic?" she guessed.

"My magic is just as before, my lady, but there's something ... new."

I thought of the twisted stream of angry energy that was not seen but rather sensed in the manner of an afterimage. It was as though I had stared briefly at the sun and then looked away with my eyes closed tightly.

"Royland says you're not sleeping," said Megan, lifting the glass gently toward her lips.

"Royland talks too much," I replied.

Megan was suddenly aghast. Her eyes widened in horror and her cheeks puffed out. The glass tumbled to the table spilling its contents as she hastily brought her napkin up to veil the lower half of her face. A soft squeak emerged.

"All is well," I quickly assured the servants and the girl's mother who was leaning in close. "She just took a fright from a story I was telling," I fibbed.

It wouldn't do for the baron's daughter to be seen with milk dribbling down from her nostrils. I was certain the incident would earn me an admonishment and a sharp cuff on the shoulder once we were out of the public eye.

Fortunately, most nearby eyes were soon drawn elsewhere as a large steaming kettle was brought forth and set before my cousin. He ladled some into his bowl. It was amusing to most onlookers that with all of Westarbor's rare and unusual treats to choose among, Royland had opted for a simple helping of peas porridge. Heads were turned as he blew on his spoon and slurped at the common dish. I didn't question it. I had long ago given up trying to figure out Royland. If there was one thing certain about him, it was that he would surprise you. I didn't know then just how prophetic this thought would turn out to be.

Not long after this, the baron arose from his seat commanding the attention of all within the hall. The initial frenzy of the feast had passed and the serving of new entrées had slowed. Our liege was an excellent orator. The cadence of the rousing speech that followed was flawless. The baron would pause in places so the audience could react and then continue, rising ever more in tone.

"Once again I bid you welcome... I am told the autumn faire progresses smoothly, and I wish our new friends, the Tomcats, an enjoyable and prosperous stay in Westarbor... It has been a strange year filled with many challenges and wonders. First, creatures not seen in a generation arose to threaten our security... These were neatly dispatched by our knights."

A soft murmuring of congratulations wafted about the room in the pause that followed.

"Next," he continued, "a goblin horde invaded from the west, but we soon sent them packing as well."

A louder stirring ensued along with a smattering of light applause. 'We taught 'em not to mess with our kingdom!' came an enthusiastic shout from somewhere near the back.

"Then the mill on which we had come to rely was leveled by foul magic... But our new mages arose to the challenge and thwarted this destroyer also in the end. Our *new* mill will be even larger and *more* capable. The master craftsmen assure me that it should be operational by next harvest season.

By this time the acclaim had risen in volume. Hands pounded rhythmically upon tabletops and cutlery struck against tin tankards to produce muted bell-like tones. The baron was hard-pressed to be heard above the ruckus. And yet he managed.

"And lastly ... with the commencement of this faire, trade has once again begun to flourish! Good citizens of Westarbor please extend every courtesy over the next week to our new friends from the caravan. We most earnestly wish for their kind opinion and swift return!"

The baron raised up his hand and waited for his guests to again settle into a hush before proceeding in a more subdued and matter of fact tone.

"For tonight's feast, we have brought a special entertainment. A man who once served the king *himself* has agreed to play a game with us. It is not a game for the faint of heart. Any who wish not to partake of it may leave now and none will question your honor."

Spellbound, the room remained silent.

"I expected no less from the stouthearted folk of *my* barony," said Lord Westarbor once the silence had stretched out. I shall leave it for the man himself to explain. Without further ado, please raise your glass to the comedic stylings of Manchester and Patsy!"

And with that, the jester I had seen previously came tumbling to the fore with bells tinkling to land just in front of our table.

"Ta-daaaaa!" said Manchester, flinging a handful of confetti aloft.

Where was this Patsy fellow?

Then I noticed a strange doll clutched in the man's left hand. It was more of a stick with a ball on the end with a painted-on face. It wore a hat akin to that of the jester himself, bells and all. It chimed merrily when he shook it. That must be this 'Patsy'. Mincing about, Manchester began to spout rhymes. He would turn this way and that, drawing the attention of both those at the high table and the audience before it at once. Thus he began:

> The baron, our excellent host,
> Arose to propose us a toast,
> But to me did defer
> And I think you'll concur,
> (It's more jolly his courtiers to roast).

The last line was 'spoken' by Patsy. The little poppet had a high, squeaky voice that was obviously affected by the jester himself as he sought to still his lips. He continued.

> So at the good baron's behest,
> I shall grant each of you a request,
> And whilst I entertain
> I shall strive to refrain
> From Patsy's poor penchant for jest.

"Who shall my first victim be? Why it's lady's choice, of course," he said as he sidled over to the baroness. "Who shall it be, my lady? Name anyone and Patsy and I shall immortalize that person with a limerick of our own invention. But have a care, for our barbs are oft known to sting!"

The Lady Westarbor seemed to consider this then said: "Do Trenton first, for I doubt me another would have the temerity to name the first heir, and I would hear what you make of my son."

She graced the jester with her beatific smile and then looked over at Trenton seated just to the baron's right. A muttering arose as the jester approached Sir Trenton whose frowning face bore a look of uncertainty. Then he began.

> While the knights of the baron made merry,
> A gryphon was plaguing the dairy,
> Trenton rose from the feast,
> Sallied forth, slew the beast,
> And its carcass was stuffed - (rather scary).

When Patsy spouted the last line, Manchester skipped over to the terrifying gryphon trophy to cower beneath it whilst rolling his eyes upward. The effect was most hilarious. As laughter bubbled up from the crowd, Trenton stood to his feet. Slamming his hand upon the boards of the high table, he declared: "I *like* this game! You simply *must* do Gerard."

Arising from his crouch, the jester cartwheeled over to Master Keaton and paused scratching at his chin.

> A worthy accountancy crafter,
> Found his efforts oft greeted by laughter,
> When he bade folks to measure
> The barony's treasure
> 'Bean Counter' they called him ... (thereafter).

This was simply too much. While the audience roared with laughter at our chamberlain's discomfiture, Manchester was making coin (or bean) counting motions with his right hand. How had the man so quickly gathered intelligence on all our local notables? He must have spent all day doing so while composing his limericks. Add to that, his antics were genuinely funny. And so it went on. Most at the high table were skewered on the jester's rapier wit and several among the audience as well. Each would get a chance to name his successor. Of course, none had the gall to name the baron or baroness, and I confess to some actual disappointment that I had not been named as yet. But eventually, Lady Megan was given up.

Manchester paced back and forth before her wringing his hands behind his back for several moments building up the suspense. Then he suddenly pointed a finger upward as if inspiration had struck.

A raven-locked baron's daughter,
Ne'er a man who had seen her forgot her,
Although young and tender
And despite her fair gender,
Rallied people the goblins to slaughter.

"Oh, Bravo!" declared Megan once the applause had died down. "I thought you might spout some banality about flowers. Well done good jester."

"I thank the lady for her endorsement and would ask that she point me to the next ego to be impaled," quipped Manny. "Anyone at all; any in the hall!"

Megan stared at me appraisingly and muttered, "I do owe you for the milk."

I quailed outwardly, but within I was elated.

"No, you want it too badly," she said with a wry grin. "Do Royland then."

"A fair maiden's wish should ever be respected," he replied, fastening his attentions upon my cousin. "Heaven only help the young man she selected."

Royland sat slurping at his soup. He didn't pause or look up as every eye in the hall fell upon him. Royland had never enjoyed being the center of attention and would often retreat within himself to escape such scrutiny. He had come a long way at Fowler Ranch, but how would he react to a prolonged inspection with mocking narration? I was surprised he wasn't even now rocking back and forth mouthing silent words. Manny stalked over to him and stared silently for a full ten count before turning to the audience.

Royland had lived life in mummery,
Although during the siege this past summer he,
Did pluck rocks from the sky,
He was blushing and shy,
(As a novice escaped from a nunnery!).

The hall erupted in loud peals of laughter. Royland sat slurping his soup.

"Well then, young man," said the jester with glee. "Who shall my very next victim be?"

He was answered by silence.

"Come now friend, we haven't got all day. Name another subject," said the jester with dismay.

Then Royland looked up. "Anyone?" he asked.

"Yes anyone is valid; those are the rules. And rules are important for both wise men and fools."

"Then do yourself," said my cousin with a sly grin.

Uh-oh. I knew that grin. I invoked my magesight and took careful note of what happened next. Royland was gesturing under the table and his discrete little packets of magical energy were emerging to cluster about his throat and also to converge on Patsy.

As the sputtering jester sought about for a suitable limerick, the poppet slowly twisted in his hand to face him full on. It then uttered the following in its piping little voice:

> (What a villainous knave was Manchester),
> (Whose insulting derision did fester),
> (He'd find out what you'd done)
> (Then lampoon you for fun),
> (And then go on to mock your ancestor)

All in the hall applauded, and a few whistles joined in. Ever the consummate professional, Manny soon recovered his wits and took a grand bow. Backing into the crowd and clutching at his chest, the man said in a melodramatic voice: "You wound me good sir, and I'm humbled thereby; I concede that you are ,,, a greater fool than I."

Royland cocked his head and smiled with half his face. He then returned to spooning up his porridge which had doubtless gone cold.

***

The next several days were busy ones. The autumn faire was shaping up into a huge success. Empowered by the baron's bounty, the good citizens of Meadowfork thronged in droves to spend their windfall on rare goods not normally available in our small hamlet. Our own merchants hastened to set up stalls of their own to showcase their newest wares. After all, the trade caravan would need to stock up with fresh goods to be sold at some other distant locale. They would also require foodstuffs, fodder for their mules, and other perishables.

"Hey Lucas!" shouted Gregor, approaching Uncle Robert and me as we inspected a display of wooden chests.

My uncle wanted to make me a parting gift of a sturdy trunk into which I could pack all of my clothes and other things for the trip. Not everything I would need would fit in my Bob. In Gregor's hand was a little flat doll of some sort. As he drew nearer, he tore off one of its arms and held it forth.

"You've got to try some of this," he said, offering me the amputated member.

I accepted the gift and warily sniffed at it. I could see that the rest of Gregor's mutilated manikin had raisins for its eyes and was further decorated by stripes of confectioners' sugar. It had a spicy scent akin to that of cinnamon, so I promptly popped it into my mouth and chewed. It was warm and delicious.

"They call it gingerbread," he said. "They're selling them at the cook wagon today. Three for a nickel. Would you like to have some, Goodman Wagge?"

"Ack," replied my uncle with a look of distaste. "Get that stuff away from me, boy. My mother used to make it all the time. Sometimes that's all my sister and I would get to eat for days on end. I think she put something *bad* in it and used the spices to cover up the taste."

"Well *I* think these are pretty tasty," Gregor declared biting the head off.

"What do you think about this one here, Lucas?" asked Uncle Robert, tapping on the largest chest on display.

"I asked Miss Tulip earlier," I replied. "She said it was too big, but that this one would be *just* right."

"If you're sure then," returned Robert, "I'll have a word with the trader."

"That'd be great, Uncle Robert, and I thank you for the fine gift."

"*Nothing* is too good for *my* nephew, say I."

When I worked though the precise meaning of this sentence, I wasn't sure how to take it, but I was certain that the phrase had been well-intended. As my uncle caught the trader's attention and prepared to dicker, I spotted Megan and her handmaidens strolling our way.

"Hey Gregor," I said, "there's a certain young lady with whom I'd like to have a private chat. Thanks for the treat, but..."

"Say no more," the young man quickly asserted, "I'll make myself scarce."

"No, I need you to distract her friends for me," I said, digging about in my coin purse.

Producing a kupfernickel, I flicked it to him and bade him to buy them each some gingerbread. We lounged nonchalantly beside the wagon until the ladies drew nigh. I engaged them in conversation. I told of the delightful gingerbread boys to which Gregor had introduced me, and my friend offered to buy them some to sample for themselves. Just as I knew she would, Lady Megan saw through our scheme at once. Claiming fatigue, she commanded Constance and Lynette to go with Gregor and fetch her some. She assured them she would be quite safe waiting here with her sworn protector. As the three strode off, we waited for them to be out of sight before making our escape.

"So what are you doing today?" asked Lynette.

"I was just talking to Lucas," said Gregor. "That Miss Tulip was showing him earlier how some chests were too big and some too small and whatnot.

The pair glanced quickly downward then glared indignantly at Gregor as he blithely prattled on, leading the way to the cook wagon and its promised gingerbread treats. When they could no longer be seen, Megan nodded, and we made our way across the courtyard and up the thoroughfare toward the mill.

"Tis almost time that you leave us, Lucas."

"It is at that, my lady," I said, feeling the sadness well up once more.

We passed by the mill and Royland's stone benches and proceeded further up the lane to the mill pond. I spread out my cloak in the grass beside its waters. The ducks gliding about in their small formations angled toward us. Megan and I sometimes brought some day-old bread to crumble and throw out to them, but today I had nothing to give.

"What good is a sworn protector if he's half a kingdom *away?*" said Megan, her somber voice blunting the petulance of her words.

"It's the law, Megan, and can't be avoided."

"I've brought you something," she said, turning away. "I wanted to give you a perfect parting gift and was quite vexed by my lack of ideas. Then I recalled your recent difficulty in achieving restful sleep."

She retrieved a green bottle from the pockets of her skirt. Holding it up, she declared: "It's a potent sleeping draught. Our apothecary guarantees it would 'lay low an ox' if enough were administered. I trust you will use it judiciously. No more than a teaspoon at bedtime."

"I will do so, my lady. In that manner, I shall think of you each night *before* I dream *as well as* during."

She punched me on the shoulder.

"Flatterer," she said.

But were those tears welling in her eyes? I knew that Megan maintained complete mastery of her body language and facial expressions. Since childhood, she had practiced her 'game' of diplomacy and etiquette. If Megan smiled, it was calculated to cheer. If Megan frowned, it was to signify her displeasure. Any reaction like a blush or a tear was well within her control. If her eyes were welling up, it could mean one of two things. Either she was purposefully affecting tears to express sadness, or was choosing to show me her true face and simply allowing the tears to flow. Either way I was touched by this and it moved me to speak.

"On my oath, which is even more binding than the king's law, if you find yourself threatened or truly in need, I shall come," I promised.

And the girl's eyes spilt over at last. Leaning forward, she thrust the glass bottle into my hands which she covered with her own. Her lips gently brushed my cheek, and I felt the wet tickle of her eyelashes as she blinked.

"Safe journey, Lucas," she whispered, drawing back from me and beginning to stand. "Come back to us one day."

And as the lady stepped toward the lane, I stood to escort her back. I was deeply honored by the lady's parting gift. And the sleeping draught might come in handy as well.

***

When the day to depart finally arrived, I was summoned by the baron once more. Rather than in his chambers, Roy and I were to meet him atop the West Tower.

The trading had by this time slowed to a mere trickle, most deals having been struck. Even the throngs that had packed the town tavern had thinned. All the songs had been sung, and news and tales from lands far and near had gone stale. As Uncle Robert put it: 'If wishes were fishes, even your fondest desire might begin to stink after more than a few days.'

Tilda had packed up her overloaded cart and set out for Fowler Ranch. Roy and I saw her off with many a hug and bade her to convey our fond wishes to Master Chadwick for his swift recovery. Cameron Ross, the caravan's master had advised the baron it was fast approaching time to pull up stakes. 'The show must go on,' he had said.

And so it was that my cousin and I mounted the battlement in the last hour of daylight. A bracing breeze tugged at my cloak and suggested the icy clutch of winter might soon be upon us. I trusted the caravan folk, experienced travelers all, would know ways to endure its onset and find us safe shelter along the way.

"Hail the watch," I said as we passed the watchmen stationed above the gatehouse.

Nearing the west tower, I espied our liege gazing out upon the barony. He turned blue eyes in our direction and bade us to approach.

"Well met, good mages," he said with a grin. "I trust you are all packed and ready?"

Royland nodded.

"Yes, your lordship," I replied.

"Then it is time you receive *my* parting gift," the man said, his face inscrutable. "The caravan will set off tomorrow at first light. As your sponsor, I have paid for your passage."

"Your lordship is most generous," I quickly supplied.

"I would not have it be said, however," he continued, "that the mages of Westarbor didn't travel in style and comfort as befits their stations. Therefore, you will join the caravan riding in my own carriage. Yonder, it rests."

So saying, he pointed below where a gleaming coach drawn by two chestnut horses had pulled up to the bridge. It wasn't gilded exactly, but it was posh. Its delicate sweeping lines and elaborate carvings made it stand out like a beacon among the stodgy, utilitarian wagons surrounding it. Furthermore, it was fully enclosed. Its passengers wouldn't be exposed to the elements in the least.

I had frequently seen the baron or his lady wife gadding about the town or out onto the roads in this very carriage. It rolled across the drawbridge and through the keep's main gates. In energetic strides the baron made for the stairway down to the inner ward and gestured for us to follow. Royland was smiling as we hustled after.

As we descended, I saw the coach traverse the cobbles of the inner ward to pull up at the castle's grand entrance. Though its wheels bounced and rattled along, its body moved steadily only swaying slightly. When I remarked on this to his lordship, he proudly told me Javier Lewis had accomplished this feat somehow with springs and other techniques he had developed.

'There's not its equal in all of Osten,' he boasted. And: 'Though perhaps besting mine in opulence, I'd wager the king himself has not a smoother ride.'

Gaining the grand entrance, I was met with a new surprise. The coachman perched atop the driver's seat was none other than Taylor Allen, the archer from Sir Trenton's lance. As Royland immediately bent to inspect the carriage's underpinnings, I greeted the man.

"Well met, Taylor," I laughed. "You are a man of many talents; it would seem."

"Your lordship," said he, first greeting the baron and somehow managing a stiff bow from a seated position. "Lucas. Roy."

"The good archer will accompany you," explained the baron. "He is commanded to deliver a full score of my homing pigeons to the capital. On his way there, he will serve as your coachman and convey you to Conclave. He will also train you in how to steer it and some other needful skills. Heed him well for he has much to teach."

Just then, the porters began arriving. They had collected all of our belongings from the mages suite. There were my trunk and Roy's. There were my Bob and Royland's backpack and a few other oddments. Then came the drum.

Among the scattered remnants of the goblin camp, my cousin had discovered an intact goblin war drum. He began experimenting with it in his obsessive way until he could reproduce all the rhythms the goblins had played and several heretofore unknown. It was eerily reminiscent of the time we had spent besieged. He hammered away in his compulsive manner until the baron ordered him to desist. The drum had been removed to the trophy room where it had lain thankfully silent and still. Apparently, my cousin had reasserted his ownership of the instrument, and his lordship had acquiesced.

As the porters studied how best to pack our few belongings within the marvelous conveyance we were to ride on the morrow, the baron lured me aside.

"Lucas," said he, "I would have private words with you. Come and join me in the library."

At this, he strode off once again, trusting I would follow. I hurried after. By this time, I knew well the way to the library, but it was never a clever idea to keep a nobleman waiting. Not even for a second. Therefore, when we arrived, the baron found me dogging his heels. His lordship claimed the largest chair amid the dusty tomes and seated himself, indicating I should choose another. As I did so, he gave me a thoughtful look before his gaze grew more distant.

"I speak to you now not as your liege, but as a father," he began.

Sitting gingerly in a chair nearby I nodded and granted him my full attention.

"My daughter shall miss you, Lucas," he continued, blue eyes flashing. "You know of our talent, and I think you comprehend what it means, especially because of your closeness to your cousin who is similarly gifted."

"What you can't know is the loneliness of keeping secrets - secrets of state. There are many who wish us ill or would have us fail or be undermined. So we people of station must remain ever vigilant against revealing our hand lest our enemies find a weakness to exploit."

"My daughter was drawn into this game early - too early. Because of her formidable talent, I knew it was of no use trying to keep secrets from her. So I presented these cold truths to her as a game. For all of her life, Megan has been privy to secrets both fair and foul, things she could not utter to another living soul save for myself."

"In giving her your vow, you have done me a great service. At once, she gained a confidant other than her father. One sworn not to repeat her secrets, and truthfully sworn, for she could tell were it otherwise. I neither know nor care what she has confided in you, Lucas, for I sense you are a man of honor."

I experienced a surge of pride to be so trusted. But I was also humbled as I considered these sad revelations. The baron was right. If I had a problem, I could talk it over with my father, but also Uncle Robert or anyone else who would listen. Megan had no such recourse.

"Therefore," said the baron "I shall entrust you with a family secret if you are willing to help share in our burden?"

"Of course, your lordship," I responded at once.

The baron produced and set before me a leather-bound book. Nothing was printed upon its cover, but flipping it open revealed its title page. "The Book of Innuendo," it said. The baron forestalled my question before I could even utter it.

"Studying this," he declared, "will allow you to write to Megan and she to you safe from prying eyes. Hide it well and keep it protected at all costs. Destroy it if you must. I will tell Megan that you have been initiated as a pawn in the game."

The baron stood.

"One more piece of advice," said he. "Beware the jester. There is something dishonest about the man."

CHAPTER TWO

The Minstrel

"A few can touch the magic string, and noisy fame
is proud to win them: Alas for those that never
sing, but die with all their music in them!"

~ Oliver Wendell Holmes ~

The caravan uncoiled itself from the keep's outer ward transforming the makeshift market once again into a line of wagons. We set out upon our journey with our faces to the rising sun and with long shadows stretching out behind. Despite the early hour, many were lined up along the main street of Meadowfork to bid the Tomcats a fond farewell. I didn't look back. It was a time for looking forward.

Once clear of the town, we took the eastern road and soon entered the Danstonshire highlands. This forested badland separated Meadowfork and its surrounds from the eastern fiefs of our barony. As newcomers to the caravan, our position was at its tail end. Thus, any dust raised by those in the leading positions would be ours to cherish.

The barons promise of a smooth ride had been no idle boast. I had tried reading for a bit, but the coach's gentle creaking and swaying soon lulled me into a light doze. Since Taylor had the reins well in hand, Roy and I had drawn closed all the curtains. We indulged ourselves in silent meditation as the forested miles slipped past. There had been a brief stop for the midday meal, and several others to stretch and to rest the animals, but so far I found traveling a humdrum affair.

"Whoa!" I heard from above.

My half-lidded eyes snapped open, and I swayed forward as our coach slowed to a full stop. Across from me, Royland sat up straighter and turned in his seat. He drew back the draperies to peer out the front window. Our first night's camp was to be on the shores of Lake Ganymede. Could we have arrived already? Curious, I opened the door. As the folding step was presently unavailable, I instead gripped the head iron and leaned out for a look ahead.

"What's the hold up?" I called to Taylor up on the coachman's seat.

"I don't know, Lucas," he replied. "We weren't scheduled to make camp for at least several more hours."

News soon came down the line that the rear axle on the fodder wagon had broken. It was even now being unloaded and moved to one side of the road. Fortunately, the caravan had skilled wainwrights within its complement. It had been decided that they would attend to the matter while we set up camp early at the next suitable site.

The Tomcats did not lack for organization and social strata. It consisted of five major groups. First, there were the administrative folks that served the caravan overall. Overseen by Master Ross, the caravan boss, were a group of wagons containing a supply of fresh water, fodder for the animals, and gear used to set up at campsites. Some space had been set aside for packages and letters to be delivered to destinations along our route. Also in this group was the cook wagon.

Next were the merchants, traders, and teamsters. Some of these specialized in a particular ware, while some others sought to haul whatever was available and could be sold elsewhere for a profit. Then came itinerant workers of every stripe. These were people skilled in highly specialized trades that were needed only infrequently in small villages like Meadowfork. The stonecutter who sharpened our millstones was one such. His profession required he travel about to find steady work. The fourth group were the entertainers.

Lastly came the passengers which at present included Taylor Allen, Royland, and me. I was soon to discover just which group served as the bottom-most rung of the caravan's social ladder.

The line of wagons in front of us began to roll forward once more.

Noah Reynolds and his brother, Aaron, were the Tomcats' wainwrights. Their own wagon was stacked with extra wheels, spare parts and the many tools of their trade. They attended to the caravan's needs and also plied their craft at each small town and hamlet along the route. I had met the two just prior to our journey's outset. After a hasty introduction, they had insisted on looking over our coach to make sure it was fit for a long haul. They must have been well satisfied, because the men had emerged from this inspection exchanging grins, nods, and assorted words of praise.

They weren't smiling now. As we overtook them, Noah was hammering at something beneath the overturned wagon. His brother lugged a great wooden stave to rest nearby then paused to look on unhappily. Soon the two were lost from view.

Before long, we had arrived at our newly designated campsite. Taylor was directed where to deposit our coach, and our team was unhitched and led away.

Though as mages, Roy and I were considered to be almost petty nobles, our lack of any real political clout detracted from how we were regarded. More than anything else, the Baron's sponsorship granted us *some* deference. But Cameron Ross had a reputation as a demanding task master who despised slackers and insisted each pull his own weight.

As Taylor began securing the coach and settling our gear, Roy and I were called over to Master Ross and assigned to assist the farrier, Olin Reed. Among the first tasks in setting up camp was care for the animals, and Goodman Reed was an expert in this matter. Hoof care was the first priority. The beasts had spent all day slogging through mud, stones, and the droppings of their foremost fellows as they lugged our conveyances toward our next destination. As others gathered wood for the campfires, freshened our water supplies, and established temporary shelters, my cousin and I bent to the arduous new assignment.

Unlike the slower oxen we used in Meadowfork, horses and mules were decidedly better for a long trek. Not only were they faster, but as equines they could stand on any three legs, a feat which their bovine brethren could only envy. This made it much easier to tend to their hooves. Even to shoe an ox was a daunting chore. The creatures needed to either be hoisted up with specialized and bulky equipment, or be forced over onto their sides and made to lie still.

Mules were interesting. I learned that each was the byproduct of a mating between a horse and a donkey. Surprisingly, these two types of creature were similar enough to spawn young. Mules could be either male or female, but since they lacked the ability to have children of their own, this distinction was rather moot. Their reputation for being stubborn actually arose from their superior intellect. Whereas a horse might willingly undertake whatever it was trained to do, a mule would sometimes decide that it knew better. I found most to have a gentle nature, and each would comply with my directions once I had won its trust.

Folks of the caravan favored mules over horses for several compelling reasons. Though not quite as strong as their sires, they were more patient, and would thus pull a heavy load for a longer period without complaint. Moreover, these amazing crossbreeds possessed the surefootedness of their dams and would happily attempt slopes and trails that might cause a horse to balk.

After patiently scraping the day's detritus from our four-footed friends, my cousin and I were set about grooming their coats. Although awkward among people, Royland had a natural way with animals. Goodman Reed seemed similarly gifted. His charges would playfully butt into him with their heads until he provided them with carrots he produced from a pocket. When at last all the mules and our two draft horses had been watered, picketed and provided with feed, we were released to explore the campsite.

It was amazing how quickly the Tomcats had settled into the surroundings. Though temporary, tonight's camp had already taken on the look of prolonged occupation. Smoke wafted up from cheery fire pits beside well-stocked woodpiles. Soiled travel garments were being scrubbed in large tubs and strung out upon lines to dry in the late afternoon breeze.

Out here on the open road, the Tomcats presentation had lost some of its luster. Their bright outfits had been replaced by well-worn traveler's attire, and their snappy banter had taken on a more comfortable cadence as they happily conversed and basked in the late afternoon sun. I made my way along the row of wagons absorbing the sights and sounds as the community enjoyed a rare measure of leisure afforded them by the early stop. Royland had ambled off mumbling something about his drum.

I spotted one man conversing excitedly with the empty air before his wagon while making broad gestures with both hands. He looked to be barking mad. Curious, I drew nearer, invoking my mage sight just in case. I grasped what he was doing only after listening to him for a bit. He was a barker, perhaps, but not a mad one. It seemed he was practicing the pitch he used to hawk his goods.

"...This is no mere wool, my friend. This is *Arborvale Woolenweave*. Gleaned from the flock of a reclusive master wizard, each fold of this lustrous cloth was spun and woven by the dainty hands of the lovely ladies of far-off Arborvale!"

Although technically true, I found the man's colorful embellishments and boastful tone to be a bit over-the-top. I was especially struck by the vision of Tilda's 'dainty hands.' Something of this must have shown on my face, for the man stopped in mid-harangue to direct a stern glare my way.

"Has something got you amused, boy?" he asked indignantly.

"Ah..." I intelligently replied, "I just had a passing fancy about some people of my acquaintance. Your cloth is truly most wondrous."

Skeptical, the man arched his eyebrows at this and made a measuring, pious face that I again found funny.

"Oh? And just what do you think you know of cloth, young man?" he challenged.

Defensive now, I shrugged and replied, "I've been known to raise up the distaff a time or two."

"Indeed," supplied Taylor Allen from just behind me. "Our Lucas here is a man of many talents."

Startled, I whirled about.

"It's too bad properly wearing a sword is not among them," he said glancing downward.

I followed his gaze to see the tip of my scabbard trailing a line in the dirt. Apparently, my belt had slid down while I was attending to the animals.

As the archer steered me aside, the cloth merchant returned to regaling his invisible customers with the many virtues of Arborvale Woolenweave.

"If you are going to bear a blade, Lucas," Taylor softly admonished, "you must handle it with proper respect. Our liege noticed your clumsiness at the feast and charged me with providing you some basic instruction. I can see we'd have to start at the very beginning. Would you care to learn this skill?"

I had never known Taylor to be loquacious. Though not as silent as my cousin, he had a reserved way about him. The archer usually only spoke up when a matter was meaningful. That he had spared four whole sentences on the topic told me it was important, so I considered carefully before replying.

"I don't seek to become a skilled swordsman, Taylor. Magic is more my focus. I began bearing the blade to honor my father. If you can show me how to avoid disgracing myself, I would learn that much at least."

"Good," he said, "We can start tomorrow morning."

"Why not at once?" I asked.

"Training is better in the mornings," he assured me. "And also, tonight you need to clean up. I don't fancy sleeping in an enclosed coach surrounded by the unfortunate reek of mules."

He was a fine one to preach. Taylor had always insisted on keeping cages of pigeons near his bedside. These cages had been tied atop the coach for the ride thus far, but I was certain I would once again become intimate with their pungent perfume the moment the weather turned foul. I sighed and tried not to think about it as we strode back to the baron's carriage.

The cook wagon wouldn't be serving dinner for hours yet, so I had best be about my business. Unlike some of the more established wagons in the caravan, our small coach had no tub of a size suitable for washing oneself. I would need to make do with what nature provided. Stopping only briefly at the carriage, I placed my sword and its belt within my trunk and set off with my Bob toward the shores of Lake Ganymede.

***

Our camp was very near the lake. Moreover, a trail had been recently broken through the underbrush by a wagon sent to retrieve barrels of water for washing. So I wended my way northward whistling a cheerful tune. Barring wild beasts, I felt fairly secure in the full light of day.

I had once wondered why there were no guardsmen traveling with the merchant caravan. After all, there were valuable goods. Wouldn't this make it an ideal target for bandits and the like? Taylor had explained it was incumbent upon each lord to keep the king's highway safe where it crossed through his lands. This was a right that the nobles jealously defended. The protection provided by their own soldiers was the very basis on which they collected taxes and tariffs. It was a feeble lord indeed who would suffer a band of mercenaries on his land who served a master other than himself. From what I knew of noblemen, that made perfect sense.

Likewise, merchants traveling in a sponsored caravan had their own sort of power. If a lord failed to protect them, that lord would soon find himself blacklisted by their influential guild.

Soon thereafter, one of two things would occur. Either traders would bypass the offender and his lands wrecking havoc with his finances, or else his own lord might strip him of his lands and titles. Appeasing a powerful merchant house was no mean feat. Travel by caravan within Osten was thus deemed safe enough, though no organized soldiers were permitted among them. Nevertheless, we remained wary.

Lord Westarbor had even offered Master Ross an escort through the Danstonshire, but the man had politely declined. Our liege had instead sent several patrols through over the preceding week. It still gnawed at his lordship's sensibilities that the brigand who loosed an arrow at Megan last summer had not been apprehended.

When the lake came into view, it was an impressive sight to behold. Unlike the mill pond and countless other small lakes that dotted the western barony, I couldn't even see its far banks. I had been told the solitary little tuft of green visible just left of center was an island of no real consequence. I recalled that far up the strand to my right lay the small fishing village of Lakethroat. Father had taken me there once when I was younger. He had built them a hoist at the end of one of their peers. They used it to unload laden fishing nets or other heavy objects from their small boats.

Drawing nearer to the lake's shore, my boots crunched on the loose gravel of its berm. Here and there scrubby little plants stubbornly clung to clumps of soil as the forest gave way to the silt and stones edging its gently lapping waters. The sky above was clear and showed the sun nearing its journey's end. I set Bob down, sat beside him, and set about unlacing my boots.

It was then that I heard the voices approaching. They were the lilting musical notes I now recognized as Elven speech.

"*Beniwia jitejhenom, sovath,*" said the deeper of the two voices.

"*Ngengi vileah vinay, Benalavioshi,*" responded the higher chidingly.

I was unsurprised to see Miss Tulip stepping to the lake's edge from out of the forest's shadow followed by her brother.

"*Weja nitevia lothnia. Lucas vilessa*," said Miss Tulip.

"Greetings Lucas. Well met as you say," she continued with a cheery wave on her direct approach.

"Well met yourself, Miss Tulip," I said. "And you also, Benalavioshi, is it?"

Miss Tulip tangled her hands up to her wrists in her lustrous golden curls and unleashed a staccato burst of melodic sounds as her face contorted in ecstasy. It was like the chiming of bells or more aptly akin to the song of a woodlark. Her brother, meanwhile sported a scowl.

"I'm sorry if I have given offense," I quickly asserted. "Did I say something wrong?"

"No. No," said she, reaching over to tousle her brother's hair. "His full name is *Benalav batlamey Najhemaram* which means 'the glory of the forest night.' Because he is ... junior to me ... *Benalavioshi* is my ... how do you say it? ... *pet name* for him. It means 'little glory.'

She stared at me expectantly while Benalav bent and picked up a stone. With a shrug and a noisy exhale of breath he then turned and paced over toward the lake.

"It is much funnier in Elven," she assured me.

"Then I take it that 'Tulip' isn't your full name either?" I politely inquired.

"It is ... how do you say? ... my *stage* name. My parents gifted me with *Toolhup vejha Sorsoos* which means 'Whisper of the wind through the trees.'

"That's charming," I declared.

Suddenly remembering our earlier introduction, I added: "You do me honor with the gift of your names."

Benalav faced in my direction and solemnly nodded. He then cocked back his arm and released the stone with a strange sideways toss that sent it skipping across the tranquil waters of the lake. From each bounce (of which there were many), a series of concentric waves rippled outward. He bent to select a new stone.

Elves are weird.

"So, Benalav is younger than you?" I asked.

"By two years only," replied Miss Toolhup. "It is rare for siblings among my people to be so close together in age. Births are very infrequent. It is why when the eightieth anniversary of my naming day arrived, I chose to wait another two years so that Benalavioshi and I could take our *Hop leng poH* together!"

Initially, I felt certain that she had misspoken and meant her 'eighteenth' birthday, but I then recalled from my reading that the Elves had extremely long lifespans. Could it be that these two vivacious youths were actually octogenarians?

Benalav skipped another stone across the lake.

"Well I suppose it's a good thing you both decided to be entertainers then," I observed.

Again the girl (old woman?) erupted in her bell-like laughter.

"No. No," she corrected. "Among the first people, selection of one's *Vallahimay* ... there is no human word ... 'wise skills,' maybe, is made later in life. The *Hop leng poH* is a time to travel around; to see the world and its marvels so that you can better choose your life path, your *Vallahimay*."

"Ah," said I, "we call that a wander year."

"Maybe this is right," said Miss Toolhup. "In our case, it can be any length of time - usually about a decade. We have traveled with Master Ross for about three years now and have seen many wondrous sights."

I let this sink in as Benelav chucked another stone.

"Why are your boots off, Lucas? Were you going wading in the lake?"

"I was going to wash and put on some clean clothes."

"Well don't let us stop you; you can do that as we talk."

"Um, well, I would be naked."

"*Chatha tutha miqua*," Benalav said, catching his sister's eye.

"Oh, we sometimes forget that you are ashamed of your bodies."

"We call it modesty, and *we* never do."

"Anyway, I have told you somewhat of the first people," she said, suddenly shy, "so it is only fair you tell me something of magic. Can you show me some?"

I had been studying her brother's technique. I thought he was getting so many skips because of the spin he was imparting to his throws. The stones' gyrations were keeping their flat sides down despite the tumbling that should otherwise result from each strike.

"Alright, Wind-Whispering-through-the-Trees," I said. "Here's something you won't witness every day."

I concentrated on a large, flat rock about the size of a dinner plate. From my magic center, I extruded numerous thin vines which only someone with mage sight could perceive. Using 'spacium girabit,' my winding mindset, I spun these into a strong ropy cord. I incanted 'levare' to unearth and lift the stone then again invoked my winding to give it a spin. It whirled so rapidly that all I could make out was a gray blur. With a final great shout of "Conicere!" I flung it directly out upon the lake.

With a series of mighty splashes, my fast-spinning rock hopped like a rabbit with its tail on fire until it was lost from our view. It wouldn't have surprised me had it reached that island off in the distance. Ringlets from the multiple wakes lapped up on the beach for a minute thereafter.

Benelav dropped the stone he was holding and began clapping his hands.

"Are all human mages so strong?" asked Miss Toolhup with raised eyebrows as she joined him in the applause.

"As it happens, I'm one of the weaker ones," I answered. "I just have a special talent for making things spin around."

"Can Royland do this as well?" she asked, looking fascinated.

"Royland is ... something *else*," I replied, at a loss for how to best describe my cousin's uncanny aptitudes.

"You must join us on our wagon tomorrow, Lucas."

"Yes," said Benalav, nodding emphatically. "We can speak more of our people, and you can tell us more about your magic."

And just like that, I had two new friends. That they were five times my age mattered not a whit. For I saw them as kindred spirits; their sense of wonderment reflected my own. The two eventually left me in peace to scrub away the stink of my day's exertions. I found the water a bit bracing but tolerable. Bob provided a bar of Madame Pennington's lilac scented soap to leave me fresh and sweet smelling. The moon was up and reflecting off the lake as I donned a dry outfit and padded back toward camp.

***

The forest had darkened somewhat. Though the sun yet strode the heavens, he was rapidly retiring toward his bed in the west. He drew his blanket of radiance after him in a silent promise to soon reveal the stars. The way back to camp was lit well enough, and I looked forward to partaking of the evening meal.

I sighted the campfires in the distance and began to hear the clatter of the camp and the murmur of its denizens. From somewhere closer by I caught a strange melody. Curious, I looked about and edged over to my right toward the odd sound. I soon arrived at a small clearing just off the trail where a man was sitting with his back to a tree and spouting nonsense in a canorous baritone voice.

dee-dah, dee-Dah! Dee-DAH!
Diddle-DAH! Dee-Dah, dee-dah...
Da-Dump. diddle-diddle,
Da-DUMP! diddle di-i-ddle
Dum! Dee-diddle-dee Dah!

His eyes were closed and propped up beside him was a stringed instrument with an oval body and an elongated neck. I recognized him as one of the three musicians who had played at the tavern in Meadowfork during the caravan's stay there. Not wanting to disturb the man, I sought to withdraw quietly, but he suddenly turned and looked my way.

"Ah," he said, his voice brimming with mirth; "'tis the very boy himself come to have a first listen. Come and join me, friend. It's almost ready to debut."

"Excuse me," I replied, "have we met?"

"It's to be introductions first, is it? I take it you haven't attended any of my performances then? No? A pity."

He took up his instrument and began tuning it. He plucked at various strings while turning little knobs on its bent neck.

"I am known far and wide as Maestro Aloysius Fenton Bok, a graduate of the Fairglen Academy of Musicians Extraordinaire. And you, of course, are Lucas Harper, a fledgling mage of somewhat more local renown. Have no fear; we shall soon remedy that. Have a seat, my boy.

As I reluctantly complied, the man stood to his feet, fretted his lute and strummed out a pleasant chord.

"I have just now worked out my newest ballad," he said. It's about your little scuffle with the goblins. Manny's limericks at the feast were my inspiration, but don't tell him I said so."

The man collected himself and stood straighter. His gaze grew distant and his voice more sober. Thus, he began.

"Hear ye then of the gruesome battle that took place only this past summer in the beleaguered barony of Westarbor."

At this, the maestro began picking out a melody on his lute. His fingers danced playfully as the pings and strums rang out rhythmically to fashion an intricate tune accentuated by a set of counterpoints that clearly demonstrated the man's skill. He wasn't even using a plectrum, instead placing his fingers directly upon each string. Soon, his clear, baritone voice joined the melodious panoply and wove the following words within.

By the gates of Westarbor Keep,
The cunning goblins did creep...
But a brave young apprentice
Confronted the menace
And caused their widows to weep!

He was, a miller's SON!
He who Put, the Foe on the run...
For blessed with the gift
To make stones fly an shi-ift
The gruesome battle he Won.

They assailed the gates with Fi-re,
And ogres swelled their Ranks!
The knights and all their Squi-res
(and even the baron gave thanks)

For when they Brought their ALL!
The GATES refu-u-sed to fall...
And how they did co-o-wer
When their siege to-o-wer
Crumbled at Lucas' Call.

"It needs a few more verses, but that's the gist. How did you like it, lad?" asked the minstrel with a knowing wink.

"It's a catchy tune," I carefully replied, "but that isn't really what happened at all. You see, Master Chadwick . . ."

"The common folk love an underdog, my boy!" the man interrupted. "No one wants to hear about a has-been like Chadwick. He's old news. Trust me. I've been at this for a long time. I should think I know better what an audience will appreciate. You just keep doing your thing and leave me to mine," he concluded with a curt little nod.

I took from this that the man wasn't interested in an honest opinion. He was merely trying to elicit blind approbation.

"What did you think, Manny?" asked Maestro Bok turning to regard the somber-faced jester.

Without his colorful costume and stage makeup, Manchester appeared ten years older and at least 20 pounds heavier. But he had at some point arrived to stand just behind me to my left. That I hadn't noted his quiet approach made me wish he still sported his bells.

"I too think the tune sounds very nice," the man replied. "And the lyrics are most appropriate when rendered by a lyre."

The minstrel smiled and turned to me. "There, you see," he smirked in self-satisfaction. "Manny knows what will please a crowd. But it's a lute, sir," the minstrel gently corrected.

The fool tilted his head to one side. "So it is," he acknowledged. "But I wasn't referring to the instrument." With that, he turned and meandered back toward the wagons.

The minstrel looked taken aback and muttered, "Everyone's a critic."

Thankful for the reprieve, I hastened after the jester making sure not to overtake him. The baron had bidden me to remain cautious of the man. Entering the warm glow of the camp and its fires, I wended my way toward the cook wagon. I hoped this new tune would fail to make its way back to Meadowfork. I was certain my liege and his knights wouldn't favor that rendition of events. I'd like as not gain a reputation all right, but it'd be as a braggart and blatherskite.

I joined the short queue at the cook wagon and was handed my trencher. The shallow bowls made of hard bread stacked nicely and kept for a long time. Having recently been restocked by the bakeries of Meadowfork, these were still fairly fresh as well. I next proceeded to a large cast iron cauldron resting atop a firepit. It was suspended from a tripod and contained our communal stew. The cook ladled out a goodly portion into my trencher.

Many of the Tomcats were sitting around their campfires exchanging gossip and good fellowship. But rather than join them, I took my dinner over by our coach to eat it in solitude. I wanted some time to think and to engage in a private activity this eve. For tonight, let them think me a recluse. There would be other evenings to better acquaint myself with the troupe.

Retrieving a spoon from Bob, I dug in. Whilst I ate the delicious stew, its juices soaked into the trencher, rendering it softer and more flavorful. I bit off chunks and chewed them with gusto until none remained. I wiped off my hands on the dirty clothing I had rolled up into a bundle earlier.

By this time, the dark of night had fully claimed the glen wherein the caravan rested. Taylor was still out and about, and the stars only knew where my cousin had gone. Stepping up into the coach, I lit the small lantern that hung in the back. I then flung open my trunk. Rooting about, I produced a burlap sack in which to stuff my soiled garments and exchanged them for a new outfit to make ready in my Bob. Digging more deeply, I retrieved the tome his lordship had entrusted to me. I deemed the time was ideal to delve into the "Book of Innuendo" and its mysteries.

At first, I was confused. The book began with a simple story written in a sloppy hand. It was the tale of a valiant tailor and seven talking ravens. It wasn't even an interesting tale, and I soon grew bored with it. Nonetheless, I persevered and read through the wearisome account to its conclusion. The pages directly following proved far more engaging. They were a set of rules which codified how to interpret ink blots.

When writing with a quill pen, if one lingered over-long on a letter, sometimes an excess of ink would spill out to mar the writing. Wiping at such puddles only made it worse. The fresh ink would smear about and ruin whole sections of one's text. It was for this reason that the scribes would often sprinkle fine sand upon freshly written manuscripts to absorb and dry any excess prior to setting a page aside.

The rules I was now reading ascribed particular meanings to *intentional* inkblots when placed upon certain letters of a page. For example, if there was an excess blot of ink on a lowercase letter 'L' within a sentence, the entire sentence was to be read as the exact opposite of its meaning. The rules were many and varied, but I immediately grasped how they could be used. The book was a primer for how to read the Arenson family's clever secret code.

I returned to the story of the tailor and the ravens, applying each rule to the imperfections I spied within its narrative. The end result was a report of the troop complement and composition of an enemy camp. One needed only to follow all the rules in order to arrive at this result.

When I overheard voices approaching, I decided to quit for the night.

"Lucas? Is that you in there?" called Taylor.

"Yep," I replied. "I'm turning in early. Did they determine the watch order yet?"

The door swung outward to reveal Taylor Allen with my cousin by his side. They discovered me digging through my trunk to retrieve the green bottle that Megan had given me.

"They did," replied the archer. "It's to be Royland on first watch and you and I on the second. I told Master Ross that both you and your cousin have extremely keen night vision."

I was relieved the caravan boss had accepted our recommendations. Early on, I had informed Taylor of Royland's atrocious snoring and we had contrived to set our watches accordingly. Eying the bottle, I dribbled out about a half of a teaspoon and drank it down.

While Royland retrieved his cloak and a few oddments, Taylor began unlashing the cages from atop the roof. As I had feared, it seemed the pigeons were to be our bedfellows. For my part, I spread out my blankets on the rear seat of the carriage and settled myself down. The bench wasn't long enough to stretch out properly, so I lay on my side facing the front with my knees folded not unlike a reclining cat. I punched my pillow and found a comfortable angle for my neck.

As the cages were slid into the space between us, Taylor established a similar nest on the rear-facing seat. Finally, with the lantern snuffed and Royland off about his watch duties, I began to drift away to the soft cooing of our avian friends. This day had given me a lot to think about.

***

"Lucas!" Taylor hissed, not for the first time.

I was being roughly shaken and a bright light pierced my eyes as I cracked them open a slit. The sleeping tonic must

57

have worked as advertised. As my waking mind arose to banish the remaining blackness of a dreamless slumber, an odd lethargy still held me in its grip. My arms were slow to respond when I raised my hands to shade my face from the glare of the lantern.

"Wuzzat?" I mumbled.

"M'wake," I hastened to add.

"It's time for the second watch, Lucas, and Royland needs the space," Taylor continued in an irritating whisper.

I sat up and sought about for my boots. I noticed the pigeon cages had all been removed from the coach, and my cousin stood at the open door peering in expectantly. I took a moment to mutter my wakefulness spell, 'manent vigilate.' This brought the room into crisper focus, and I was soon joining Taylor atop the carriage on the coachman's bench.

"Did you bring your sword?" Taylor asked.

"Yes," I replied," and my crossbow as well."

If something disturbed the camp at night, I felt much safer confronting it with my crossbow. After much practice, I found I could use my talent for winding to crank back the string almost as swiftly as thought. It had served me well during the goblin invasion.

"Aye," said Taylor. "It still confounds me how quickly you ply that thing. Here I devoted all those years mastering the longbow. And though I'd wager my sister's virtue that my aim is more true, the draw on your string defies reason."

The secret of that was simple (or at least well known to me). My magic center was a green field I called my 'inner garden.' It was far less potent than was average for a mage of my years. However, I also possessed a special talent that attuned me to the turning force of the earth. This allowed me to apply spin to an object with very little effort. Master Chadwick had instructed me by having me wind back a crossbow. The bow I used presently was made of witchwood and required tremendous force to draw it back.

Taylor and I settled down to begin our watch. He sat in the coachman's bench, and I sat atop the coach itself facing in the other direction. Between us, we commanded a view of most of the camp. I invoked 'visio tenebris,' a spell I had learned which vastly improved my night vision. It drew only a trickle of energy from my inner garden. I had used it for countless hours when watching over the flock back at Fowler Ranch. Along with the wakefulness spell, it made one into a superior sentry.

Nothing bothered the camp through the rest of the night. I spotted a few shadowy shapes slinking under wagons and around the temporary structures. Mostly, these were opossums or skunks attracted by the food smells. They found naught to keep their interest; Master Ross always insisted on keeping a clean camp. They soon scurried on their way. Once or twice, I glimpsed larger figures prowling near the forests edge, but none of these violated the sanctity of our firelight.

The picketed line of mules might have been our best means of alert. On several occasions, they became unsettled when they heard something or caught a scent they disliked. Taylor cautioned me to be especially vigilant at such times. But soon these commotions would cease, and the night passed uneventfully.

As the faint light of false dawn painted the horizon to the east, the camp started to stir. With a muted clatter, the cook began preparing the morning meal. Soon others were emerging to attend to their morning ablutions or commence their daily tasks. The mules were given water, and the air was soon abuzz with genial conversation punctuated by an occasional shouted order.

"Come and join me on the bench here Lucas," said Taylor placing his hands behind his head and giving his back an all around stretch. "It's time for your first lesson."

I arose to comply and gave my own stiff joints a quick shift to get the blood flowing aright. Sitting beside Taylor, I awaited his instruction.

"Do you see that man in the red shirt building up the cook fire?" he asked. "What do you make of him?"

I found the question a bit odd but answered it as best I could.

"I've seen him around," said I. "I think his name is Harold. He's a roustabout who works for Master Ross, I believe."

"Mark how he moves, Lucas. Do you see how he straightens before he turns? And when he bends to retrieve a stick, he plants a hand upon his left thigh. Muscles have memory, Lucas. Even when he's not wearing it, that man bears a sword."

I considered the matter thoughtfully as Taylor continued.

"Doubtless, this Harold Hunt served for many years as a soldier or in some similar occupation. Although caravans aren't allowed mercenaries, I'd hazard that Master Ross hired him for more coin than is typical for a lowly 'roustabout.' As a mage, Lucas, you have the right to wear a blade, though few mages ever claim it. To overcome your awkwardness, you should keep your sword belted on each day of our journey south. In this manner, you shall learn to move with more grace when the occasion again arises to wear it ceremonially."

I nodded once. This lecture was more than I had ever heard the quiet archer speak all in one go. I belted on my sword in the manner I'd been shown.

"Let's hop down and run some drills then," said Taylor. "I need to answer nature's call, so meet me back here anon."

How old was Taylor, anyway? No one said 'anon' anymore. The man set off into the woods with a determined stride and was promptly lost from view. I climbed on down myself. I thought about waking Roy but decided against it. My cousin always seemed able to rouse himself when there was breakfast to be had. Instead, I sought an appropriate tree of my own to water.

Returning, I found no trace of Taylor. I guessed that 'anon' wasn't synonymous with 'shortly.' I found that 'anon' was roughly time enough for me to grow annoyed anticipating my upcoming lesson. I released my spell of darksight; the glen had brightened. I unsheathed my sword and made a few practice swings to warm up.

"O-ho," said Taylor as he ambled up with a basket in one hand. "Eager to be at it, I see. Your enthusiasm is good; your form - far less so."

"What's in the basket?"

"Pinecones," he replied.

I refused to continue asking pointless questions and waited to see what the man had in mind. Taylor told me to hold the sword straight out before me with the blade facing downward and bade me to still its tip. He then said that I was standing too stiff-legged and required that I 'loosen my knees.' After making many more such corrections, he said I was to hold this pose and was not to move my feet.

It seemed simple enough, but after a minute or so it began feeling uncomfortable. It grew difficult to keep the point of my blade steady.

"We shall begin with a game," said Taylor, turning to step about ten paces away from me. "I shall throw pinecones at you. You may not shift your feet, but you may angle your body, duck, or dodge to either side. If you feel you cannot evade my toss, you may bat it aside with your sword then return to this stance. Begin."

The game lasted for a good twenty minutes with brief pauses for Taylor to regather his arsenal. My arm was aching by the time Royland put in an appearance. He looked on with undisguised amusement while I was pelted. Where was his blue magic shield when I needed it? Pinecones stung a bit the way Taylor threw them, and the man had a cunning knack for piercing my defenses and striking me in humiliating places.

With a laugh, Taylor at last called a halt. We headed to a hearty breakfast of oatmeal with raisins which I ate with my left hand.

Later, as the caravan moved out, I sat on the bench beside Taylor. I had informed him of my invitation to ride with Toolhup and Benalav, but he recommended I wait until after the mid-day stop. For this morning, he had me draw my blade and hold it straight out before me as we rode. It soon felt heavy, and every slight bump in the road sent a stabbing pain up my arm. If I let the point dip downward, the archer would slap the back of my head to inspire me to greater efforts. For a mercy, he would sometimes let me hold it straight out to the side instead.

By the time Master Ross called a halt at mid day, my arm dangled useless and boneless like the threads from a distaff. I stalked back into the underbrush, seeking relief. Back at Fowler Ranch, I had found a most useful side-effect of my affinity for plants. Whilst weeding Tilda's gardens, I discovered I was unconsciously siphoning strength from the plants I was uprooting. As the weeds withered away, my inner garden became more energized, and the excess energy banished my fatigue.

I sought about for a suitable victim. Not too far in, I spotted a stately elm. Wound about its trunk and along its branches high above grew a parasitic ivy all but choking the life from its poor host. Concentrating on my gift, I knelt beside its base, gripped the pernicious creepers, and tugged. At once, my inner garden responded. Green tendrils visible only with mage sight issued forth to twine down my arms to my fingertips. As the leaves of the villainous vine wilted and began to decay, its shoots and roots released their relentless grasp upon the beleaguered tree. The tendrils of my magic lapped playfully against the trunk of the elm, depositing any surplus vitality as my inner garden was refreshed. With a final tug, the ivy vines came loose from the ground and away from the tree. A shower of brown detritus descended from above and wafted off on the breeze.

Typically, I used this technique to refresh my magic. Since I had only a modicum of stamina as compared to other mages, it was quickly spent in any endeavor I undertook. My rock skipping feat at the lake had almost completely depleted my store of magic. Today, however, I was interested in a curious byproduct that Master Chadwick had noted. Besides restoring my magical strength, such transfers sped up my natural healing and contributed to my general good health. Sure enough, as I flexed my weary right arm, I noted only the dim remnants of the aching from Taylor's tortuous lessons.

I headed back toward the wagons with a new spring in my step, eager to resume discussions with my new friends. After assisting Olin Reed with hoof care for our animals and sharing a quick, cold meal at the cook wagon, I sought them out. Miss Toolhup and her brother had their own wagon, which they used to transport all of their paraphernalia and a few consignments bound for destinations farther down the line. The two welcomed me. Their wagon was up nearer the front of the caravan. And a space had been cleared in its bed where one could sit in relative comfort up near the driver's bench. The sky was clear and the breeze refreshing if a tad brisk. I looked earnestly forward to learning more about the first people and their ways.

***

The afternoon sun shone warmly on my face after we had cleared the forest of Danstonshire. The hours had slipped away while we exchanged stories from our lives.

Benalav held the reins. He managed the mules with only subtle tugs and voice commands. Taylor had done likewise but had occasionally used a coachman's whip to encourage our horses when they were flagging. He didn't strike the animals. The sharp sound alone caused them to lay their ears back and urged them to greater efforts. On the few occasions I had driven an oxcart back in Meadowfork, I had used a long, pointed goad for the same purpose. But I suspected I was well out of my depth with these equines.

Miss Toolhup was by far the more talkative of the pair. She would leap from one subject to another with an exuberance that was most innocent and endearing. She seemed fascinated by magic and was always imploring me to show her some small feat of levitation or to tell her why Royland so easily commanded insects.

I explained that each mage had a reservoir of magic which he envisioned in a certain way. Mine was like a green field from which I caused vines to sprout. They weren't actual vines, and no, I couldn't show them to her. But because I viewed my magic in this way, and no, I couldn't opt to view it differently, I had a special affinity for working with green and growing things. What was Royland's magic center? Well, it resembled a very large hive of hornets. His little packets of magical energy flitted about and would swarm and gather to do his bidding.

Although he spoke rarely, I had a sense that Benalav listened far more intently. Slow to chime in with his more thickly accented speech, his rare observations proved insightful and much more focused on the matters at hand.

63

When the topic changed to the first people and their history, I was unprepared for its grim beginning. I knew from my studies that there had once been war (or at least a long-standing, contentious struggle) between the men of Osten and the land of Lorédon. But whereas I considered the conflict a historical matter, the first people held it much closer to their hearts. They called it the *Iway jagha poH*, or 'blood enemy times.' Toolhup and Benalav had not yet been born when the feud had been raging, but their parents had taken part in it. Even among the younger Lorédonians, almost everyone had lost a beloved uncle or grandfather in the misguided conflict. The people of Osten thought the elves haughty and spiteful because they held onto any slight or affront for decades and sometimes even centuries. But it was really only a matter of perspective.

I suppose we owed the eventual peace to the depravities of the dark druids. This group of strange mages from the south had extended their influence all the way to the southern borders of both warring kingdoms. They brought strange, aberrant creatures, blights, swarms of rare insects and all manner of foul magic to plague the people in their northward advance. The elves were hardest hit, having fewer mages and being entirely dependent on the natural bounty of their land. The dark druids quickly made inroads into Lorédon.

It was at this time that King Raymond Osten (the first) made an unprecedented move. Though hard-pressed along his own southern border, he opted to lead an army into the beautiful Elven land to help repel the invaders. Although successful, King Raymond never returned home from that battle, being stricken by a deadly illness for which the elves had no cure.

Thankful for the reprieve and stunned by this charitable and courageous act, the Elven leader journeyed to Osten's capital of Fairglen with the body of the great man. There she met with King Raymond Osten II, grandfather to our current ruler. Grief stricken and new to his crown, the young king was adamant. No more aid would be spared for the elves. After much debate, a compromise was struck. The two kingdoms would be merged into one to face off against the graver threat. As Osten was by far the larger, the new kingdom would be named Osten and

Lorédon would become its eleventh duchy. This obligated its king to provide aid and succor to the elves.

For her part, the Elven leader affectionately called 'the bright one' by her people was raised up to the nobility and adopted a human name. Henceforth, she would be known throughout greater Osten as 'her grace, Lady Brighton Duchess of Lorédon.' Within her own lands, she was oft referred to as *wova zeja bosch tazbeth*, 'our bright and shining queen.' But she forbade use of the term '*tazbeth*' outside of her borders. Thus, an uneasy truce was accomplished in the Great Accords of Fairglen. All this had happened more than a hunderd years ago. And though King Raymond Osten III was now almost in his dotage, the 'bright one' still reigned over the elves as the last living signatory of the Great Accords.

I tried to take part, supplying details from my scholarly pursuits regarding those times. But though the elves agreed with many of the essential facts, they laughingly disputed many others. They deemed them the scribblings of old men who weren't there, based upon stories recounted by people one had never met. The elves preferred an oral tradition and often had access to direct witnesses of recent events. By 'recent,' they could mean anytime in the last several centuries. It boggled the mind. I doubted the concept of historical sourcing would ever catch on among the first people.

I was so fascinated by the tale, that I almost failed to notice we were arriving at a crossroads. Riding back along the line of wagons on a saddled mule, Harold Hunt spread the word that there would be a short break to stretch and to water the animals.

"Ghee," said Benalav, echoing the command given by the leading wagons and causing our draft team to turn right and off the road.

Up ahead, where the road east out of the Danstonshire met the highroad running north to south, stood a life-sized statue of a mounted knight facing west. It towered above the crossroad on an enormous block of marble.

"What's that about?" I wondered aloud.

"You have not seen it?" asked Benalav. "It honors your baron and his brave men. Come. Let us approach and reflect on it."

So he climbed down and I followed. Recalling my manners, I offered a hand to Miss Toolhup to assist with her descent. Ignoring my chivalrous effort, she flashed me a smile, turned about and did a backflip with a half turn to land facing me. She then swept her arm out and bowed low.

Oh, yeah. Juggler.

We approached the monument at a steady jog. Many others followed at a more sedate pace. We arrived at the statue. Sure enough, chiseled into the base it read: 'Sir Vincent Arenson, Knight Commander of the Battle of Goblin Flats.' There followed a lengthy list of names commemorating those who had perished in the campaign. I read each one then bowed my head and thanked them for their sacrifice.

Sir Nolan had once regaled us with the tale of this conflict. He claimed it was but a simple prelude to the guerrilla warfare which was to rage through the forest of Arbordel in its aftermath. Here on the level farmlands that once comprised the western fiefs of Downham, the vicious little goblins, though numerous, stood little chance against the mounted lances brought north by Sir Vincent. They were quickly brought to heel and fled west.

Perhaps it was some genius of the sculptor's artifice, or mayhap I was projecting my own feelings on his creation. But the eyes of this more youthful Sir Vincent seemed to convey both a fierce determination and a profound sadness at once. Yes, I had heard the story. The stone horse atop which the man-who-would-be-baron sat was his favorite war mount, Reprisal. In accordance with stonecutter traditions, the steed was portrayed *passant*, with his right forehoof raised. This signified that Sir Vincent had been wounded in the battle. It struck me that *this* Vincent was precisely the same age as his son, Sir Trenton, at present.

When we had returned to our wagons and resumed our travels, we turned south. Continuing directly east, one would soon arrive at the Powell Fief, home to Sir James' squire, Blake, and to Lady Megan's handmaiden, Lynette. Because the

Tomcats had been hosted there on their way into Meadowfork, Master Ross preferred to follow a different route on the outbound trip. Therefore, we would end our day's journey at the Lester Fief some distance southward.

This time it was Miss Toolhup's turn at the reins and this afforded us a more rollicking ride. The baron's comment about his coach's unique system of suspension had been an understatement. For spoiled by its gentle swaying the previous day, I now felt each bump and imperfection in the road most keenly upon my backside. As the sun crept toward the horizon to our right, talk among us turned to more personal matters.

"So, Benny," I said, trying out a new nickname, "what do you have in mind for your Vallhallamar thing?"

Benalav blinked.

"I think you mean *Vallahimay*," corrected Miss Toolhup from her perch atop the driver's bench. "Benalavioshi has always known what he wishes for his life path. He would follow in mother's bootsteps and become a *puachoqua*, one who preserves the land."

As the two explained it, this unusual profession was very respected among the first people. There really was no human equivalent. The game warden that protected the lord's hunting grounds was the nearest match I could conceive. Due to their extended lifespans, the elves saw direct benefit from some very long range planning. The *puachoqua*, or 'Sylviculturalists' as I came to think of them, advised the queen on matters of the health of the land. They noted which animals were in overabundance and which were becoming too scarce. They marked which trees might be felled so as to improve the forest, and which areas would benefit from new planting and the like. It was why their land of Lorédon had become such a wonder to behold.

They went on to complain about how the other duchies of Osten were so badly mismanaged. The short-lived humans (no insult intended) were too quick to exploit any natural resource to its exhaustion. They should instead adopt the Elven view that they were not owners of the land, but rather its custodians for future generations.

"What about you, Tula?" I tried again. "What will be your *Vallahimay*?"

"I am ... how do you say it? ... undeclared," she declared, flicking the reins and narrowly avoiding a chuckhole. "I will decide in a few years - *after* I have seen *much more* of the world. Perhaps I will become a dancer!"

Benny only smiled and rolled his eyes.

We talked of many things. I learned some useful greetings in Elvish to broaden my repertoire. I already knew a few phrases in gobbledegook from during the siege, but I expected these were all curse words and insults. Still, they might come in handy. After all, what else might I have to say to a goblin?

The sun began setting, and still we pressed on. That broken axle yesterday had put us far behind schedule, and Master Ross seemed hellbent on making up the deficit. We had entered the Lester Fief and were now on the outskirts of Aeriston. This small 'town' had sprung up around the copper mine and was our destination for the night.

The caravan master had negotiated an arrangement for us all to sleep in a barn safe from the elements. It had been an over full day. After tending our weary animals, I rejoined Taylor and Royland at the coach. Owing to the late hour, it had been announced that only cold food would be available at the cook wagon. They would make it up to us with a hot meal at breakfast. I laid myself down in a sweet-smelling bed of hay and awaited the blessed oblivion wrought by a full teaspoon of my lady's emerald elixir.

CHAPTER THREE

The Tailor

"I go to a better tailor than any of you and pay
more for my clothes. The only difference is that
you probably don't sleep in yours."

~ Clarence Darrow ~

I awoke with a throbbing headache. Something was wrong. I knew it before I opened my eyes. Though I could recall no unpleasant dreams, there was a sense of something lurking just at the edge of my awareness. I had become convinced that the writhing line of force I had felt at the keep was none other than the witch's ley line. Abigale had once mentioned it was closer to the surface there than anywhere else she had perceived. And sure enough, as we had traveled, it had slowly receded until I had almost forgotten it. Now, it had returned with a vengeance; it would seem.

If it was indeed the ley line, why could I discern it at all? Had Grandma Abbey not mentioned it was available only to one having her affinity? Perhaps the nearby copper mine had disturbed the natural order. Or maybe it wasn't only the witch's memories that had come to rest within me upon the shattering of her heart-shaped crystal. Regardless of the reason, I knew I should tell someone. I wished I could ask Master Chadwick about it, but he was far too distant to get a ready reply. Royland. I would tell Royland.

While striving to order my thoughts, I fought through the lethargy that resulted from Megan's elixir. I sluggishly heaved myself up to my feet, brushing the hay from my tunic and breeches. I wanted to retch.

The others were still soundly asleep, and I had no desire to waken them in the wee hours of the morning. I therefore quietly pulled on my boots and made my way out of the barn and into the brisk night air. I concentrated on the angry boil of energy which prowled at the periphery of my thoughts. I reached out to it just as I had so often sought my inner garden, but it failed to respond. Baffled, I strode over to the picketed line of mules. They stirred, and some raised their heads at my approach. Stroking the neck of the one nearest, I was comforted that at least my nightmares had ceased. Thus, I passed my time in quiet thought until Taylor emerged from the barn for our next lesson.

This time, he threw acorns at me and I was much harder pressed to fend them off. Pinecones had merely humiliated me. These acorns hit hard enough to raise welts and soon had me drenched in sweat from the heightened efforts this inspired. As the caravan made ready to depart, I cleaned up as best I could. The Tomcats were again resplendent in their finery. Ollie Reed had woven the ribbons into the mules' manes and re-affixed their gay plumage. The traders clearly meant to conduct some business at the next stop.

As promised, a hearty meal was available at the cook wagon, and we all appreciated the rare bit of ham and eggs that sat steaming in our trenchers. I joined the others as we partook of the nourishing fare. Aeriston had few structures of any significance, but there seemed to be an abundance of stone in their construction. I reckoned its availability was due to tailings from the mine nearby. The largest building was the smeltery that had been recently raised to process and refine the malachite ore into ingots of pure copper.

Nor was the area overpopulated. At breakfast, we were approached by a smattering of local miners intent on obtaining some few needful wares. These deals were struck quickly and easily by the bored traders. They didn't even deign to dicker.

I took my seat next to Taylor on the coachman's bench. We soon set off from the small settlement toward Sir Lester's estate in the village of Belsby. We were joined on the road by a new wagon. Heaped high with hay, it resembled one of our fodder wagons and took its place among them. It was hauled by a full team of four mules. And by their straining, I deemed it to be much heavier than it appeared on first glance. I remarked on this to Taylor as we got underway.

"Pay it no mind, Lucas," said the archer. "Draw your blade and prepare for lesson two."

Instead of merely holding my sword out and stilling it, this time Taylor bade me to make small figure-eights with its tip as we bounced along. This was supposed to develop some fine muscle control. Taylor seemed impressed that I could hold this pose after yesterday's unaccustomed drills. I explained I was a quick healer and neglected to mention the why of it. Nevertheless, before long, exhaustion once again crept up my beleaguered limb. Not only my upper arm was beset, but now too was my forearm aching from the abuse.

"That's enough for today, Lucas," the archer finally decreed, to my considerable relief.

Re-sheathing my sword, I hugged my tender arm close and looked out upon the farms and tenancies that outlay the humble village that was our destination. Like the rest of the eastern fiefs, the Lester lands lay flat and even. Not a hillock marred the uniformity of the countryside. Much of this acreage had been put to the plow, but now lay fallow and bleak in the dreary months of early winter.

My thoughts returned to my morning's rude awakening and the ley line that now disturbed my inner peace. I recalled my resolution to share this knowledge with my cousin, but the opportunity to do so had not yet arisen. Just as I had made new friends among the Tomcats, so too had Royland. Upon observing my cousin dabbling with his drum, Maestro Bok had approached him about sitting in with the musicians. According to the maestro, their band would be benefited by a bit of rhythm. Apparently, the others agreed because Roy now sat among them in their leading wagon where they were preparing to perform. Their trio had become a quartet.

Up in the distance, I saw the low structures of Belsby proper. It was home to Sir Harrison Lester and his goodwife, the Lady Daphne. Just then, the ensemble struck up their lively tune. The caravan seemed to come alive, and even the mules appeared to step in time to the jaunty rhythm that flowed back to envelop us in its gladsome grip. I looked forward with interest to being on the receiving end of the ceremony of welcome.

***

The welcome at Belsby wasn't nearly so grand a display as that put on by our baron. But it was a fine effort withal. The townsfolk were gathered on the streets to witness our approach. Lacking Westarbor's spacious outer courtyard, the wagons all came to rest in a row. They lined up on one side of the wide avenue which led to Sir Harrison's manor house.

The good knight rode forth to greet Master Ross. He was accompanied by his squire, Devon Klein. The heraldry of the house of Lester featured the cinquefoil, a five-petalled yellow flower denoting joy and plenty. It was emblazoned on Sir Harrison's shield and much evident on the many banners flown above the house. Also present was Sir London, attended by Sir Trenton's squire, Derrick. After the official welcome and at Sir Harrison's signal, a large bonfire was lit at the end of the lane by an archer's flaming arrow.

As our teams were unhitched, and the wagons were made ready, the good people of Belsby converged upon us. Several stood gawking at our coach, but Taylor shooed them away briskly saying: 'Passenger wagon only here. Move along.'

Not long thereafter, we were approached by a young page sporting Sir Harrison's cinquefoil livery. Taylor let him pass. The young fellow doffed his hat and graced us with a half bow.

"Is this the coach of Lord Westarbor?" he asked.

"It is," I confirmed.

"And do I have the honor of addressing Journeyman Aspirant Lucas of Meadowfork?"

"You do," I replied, amused by the formality.

"I've been bidden by my lord to invite two visiting mages and their attendants to dine with him this evening. Rooms have been made ready for your use and the full hospitality of Lester Hall shall of course be at your disposal during your stay here."

I had heard of *noblesse oblige* but wasn't certain whether my rank rated it. Still, I knew nobles could be very prickly and quick to take insult. Sir Harrison was one of the better ones. I had fought beside him during the siege, and he seemed an open and friendly sort. I decided to accept at once. Just for fun, I put on my most haughty manner.

"Tell your lord that Lucas and Royland of Meadowfork would be honored to sup at his table this eve. Our *attendant* and we will present ourselves... anon."

This time, by 'anon' I meant as soon as I could figure out the proper protocol for doing so, round up Roy, and head on over. Maybe Taylor had struck upon a winning idea with this useful little archaic adverb that could mean anything from 'immediately' to 'sometime tomorrow.'

"Very good," returned the page. "If you will instruct your lackey to drive the carriage into yon coach house, our groomsmen will attend to your animals and see to its cleaning."

With that, he turned and hustled back the way he had come. Taylor was looking at me strangely, and only after the lad was well gone did he burst out laughing.

"Very good, m'lord," he said in a stilted voice. "Shall I see to the 'orses then?"

"Do so," I said with a grin and a disdainful flap of my hand, "whilst I retrieve my fellow mage from his dabbling."

I headed up toward the musicians' wagon to seek my cousin. When I had traversed nearly half the distance, I spotted a commotion. Clustered around a wagon stood a group of citizens. Atop it was the cloth merchant I had met earlier. I had since learned his name was Samuel Robinson or 'Trader Sam,' as he preferred. He was extolling the virtues of his Arborvale Woolenweave to any who would listen. The attentive townsfolk seemed skeptical of his outrageous claims, but those who stepped up soon grew enamored of the shimmering bolts on display. As I approached, I noted a child trying to press his way through from the back and meeting with little success.

"Make way you filthy lummoxes," he chided in a decidedly non-childlike manner. "Step aside you churlish looky-loos and make way for an honest tailor!"

Several of those in the crowd edged aside from the pint-sized man's rebukes. He pushed through to the wagon and glared upward at Trader Sam.

"The name's Winkle, William Winkle," he said. "Disparage my size, and I'll spit in your eyes."

"Rest assured, good sir," replied the merchant. "None here seek to further belittle you."

This remark drew a tittering of laughter from the watching crowd.

"Aye. Have your sport, then," said the little man, folding his arms before him. "Believe me, friend, I've heard them all and from better 'n the likes of you. But I've a commission from Sir Harrison himself for his household livery, and that bolt of yellow might be just what I'm missing. If you want my custom, you'll politely hand it down with no more funny business."

Trader Sam made his most pious face and did so. The haggling that followed was so banal and predictable that the crowd began to thin. After agreeing on a price, the tiny fellow produced his purse and counted out a sizable pile of coins. These he placed on the wagon's rim, almost above his reach. Trader Sam scooped them up. As Goodman Winkle strode away with his glimmering golden prize slung over one shoulder, the merchant couldn't resist taking his parting shot.

"It was a pleasure doing business with you, goodman," said he. "I'll count them out again and let you know if you're a little short."

Wincing, the man stalked off grumbling about Trader Sam's ancestors having carried out a variety of unnatural acts. I continued onward skirting the crowd and soon arrived at the musicians' wagon.

"There's no proper tavern in this town," Maestro Bok was grumbling. "If there were, the four of us would surely clean up. Your tempos are top notch, Royland, and blend superbly with our pieces. Where did you study, friend?"

"I'm self-taught," Roy replied blushingly.

"As are most of us, Aloysius," griped the piper. "Why must you always go on so about your hoity-toity education? I bet we could get him guild-certified lickety-split if it wasn't for that mage thing he's gotta get on with."

I caught my cousin's eye (and his eyes were hard to catch).

"Speaking of getting on," I announced, "Royland and I have an engagement with Sir Harrison for which we should prepare. Your music sounded splendid, and I'm glad you enjoyed my cousin's drumming. But if you gentlemen will excuse us ..."

"Remember, practice is at sundown in widow Henderson's parlor," shouted the maestro as Royland hefted his drum and hopped down. "Be there or be forsworn!"

Roy actually smiled and nodded up at the three. On the short trek back to our coach, I brought him up to speed about our temporary new living arrangements. I also wanted to tell him about my problem, but there simply wasn't time. We arrived to find Taylor had re-harnessed the horses and was prepared to move out. I was sure it would prove an interesting evening at *Chez* Lester.

***

After settling into our rooms, Royland, Taylor and I had a warm bath drawn. Cleaned up and freshly shaven, we donned our finest attire and prepared for an evening meal with nobility. The room was delightful, and the scent of fresh rushes wafted about. The fragrance was tainted only by the faint whiff of pigeon droppings that accompanied it. For as usual, Taylor insisted on twenty tiny additional roommates in our chambers. The man took his responsibility seriously.

My arm still ached from this morning's drills. I cradled it close and worked my shoulder to relieve the stiffness. I had seen no significant greenery with which to ease the condition.

There came a knock upon our door.

"Enter," I said, thinking it was perhaps the servants come to retrieve the washtub.

There was a pause, and then the door swung inward. Framed in the entryway stood Derrick Lester.

"It is customary," said he with a gap-toothed grin, "to greet the son of one's host at the door. Or at a minimum to direct a servant to do so."

I arose and quickly crossed the room to clasp his hand with a hearty exclamation of 'well met.' I had first known Derrick when we were boys back in Meadowfork. Although a year my junior, he was the page of our good baron, and I - a modest miller's son. Soon after my magery was discovered, Derrick had been selected as Sir Trenton's squire. He and I had fought the mygaloms together at Tillerson Ranch and had been brothers at arms during the second goblin war and its horrific siege. Since attaining my raised station, I had relied heavily on Derrick to assist me with matters of proper protocol and the like. As the baron's former page, he was brimming with useful facts about the ways of nobles.

"My apologies, Derrick. We thought you might be someone else. Shouldn't you be attending Sir Trenton, by the way?"

"I switched with Sean Henry and came with Sir London when the baron sent the last patrol out this way. I didn't want to miss a chance to visit family."

While we were talking, Roy had padded over and extended his hand saying: 'Derrick, well met.' Derrick gripped the offered hand absently and shook it. I wondered whether the young squire recognized the rare gift he had just been given. For Royland only suffered direct contact with others whom he trusted implicitly. Standing beside my cousin, I marked that Derrick had grown at least four inches since this summer and filled out withal. His new regimen as Trenton's squire had packed on enough muscle to make Roy look like a scarecrow by comparison.

I cradled my right arm again and winced as I flexed it.

"Sword practice?" Derrick guessed, glancing briefly downward.

"Yep," I admitted. "Taylor's been putting me through my paces each morning."

"And just where *is* Goodman Allen?" he asked. "I heard he was accompanying you."

"I believe he's off requisitioning more seed from your steward for his avian charges," I replied, indicating the stacked cages in the room's corner. "He said he'd return anon."

"Ah," the squire remarked. "That would be just like him, wouldn't it?"

I recalled that Derrick and Taylor were both members of Sir Trenton's Lance, so the young man likely knew well the archer's habits.

"I came to see if there is anything you require. Dinner will be served by the next bell. I'd be happy to escort you down there if you like."

"Isn't that the page's job?" I asked. "What's *with* him, by the by? The little squirt speaks as though a book of court etiquette had gotten lodged in his throat."

"Milo is new, Lucas," Derrick explained. "He's only eight, and he gets a little overexcited about what he's learning. Father has been teaching him aught of courtly manners and diplomacy."

"Have you heard how my Uncle Robert defines diplomacy?" I asked with a grin.

Without missing a beat, Royland finished it for me, his expression deadpan.

"It's the fine art of saying 'nice doggy' while you fish around behind you for a suitable rock," he reported.

"Well, I suppose that's true enough," said the squire jovially. "Fear not, Lucas. Your arm will soon toughen up. Meanwhile, I'll let you in on a secret we squires use. There's an ointment the groomsmen employ when a horse's fetlock becomes swollen or inflamed. It works wonders on a tender sword arm. I'll fetch you some this evening."

So, we seated ourselves and chatted amiably while we awaited Taylor's return. Once we were united with our fourth, Derrick led us down to the dining hall of Lester Manor. Though nowhere near the size of the baron's great audience chamber, the room was well appointed and spacious enough for several tables.

Most who were to join us had already been seated. Royland and I were ushered to seats near the table's head. As our attendant, Taylor would stand behind our chairs. Sir London was seated next, attended by a household servant. Normally, this would be the place of his squire, but as Derrick was a son and heir to this house, he was himself to be seated near to his father's side.

Lastly came our host, Sir Harrison Lester himself, escorting Lady Daphne. We all rose at the lady's approach and resumed our places after she had taken her seat. Like the baron, Sir Harrison was brief.

"Ladies and gentlemen and honored guests, be welcome in the house of Lester. May our joyous and plentiful repast refresh us both in body and in spirit."

At this, he raised his goblet and drank deeply.

Many delicate dishes were brought forth but prominent among the entrees were all manner of fish. As I indicated one of these for Taylor to serve me, Sir Harrison noted my selection.

"An excellent choice, Lucas," he said. "Our *poissonier* prepares a marvelous eel. Those were fresh caught yesterday morning up at Lakethroat Village."

Upon noting my expression, Derrick was barely able to contain himself. He hurriedly whispered in my other ear that a *poissonier* was nothing inimical, but rather a chef who specialized in preparing fish. Relieved, I sampled a bite. It turned out that I liked eel. It was soft without being blubbery and had just a hint of sweetness with none of that fishy aftertaste.

"Here," said the knight, "You should dip it in some of this cameline sauce. That should spice it up and complement its flavor nicely."

He wasn't wrong. Though I may have lacked an educated palette, I could definitely appreciate the soft savor of cinnamon in the mix. Thinking I should contribute to the conversation, I sought about for a topic to share.

"We stopped at Lake Ganymede on the way here, Sir. It's a lovely sight."

"Isn't it, though? I get up there whenever the opportunity arises. I love to fish. When the bream are biting I ..."

"Don't get him started on his fishing stories, young man," interrupted Lady Daphne. "You'll soon as wish you hadn't the way he'll go on about it. Talk of something else, dear, lest you bore our poor guests to tears."

Frowning, the knight complied.

"Tell me," said he. "While you were up there, did you perchance glimpse the monster of the loch?"

I had heard of the fabled beast, but considered it a myth to frighten children. No one actually claimed to have found direct evidence of it. I said so in the most diplomatic terms I could muster.

"I'm convinced it's real," insisted Sir Harrison. "The locals at Lakethroat sometimes discern its gargantuan shadowy shape down in the depths when they venture out too far. They think it might lair on that island out in the center and avoid that area like the plague. And once, just for a moment, mind you, I thought I glimpsed an enormous reptilian head break the water's surface."

"I understand my husband drinks quite heavily on these little fishing jaunts he takes," supplied Lady Daphne with a wink.

And so the meal ran on. The Lesters were most congenial hosts, and all twenty or so guests were pulling back their chairs in satisfaction when Sir Harrison arose.

"For tonight's entertainment," he announced, "I have invited the caravan's minstrels to serenade us with their latest melodies. It is with an eager heart I rise to welcome Maestros Bok, Gordon, and Farrell."

As the knight reseated himself, the three entered and made their way toward the open space near the door. There was Maestro Bok with his lute, followed by the piper carrying both his recorder and the vielle of the third musician. Finally came their vielle player. He was lugging Royland's goblin war drum.

Sir Harrison frowned, and his eye twitched.

"Get that godawful thing from my sight," he exclaimed. "During the siege, I vowed that if I never heard those drums again, it would be too soon."

Working through his syntax, I realized his oath made no logical sense, but I strongly suspected he didn't favor the percussion instrument in question. As the stunned musicians scrambled to comply, Royland stood.

"It's mine," he proclaimed. "I took it as a trophy of war."

I could see the conflict rage on Sir Harrison's face. Having issued a command, he would appear weak should he rescind it. Having mentioned a vow, he might even appear to be forsworn. Pitted against this was the hospitality due a guest. I was amazed that Roy possessed the temerity to assert guest privilege over so trivial a matter. I was even more amazed that his gambit proved successful. The tension eased from the knight as his eyes fell upon my cousin and his genteel nature won out.

"A war trophy, you say?" he confirmed with a sheepish grin. "Well that's a different matter entirely. It would honor my hall to take our enemy's pride and place it at the service of our own amusement. Pray, let us see what the good minstrels intend."

There followed an uncomfortable silence as Royland moved to join the trio and seated himself. As the band struck up the first tune, a strident melody, Roy joined in. Rather than the hollow booming favored by the goblins, Roy produced a gentle tapping. Instead of using strikers, Roy only tickled the stretched hide of the drum's head with his fingertips and occasionally with his palms. The rhythms he elicited from the instrument were complex and blended beautifully with the melodious notes of the other skilled musicians.

The low buzz of conversations soon returned to the room, and I noted many smiles and heads bobbing in time to the music. Song after song was performed in this manner until at last Sir Harrison rose once more.

"We have fain enjoyed your music, good maestros," he declared. "And I would deem this evening a complete success if you could play for us 'A Knight's Lament.' Do you know it?"

The musicians briefly conferred.

"Of course we know it, good Sir," said Maestro Bok with an offended air. "Tis an old favorite sung to honor the dead of a war fought twenty years ago. Hear ye then, the song of an anonymous knight whose squire was slain at the Battle of Goblin Flats."

The maestro then bowed his head, and Ben Farrell blew out a short introduction on his recorder. Then began a song that was at once triumphant and melancholy. It lifted one up, then stabbed at the heart. While the recorder piped out its mournful main melody, Maestro Bok plucked a counterpoint upon his Lute. Liam Gordon sang the lyrics in a powerful, baritone voice. I wondered whether he would play his vielle. My question was soon answered when he began bowing it here and there starting in the second verse.

There was a chorus between each verse that always began with a set of 'Heigh-Hos!' By the second verse, those at the table joined in on these. By the third verse, I did as well.

By this time I was caught up in the story. The knight was describing his squire and the reasons they had come north to defend the kingdom. When they became embattled, the squire had kept to his vows and fought although they were 'sore outflanked.' When the knight fell from his wounds, the squire remained standing over him and defending him until he was overcome. Somehow the knight survived the ordeal to sing about it afterward. I think it was the final verse that gave me chills and raised the gooseflesh upon me. I wanted to grieve with the knight.

Though the knights had won the day!
My thoughts upon him dwell.
On the crossroads plaque nearby the attack
He will be remembered well.
Heigh-ho! Heigh-ho!
What a knight he would have made
Heigh-ho! Heigh-ho!
Still I mourn the price we paid...

As the final soulful notes of the recorder trailed off, silence reigned within the hall. There was no applause. None was needed. All bowed their heads in silent thanks to the men who had defended us on that day. Some openly wept.

When the statue at the crossroads had been dedicated, the knight who wrote the ballad had asked to remain anonymous. In that manner, all who had fallen might be equally honored. Some suspected it may have been Sir Vincent himself, for he was known to have lost his own squire on that day.

It was then that Sir Harrison stood yet again. Pinched between his thumb and forefinger was a coin. By its color, it could be nothing less than a golden crown. This he tossed in a high arc toward the musicians. As it rang on the stone tiles of the floor, others hastily stood and scrambled for their own purse strings. The coin was soon joined by many others which showered down in a jingling approbation. The astonished minstrels began gathering them up and scooping them into Maestro Bok's upturned hat.

***

Once again I awoke with my head pounding. Though it smelled strongly of wintergreen, Derrick's ointment had worked wonders, spreading its cool relief down my aching arm. I would be ready for Taylor's next torturous drill. My head, however, was a different matter. It was as though in denying the dreams I was overlooking something important. That was it. I felt as if I had forgotten something and couldn't bring it back to mind. The ley line had withdrawn again since leaving Aeriston, but it still flitted about just out of reach.

I stilled my thoughts and reached out to it again. It hovered encouragingly closer, but still beyond the sway of my will. Then an idea struck. Grasping instead at my inner garden, I drew forth a thin vine-like tendril and extended it out toward the alien manifestation. It worked. When they touched, I felt a pulse of energy shoot down the length of my vine to its roots. It burned like acid and my poor little vine twisted and blackened finally to fall away limp and spent. It left at its base an ugly little blister upon my inner field of green.

What had just happened? When I focused on this ulcerous hump, I found I could move it about, but not much else. I desperately hoped I hadn't permanently marred the perfection of my inner landscape. I tried moving the pustulant little cyst out of my inner garden, but it stubbornly clung to the edge. I let it lie there, next to my magic's source. I sat up. What could it mean? I needed to think this carefully through. I called upon my wakefulness to overcome the hebetude of my nightly medication.

As had recently become my habit, I quietly laced on my boots, pulled on my tunic and padded out the door. The layout of Lester Manor was straightforward, and I soon arrived at the main entryway. It was barred for the night. As quietly as I could, I eased the beam upward and slipped outside.

It was a clear night. The stars were visible, but only dimly perceived because of the large bonfire that still flickered lazily at the manor's front. Sir Harrison had ordered it be stoked to burn throughout the night. The Tomcats cook would use its coals to prepare their morning meal. The fragrance of a wood fire overpowered any other scent the night may have brought. The Tomcats' sentries and those of Sir Harrison had surely spotted me. But no one disturbed me as I ambled over and took my seat beside the crackling fire. A low-lying mist had rolled in and made hazy anything much lower than a man's knees, and there was no breeze to stir it.

Into this scene came a point of light from down the lane past the wagons. It grew and resolved itself into a small figure bearing a candle. He waded through mist up to his waist. He continued to advance down the avenue in my direction in ghostly silence. When nearer he trod, I recognized him. It was the tiny tailor who had dickered with Trader Sam. I had discovered over dinner that the man was somewhat of a legend in this town. He had been around for as long as anyone could remember. And his tiny hands could quickly make stitches so fine they could scarcely be discerned from the cloth itself. Moreover, he suffered a sleeping disorder. Perhaps he and Royland and I should found a support group.

According to the gossip, Goodman Winkle got up and roamed about in his sleep. If you didn't secure your doors at night, you might well find him snoring away at your kitchen table when morning came. His somnambulant adventures had become a cautionary tale for children who stayed up past their bedtimes. 'You'd better go to bed, or Wee Willie Winkle will come take you,' parents would say. To be fair, the man wasn't known to have abducted any children, misbehaving or otherwise. But his legend persisted.

He approached the bonfire wearing nothing but his nightgown. I had been told it wasn't wise to wake the man, so I sat stock still. He stared about unblinking for a minute and then sat down on the log beside me. A few moments later, his eyes closed. Then his head lolled to one side and a soft snoring issued forth. I wished my cousin could take some lessons from the man. This I could tolerate.

I was returning to considering my own problem when the man suddenly sat bolt upright and his eyes snapped open wide.

"Hog hocks and horny toads!" the man exclaimed. "I've done it again, ain't I?"

"If you mean walked about in your sleep, then yes," I replied.

The man picked at a scab of molten wax that had dried on the back of his hand and grinned at me sheepishly.

"I hope I didn't disturb you overmuch, youngster," he remarked.

"If you don't mind my asking," I prefaced, "how old *are* you, goodman? No one seems to know."

"I won't answer that," he returned gazing plaintively into the fire, "but I'll tell ya a story if you'd hear it."

I nodded solemnly, not wanting to ruin the man's mood.

"There once was a man who trapped small animals and birds. He had a sweet wife and a loving son. One fine day he was checking his traps and came upon a tiny bearded man caught in one. 'Free me,' says the little man."

"Were *you* the little man?" I asked.

William looked offended and said: "No! It was a tiny little man, no bigger than a cat."

"Anyways," he continued, "the trapper knew he should free the little fella, but suspected he may have caught himself a fairy, so he hesitated. 'Why should I free you?' he asked instead. 'I'm a leprechaun,' the little man replies, 'and if ye free me, I shall grant ye a boon.' The trapper asked what boon the leprechaun would give him, for he had heard of the deceitful ways fairies kept their bargains. 'You may name it,' said the leprechaun."

"The trapper thought and thought. Wealth was no good for fairy gold was known to disappear. He had several other grand ideas, but he didn't want to waste his boon foolishly. It had to be something the fairy could give him he couldn't likely get in any other way."

"To play for time he asked 'If you're a leprechaun, why can you not free yourself, then?' To this, the little man replied 'Your trap is made of iron and we of the fair folk possess no power over such.'"

"Finally, the trapper had his answer. 'You fairies live long, healthful lives free of the ravages of disease and old age. Can you grant such to me?' To this the leprechaun said: 'Only that? Tis easily done.' At this the trapper opened the trap and set him free."

"Did the trapper get his boon, goodman?" I asked in fascination.

"Yes and no," said Willie. He stared into the fire for a long moment before continuing.

"From the pocket of his jacket, the wee man produced a bean. 'Take this home and boil it for a good hour in a cup of cow's milk. Consuming the full cup of broth will grant ye the benefit ye have requested,' said he. Elated, the man returned home intent on followin' these instructions to the letter. On arriving, he found his worthy wife in tears and his son stricken with the plague. 'The reaper shall not have my boy,' said the trapper grimly. He promptly boiled that bean and bade his son to drink it straight down."

"Did it work?" I asked.

"Aye. The sickness left the boy, and he has never aged a day nor grew an inch since. The bean was meant for one already mature, you see..."

"It's hard to see all the ones that you love grow old and die. What's more, the fairies don't properly sleep. And now nor do I. I can't so much as lose my milk teeth. I expect the fairy knew of the boy's affliction - perhaps even *caused* it. Be careful, youngster, when dealing with the woodland fey. They can tell a true heart from that of a greedy bastard. The trapper should've freed the little man straight away, or at least accepted whatever boon the fellow chose to bestow."

At this Wee Willie rose and wandered off into the night.

There followed several more days of lukewarm trading before the Tomcats were ready to depart. Derrick returned to Meadowfork with Sir London after the arrival of the following patrol. This group bore a letter from Lady Megan. It was scribbled in a carefree hand that I now understood to be intentional. I took it back to our coach, dug up the "Book of Innuendo" and deciphered it. It was fun; like working a puzzle.

My favorite line was: 'With Constance and Lynette to keep me company, I'm not missing you at all.' The darling girl had smudged one of the 'Ls' in the word, 'all.' Another one that puzzled me somewhat was: 'Don't pay too much heed to Taylor; he's only there to serve you.' The 'L' in 'Taylor' also bore a smudge. My lady was advising me that there was much more to the archer's mission than he let on and that I should behave exactly as he instructed. Interesting.

I said my goodbyes and thanked our hosts before we set off. I could detect no change in the pimple conjoined to my inner garden and decided not to bother Roy with it. After all, what could he do about it? I was certain someone down at Conclave could sort me out. Perhaps when I was assigned as a journeyman to a new master, I would find some answers. For the present, I just leaned back and made figure-eights in the air as we left the Lester Fief heading for Downham.

CHAPTER FOUR

The Tyrant

"If this is where the monarchy is headed, count me out!"

~ Zazu, a wise little hornbill ~

The young man seated beside me seemed more able than I would have credited. As the miles stretched out behind us, he continued spinning the sword in lazy arcs. I had come to suspect the boy's magic was in play. Most that I had instructed in the sword were reduced to tears by this point. I shouldn't be surprised. Both he and his young cousin had oft proven most resourceful in their respective pursuits.

Truth be told, I owed each of them a weighty debt. Lucas had hefted that gigantic spider from atop me at Tillerson Ranch. Had he not, I may well have suffered the same fate as the late Kyle Digby (stars rest his poor soul). And though I blench to recall it, Royland's disgusting 'remedy' afterward had likely saved my good right eye. The lad had an *unnatural* control of insects. I still bore a scar along my right cheek. Once, I had tried playing it off as a memento of a lovers' spat, but Sir Trenton had called me on it. 'As I recall,' said the young lord, smirking all the while, 'the lady in question had eight hairy legs, and the flames that day were not those of passion.' Whenever had the stodgy youth developed a sense of humor?

As we were conveyed toward the lands of Downham, I spared little attention for the road. The horses knew well by now to follow the wagons before us in their plodding gait. Instead, my thoughts dwelt upon the dangers which lay ahead. In recent days, Guy Lord Downham had proven a plague upon the peace of Westarbor. He sat like a great spider weaving his webs of deceit and ever advancing plots to serve his overweening ambition. Moreover, Northford 'duchy' still lacked a proper duke to take him to task for it.

The Northford uprisings remain a distressing stain upon the baronies of the north. How well I knew of the treacherous misdeeds of 'his former grace,' Ferdinand Cummings. The disastrous rebellion he launched had merely caused the former duke to be stripped of his title. He and his family were exiled to an island of Indigo Bay, there to dwell in disgrace as wards of his brother lord. It was a far cry better than the gruesome punishments meted out to those poor wretches who had sided with him.

Nor had a new duke been raised up in his place. The king had instead opted to oversee the barons of our province more directly, including both Downham and that of my own lord, Westarbor. Despite persistent hints and gossip that the naming of a new duke was imminent, nothing of the sort had yet come to pass. I suspect his majesty revels in keeping his barons guessing and vying for his favor.

My ruminations abruptly ceased when my attention was drawn ahead. The wagons had turned off the road, and their occupants could be seen scrambling about in their beds. I spotted Harold Hunt galloping rapidly down the line on his saddled mule, raising a cloud of brown dust in his wake.

"Make ready! Prepare yourselves!" cried the roustabout.

"Is it bandits?" Lucas shouted, pulling his sword close and half standing.

"Worse," returned Harold as he drew up near our coach and turned about. "Taxmen! Bandits we could fend off, but these fellas will fleece you like a ewe in spring."

By this time, the wagons were lined up to one side of the roadway. All had spread open their tarps for inspection. I guided our animals aside and climbed down to the grassy berm. With a sour grimace playing upon his face, Goodman Hunt spurred his mule into motion and headed back up the line. The door swung outward and Royland appeared, staring blinkingly after him. As an afterthought, I lowered the folding step of our carriage, and the lad stepped down to join us.

"Welcome to Downham Barony," I quipped, "where taxes are high and the peasants are kept low."

Up at the head of the caravan, Master Ross was exchanging words with a group of mounted soldiers sporting the red and black checkered livery of their lord. Hopefully, our worthy caravan boss had prepared a suitable bribe, and the inspection would be but a cursory one. Our special cargo should remain covert. I thrust such thoughts aside and blanked my face as the assessors spread out among the wagons.

"A passenger coach," remarked one of them heading our way. "Have you aught to declare?"

"Only travelers and their personal goods," I replied. "The pigeons atop the coach are bound for his majesty's aerie at Fairglen. As such, they are not subject to tariff."

The man looked at me skeptically.

"Do you have papers to prove that claim, goodman?" asked the man, peering suspiciously into our open coach. "And who are these passengers? I saw no mention of such on the bill of lading."

"Two mages fresh from their apprenticeships," I replied. "They'll be reporting to Conclave to begin their service to the king. We joined the caravan for safe passage. I'll fetch their documents at once."

"Mages, you say," declared the man, looking stricken. "No, that won't be necessary, goodman. I'm satisfied all is in order here. Carry on, then."

With that, he promptly wheeled about and urged his mount back toward his fellows.

It was no laughing matter, and yet I laughed (inwardly, at least). Downham's bullies knew well their reign of fear was propped up only by their martial superiority over a cowed populace. They therefore rightly feared anything that might call into question the supremacy of the sword. And magic had always been a wild card in the game. It was why the king was so insistent that all mages be brought into the guild and made to serve him. All in the game recognized the importance of this dire trump card that lay ever at his majesty's elbow.

It wasn't long ere we were back underway. By day's end. Master Ross planned to arrive at the hamlet of Kentonbrook in the fiefdom of Sir Travis Mendel. This was deemed the ideal stopover on our way to the baron's castle at Downbury. I had therefore arranged to meet my informant at what passed for a tavern there.

"That's enough for today, Lucas," I said when the boy dutifully raised his sword once more.

***

The stay at Kentonbrook had been unremarkable and brief. It was but another of Downham's fiefdoms built upon the backs of his downtrodden serfs. Sir Travis *did* direct some of his household servants to secure several items for his manor house. Apart from that, trading was subdued and for the most part unprofitable. The threadbare citizens of this miserable hamlet could only pay in cabbages and wanted for nearly everything. What trading did occur was done more out of pity than from any desire for mutual profit. As with Aeriston, we set out again immediately on the following day. We'd all be eating those cabbages for long enough as it was.

In late afternoon, we entered the outskirts of Downbury. The monotonous farmsteads were replaced by other facilities which heralded closer habitation. We passed a tannery, and our mules nearly balked at the stink. Several mounted patrols had passed us by. They shot us offended glances at having to leave the road, but made no great issue of it. It was far simpler for horses to give way than for a row of wagons to do so.

Lucas climbed once again nimbly up to sit beside me on the coachman's bench.

"Why isn't your arm tired, Lucas?" I was finally forced to ask outright.

"You said that muscles have memory," the boy remarked. "I think magic must have memory too. For each time I take up the sword now, my vines come twining down my arm and help me to grip it and hold it steady. Should I stop them from doing that?"

This would explain the boy's newfound endurance.

"There is no *fair* in swordplay, Lucas,". I answered him. "My old drill sergeant once told me to 'use whatever you got and try 'n keep 'em guessing.' If your magic comes unbidden, then learn to use it to your advantage."

I hadn't thought of that old man in years. The last I had seen him, he was being marched away to the king's mines with my father for taking up arms against the crown. I was spared the same fate only for the undeserved mercy of being underage.

"Are you okay, Taylor?" asked the lad.

He was looking at me strangely. And I'd thought it was the other one who could read minds, but *that* lad seemed to lack all empathy. Lucas was too clever by half. Had he not spotted our disguised cargo wagon almost at once? In truth, I owed the boy more than my life. For it had been his keen awareness that had salvaged my honor. Rather than turning me in, the boy had come alone to confront me at the tavern.

As a younger man, I might have run him through and fled, but I'd been teetering on the brink for some time by then. When I'd first come to Westarbor as the king's spy, I thought all nobles abused their power and unjustly took advantage of their station. Their claim to rule for the good of their people according to some knightly code was mere lip service. But I soon discovered that Westarbor was the genuine article. And somehow he tempered his nobility with a pragmatism in his dealings that avoided the pitfalls to which so many such men succumbed. One couldn't help but admire the man. Lucas' earnest plea found my better angel that day and had changed my fate into something I could live with.

"Just some bad cabbage, I think," said I, extending my hand toward the boy. "It might help if you would pull my finger."

The boy's eyebrows descended, and he quickly slapped my hand aside.

"No thank you," he declared. "Uncle Robert initiated me into that game almost before I could walk. Take your flatulence elsewhere, Taylor, and attend to it yourself!"

In reply, I noisily broke wind anyway and fanned it in his direction.

"Why did you come up here, anyway?" I chuckled.

"Royland is snoring again," he replied resentfully. "I thought to come out and get some fresh air. You can see how well *that* idea panned out for me. Egads, Taylor, that's worse than the tannery we passed. I am no longer surprised that you are unmarried."

We rode on in silence.

Once again, I noted a curious thing. Though our coach swayed only gently as we passed over the troughs and furrows of the roadway, I could previously hear its wheels clattering. And now I could not. It seemed to happen whenever Lucas was present. Initially, I had believed we had merely found a level stretch of road. I became more attentive and focused on the wagon ahead. There. It had bounced sharply as it encountered a furrow. When we reached the same spot, we glided smoothly across it.

"Lucas, are you doing something to the roadway or the carriage?"

"I don't think so," the boy replied.

I explained the effect I had noted.

"I'll check," he said.

The young man's shoulders relaxed and his eyes grew distant. From this I surmised he was communing with his magic.

"You're right, Taylor," he finally said as he turned startled eyes my way.

His lips tightened, and he turned his head aside. But after a moment he turned back to face me and the tale came out in a rush.

"Several nights ago, I connected with a . . . peculiar energy. It left a blemish upon my inner field. I thought it would go away, but it hasn't. It has grown into a funny little hillock adjoined to my magic's source. I can't be certain . . . but I think it has to do with the witch."

He wrung his hands, and his brow knit in concern. I considered the lad's confession. I knew naught of such matters. But I wanted to reassure the young man.

"Well, your grandmother was an earth shaker. Mayhap you have just inherited some of her talent and it is only now coming to the fore."

"I've never heard of anyone having a secondary affinity, Taylor," he babbled. "And now it's doing things I don't intend. I'm afraid it might be *her.* I don't want to be *controlled* again. That was awful."

"Here now, lad. You just said it yourself. Magic has memory. Holding the sword out hurt your arm when the wagon bounced; didn't it? What if your little hill thingie is just trying to help - like your vines? Couldn't that be the case?"

Lucas drew in a steadying breath, and his face took on a puzzled look.

"You may be exactly right, Taylor. I shall have to study this phenomenon further. Thanks."

And with that, he swung back over the side and climbed back into the carriage.

"Wake up, Royland!" I heard him shout. "I've something to share."

He was a wordy little chatterbox, but he kind of grew on a fellow. It wasn't how I had pictured advising a teenager on care for his pimples.

Bump, went the wagon's wheels.

***

We set out upon the final leg of our trek to Downbury. Once again our caravan sparkled, and the minstrels sat prepared to announce our imminent arrival. Far sooner than expected, the wagons slowed and stopped. Up ahead, the roadway was blocked by a contingent of militiamen wearing the red and black checkered livery of Lord Downham. Out from among these, there emerged a glittering coach which dwarfed our own in both size and grandeur. It was hauled by a full team of four snow-white stallions. As it approached, Master Ross stood from the bed of the leading wagon and doffed his broad hat with a bow.

What was this? Was the ceremony of welcome to occur here outside the city's gates? Or did his lordship have something else in mind? The door to the carriage swung wide, and a young footman hopped down. He set a plush red footstool before the opened door. Down stepped Guy Lord Downham. He was a giant of a man. He stood at least six-and-a-half-feet tall and was well filled out withal. It was as though a great bear had emerged from the gilded conveyance and stared at us in challenge. His black doublet sported the image of a blood-red hawk, and many rings of gold adorned his fingers.

He was soon bracketed by several ranks of guardsmen as he approached the leading wagon. Master Ross remained supine but lifted his eyes to meet those of the baron as he awaited the words of welcome. Taking his time, the baron first stared down our line of wagons. When his eyes alighted on our coach at the rear, he smiled. Some hasty words were exchanged and Master Ross sagged back erect. Harold Hunt was soon dispatched and rode back toward us. One by one, the other wagons were pulling to the curb.

"You're to join his lordship up at the front," Harold instructed as he drew up his reins beside us.

I resumed our coach's forward advance, passing the wagons of our fellows. I figured his lordship would meet the two new mages from Westarbor. Surely I was not significant enough to merit such notice. Not to be outdone, I leaped down from my seat as the horses drew to a halt and lowered the folding step. I opened the door and stood silently at attention beside it, eyes front.

Lucas emerged and stepped down. At least he'd had the good sense to don his green doublet. I smiled inwardly at the graceful way he managed his belted-on sword. He was joined by his cousin who had climbed down from among the musicians two wagons back. Lucas bowed and said 'your lordship' as did Roy a moment later.

"So these are the mages of Westarbor," said the baron.

His voice rumbled forth in a deep basso profundo, but his tones were gentle.

"We have heard of your deeds and couldn't forego the opportunity to greet you in person," he continued. "Rooms have been made ready for your arrival and all the amenities of my castle shall be yours to enjoy. The caravan has been welcomed. Let us lead the procession through the gates of Downbury that my people may see we host dignitaries sent by our brother baron to the west."

At this, he turned and stepped back toward his coach. By this time, it had been turned about in preparation for the return journey. His footman bent and steadied the stool as Lord Downham surmounted it to alight within.

As we progressed through the gates, the caravan's musicians struck up their jaunty tune minus one drummer. With the baron's ostentatious coach leading the way and our quaint little buggy meekly following, we led the caravan through the teeming streets of Downbury. It was a contrast I am certain his lordship intended. It was then that a large coffer atop Downham's coach was flung open.

"A largesse!" boomed the voice of the baron's harker atop the coach. "A largesse from his lordship, the Right Honorable Guy Lord Downham!"

At this he began flinging handfuls of coins to scatter among the milling crowd. It was brutal. The gaunt denizens of the lower classes surged forth at once, trampling one another in an effort to claim a glittering prize. Those who approached too closely to the coach were not spared the whip. I witnessed one boy who had nimbly snatched up a coin being tackled to the ground by a group of thugs who promptly relieved him of it. This is what passed for sport in Downham. At least Westarbor didn't have to bribe his people to attend such events.

Once upon a time, I had been that very boy. Growing up on the mean streets of just such a burgh, I had eked out an existence in whatever manner I could. Largesse robs one of dignity. What sense does it make to tax a man to within an inch of his life and then dole some back to him with an indifferent hand? Better to give a man honest work and the pride that goes along with it. Then simply allow him to enjoy the fruits of his labor in peace. The truly needy would find sustenance from the charitable acts of their more able brethren. And such charity would possess meaning as largesse from a noble did not.

It was what the Northford uprising had been all about. Oh, father! Had we but known our efforts would be for naught, would we have risked it? But I knew that answer. My father would and did risk all for the hope of a better life. If men kept striving for this ideal, then one day, perhaps in some distant place, sanity and justice might win out. We could finally sever the bonds of serfdom that made us slaves to the land. Till then, we should just suck it up; I suppose.

***

"Just stack the cages over there," I instructed the porters.

Traveling with mages had its advantages; it would seem. A hot bath had already been drawn, and our soiled travel garments had been taken away to be laundered. A fellow could get used to such service. It beat darning your own socks.

"I'm looking forward to a proper bath and a shave," said Lucas to his cousin.

The other young man only nodded and sat down in the washtub.

"Since it's already got a few days head start, I'm considering growing out a mustache."

"Ridiculous," I opined. "It'll be years before that peach fuzz of yours can form anything resembling dignified whiskers."

"If you say so," he said prodding at his upper lip to assess the growth in question.

"Taylor? What's a peach?"

"It's a fruit grown down south where I was stationed for a while. Kind of like a plum but larger and orange."

"And they've got *hair*? Then the southerners can keep them," he declared.

I stifled a grin. We were to meet his lordship atop the parapet after we had cleaned up. He said he had a treat for us. While the two young men took their turns in the tub, I set about securing the perimeter.

"What are you doing, Taylor?" asked Lucas as he approached wrapped in a towel.

For a little guy, he appeared to have some well-developed muscle. I raised my finger to my lips in a shushing gesture and pointed to the peephole I had discovered. As I considered my options, Lucas stepped over to the bed nearby and began rooting about in the backpack he called Bob. Straightening, he turned and tossed me a small gray brick. It was a hunk of raw clay, like the potters fired in their kilns. I promptly worked a bit loose and pressed it over the opening. I doubted I'd find them all, but we might as well make the baron's men work for their intel.

We were soon off to meet the baron. Led by a stern-faced sergeant of the guard, we ascended through an outer tower to the battlement of Downbury Castle. Say what you like about the tinpot dictator, but his ancestors had chosen their castle architect well. The forty-foot walls were crenelated along their length and commanded an excellent view of the courtyard below. Unlike the smaller keep of Westarbor, the inner ward of Castle Downbury could accommodate the entire troupe within its gates. I could see the wagons of the caravan doing a brisk business, despite the chill. The overcast skies obscured the sun, and the clouds hung laden with what might be the first snows of the season.

His lordship stood before a set of cages the like of which I was intimately familiar. A soft cooing emanated from within them. The baron styled himself 'The Hawk of Northford' so I suspected I grasped what he had in mind. The great calf-leather gauntlet that ran up well past his elbow was the main tell. The man beside him was unknown to me.

"This is my falconer, Percival," the baron announced jovially upon our approach. "Percival, these are the two chaps I was telling you about. New mages from Westarbor: Royland Wagge and Lucas Harper with their attendant."

He then reached into the cage that rested atop the others. When his gauntleted arm reemerged, there was a large bird of prey perched atop it.

"And this lovely lady is Petra Accipiter. She's a bastard hawk. Her origins are unknown, but I suspect she may be a rock falcon by her coloration."

Falconry was the sport of kings. And most were well aware that only royalty had the right to hunt with a peregrine or gyr falcon. Less commonly known was that rock falcons or 'falcons of the loch' were reserved for peers ranked as duke or above. I saw Lucas exchanging a look with Royland. Both lads were clever and well read. Royland would hold his tongue, but before Lucas could spout something stupid, I'd best assert myself. If Downham hadn't marked me as a player, he soon would have had in any event.

"By her coloration... or your *inclination*, your lordship?" I asked.

The baron blinked.

"Perhaps a bit of both, Goodman *Allen*, is it?" he replied. "I find it odd that when yon traders fodder their mules, they seem to avoid that one wagon. Though it's heaped high with hay, they take only from the other two. It looks heavy."

He was a sharp-eyed old buzzard; I'd hand him that. He turned to the boys and spoke on amiably.

"Petra here is a well trained bird. Since she was hatched, she has taken food only from my hand or that of my falconer. Although retaining her instinct to hunt, she doesn't associate the kill with sustenance. Thus, she never takes what is *mine*. I wonder if your Goodman Allen is as well trained."

"He's always been well mannered and convivial in our presence, your lordship."

"With regard to the wagon," I added, "We have no intention of depriving Downham of its rightful tariff. Our liege supplied me with a generous amount that should cover it quite nicely. Your assessors will, of course, be granted full access to said wagon to verify our accounting. But I ask that this business be conducted in private. We fear highwaymen farther along our route might be tempted should they suspect our cargo. We appreciate *your grace* and forbearance in this matter."

At this, I handed him a purse of gold coins somewhat in excess of the needed sum. From the frown I'd seen on Gerard's flushed face when he'd delivered it to me, I imagined Westarbor was gambling the farm on this venture.

"Ah, *my grace*, indeed," he rumbled. "I enjoy the sound of that. Percival, release the prey."

The falconer opened a cage out from which flew a pigeon. The poor thing didn't make it a hundred feet before Petra was upon it. Her piercing cry caused those below to look up and marvel at the aerial carnage. Several more were released. Each time the baron's bird returned with the carcass, neatly dropped it at the baron's feet and was then rewarded with a treat.

Roy and Lucas seemed fascinated, but I quickly had my fill of it. Most falconers hunted wild birds. The symbolism did not escape my notice: Westarbor is the pigeon, and the hawk represented Downham. Message received. This pointless exercise in cruelty was also what passed for sport in Downham. At least Westarbor could properly kill a bird he'd already caught.

***

I stood behind the lads near the table's head. As the guests of honor, Lucas and Royland were given preference even over Lord Downham's knights in residence, who outnumbered our own by at least half again. Many cast us sullen looks as they spoke to their primping, overdressed ladies and were attended by their squires. Aside from the baron himself and his lady wife, only their son, Sir Eric, had been seated after us (if you could call what I was seated).

The baron had welcomed the visiting mages and profusely praised them for having 'saved Westarbor' from a disastrous defeat by the goblins. Best to stay sharp and try to figure out the old buzzard's angle. Methinks his lordship was a trifle to quick in accepting our belated payment. After sipping ceremonially at his goblet, he set it aside and turned toward my charges.

"I think you young men will enjoy this feast," he said as the first of the covered dishes arrived. "We have taken care to provide some of your favorites."

As a tray was uncovered, he cheerfully announced: 'Cameline eel for you, Lucas.'

Turning to Roy, he lifted the lid of a large silver tureen to reveal its contents.

"And for Royland, of course, the soup du jour," he continued, broadening his ingratiating grin.

"Your lordship seems adequately informed," Lucas said quietly with a hint of suspicion.

Good for him, I thought.

"We may lack the quaint little messenger birdies of your own liege, but we try to make do," parried the baron.

"You know, your 'doojer soup' is a lot like the peas porridge they serve back in Westarbor," the boy observed.

And . . . it was *gone*. The lad took to diplomacy like a fish to dry land.

"Ahem, quite," replied Downham, turning back to uncover his own dish. "Eat up, my boy. I think you'll find our chef to be a cut above what you're used to."

His page filled the baron's plate with three of the pigeons he had slaughtered earlier, and he began stabbing at them with gusto.

"I'll have some of that ham," said Sir Eric to his own servitor. His seating and the 'Sir' were both honorary. I understood the lad was a squire yet to earn his spurs. He possessed the considerable frame of his father, but rather than a bear, the young man put me more in mind of a toad. I think it was how his eyes shifted about without moving his neck.

Turning to his right, Lucas spoke to the knight seated beside him.

"I think I remember you. You're one of Trenton's friends," said the boy conversationally to Myles Nieves.

The man looked startled; and well he should. Far from being friends, he and Trenton, though fellow squires, had been rivals at best and bitter adversaries at worst. At Westarbor keep, he had long been identified as Downham's man and had been dismissed from the service of his knight there.

"Yes," the snake replied. "We were squires together serving your baron. I had to return home due to a family emergency, but there was *much value* to all I learned there. I have since arisen to the knighthood and now serve my *proper* liege.

"I see you are sporting a sword, Lucas," remarked the baron. "That's unusual for one in your profession. Are you skilled with it?"

"I took it up but a fortnight ago, my lord. Taylor's been training me to wield it properly."

"Has he now?" said the baron with a predatory gleam in his eyes reminiscent of the bird that was his symbol. "Perhaps you and our Eric here could have an exhibition bout, and we could observe how you're progressing. Give you a few pointers, eh?"

Lucas looked stricken. Be careful, lad, I thought. Eric paused in his sloppy dining and graced his father with an upturned lip.

"I don't know if I'm ready for that, my lord."

"Nonsense, my boy," supplied the baron. "There's no time like the now. I'm sure Goodman Allen has prepared you well. Tis dishonor to refuse. I'll set it up for tomorrow afternoon."

With the matter settled to his satisfaction, the baron returned to stabbing at his meat. His son followed suit and began inhaling his large platter of ham.

"I think you and Eric will hit it off," continued the baron after he had swallowed. "Tell me, are you close to the lady Megan as we have heard? I understand you are her protector. Have you any sway with her?"

Some color returned to Lucas' face as he warmed to the topic. I sincerely hoped the boy would never take up the game of poker.

"I am indeed the lady's protector," announced the boy, "and I dare name her a friend as well."

"In that case," said the baron, "Perhaps you could write to her and recommend my son as a suitor. Long have I sought an alliance with Westarbor, but my brother baron is slow to respond to my missives. There is much I could do to assist your barony were our relations strengthened. If you truly have the lady's ear, surely a word in it wouldn't go amiss."

"It would please me to draft such a letter, your lordship. I feel certain the lady would be honored to meet with Sir Eric. But you should know that Megan is very discerning and keeps her own council. If your son is a man of worth, she shall know it at once."

It was a big 'if.' It lay there like an unhatched egg upon the table, waiting for the baron to crush it. The nearby knights all paused in their dining to witness their lord's reaction. Lucas' innocent blunder might land him in the stew should Downham choose to take issue with this phrasing. Welcome to the exciting and potentially lethal world of *faux pas*, Lucas. Suddenly, Royland spoke up.

"Because," he said softly into the charged atmosphere. "My cousin meant: '*because* your son is a man of worth.' Sometimes my cousin trips over his own tongue. He flaps it about too much and I think it's grown loose."

After a pregnant pause, the baron began roaring with laughter. It was a mighty bellow that nearly blew the foam from his tankard of ale.

"And here we thought *you* had no tongue of your own," he guffawed, "*Grown loose*, indeed."

The diners settled back to their meals and musings and were soon settling back in satisfaction.

"My people," began the baron, "this evening I should like to grant you all a rare treat. The Tomcats' jester has been retained to show us all a bit of his humor of which I have heard tell. The reviews drifting out from Westarbor have been most complimentary. We shall judge for ourselves. Please welcome Manchester Kidder and his amusing antics."

With that, Manny came skidding forward bells ajingle and promptly tripped and fell over onto his face. Fishing about in his pocket, he rolled to one side and lofted a handful of confetti about two feet above his recumbent form.

"Ta-dah?" he said weakly.

When the baron chuckled, so too did his knights. There was little of joy in the sound. It came out forced, as though from duty. Manny rose unsteadily to his feet and brushed himself off. Was he drunk or was this merely part of his act? Underneath his painted smile, the man looked unhappy.

Your excellent liege-lord, the baron,
His funny bone he sought to wear in,
Required through informants,
A command performance,
In this hall thus, I find myself . . . (therein).

This wasn't up to Manny's usual standards. Wait a moment. That phrasing... I suddenly recognized it to be set in the code of the king's spy network, a brotherhood I had forsworn only a few scant months ago. Was Manny trying to tell me something?

To honor the good baron's guests,
I shall grant some of you requests.
Name a man from Westarbor.
And I'll be his barber.
And put my poor wit to the test.

'M-E-E-T A-T T-A-V-E-R-N,' this revealed.

"Who shall my first victim be? Why it's lady's choice, of course," he said as he staggered besottedly toward the baroness. "Who shall it be, my lady? Name any man of Westarbor and Patsy and I shall portray him in good fun."

The Lady Downham shivered squirrelishly in her high seat. She was a quiet one. At a nod from her husband, she spoke in a quavering voice that smacked falsely of rehearsal. "Do Trenton first, for he seems a buffoon most worthy of ridicule."

"As my lady commands," said Manny, puffing out his chest and strutting about like a peacock.

He transferred Patsy to his right hand and began wielding him like a sword.

"I am the brave Sir Trenton," he decried in a voice which had lowered by an octave and was over-accented with noble tones. "I'm a knight now 'cause I've killed a chicken with the body of a cat!"

"Here kitty, kitty," Patsy added to a tittering of laughter.

"Most apt," spouted Sir Myles. "You simply must do their gardener, for I hear he is a tragic oaf most memorable."

Manny immediately stooped over, crossed his eyes and made motions of laying something on the ground.

"I M-m-m-must lay out the b-b-baron's sod," he said as he 'worked.'

"Green side up! Green side up!" chided Patsy all the while.

I saw Lucas scowl at this portrayal. The boy may as well carry placards about that announced his mood. 'I'm Hungry' or 'Now I am Sad' they could read.

And so the tedious affair ran on. Each knight at the baron's table arose to designate a fresh target for Manny's hollow mockery. To his credit and despite overdoing it, some of the skits did have the rudiments of comedy. I suppose he couldn't help himself. The man was an artist. And he seemed to know his audience. Though his act now consisted of pratt falls and low humor, the gentry of Downham seemed to lap it up. The final knight stood.

"Do Royland, then," said he.

Manny cast an apologetic gaze toward the elder of my two charges. Royland returned his gaze squarely with the courage of true martyrdom and nodded. Manny began rocking forward and back on his heels and his mouth worked soundlessly as he gazed up at the ceiling.

"What's that?" asked Patsy. "I can't heeeear you. Are you a mage or an oil painting?"

Royland smiled. He next began slowly and rhythmically to clap his hands together.

Some of the surprised onlookers joined in. Before long the hall was awash with good cheer as the very subject of their mockery demonstrated that in Westarbor we could laugh at ourselves. I doubt many of them were aware such freedom of thought and expression could ever exist.

"All in good jest," boomed the baron over the unexpected approbation. "We harbor no ill will for our brother baron to the west or his minions. Well-done, worthy jester, your skills have proven worth the coin. Now get you gone from my hall. As to the rest of you louts, drink up; the kegs are beginning to run dry!"

On that sour note, the feast was dismissed.

***

Nester's Flagon was Downbury's premier tavern. Lucas was surprised there was more than one such drinking establishment. I'd been through here a few times before, but they'd expanded the old girl since those days. Despite the early hour, Nester's was doing a fine custom. I credited this to the caravan's minstrels being newly arrived.

The jester was so well disguised that I failed to recognize him at first. He sat at the bar looking scruffy, ragged and disreputable. I took him for some vagabond or other shiftless denizen of this worthless borough. I had taken my seat at a table nearby and was thoroughly enjoying the Tomcats' quartet. They were playing a melody about the battle with the goblins at the gate. Their lyrics ascribed all the credit for the victory to Lucas, as if he had single-handedly routed the entire horde. It was a catchy tune. I propped my feet atop the stool opposite my own.

107

Ever since the baron's display of falconry up on the battlement, Lucas had been insistent on knowing what was in the wagon. I had finally relented and briefed him. He would know soon enough in any event. At Aeriston, we had taken on a wagon with a shipment of Westarbor's copper ingots. It was enough to complete a large order. On safe delivery to Eagle's Keep, the consignment would earn the baron funds sufficient to ease his financial woes. This was one of my missions. It had to stick in Downham's craw that the valuable metal had been mined from lands that were once his.

Delivering the boys safely to Conclave was another of my tasks. But using me thus hinted at a third, subtler mission. I believed his lordship wished to send a message to the king. The message was twofold. First it read: 'We have discovered your man among us. He works for me now.' Secondarily, it said to all other players of the game: 'Taylor has twenty of my fast messengers ready to release at a moment's notice. Interfere with this shipment at your peril, for I shall know of it at once.'

"That drummer's an 'andsome one, " I overheard one barmaid say to another. "All skinny and delicious. I'd like to give 'im a proper tickle; I would."

My attention was drawn to the bar where an irate barkeep was admonishing my contact.

"Oy. I know your like," exclaimed the man. "Of course there be food here but it ain't for free. Them stools is for payin' customers; they is. Unless you're buyin', don't be sniffing around here for handouts. Smellin' it won't fill your belly anyways."

At this, vagabond Manny raised his hand and with a whirling bit of prestidigitation caused a silver coin to appear pinched between a thumb and forefinger. Flicking it aloft, he caused it to land with a ringing sound atop the bar, there to spin and settle. When the barkeep reached for it, Manny adroitly snatched it back.

"There my friend," he explained. "Now you've had the sound of my money. I believe it was enough to purchase the smell of your food. Are you satisfied?"

Some people just couldn't help themselves. As the barkeep stood puzzling out whether to be angry, Manny caused the coin to reappear and roll toward the man.

"If not, set me up with two tankards of your spiced mead, then," he added.

When the man had filled the order, Manny took up the tankards and strolled my way. I pulled my boots down from their comfy rest as he slid one over toward me.

"The first one's on me, friend," he said with a subtle hand gesture.

It was so quick that I wouldn't have noticed it had I not been looking for it.

"Pull up a stool and join me," I replied.

"Your tail is at eight o'clock seated at the bar," he muttered. "The obvious minder I'm sure you've already spotted. It's the captain of the guard seated at that table to your right."

"Nothing suspicious about a couple of caravan mates meeting to knock back a few," I returned. "So why'd you break cover? I hadn't made you as yet - not for sure."

"I need your help," he said.

"I thought I was *persona non grata* in the brotherhood by now."

"You are. For a wise man once said: "No man can serve two masters: either he. will hate the one, and love the other; or else. he will hold to the one, and despise the other.'"

"I believe another wise man remarked that the devil can cite scripture for his own purpose," I returned.

"Then let us cease mincing words. Your baron has brought risk upon us all."

"It's not *my* baron you need worry about."

"Exactly. Your shipment, and thus my caravan, is in jeopardy. Our interests coincide."

"I thought it was Master Ross' caravan."

"He does what I tell him. It's the same as being mine."

"What do you want me to do?" I asked.

"There's a tinker you should speak to. He goes by the name of Jeremiah Blessings. The code word is 'cantankerous.' And lose your tails - both of them.

"Is that all?"

"You might want to look into Trader Sam's checkered past," suggested the jester, draining the rest of his tankard and sliding back his stool.

I considered the retreating jester as I sipped at my own flagon. It made sense. A traveling caravan would be welcomed anywhere in the kingdom. Manny could gather intelligence on the notables at each stop without suspicion in the guise of preparing his limericks. As to Trader Sam's past, did that mean he was Downham's agent? If so, the man had a smooth cover himself. Checkers was code for Downham's red and black livery. It amused me to think that while Downham played at checkers, *my* baron was playing chess on the same board. The analogy was apt, given the goals of the respective games. In one, the object was to become king; in the other, it was to protect the existing king at all costs. That was my baron, loyal to his core.

I thought I'd be done with all this skulduggery when I'd come clean to Lord Westarbor. But the man had promptly cast me in a very similar role. And since he held the charge of espionage in abeyance, he now had me by the short and curlies. It was odd that he would so readily trust a man who was already forsworn. The rumors about him must be true. Those blue eyes could see through to a man's heart. And my heart was with Westarbor these days; the king be damned.

I sat and listened to the music. I ordered a few more drinks and waited for my minder to get bored. Even a dedicated man had to use the piss pot eventually. Then I'd lose Captain Obvious in some other manner. Here's hoping the mead hadn't muddled my mind.

CHAPTER FIVE

The Tinker

"No proceeding is better than that which you have concealed from the enemy until the time you have executed it."

~ Niccolò Machiavelli ~

When I returned to our rooms, Lucas was in a panic.

"*There* you are, Taylor," he said. "The baron set the time for my exhibition match with Sir Eric. It's to be just after the noon bell. I'm to fight him in the main courtyard, and I haven't a clue how to prepare."

"Prepare to lose," I advised.

"I had hoped to make at least *somewhat* of a showing. You know, 'do Westarbor proud' and all that?"

"Lucas, it takes *years* of dedicated practice with the blade to become a swordsman - years Sir Eric's had and you have not. You've watched Trenton sparring with others. Do you think you could long stand against him?"

The young man frowned and shook his head emphatically.

"Your goal should be to avoid getting hurt. Oh, make a bit of a show of it to satisfy honor. Don't give up without at least taking a scratch or a good thumping or two. But even if you somehow could win, it wouldn't be wise to do so. For crying out *loud*, Lucas, he's the son of a baron and not an honorable one at that. Just remember these words: 'I yield me,' and learn to savor the taste of your pride as you swallow it."

"Right. Got it. He's an S. O. B." Lucas smirked.

Unbelievable. *That* was his takeaway? After checking in on the pigeons, I headed for the door.

"Aren't you going to help me prepare? Where are you *going*, Taylor?"

"Nah. I need to see a man about a lantern. I'll join you later in the courtyard."

I could feel the boy's distraught eyes pressing on my back as I stalked off. I crept across the fairgrounds, doubling back several times to make sure I wasn't still being followed. I made my way surreptitiously toward our coach. Wait. Was that *motion* I detected? Someone was within. I don't think we left anything of value when we had moved into the castle. But I knew the baron's men might come to ransack it, or perhaps sabotage us in some way. Thinking to confront the scoundrel, I quietly drew out a knife from my boot.

"I know you're in there!" I shouted. "Come out and face a reckoning."

The carriage rocked again, and I prepared myself to face whoever might emerge. After a few moments of silence, I grew impatient and was just reaching for the handle of the door when it swung ajar to reveal Royland. He glared down at me with his lips pressed tightly together. His hair was disheveled, and his face flushed.

"Weren't you just at the tavern?" I asked in surprise.

"We finished the set," he replied. "We're on a break for lunch."

"Who is it, Royland?" came a feminine voice from within.

"It's just a servant, Laura," he answered while casting me a pleading look. "He'll be *on his way* soon."

"Laura works at Nestor's," he mumbled. "I was showing her the carriage. Is there something you need, Taylor?"

Amusing as it was to discover Roy was a closet Lothario; I did have business to get on with.

"Hand me down that lantern; will you? And you can disregard that 'reckoning' stuff. I'm just a bit jumpy. I've been known to 'show a woman the carriage' a few times myself. It's customary, however, to hang something on the door handle to guarantee privacy."

"Done and noted," he replied as he complied.

Then he quickly eased the door back shut.

I swung the lantern in a high arc and brought it crashing down hard upon the flagstones. The dull, ringing impact was accompanied by the crunch of broken glass as the oil reservoir shattered and dribbled its contents out upon the pavers. I then made my merry way toward Smithy Rowe while presenting an unhappy face to the world at large.

The shoppe was called, "Blessings of Tin." It was nestled between "Thomson's Smithy" and a structure that appeared to be a repository for coal. I was frowning as I rapped upon its closed door for the third time.

"Go away; we're closed," came a muffled response.

"My business is urgent. I've a lantern that needs fixing."

"Not my problem."

"Open up, you *cantankerous* old curmudgeon!" I exclaimed.

After a brief pause, I heard a bolt slide back.

"Come in. Quickly then," whispered the man whose bearded face appeared suddenly from around the door jamb.

After ushering me within, he secured the door. The back of the shop was a riot of pots and pans and other dented or broken items. Here at the front stood a massive workbench with a variety of tools for scraping and shaping hung neatly above. Nearby a modest iron cauldron hung within an ingle over a low-burning fire. The tinker's eyes took me in, then roamed down to the lantern I held.

"Cantankerous," I repeated in a calmer voice. "What's the cackle?"

His shoulders took on a stubborn set, and he eyed me warily.

"Hold on a minute," he said. "This one is big. If you want it, you need to do me an earnest."

"And what would that be?"

"I want out," he declared. "The lay is getting too grand for my gullet. Take my wife and me and our two children out of this wretched barony. You've got wagons. You can hide us and take us past the border south of here. If I sing, I want your guarantee you'll do that.

"That's quite a big ask. Is your cackle worth the seed corn?"

"It's worth your life."

"Then speak on," I said.

"Here's the peach, then. The night before last, I was in the back when a pair of checkered wabblers came in. I was taking a nap, so I just let them think I was out. Before they left, one remarked to the other how there's to be a meeting outside the city walls."

"Who were these men?"

"I'm getting to it," the tinker forestalled. "Thinking to earn some buttons, I put on my best slither and strolled past the bus nappers that night out to where they were diving. It was a bunch of rum padders - the well-equipped sort. There had to be three dozen at least. And the wabblers were there with them."

"How do you know it was Lord Downham's men associating with these bandits?" I asked. "Couldn't it have been other bandits merely posing as soldiers?"

"I *knew* one of them. It was that Myles Nieves fellow. Doubt me not."

"Then I had a spot of luck," the man continued. "I couldn't hear what they were saying, but when Downham's lot were leaving, I ducked back into the brush. One stepped down off his prad to take a pee, not twelve paces from where I hid. I saw a parchment poking out from the man's saddlebags like it was wanting me to take it. Being a fair bung nipper, I relieved him of it quick as a blink."

"What was in the note?"

"I couldn't read it. So I offered it to the jester. He knew how to break the checkers' code. When I asked him my earnest, he said he wasn't allowed to 'free assets,' but that *you* could. I don't give a tinker's dam whether some royal's rust gets nipped. But if the wabblers see me as a hole that needs plugging, I'll be crashed and my family will be having tea with the pigs. Will you do it?"

I was wavering. The baron was likely even now stationing more loyal and competent assessors along our southern route. It wouldn't be easy to hide a family of four. But if Manny had left it up to me, he would likely help. Suddenly it made sense. Master Ross told us late yesterday evening that we would move on tomorrow morning. I should have thought a big burgh like this would merit at least a week's stay. The caravan boss had spouted some drivel about winter's onset, but now I could see it probably related to this mysterious note.

"Here now, I squealed, now where's the cheese?" the tinker prompted yet again.

"All right," I agreed, "we'll do it. Take your family to the fair tomorrow morning early. Be ready on the main street just outside the castle's gates. Have your belongings packed up and ready to go. No more than a single travel bag apiece. Leave them in the back and stack that clutter atop them. *Don't* say any tearful goodbyes to friends or relatives. *Don't* be seen acting in any unusual way, such as selling valuables. If you leave here, you're starting from scratch."

The man's eyes widened as he considered the natural consequence of his decision, but then he nodded as his beard bunched up around stiffened lips.

"In that case," he said, passing me a parchment, "the jester said to give you this. It's to be a two-'fer: Westarbor loses the shipment, and Leopold takes the blame."

I perused it. The plan was diabolical. A heavily armed group of highwaymen was being sheltered and provisioned in the southern wilds of Downham Barony. When the caravan set out, they would swiftly and quietly relocate, infiltrating the lands of Lord Leopold Stein to the south. Their forward camp there had already been established. There they would lie in wait and fall upon us in numbers too great to be repelled. Should anyone survive the raid, Lord Leopold would be discredited for his failure to protect the Tomcats and the king's highway.

I had been briefed about the lord in question. Contrary to the custom of adopting the name of his barony and insisting on his title, the charming old gentleman favored the moniker: 'Lord Leopold.'" He claimed it had a dignified ring to it. Sadly, my intel also had it that the old gray wolf was fast progressing toward senility and losing his grip upon his barony. Heirless, his wife, the lady Wilhelmine Stein, was holding it all together with the help of his loyal knights.

They were staunch supporters and allies of Westarbor. They too kept messenger pigeons, but in a manner not nearly so grand as that of my liege. They had spent the last of their birds raising the alarm over Downham's insidious machinations regarding the border last summer. Restocking their mew with blue-banded birds was one of my tasks for this journey.

That was neither hither nor yon. I could apprise Westarbor of our situation. But lacking any gray-banded pigeons myself, I couldn't convey a warning to the Steins. We were on our own. We would simply have to run the gauntlet and pray we could emerge unscathed.

***

A gentle flurry of wispy snowflakes drifted down from on high as the bell tolled noon. The dark heavens had not yet unleashed the fury they promised, but foreboding black clouds amassing above portended heavy snowfalls to come.

Although the outcome was never in any doubt, it would unexpectedly prove an exciting mismatch. The boy stood poised to confront his first opponent in the sword. I approached the ring of the baron's knights and wove my way through to stand before my charge. Royland had abandoned his womanizing to stand at his cousin's side. Our side of the circle seemed a bit desolate. Most clustered about the boy's opponent, grinning and offering bits of advice.

Sir Eric stood amid this pack of jackals armored from head to foot in expensive-looking mail. That didn't necessarily mean anything in a practice match. In fact, it might slow him down. That was all to the good. Both combatants had been equipped with suitable wooden practice swords well-matched in heft and reach to the blades with which they were accustomed. Such a blade might not lay one open, but it could raise a nasty bruise or three. And broken bones were not uncommon when wielded with too much vigor.

The baron himself sat in the judge's chair sporting a reckless smile. His dispirited citizenry stood well back from the chalk circle which had been traced upon flagstones of the outer ward. They looked on with muted curiosity from the sidelines. Whatever was going on? This was far more elaborate than any simple practice bout had a right to be.

"Any last bits of helpful advice?" asked Lucas as his sullen gaze swept over to greet me.

"Nope," I returned. "Any final words?"

"You're not funny, you know."

"I shall have that engraved on your marker," I promised with a wink.

It may have seemed cruel to some, but I had noted Lucas responded well to humor. Even now, though his offended glare excoriated me with words he'd never utter, I saw some of the tension ease from the lad's shoulders. And was that a smile struggling to escape from behind his firmly clenched jaw?

Royland's eyes met mine, and he nodded.

A harker stepped forth ringing a brass hand bell, calling all to silence.

"Hear ye one and all," he proclaimed. "Our gracious liege, the baron, invites all to attend this exhibition match between his son, Sir Eric of Downbury and Lucas, the hero of Westarbor."

Oh. So that was his game. The minstrels' fanciful depiction of Lucas defeating the horde had by now made the rounds. Many would mark him as Westarbor's champion rather than the neophyte student of the blade he was. This match was to impress on his people the superiority of Downham's fighting men. A mere squire, his son, no less, would administer a beating to the best Westarbor had to offer. Regrettably, belief in such a notion was as likely as it was despicable. As the knights cheered and banged upon their shields, the apathetic onlookers weakly joined in.

When Lucas stepped toward the center, Sir Eric began taunting him.

"Is that what passes for finery in Westarbor?" jeered the larger boy.

"Hey. This is my second best outfit!" Lucas returned.

"Then tis most fitting," said Eric with a smug grin, "since that is assuredly where you'll place in this contest."

In response, Lucas struck his pose. The boy's balance and stance were mostly correct. He spared no further breath for words. As was proper, he would let his deeds speak for him.

Sir Eric went straight for a fancy disarm. Lurching forward, he lunged in and spiraled about Lucas' blade once, twice, and then a hard snap to the wrist. This should have sent Lucas' sword sailing away. But surprisingly, Lucas maintained his grasp on the weapon. It likely had something to do with his magical vines improving his grip. I watched in fascination. Lucas' sword had been drawn out of line, but confident of the maneuver's success, Sir Eric failed to take advantage of the opening. Lucas returned to his battle-ready stance.

"Show him his proper place, Sir Eric!" his knight bellowed in encouragement.

Seeing that Lucas was completely committed to defense, Eric next attempted a series of rolling swipes. There was a great deal of power behind each stroke. Rather than block these head on, Lucas twisted and ducked to one side, then the other.

"That's it, Lucas!" I cried out, getting caught up in the spirit. "Dodge them acorns!"

"Oh!" I hastily added. "And you're allowed to shift your feet now!"

"Stand still and cross blades with me like a civilized man!" Sir Eric shouted in frustration.

Just then, in ducking a blow, Lucas chose to roll to one side and lashed out at Sir Eric's armored greaves. I heard the clank of wood on metal as Eric lurched briefly to one side. Had our boy just scored a touche? It was a blow no armored opponent could have delivered. And though perhaps it was ignoble, such an attack was certainly unexpected.

"My teacher says, there is no 'fair' in swordplay," the boy panted out as he resumed his stance.

Unfortunately, this cost Lucas his momentum. Having learned some caution, Sir Eric approached warily and sent a few feints at Lucas. Acorns never feinted. Lucas overreacted to every one of them. Having discovered this weakness, Sir Eric gleefully let loose with a punishing volley of feint-jabs, connecting with each.

Every strike upon his unarmored body caused Lucas to flinch as he was steadily driven almost out from the sparring circle. Rather than grant him this mercy, Sir Eric paused. After a high feint, he came in low and swept Lucas' legs from beneath him. The boy's knees buckled, and he grunted as he struck the ground. His practice sword clattered upon the flagstones beyond his reach.

"I yield me," Lucas croaked.

Again Sir Eric paused, but the harker failed to sound the bell of ending. With a shrug, Sir Eric hefted his weapon high above his head and brought it down.

It ended as it must. The smaller, weaker combatant was scrappy and spirited, but the outcome was inevitable. He was vanquished; laid low by the steely resolve of the heir of

Downham. It exemplified the contention between Downham and Westarbor, which was doubtless the baron's true aim. It was not his intention, however, to leave any with the impression that the smaller contestant might be spared the final blow by magic.

"Crack!" went the wooden weapon as it encountered a dim blue disk.

And there stood Royland with his arms outstretched. The thumbs and forefingers of each hand were pressed together to form a triangle, and he muttered inaudibly as he gazed through it.

There was silence for a moment, then the angry muttering began. Regaining his wits, the harker belatedly sounded the ending bell.

"Foul!" shouted Sir Eric. "I cry foul! Magic was not to be used in this bout."

"Cry all you want," Lucas declared, arising to his feet. "The bout was properly over before my cousin intervened. I had yielded me, Sir!"

The boy's blood was up. Though Eric was the superior swordsman, I'd give odds on Lucas in a battle of contumely. He was a smart-mouthed little chap.

"The bell hadn't sounded," Eric returned with a sneer.

"Enough!" boomed Lord Downham, cutting through all the chatter and stilling it at once.

The baron steepled his fingers, and the light flashed and played over his many bejeweled rings. Like Solomon, he sat in judgment. In a deep, stentorian voice, he rendered the decision.

"I find Westarbor to be at fault for bringing proscribed methods of combat to the contest."

Cheers that erupted from the knights were quickly silenced by the baron's raised hand.

"I further find Downham to be likewise at fault for offering harm to a surrendered adversary. Such behavior is unknightly and not sanctioned by this lord. The outcome, however, is quite clear. Victory this day belongs to Downham."

The knights' ovation resumed, accompanied by backslapping and congratulations for their man of the moment. The baron let this run on a bit before continuing.

"All such ballyhoo aside, both young men have acquitted themselves most . . . creatively. The honor of the field is thus satisfied. Let's give them both a round of applause."

It sounded gracious, but of course it was meant to sound thus. I didn't have to wonder about why the ending bell hadn't sounded in a more timely fashion. Such things didn't happen merely by accident. Still, it was but a trifle when weighed against the bandit attack we somehow had to survive.

Royland and I supported Lucas between us. The boy had insisted on walking unassisted from the field and across the outer ward to the castle, despite severe bruising on his wrist, knee and ribs. I admired his spunk. He had then promptly swooned.

"Hold there a moment," I heard from behind us.

I would have cheerfully ignored any other voice, but a baron (even an evil one) commanded respect within his own halls. Lucas shrugged loose from us, turned, and crossed his arms before him.

"Yes, your lordship?" said Lucas.

"I wanted to remind you about the letter you promised to write to Lady Megan. Your caravan master announced his intention to leave us on the morrow. We had hoped for a longer stay, but he cited the inclement weather and refused, in insolent disregard of our wishes. If you draft the letter tonight, you may leave it with us. We shall see it is conveyed with alacrity to the lady's gentle hands. You may use our library. It's well stocked with paper and quills."

"That won't be necessary, your lordship," Lucas replied tersely. "I have my own writing supplies, as does Taylor."

The baron frowned at that reminder. Score one for unintentional diplomacy.

Back in our rooms, I rooted through my belongings for my quill set. Lucas already had his out, Bob having 'given it' to him.

There, I grumbled inwardly. Always in the last place you look. I laughingly looked in two more places just to give lie to the adage.

"Hey Taylor, how do you spell 'boorish lout?'"

"You know he's going to read that, don't you, Lucas?"

"Just kidding. I'm well aware. I haven't yet learned to do that thing Master Chadwick does on his seals."

"Oh? And what's that?" I asked.

"He spells them so that something unpleasant happens if his letter is opened by someone apart from its rightful recipient."

"What happens?"

"I don't know exactly. I've never opened one. I imagine it bursts into a great ball of fire or some such."

"Good to know," I declared.

"What's that you're writing, then?" I asked while sidling over to peer over the boy's shoulder.

"Just what the baron asked for," he replied.

Incredible. Somehow the boy was privy to the Arenson family's secret code. The letter was fraught with minor ink spills and other such 'mistakes' that only a player of the game could read properly. Regarding Sir Eric, Lucas had smudged the 'L's on several sentences like the following:

'He's a very amiable and handsome young man.'

'You would like him a lot!'

'I'm sure you would find such a match very pleasant and agreeable!'

'You should tell your father you would like to meet him.'

I saw nothing more sophisticated than something a pawn might know, but it surprised me that Lucas was an agent at all. He scarcely seemed the type. Lucas couldn't keep his emotions from his face to save his life. My baron was recruiting them young these days; it would seem.

Perhaps I was doing him an injustice. The boy did have a good heart. Moreover, having an agent in Conclave could be useful. I was warming to the idea. I flashed him the hand sign for a knight, but there was no response. Well, trust had to begin somewhere.

"Royland, please come over here," I requested.

The young man set down his book and wandered over.

Then I shared the news we had discovered about the ambush. I hadn't wanted to burden them earlier. They had enough to worry about at the time. Now, however, they needed to be prepared. As expected, Lucas peppered me with numerous questions while his cousin just stared into the distance, soaking it all in. Both seemed horrified that the danger was sponsored by the very man hosting us at present. Lucas had many ideas. None were feasible given what I knew. They ranged from just leaving the wagon here with its king's ransom in copper to somehow exposing the corrupt lord.

"Listen, the danger isn't immediate," I said. "In the morning we will set out as planned. I'll send you to safety before it becomes an issue. Nothing will happen until we leave Downham."

"Oh," I amended, "And we'll be smuggling a family out of the city. We may need to stash a couple of them in our coach."

I forestalled any further questions and returned to my own writing. I could hear their quiet whispers as they discussed the news. Nothing attracts your attention quite like a whisper. I think I could more readily ignore the distraction if they were yelling to one another.

I thought carefully before scribbling out the message for my liege. No matter how tiny the writing, only so many letters would fit on the thin strip of parchment that could be carried by our birds. I selected a healthy-looking pigeon from among those in my cages, drew her out and affixed my note securely to her blue-banded leg. I carried her over to a window, prised it open and released her. In a sudden burst of fluttering wings, she arrowed away.

I was startled when a shadow passed overhead. A familiar piercing cry announced that Petra was present and on the hunt.

Fly little pigeon, I thought as fear scraped his icy cold fingers down my back. Although I had nineteen more birds with which to try, I didn't fancy my message being dropped neatly at Downham's villainous feet.

The hawk dove, but to my enormous relief, her intended prey was a bird other than my own. *My* bird achieved the tree line and disappeared from view. Godspeed little messenger, I fervently exhorted her.

***

I walked over and retrieved my trencher. I took my seat at the fire beside Trader Sam.

"How's business?" I asked politely.

"It's going well, my friend. Already I have disposed of nearly a quarter of my stock."

He took another bite of his own breakfast. The wagons nearby were being prepared for the road as Ollie Reid led the mule teams out from the baron's stables. I could see their steaming breaths emerge from their nostrils in the crisp air. I huddled closer to the fire.

"I wish we could stay longer at this stop," the merchant continued around a mouthful of food. "There is little call for my superior product at the bodunk hamlets we'll hit next. The sumptuary laws being what they are tend to restrict me to a rather exclusive clientele."

He yawned, then shook himself and took another bite of his trencher.

"Well, you know," I remarked, "old man winter is on the prowl. I think Master Ross hopes to reach the caravansary south of the Stein Barony before the heavy snowfalls hit. We can weather out the worst of it in relative comfort."

He yawned again and rubbed at his eyes.

"You know, I can't seem to muster any enthusiasm for the trek south today. I feel as though I'd been up late making merry at the tavern, though on my honor I was not."

"You look unwell, my friend," I droned. "Perhaps you should have a little lie down in your wagon for a bit. Here, I'll help you over there."

"That may be wise," said the man as I stood. "I think I..."

As his eyes rolled back and the half-eaten trencher fell from his slack hand, I relieved him of his jacket. I then seized his arm and lifted his dead weight into a side carry.

Approaching his wagon, I found a large roll of cloth already spread out directly behind it. Depositing the man thereupon, I quietly and precisely rolled him up therein. Lucas came around from the front accompanied by Trader Sam. As the merchant donned the jacket, the lad was staring up at him round-eyed with astonishment. The boy was still a mess of bruises from the beating he took yesterday and walked with a limp, but he was soldiering through it well enough.

"Thanks, Lucas," I said, handing him the green bottle.

"The likeness is amazing, Manny," the boy declared. "You could be his twin."

"Oh?" returned the jester, arching his eyebrows and making a pious expression. "And just what do you think you know of disguises, young man?"

Lucas' jaw dropped. I mean it literally dropped, and his mouth hung open. This didn't still his eager tongue for long, however.

"Your voice! That's just uncanny!" he exclaimed. "If my mage sight weren't silent right now, I'd *swear* you must have the gift."

Turning to me, Manny said: 'It's nice to be appreciated. On to stage two then, and don't forget you promised us the moon for our assistance.'

At this, he mounted the drivers bench to await our departure. I hustled back to the coach where Royland already had the team hitched and ready.

Rather than trailing behind, our coach was to lead the hasty exodus and Master Ross' grand wagon was to be at its rear. Thus, we could simply turn in place and be off.

"Are you certain you can do it?" I asked Lucas as he climbed to the seat by my side.

"Just get me close," he said.

Slapping the reins to our horses buttocks, I set the carriage into motion. This was the signal for the others to do likewise. The castle guards began taking notice. I held the horses to a casual walk as we approached the gates.

"Hail the watch!" I cried down jovially.

A bewildered guardsman stared up at me.

"Well, open the gates, man, It's time for the caravan to depart."

"The gates aren't to be opened until the dawn bell," he pedantically recited.

"Your baron granted us leave to depart early. Would you hamper the king's mages, then?"

All the while, I was edging us closer to the gatehouse while giving the appearance that it was merely the horses' restless shifting about. The gates themselves stood open at present, but the portcullis was down. This huge framework of iron bars was lifted and lowered by a winch within the gatehouse that required a team of men to operate. Wound about with heavy chains, it was a sophisticated feat of ironmongery worthy of our own Javier Lewis. From where we had arrived, I could only just spy the winch within.

"Ah, I see your men are unbarring it already", I lied. "I can see at least *someone* around here has some proper sense."

At this I waved at the imaginary men beyond him who were supposedly carrying out this deed. Confused, the man spun about. Lucas did not disappoint. For while the man was distracted and the boy's gaze grew distant, the winch began to turn.

As the portcullis gradually rose, the man hustled back toward the gatehouse, hollering: 'Here now! Who ordered this?' When I deemed the gap sufficient, I urged the horses forward. On sensing our rapid approach, the man skidded to a stop and turned about, nearly tripping on his greaves. He stood in the center of the road with his hand raised before him. It was no time for half measures.

"Crack," went the whip.

The horses broke into a reckless canter. I'll give him points for loyalty. We were almost upon him before he rolled aside from our path.

"Sorry friend," I said as we passed by his recumbent form. "But we really must be off."

The other wagons thundered after. Other guardsmen in the inner ward were congregating and had begun to organize a pursuit. As the last wagon cleared the gates, I turned to the boy beside me.

"Well done, Lucas. You can stop now."

With a deep release of breath, the boy relaxed. At the same instant, the portcullis dropped. The sudden jangling of heavy chains preceded a great ringing boom as it fell unrestrainedly upon shattering flagstones.

"Take the reins, Lucas," I said. "There's some business I must attend."

Tossing the reins to the startled boy, I leaped from the careening carriage to roll upon the roadway. Regaining my feet, I turned and awaited the trailing wagons to catch me up. The caravan was in almost the opposite of its usual order. Despite the early hour, curious onlookers were emerging to gather at the roadside. Aroused by the ruckus of our hasty departure, they grew more numerous as the moments ticked on.

The dust began settling before the closed portcullis. I could see the barons men impotently swarming it like a pack of angry hounds. Soon enough they would work it back open if my young friend hadn't damaged its mechanism overmuch. In the confusion, I saw four cloaked figures slip under the tarp of the juggler's wagon. Good.

Master Ross' wagon was the last in line. I jogged alongside it and swung up into its bed. A few of the baron's more quick-witted men had already emerged from the sally gate, finding its key more swiftly than I'd have credited. The main force trapped behind the portcullis appeared to be trying to lift it by . . . well . . . main force. Straining in unison, they had managed to draw it up a foot or so, but none yet dared to roll out from beneath it.

"It's time," I said to Master Ross.

Nodding, he threw open a deep chest before him in the wagon's bed.

"A largesse!" he cried. "A largesse in honor of Sir Eric's naming day!"

At this he began flinging handfuls of coins to scatter in the roadway behind our wagon. If the good people of Downbury wondered why a caravan master would be in charge of such an event, they didn't question it. With a gladsome cry they surged forth into the street, there to brawl and contend for these pitiful baubles while foiling any swift pursuit.

The wagon recommenced its trek down the lane, all the while spewing low-value coins onto the cobbles. And as it did, I turned about, dropped my britches and bent low. I let the vertical smile of my hairy arse grace Downbury Castle and all of its denizens and especially its lord.

***

I had returned to our coach at the head of the line. Lucas still sat on the bench beside me, and Royland rode within. Pursuit should overtake us ere long, but I hoped to delay that encounter as much as possible. In revenge for the dignity of his castle, the baron could set his knights upon us. Then we would be doomed. Or he could simply herd us into his trap. Downham was a calculating bastard. I was betting on the latter. The former solution was inelegant. It would defeat the very purpose of his preparations and bring down upon him the full wrath of the Merchants Guild of Fairglen.

The brigands to the south would require time to infiltrate Stein Barony and set their trap. This was time I didn't intend to give them. It was toward that end I had asked Master Ross to let us lead the wagons.

"It's time for your sword practice, Lucas." I announced.

The boy stared daggers at me.

128

"*Really,* Taylor?"

"No, not really. But pretend you're holding your sword out before you. Talk to your little hump. Convince it you want to flatten the road ahead as we ride."

I saw enlightenment grace the young man's face. That was our Lucas; quite quick on the uptake.

"Okay. I'll try," he said.

At once, I felt the coach's trembling cease, and that smooth, gliding motion ensued. Testing my idea, I urged the horses up to greater speed. It worked. The boy was actually doing it. Moreover, the wagons trailing us were easily keeping pace. We didn't gallop; that couldn't be sustained for long. But we were moving along at a fair clip one wouldn't expect from a mule caravan. And every minute we gained was one unexpected minute sooner we'd arrive at Stein's border.

I wondered whether Westarbor had received my note. Given the relatively short distance, it should've taken only a few hours. Would Peter have delivered it to him in the middle of the night? Could my baron even now be wording an outraged missive for the king? He couldn't send word to Leopold. His stock of gray-banded birds was thoroughly depleted. That was one of my tasks for the return journey.

I should *live* so long. Would the king have the good grace to let me leave his service unscathed, or would he consign me to some dark cell for my 'treachery?' How could I even make the return journey through Downham Barony? All I could do for now was to focus on the task at hand: getting the copper shipment to Eagle's Keep after slipping the noose set by that evil prick who fancies himself the next Duke of Northford. I was so caught up in these thoughts that I was surprised when a mule drew abreast of our coach.

"Checkers to the rear!" announced Harold Hunt, overtaking us.

Glancing back beyond the end of our line, I saw he was correct. There was indeed a small contingent of mounted men on a fast approach. I slowed the coach. I pretended not to notice the shouts from our rear until they parted from the road and drew up closer.

"Ho there, wagoneer! Halt this mule train at once."

It was the guard captain who had followed me around Downbury. According to my intelligence, his name was Robert Dumont, and he was rumored to be an accomplished sword master. But I would always think of him as 'Captain Obvious.' Snapping the reins, I steered the horses aside, and we clattered to a full stop.

"Are you addressing me? I've done as you wish, sir, but as you can see, I'm a coachman, not a *wagoneer*."

The other Tomcats were stepping down from their respective wagons and gathering near. If it was to be a fight, odds were with the armored men, but they might find some unexpected skills among us. Cameron Ross quickly stepped to the fore.

"I'm master of this caravan," he announced. "What would you have of us, captain? We've hitherto met with your assessors and cleared the tariffs . . ."

"Cease your annoying prattle," the man interrupted with a wave of his hand.

He unrolled a parchment he produced from his saddle bag. On it was a fair rendition of Jeremiah. He held it up.

"We are seeking this man; have you seen him?"

"Hmmm. I can't say that I have," returned Master Ross. "What do you want him for?"

"His name is Jeremiah Blessings, but he sometimes goes by the alias: 'The Tinker.' He is wanted for questioning. He's a dangerous man. If any are harboring or abetting him, the consequences will be most severe."

His eyes surveyed the crowd. When they alighted upon Trader Manny, they paused. Manny flashed him a brief hand signal, and Captain Obvious unconsciously nodded. What was that? Was this to be a betrayal, then? He claimed he worked for the king, but what did I really know about the jester? Returning his gaze to Master Ross, he said:

"You're making good time - suspiciously good time. One might think you were fleeing from some misdeed."

"I think your baron is to blame for that, captain," said the caravan boss with an earnest smile.

"Oh? And what blame would you lay upon our good liege?"

"I must compliment his lordship on the excellent condition of his roads."

The captain nodded at this, having doubtless noted it himself. He seemed to be appeased, but in his eyes there remained the glint of suspicion.

"Perhaps I should have you turn out all your wagons for a full inspection."

Just then, there was a movement in the bed of a wagon from beneath its securely lashed tarpaulin. A hand emerged and sought about for the lashings.

"I confess," said the quavering voice of Jeremiah.

The man crawled out from his canvas womb accompanied by a strange jingling sound. His beard had been shaven to alter his appearance, but more than that disguised his nature. The man stood before us atop the wagon bedecked in the full outfit of a jester. Hopping down, he approached the mounted guard captain with a cringing and fearful demeanor. He turned pleading eyes up to the captain and his frightened grimace stood out even beneath his mask of white greasepaint with its painted-on smile. He then righted himself and presented Patsy as a priest presents a cross, proclaiming:

Like the devil below,
I confess to the crime.
And rather than keeping you guessing,
I think you should know,
Without wasting your time:
(I'm a man who has seen many blessings!)

Captain Obvious looked disgusted saying: 'Begone, fool. We've no time for your antics."

Turning to Master Ross he said: 'Know you are not in the clear. We are investigating the havoc you caused at the gate this morning. When the truth comes out, we may appeal to your guildhall for damages.'

In a wounded tone, Cameron countered.

"My guild will certainly hear of the discourtesies done to us and the shoddy maintenance of your equipment as well," he blustered. "We could've been killed when that gate fell . . . "

"Enough! We haven't time to stand about bandying insults with a merchant and his fool. We've other business to attend. Come men."

And with that, they rode off in haste, churning up more divots in the road's earthen surface. As the hoofbeats clattered off and diminished, I marked further movement from beneath the tarp.

"Are the prad prancers away, Papa?" she asked in a girlish soprano. "Can we come clear?"

"Yes. My angels, the bloody-backed buggers are off. Come ahead then," he replied.

And with much squirming, two more figures emerged. They were dressed head to toe in the bright working clothes of jugglers, and each had the slender build to match.

If one is to hide in plain sight, I suppose it's best to go all in.

"These are my daughters. They're my pride and joy, my dear angels," said the doting tinker.

They were a well-matched set. If not for a slight difference in size, they might have been twins. They looked to be about Lucas' age.

"On the right is Angelica, to the left, Seraphina. And coming up behind them is my wife, Adeline. Addy wouldn't wear any make-up. We thought we could pass her off as a helper at the cook wagon."

Behind them the tarp heaved yet again, and a woman sat up. Her only nod to a costume was the cast iron frying pan she held.

"No I wouldn't wear no make-up, Jerry. Our daughters look like *harlots* in them get ups," she croaked.

This was all well and good, but we couldn't afford to lose more time.

"Well played, 'jester,'" I praised. "It's nice to meet your family, but there's no time for pleasantries."

"Everyone!" I shouted. "You have five minutes to attend to necessaries and take your places."

The Tomcats dispersed, each to his own business. I sought out the Reynolds brothers and asked them whether the wagons were fit to handle our increased speed. They assured me they were. 'That and then some', I believe were their exact words. Next I approached the jester, the real one.

"What was that hand signal you made to Captain Dumont?" I demanded darkly.

"Oh that? I just flashed him the all clear sign in Downham's not-so-secret code. I've seen Trader Sam do it repeatedly over the last several days."

"You surprise me again, Manny. I didn't know you spoke asshole."

"It's not so hard," the jester quipped, "But I find that 'asshole' is a dialect best delivered tongue-in-cheek."

I returned to the coach. I was under no illusions. We had little hope of encountering the baron's trap without springing it. The men who had ridden ahead would undoubtedly tell their bandit confederates to set the wheels in motion. Even if we could make the border by nightfall, I doubted we could outrun this thing. My next best hope was that we could warn Leopold's own border guards. Surely, the Knights of Stein could rout the blackguards and thwart the baron's evil scheme. But this hope too, slim though it was, was soon to be dashed against the shores of our misfortune.

***

Lucas was clearly flagging, his arcane energies having been altogether spent. When we approached the border of Barony Stein, he was barely able to ease our way. He claimed his little hillock now lay limp and flaccid, resembling more a puddle of mud than it did a mighty mesa. Whatever this magical mumbo-jumbo might mean, I could tell the boy was worn out.

We had arrived before the fall of night. But the glow diffusing down through the dismal gray blanket above was diminishing rapidly.

We were stopped on the Downham side, and Stein's border guardians could be seen waiting for us in the distance. They wore the gray livery of their baron with the head of a wolf embroidered on each tabard. The Downham stop proved perfunctory. To the checkers, Master Ross presented the bill of lading, and we were passed through without much fuss.

Just as we pulled up on the Stein side, however, a muffled thumping erupted from one of our wagons.

"Mmm-mm-mph!" said the roll of cloth, as it wriggled and rolled in the back of Manny's wagon.

It was the cloth merchant. Maybe I should have dosed him more thoroughly, but Lucas had told me a teaspoon or so would do the trick. The guardsmen hadn't noticed just yet, busy as they were reviewing Master Ross' list. I had thought we should get the formalities settled before approaching them with our warning. Addy Blessings appeared, striding with a purpose from around the back of the cook wagon still sporting her frying pan. She peered at the twitching bolt of cloth, then struck it once - hard. This drew the guardsmen's attention.

"Here now what's this then!" she hollered, jabbing an accusing finger at Manny up on the driver's bench. "Rats!" she declared. "I told you yesterday to keep your infested lage of duds well back from me cook wagon, you misbegotten dandy prat."

Not missing a beat, Trader Manny hopped down and replied just as hotly.

"Lookin' fer meat for your stew is ya?" he accused, "Get ye back to your cook wagon. And keep yer mitts from me whiffles, woman, or I'll give your nazy neck-stamper his bastings!

The matron looked ruffled, but as she hefted her skillet and sauntered back toward her cook wagon, she began humming a little ditty. Was that 'Bunny Foo Foo?" As the mystified patrolmen muttered to one another, Manny headed my way.

"Did you hear what that cheeky wench said?" he groused, while at the same time flashing me the hand sign for 'danger' in king's code.

As he arrived at my side, I placed a consoling hand on his shoulder and appeared to commiserate with him.

"The guardsmen," he muttered. "They wear his livery, but they're not Stein's men. Don't trust them."

"Best you just avoid the batty old egg cracker, Sam," I said aloud while giving his shoulder a squeeze.

Soon we were past the border patrol and in Stein Barony. What now? It was ludicrous. We'd known about the baron's ambush for days. Yet every step along the way seemed to sweep us nearer to it. For a tactic which relied on surprise, this one was proving devilishly difficult to evade, even given adequate foreknowledge.

I huddled with Manny and the others over Cameron's spread-out map of the area. The caravan boss looked ill at his ease as he described our few options.

"They'd most likely set up on this ridge. *I* would. It commands a view of both the eastern and the western road. Once we choose our route, they'll just ride down to greet us."

"I think you're right, Cam," observed the jester. "What about this little trail here?"

"No good," Cameron sighed. "That dead-ends at a logging camp."

"Well the western road runs close by Castle Stein," Harold Hunt noted. We should take that one at the fork. It's more likely to be patrolled. Or maybe I should ride on ahead and try and make it through to Lord Leopold."

"I wouldn't ask that of you, my friend," said Ross. "They'd cut you down in an instant. Likely they've got eyes on us already. If we fail to move ahead, they may bring the fight to us. But thanks for the offer. So what will it be, east or west?"

"Neither," I said. "Royland, go wake your cousin."

I had an idea. I told the others to get some rest while I explored a possibility.

Lucas was surprisingly easy to awaken. The boy had abruptly nodded off after the border stop. We had laid him in the coach and tried to make him as comfortable as possible. Fortunately, he hadn't taken any of that green stuff before the fatigue had caught up to him. Once awakened, however, he seemed to instantly snap to. He claimed it was his 'shepherd spell of wakefulness' or some such nonsense.

"Lucas, if you can smooth a road, can you also mess one up?"

"Probably. But I can't do anything until I've rested more. As I told you before, my hill is flat."

"What about that thing you do with the plants? Doesn't that restore your magic?"

"My green field is fine, Taylor." He said with annoyance. "That's a separate thing."

"It needn't be," supplied Royland who was listening most intently. "According to Narfaggle's Law, a conduit can be established from a primary affinity to an enchanted object. Theoretically, a secondary affinity should be subject to the same meta-distancing."

We stared at him in stunned silence, as though our roles had been reversed completely. I had only understood about one word in three, but was liking that 'needn't be' bit.

"What?" said Royland into the silence. "I read a lot. And I can talk when I need to."

"What's a conduit?" asked Lucas.

"That's why I often don't," said his cousin. "That and habit, I suppose."

"What's a conduit?" repeated Lucas excitedly, "And how do I make one?"

Royland gave me a long suffering look. It was as doleful as that of Mother Hubbard's hound back in Meadowfork.

"You two work it out. I'll get us moving again. The game is back on."

The others were skeptical when I informed them we'd be taking Manny's little trail to the lumber camp. True, it led to a cul-de-sac. But the bandits wouldn't be expecting it. They perked up when I explained how we'd be carving our own road thereafter. So in the dark of night, we drove our caravan down to the turn off and departed the king's highway. The animals were unhappy. They'd been hauling all day and were unused to nighttime treks. So far, though, the beasts obeyed.

I had to call a halt, so Lucas could practice his newfound ability. The brigands ahead had to be wondering why we were moving at night. Toolhup and Benalav sighted some of their sentries, but I instructed the elves to stay well back from them. It was much easier for the bandits to track the progress of the caravan than it was for us to spot their men in the dark, Elven eyes notwithstanding. Cameron had the cook wagon issue Ollie Reid a whole bushel of carrots to keep the animals content.

I was getting a little tired myself. It had been a long and active day. But to rest now was death. Harold now wore his sword openly, niceties be damned. It was a beauty. Unlike Lucas' broadsword, which was great for slashing, Harold's more modern longsword was sharpened along both edges of its blade. Its cruciform hilt would be long enough to use both hands if one had the notion to. I had strung my bow, and the others all carried some favored weapon, or at least a makeshift one. The caravan now had teeth.

When I returned to my mages, they were excited about something. It involved Lucas walking barefoot in the grass and laughing. As I approached them, I noticed his limp was gone.

"I shall call it 'ambulare interitus,' my withering stride." The boy proudly announced.

"Why would we care what you call it?" I impatiently remarked. "Just get on with it."

"Master Chadwick said it was important to affix a verbal trigger firmly in one's mind. Otherwise, we might start doing it unconsciously. I don't fancy going for a stroll and blackening all the bushes as I pass by. That's the sort of thing that gives mages a bad reputation."

"Well in that event, at least folks wouldn't think you a hedge witch," remarked Roy in a droll voice.

This pun was in honor of their old master; I was later to learn. I think I liked this new Roy, but it still disturbed me somehow. The transformation seemed too sudden. First the music, then the girls, now this speaking more normally. Sometimes a person could lose himself if he strayed too far from his roots. I resolved to keep a close eye on the lad if we all survived the day.

It was too dark to see properly what was going on, but apparently Lucas was satisfied with his ambu-inner-thingy. I set him straight to work. As the wagons pulled onto the old timber trail, Lucas followed them on foot. He blackened the overgrown grass and weeds around himself as he siphoned off their energies and fed them into his 'hump.' Every couple of steps, he would pause and the dirt beneath the dead weeds would fragment, developing deep furrows and jagged trenches. It was slow going at first, but as we progressed, he grew more proficient at it and the gaps grew larger.

Royland paced beside his cousin. His darksight was active and he stood prepared to shield Lucas from any harm. Should the bandits' scouts take a notion to end our endeavor with an arrow, Roy'd be ready.

As we neared the trail's end, I became concerned. Had we just painted ourselves into a proverbial corner, or could the boy get us out? The logging camp was abandoned, or rather, it was closed for the season. By this time of year, all the firewood had been felled and split into cords enough to keep the folks cozy in their homes. My young charges came up to the front.

"Give me a minute, Taylor," said Lucas. "My magic is replenished (topping over, really), but my feet are freezing!"

The boy's face looked flushed, and not merely from the cold. Roy had briefed me that Lucas could get a little over-energized after deriving strength from a plant. I hated to ask more of the boy, but he was the only one who could do it. And he seemed willing enough. From this point on, Lucas would carve out a new road in as direct a line as possible toward

Castle Stein. I sent the Elves to scout the easiest path and blaze him a trail. From there we'd . . .

Then I heard it. A mighty screech from above rent the night. More hunting falcons? But no; it was too grand. All paused to search the heavens for the source of the alarming sound. A light dusting of falling snow tickled my face as I scanned the darkened sky. Naught was visible beyond the ring of lanterns flickering dimly from our circled wagons.

Then another sound arose. It was a sound most welcome, and I cherished it. The clangor of the harker's bell fell rhythmically upon our ears. Was it to be some perilous new minion of our adversaries or our salvation? I raised my bow and prepared to sight on the former, but I stayed my hand lest it turn out to be the latter. To my startled mind, it seemed to be both at once. For with a great beating of wings, a monstrous avian thudded down alarmingly a dozen paces off in the clearing. But perched atop this dire bird sat a small figure prominently and proudly wearing the livery of my lord.

The mules were in a panic, nearly tearing down their picket line in their agitation. It was all Ollie could do to resettle them. The harker dismounted and approached. He produced and unrolled a scroll, which he squinted at and proceeded to read by the faint light. We shivered in anticipation of the tidings he might bear.

"Good 'P'... pee-oh, peep holes? Oh, People!" he began.

The harker couldn't read or could do so only haltingly? Despite the strangeness of the situation, I felt my shoulders sag and I returned my bow to its back sling. This could take a while. I saw others doing likewise.

There was something wrong with that bird. It now stood awkwardly upon its talons with wings folded. It was shuffling nearer in a strange, hopping gait, but was brought up short by its master's raised hand. It halted just at the edge of our lanterns' light It then turned its great head in profile and began preening at its neck. I gasped at the truth this revealed. For from this angle, I could see its feathered neck met a body that was that of a lion. It was a gryphon the boy had ridden! Nor was this to be the only startling revelation this night. The harker continued:

"Good people of the 'T'...tom, tommy? Oh, hells bells!" he exclaimed.

As the harker stuffed the scroll aside and proceeded in a more natural voice. It dawned on me that the child was in fact a young woman. My baron had sent a little girl to aid us in our time of need? To be fair, he'd also sent a gryphon. To the relief of all, she cleared her throat and continued the proclamation in an ad lib fashion.

"Good people of the Tomcat caravan. Good baron Westarbor sends greetings. He heard of your danger and sent me and Wynken to help out. We flew here to bring the news to old Leopold at his castle. It was hard to find being dark as it is, but we managed. Castles stick up pretty good from the woods around them. The baron's archers would have shot us from the sky, but Wynken was too fast and clever for that. Lord Leo is gathering his men and plans to find these bandits that are threatening you. He'll put an end to them. Fear ye not, the baron's looking out for ye!"

Her message delivered, the girl suddenly looked lost.

***

"And so I told her straight out: 'You can't catch me; I'm the gingerbread man!'"

Everyone laughed. The cook was regaling us all with an amusing anecdote that had occurred back at Westarbor's autumn fair. We were reclining around the large bonfire we had built in the clearing. There had been wood aplenty available at the logging camp to construct it. The animals were all safely corralled in the logger's pens. All save for one, that is.

After the young harker had discharged her duty, she had fallen silent. It was clear the young woman was all but asleep on her feet. Goody Blessings said, 'Oh, you poor little darling' and approached her. The gryphon screeched a warning and half-revealed its impressive wingspan.

"It's all right Wynken," said the girl, with sudden alertness. "These are our friends. *Friends*, Wynken. *Who's* a pretty girl? *Wynken's* a pretty girl!

The harker's soothing words caused the great beast to fold closed its wings and lie down like a cat. And was that purring emerging from the juxtaposed monstrosity?

"She's just hungry," the girl declared.

"Have you any fish?" she asked of the beldam.

"We've some salted grayling we got at Lester fief," returned the matron after considering the matter.

"Salted? Too bad. Wynken only eats fresh. Have you any rabbit then?" asked the girl with a wide yawn.

Goody Blessings turned to Lucas and Royland expectantly. When the two men made no reply, she prompted them.

"Well you're mages, ain't ya? Can't you lot pull such from your hats? No? Bootless lurdans. I'll go see what we've got on the cook wagon, then. Wait here, miss."

"Is that creature dangerous?" asked Master Ross, stepping forward.

The girl laughed, yawning once again.

"Of course she is, mister. But let's get introduced. I'm Marjery, and you all know Wynken, of course."

Did the creature just preen and nod its (her) head? One by one Cameron named the members of our troupe. I'm not sure if she heard any after the first few because her eyes were drooping closed. After the gryphon was fed, the little redhead cuddled up to her side and promptly fell asleep. Wynken's stomach was her pillow; Wynken's wing, her blanket. None dared approach after that.

So here we all sat by a raging fire in the late night hours while a bird-headed grimalkin kept watch from nearby. It was funny what you could get used to. We were tired, but we were all too excited for any to shut an eye. On a ridge to the south, or perhaps on the very approach to our camp, a fierce battle raged. Our erstwhile tormentors were even now being routed and gathered up to be tried for their misdeeds. Or perhaps they were being granted some swifter mercy by the blades of the Knights of Stein.

The musicians had brought their instruments over by the fire with some notion of playing a tune or two. But our mood had called for something more restful. Only amiable gossip and cheerful comradery disturbed the stillness of the night.

"Watch your daughters around this one, Jerry," I said while indicating Royland. "He's a known philanderer. Mark my words; he'll leave a brokenhearted maiden at every tavern along the way."

Royland reddened. He turned to stare into the fire. I thought that would be the end of it until the young man suddenly shot back.

"I wonder how many maids in Downbury were devastated by the sight of Taylors retreating derrière, if you'll pardon my French."

He then beat out a quick three notes on his drum. Ba-dum-BUM!

"Mayhap that should be the subject of my next ballad," said Maestro Bok when the merriment had died down. He picked out a familiar melody and sang:

On the Gates of Downbury Keep,
Taylor's brown-eyed cyclops did peep!

He could play no more of the tune because he was bent over in a most unmanly giggle-fit. I think Manny actually shed a tear.

"I shall insist on a more original tune and half the tips," I responded weakly. "Speaking of arses, are you sure Sam Robinson can't escape from the woodshed where we secured him?"

"I tied him up right proper," said Harold, "He'll not be wiggling free of those darbies till we get him to Lord Leopold for justice. What I want to know is how Manny here came to work for the king. I've heard it bruited about he was once the top joker in the deck. While we're cooling our heels here waiting for news, let's play a game. We may as well have the story."

I confess I was curious about this myself. We all turned to the jester. He had abandoned his 'Trader Sam' guise and again sat among us as a nondescript man of middle age with his hair running to gray about his temples. His lips tightened, and he shrugged in acquiescence.

"As you may be aware, his majesty favors the theater. Years ago I was but a struggling actor in the capital. I belonged to a small troupe and had no loftier aspiration than to tread the boards and bestow some happiness to uplift the dreary lives of ordinary citizens. My preferred venue was the 'Silverlight Grand Theater of Fairglen.' Ah, the bright costumes, the smell of greasepaint, the taste of a famous soliloquy tripping from one's tongue and the thundering approbation for a job well done. The maestros here know what I'm talking about."

"Indeed we do," confirmed Maestro Bok.

"Alas, my lifestyle was humble and my purse remained light until that fateful day. It was during a performance of 'The Pirates of Indigo Bay.' I was playing the role of Horatio, a valiant sea captain. My boot became unlaced at an inopportune moment, just as I was enacting a dramatic duel with the pirate king himself. I stumbled into the man. In an attempt to remain standing, I grabbed him about his waist. When I slid down to the deck, I drew his breeches along with me. And there stood the pirate king in all his glory, striking a regal pose in his nether garments."

"No you did *not*. Say on man; what happened next?" urged Jerry Blessings.

"It happened that the king himself was attending that night up in his royal box. The silence of the stunned audience was broken as his laughter rang down from above. 'Who is that man?' he said. 'I want him for my court. I've chancellors and groomsmen and constables aplenty. But I need a man who can make me laugh.'"

Manny inclined his head and picked at a thread at the hem of his cloak.

"Bullshit," I said.

The jester smiled at me. A true smile.

"You're right, of course," he said, spreading his arms wide and turning his palms upward, "Still, it was a pretty good story; don't you agree?"

"Deceiver," said Liam Gordon.

"Charlatan," added Noah Reynolds as he threw a twig at him.

"*Washtojavi!*" put in Miss Toolhup for good measure.

"Hey, I know," said Patsy "Let's change the topic! We've rescued you from Downham like we promised. What are your plans now, Jerry?"

It was conceivably the most blatant misdirection ever. Yet we allowed it to succeed.

"Addy and I were just discussing that," Jeremiah answered the puppet. "I think we'll stick with *you* lot, if you'll have us. I paid for this ticket with all I had. There's always work for a traveling tinker or piepowder. And we noticed this extra cloth wagon needs a steady hand at the reins. What do you say?"

Master Ross tapped on his chin for a moment before delivering his reply.

"I say . . . Welcome to the Tomcats. We could definitely do with a few more Blessings upon the roads we travel."

The tinker beamed and hugged his goodwife close.

"Who's hungry, then?" asked Addy. "As the cooks new apprentice I should be the one to see to that. After feeding that beast the last of our stew meat, I'm not sure what I can scrape up. But I do feel a bit peckish myself."

As the woman sauntered off, Cameron spoke again.

"Since we seem to be playing Harold's game, is there someone you'd like to ask a question, Goodman Blessings?"

"I do confess myself disappointed that the jester was just spinning us a line. I find the caravan's tunes most merry and would fain know how you learned to play, if it isn't too much of a bite."

"Not at all good fellow," said Liam. "It's no imposition at all. I'm sure you know Maestro Bok's origins, since he never stops going on about them. Now me, I'm a self-taught musician. I learned the vielle at my father's knee as all of us Gordons have for generations. As a member of the famous 'Fiddler's Three,' I rode the king's highway as part of Master Cole's caravan. Loved the man; but I couldn't stand his foul-smelling pipe. We made quite a name for ourselves back in the day."

"What happened to the other two fiddlers?" asked Lucas.

"We separated over creative differences," said the man with a pained expression. "I'm not sure what they're doing now. I became a solo act. It didn't work out. It just didn't have the same magic. Nobody would pay good coin to hear the 'Fiddler One' or the 'Lone Fiddler.' So I joined up with this sorry lot. Take it or leave it, but that's all I got."

"As for me," Ben Farrell began unbidden, "I spent a lot of years on the circuit. Nothing so notable as Liam, but I made a good honest living at it. I kept a wise head and avoided drinking up my profits. Each time I swung back home, I gave Lila a fat purse. She was a right prudent little woman, my Lila, no spendthrift she. After all those hard years on the king's highway, I finally went home for good. We'd saved up enough to retire!

"Then why are you here?" asked Royland with a puzzled look.

The piper's cheeks reddened, and his grip tightened on his recorder. I hoped it was a sturdy instrument. It appeared Roy had struck a nerve.

"It's for Tom, my Tom!" said the piper. "He's my son."

The piper raised grief-stricken eyes to stare around defiantly before continuing his tale.

"Tom was a good boy, but lacking the stern hand of a father I must confess he never grew into a proper man. I blame myself, for you see, I was always out on the road looking after my own concerns and my Lila doted on the boy. Tom knew he could always count on Lila to put him up and give him a proper meal."

"She spoiled the child," I said with understanding.

"That she did. Tom would drink or gamble away any money he made from the odd jobs he could hold down. When I came home and put a stop to the handouts, Tom took to thieving. Stole a pig; he did and run off with it. He got caught, of course, but by then he'd cooked and eaten the pig. The baron fined him fifty gold crowns. *Fifty!* For a pig worth no more than a hundred and twenty pence. Needless to say he couldn't pay it. They were gonna flog him and toss him to rot in the baron's gaol."

"And did they?" asked Benalav.

"They sure would have. But my Lila wouldn't hear of it. The woman was on me like a bear on a fish, demanding I *do* something. We paid the fine, but that didn't leave much scratch for us to live on. So here I am back on the circuit and saving my coin. I figure about another thirty years or so will do it. *Stop* that. It ain't a matter to be mocked!"

This last admonishment was directed at Liam Gordon. During the last part of the story, Liam had begun to play a soft, slow accompaniment to the tale on his vielle. The tune was mournful and put me in mind of the hokey melodies played at dramas when they wanted people to feel sad.

Just then, our meal arrived. Addy Blessings was toting a large covered basket, which she set down and unveiled.

"Awww," groused Ollie Reid. "Not cabbages again. I've been trying to feed them to the mules, but now they won't eat them either."

"Yep. It's cabbages not-so-fresh from the market at Kentonbrook Farms! We pickled 'em so they'd last longer. I was thinking we could roast the last of the buggers over the fire on sticks. It was either this or the leftover peas porridge from Westarbor. But you wouldn't want that. It's nearly nine days old."

"Well I'll have one" said the little harker. "I'm so empty my bellybutton is scraping at my spine. What are you all doing up so late?"

The little redhead had awoken and quietly approached our fire.

"We're telling stories miss," reported the piper. "And since I just told mine, I get to pick the next teller. I'm sure we'd all love to know how you came by your huge, near-mythical friend over there and how a small girl came to work for a baron. I don't know what prompted Harold to start this game, but I find it agreeable. Glad I was to get all that off my chest."

"I once spent some time traveling with a man named Geoffrey," Harold explained. "Chaucer was his surname, I think. He kept us well entertained all the way to our common destination. It was his game originally."

"Fine," said Marjery. "But let me get something to eat first."

As the little lass began settling in, I overheard Lucas having a side-conversation with Royland.

"I'm curious what Master Chadwick said about us in our letters of introduction. I wish I could have a peek at mine."

"That wouldn't be wise," Royland remarked.

"I know," Lucas sighed. "Master Chadwick laid a complex enchantment on the sealing wax."

Manny leaned closer to me and muttered: 'I think the time has come, my friend, to talk of many things. Let's avoid the ravages of cabbages . . .'

I didn't miss the reference. It was to be the king's business.

"Waddle on, then," I replied. "Although I stink at carpentry, I'll let you be the semi-aquatic fellow."

What in the nine hells could the man want now? I arose stiffly to my feet and followed him toward the broken road. The young harker was just warming to her tale. And from the sound of it, it was shaping up to be an exciting one. I listened as her chipper words faded with distance.

"You see," said she, "I always hated my name. It sounds like I belong on a spice rack or was something Ma scraped up from the bottom of her butter churn . . ."

"Who are you really?" I asked as we walked along.

"I am known by many names. Manchester Kidder is but one."

That the king enjoyed theater was true enough. His majesty's spy network called themselves 'The Brotherhood of the Board,' as in: 'treading the boards.' It made reference to the entire world being a stage and all of us mere actors upon it. I was just a bit player, but I had revised my opinion of Manny upward each time the danger had mounted. By now, I suspected he was at least a leading actor, perhaps even the director himself.

"You have played your role well, Taylor Allen. I could have cut you loose from the caravan when your shipment became a danger, but I wanted to see whether you were worthy. You have passed my little test. My report to the king will be most favorable. I allowed you to lead during this time of crisis, and you led well. Though ultimately saved by happenstance, you were creative and most loyal to your goals."

I had once been saved from the streets by a fletcher who took pity on a young man. From him, I had learned to craft bows and to fletch arrows. He gave me occasional odd jobs. And by odd, I mean really odd. It was only years afterward that I learned I had been quietly recruited into the brotherhood. How strange I found it to be serving the very crown father and I had once rebelled against.

"You will be allowed to continue in your service to your new master. He, too, is an important actor. As long as Westarbor remains loyal to the crown, you may call on the brotherhood to assist you. Our cast is large and there's room enough for one more voice in its chorus. But know this. Should ever Osten and Westarbor come to cross purposes. The hook will descend, and the final curtain will close upon you."

That didn't sound ominous at all. I think I preferred the Manny persona to this sorry bag of melodramatic metaphors.

"I've heard that dying is easy," I said with a shrug.

And the jester smiled.

PART II

A Harker's Tale

(Havoc in the Henhouse)

CHAPTER SIX

The Midwife

"A woman is like a tea bag; you never know how strong it is until it's in hot water."

~ Eleanor Roosevelt ~

I hate my name. It sounds like I belong on a spice rack or that I'm something Ma scraped up from the bottom of her butter churn. Why couldn't *I* have been the one named for our mother? 'Helen' is a beautiful name. Instead, they saved it for Nellie and saddled *me* with 'Marjery.' Still more unfair, Nellie even looked like Ma with her wavy, honey blonde hair and her creamy complexion. Drew and I both took after our father, unruly red hair, freckles and all. How Nellie had escaped the Cunningham curse, I couldn't figure. But now that she'd finally earned her bonnet, things had only gotten *worse*. 'Don't you two look like sisters?' Papa would say. Or, 'Nellie is your spitting image, my dear,' all the while treating *me* like I wasn't even there. It sometimes made me so mad I could just spit *myself*.

Don't get me wrong. As the eldest child, I was still at the top of the pecking order. I just sometimes wished Papa would remark on *my* looks or something *I'd* done. Not that I ever did anything exciting, just milking the cows and my other chores.

Yesterday, a harker had ridden through announcing there was a criminal in the stockade. Papa wouldn't let us go into town to see it. I wished he had. No, instead, Nellie and I had to babysit, so the Hendersons could go. The young couple had moved in at the old Lawson place a few years back.

I missed the Lawsons. Although the mother was a little batty, the children were very near our same ages. They were always up for a game of 'Red Rover' or 'Blind Man's Buff.' I especially missed their oldest boy, Peter. About three years ago, their dad had dropped dead on a hot day while plowing his fields. That was the day all the games had stopped. All the Lawson kids had to pitch in to bring in the harvest that year. We did what we could to help out, but it was like all the cheer had left them. When the baron stepped in and relieved them of their tenancy, we were all afraid for how they would get by and we prayed for them. But we needn't have worried. They're all living in the baron's keep now and tending his lordship's chickens and geese. I wondered what it would be like to live in the castle.

Anyways, over breakfast today, Papa told us all about what happened at the stocks. It seemed the boy being punished was no criminal at all. It was that Lucas boy, the apprentice miller. When some strange miracle had caused the mill stones to fly about, he'd knocked the baron's son down into the mill race, maybe to save his life. The people thought the punishment unfair, so they celebrated Lucas by raining down flowers on him and booed Trenton out of the town square. I wished something that exciting would happen around *here*.

Instead, here I sat on my stool in the barn milking old Bessie, encouraged by a chorus of cats. The mangy old things had lined up at the edge of the stall and yowled nearly non-stop. They knew I would give in and occasionally send a squirt their way. I tried hitting them in the eyes, but they were pretty skilled at catching most of the flow in their open mouths and seemed equally content to lick the creamy white offerings from their paws. I was careful not to give them too much. Cats needed a little hunger to encourage them to keep the mice from nesting in our barn.

Papa had already returned from this morning's trip into town and was at the back of the house washing out clay milk jugs that people had returned. Ma was inside, and I'd seen Nellie head out to the chicken coop. The stars only knew where *Drew* was. The last I'd seen him, he was proudly presenting a brace of rabbits for Ma to skin. It looked like it would be rabbit stew for dinner again. We'd been eating rabbit ever since Papa had come home with Dillon.

You see, my father was rarely ever paid in good coin for his milk. Only the baron did that. Although people appreciated a bit of fresh milk, they knew it wouldn't keep for very long and that he needed to sell it quickly. Most took shameless advantage of this and only offered up trade goods. One never knew what might come home on Papa's handcart. Once it was a new butter churn for ma, fresh from the cooper. Another time it was a whole bolt of cloth from one shop in town. Today it was only some vegetables, a sack of cornmeal, a few loaves of bread from the bakeries, and his tired old self.

"Kee-eeeee-arr!" I heard from outside.

Bessie got unsettled by the sharp sound from above. I quickly snatched back the bucket lest she kick it over. The cats became hopeful for just such an event, but they soon scrambled to make themselves scarce when it sounded again, this time much louder and closer. I stood and stroked the cow's neck to try calming her but had to back away quickly when she lowed mournfully and nearly trod on my foot.

It had been raining earlier and had drizzled for much of the morning. It was still a bit shady, so I almost missed the change in light when a large shadow passed over. I stepped over to the barn's open side and looked up into the sky above. Then it passed over again. It was some kind of gigantic bird gliding above the pastures. It looked to be carrying off a large cat. No, that wasn't quite right. It was a single creature upsetting our herd with its frightening hunting cry.

Frozen with terror, I clung to the pole at the barn's entrance. Then I saw Nellie. She was coming out of the chicken coop with a basket of fresh eggs and a questioning look on her face. She was looking all around, but she never thought to look up. The bird creature cocked its head toward her and slowed to circle back around. I didn't stop to think. Dashing out into the open, I waved my apron at it and screamed. This attracted the creature, alright. It turned away from my sister because it had spotted a livelier target. Now certain I had its attention, the full measure of my foolishness occurred to me.

Sometimes in the spring, you could get targeted by an angry bull. This felt like that. Papa told me it was important to stay calm in the face of such dangers. So as I fled back into the barn, I hurried to tug loose my apron strings.

Hot on my heels, the monstrous thing touched down and charged the opening. Just like Papa had taught me to fend off a riled bull, I fluttered my apron off to one side whilst standing stock still behind the pole. It worked; thank the stars. My apron got snatched away. The monster was now wearing it like a hood. He went barreling by whilst raking at it with his fore-claws. I was spun about and knocked roughly onto the ground as it went past, but I'd bought a little more time to keep breathing.

My heart was hammering away. If there'd been cream in my belly, it'd be butter by now.

I was saved only because poor Bessie was there. When the winged critter's pounce brought it fully inside the barn, its wildly wheeling claws met the terrified cow head on. Bessie mooed her misery with a deep lowing sound as she was knocked on her side and torn into. The savage beak came down hard and made quick work of Bessie.

I scrambled to my feet and sprinted toward the house. The creature tracked me but made no move to follow as the bright blood pumped from Bessie's torn neck and her hooves kicked weakly on.

Nellie had dropped her basket and stood frozen in the yard.

"Run!" I hollered, begrudging the breath this took as I passed her by.

She sluggishly moved to follow, and Papa leaped down from the back stoop and ran to us.

"Are you hurt?" he asked, eyes wide.

I didn't answer until we had reached the safety of the house and were pulling the door shut behind us.

"I'm fine, Papa," I replied through deep, struggling breaths.

More truly, I was just starting to feel the blood well up from a deep scratch on my forearm. But underneath all the mud, it didn't seem so bad.

It was then that Drew came running over.

"Where's your mother, boy?" demanded Papa in a frantic voice.

His eyes got wider as the boy quietly pointed his trembling finger to the open front door. Papa ran over, and we followed him. Peeking out, we saw Ma at the roadside talking excitedly to a knight with a lance and pointing toward the house. Before long, the knight spun his horse around and trotted across the side yard. Ma hoisted up her long skirts and ran unashamedly back toward us.

"What were you thinking, woman!" Papa shouted at her.

"Providence has blessed us, husband," said ma, suddenly meek. "One of our liege's knights was happening by just in the time of our need. He nearly rode on past. I had to get his attention for the children's sake."

"Helen, my dear, I fear you may have sent that young man to his death," Papa muttered. "Did you not see the size of that beast? It's eating a cow, for stars' sake!"

We returned to the rear door and eased it open to watch.

There followed an epic battle the like of which I had only heard in tales of old. Unlike those tales, it all happened all too quick. I stared without bothering to blink while the knight reared up his steed and charged at the creature. I feared for the knight when he was thrown to the ground. But he rose as quick as thought to brandish his sword. The foul catbird clawed at him, but the knight soon stabbed it through its neck and it fell over on its side and lay still.

This scene will forever play back in my head as a prime example of how a knight ought to act. The knight came swaying over to lean against the very post that saved me from a mauling, as Papa took up a pitchfork and warily stepped out.

"Down," commanded the knight.

This seemed to calm his jittery mount.

Papa doffed his hat and humbly hollered, 'What is your name, my lord, that I might commend it to all who would hear the tale when I bear witness to this deed.'

"Trenton Arenson," replied the knight, "squire to Sir Declan Highcastle."

'This was our good liege's son?' I thought with wonder. I was certain he had indeed been sent by providence. He made me glad to live in Westarbor protected by such men. But in spite of my earlier thoughts, my new wish was that nothing exciting would happen around here ever again. It was an awful shame you didn't get all the stuff you wished for.

***

Papa didn't have to go into town on the following morning. It seemed that everybody and his neighbor had a sudden hankering for fresh milk the next day. Some of the lord's men were sent out with a wagon to collect the beast that was smelling up our barn. And while they were figuring out how best to lift it, a lot of people came 'wandering by' to have a look. Some didn't even have the excuse or good manners to buy any milk.

I didn't get to see much. Papa wouldn't let me go near the barn last night. This morning, the cows still needed milking. So here I sat on my stool out in the pasture, hoping the milk wasn't soured by yesterday's frightening overflight. It was raining yesterday, so the pastures were a mess. The cats had already found my new place of business. One swiped at a butterfly that unwisely came in its reach. I wondered who had named them butterflies. They were nothing like pesky flies and had nothing at all to do with butter. If he'd asked *me*, I'd have told him to call them 'flutterbys.'

Suddenly, the cats abandoned their post and streaked away in fright. I looked up, fearing another griffin. But such wasn't the case. It was only *Dillon* terrorizing the cats. The crazy thing was sniffing around where the cats had sat and rolling in the grass nearby. I saw my brother running toward me. Drew was waving to get my attention.

"You gotta come see, Marjery."

"See what?"

"I was out scouting rabbit burrows and found the most amazing thing."

"This isn't another hornet nest, is it?"

"No, sis. I *swear* you'll want to see it for yourself. You and Nellie both."

"Well I'm near done here. I'll go hang this pail in the well to keep cool, and you can go see if Nellie wants to come. Let's go see what's so all-fired amazing. It'd have to be something special to top what's in our barn."

"And don't tell ma," I warned. "She'd like as not keep us all near the house."

I watched Dillon scramble up to my brother's shoulder as the boy made for the house. I finished up as quickly as I could. I knew it must be something. Only the fear of Papa's hickory switch had kept the boy from trying to catch a glimpse of the doings in our barn this morning. And here he was stepping right past, sparing it nary a glance.

We made our way across the pasture and toward the road. As we did, we saw an oxcart coming from the direction of town. This one didn't stop at our house but kept coming. We hurried across the road and hid in the bushes to watch it. It was driven by an old man, and on the back were two boys. One was a stranger, but the other was Royland, that quiet boy from the Wagge farm. Word was he was touched in the head, but he always seemed nice to me. We hunkered down as they drove past.

"The word to throw it is 'conicere,'" the old man was saying as they drew nigh.

Then I saw it. Above Royland's hands was a stone, and it was floating right there in mid-air!

"Conicere," he said all serious like.

And I swear that stone flew down the road like a mouse from an angry cat! I grabbed Drew by the shoulder and said:

'Drew. That was amazing, but how'd you know they were coming this way?'

"That wasn't it," he said, scrambling deeper into the thicket. "C'mon, it's this way."

So we followed while collecting scratches on our legs and arms. Nellie's skirt caught on a grasping root and tore a bit when it came loose. Ma wasn't going to like *that*. Finally, Drew came up short and pointed.

"I found an eagle's nest," he proudly proclaimed.

And there before our wondering eyes was a gigantic round nest of twigs and branches. Nestled within was a clutch of the biggest eggs I had ever laid eyes on. Any one of those three gigantic eggs would be enough for a family breakfast. I swear each was as big as a hog's head.

"What should we do?" I wondered aloud.

"Dillon and I found 'em," declared Drew hotly. "Before you get any grand ideas, remember it's finders keepers. I only *showed* you to be nice. And because I need your help to carry them back home."

"What do you want them for?" Nellie asked.

While I was still stunned by the sight, Drew had had a while to ponder it. His plan came out all in a rush.

"Eagles eggs have to be worth something, sis," he said. "Instead of selling them, though, I want to hatch 'em. Baby eagles can be trained to hunt, just like Dillon here, and they got to be worth a lot more. Maybe we could sell two, and I could keep one for my own."

"Fat chance, little brother," I said. "If eagles are so valuable, I'm sure the baron'll take them just like he's taking the griffin."

I didn't truly begrudge that. If Sir Trenton hadn't come along when he did, we might all be food for the crows by now. Besides taking the griffin, the baron's men were also loading up the remains of Bessie. The poor old thing had been dead for less than a day, and the baron was paying Papa handsomely for the carcass. He wanted to smoke whatever meat could be salvaged by Master Verney for a feast to honor his son. We might even be invited to partake and say a few words.

"All right. But if we help you tote them back, then we each get one," I decided.

"No *fair*," Drew protested. "I found 'em Marjery."

"*And*," I further added, "we'll help you hide them and not tell ma."

That shut him up.

I let Drew use my apron as a sling to carry his, and Nellie and I used our skirts as we quietly picked our way back through the briers. It was well known that bunnies liked to make their burrows near to gorse bushes, so it was unsurprising that Drew had been crawling around back in here. Crossing the road, we slipped between the fence railings after first passing our enormous cackleberries carefully through.

The folks were still gathered about our barn, and luckily no one looked our way when we crossed the pasture and slipped into the henhouse.

"Over here," Nellie whispered. "Ma hardly ever comes out here. And when she does, she doesn't check this one."

It had become Nellie's chore to collect the eggs each day. I was glad to be shed of the foul task. Nellie had befriended each of the hens, and they let her collect the eggs without any fuss. Back when I had done it, the chickens were meaner. They would peck me something fierce. And the meanest one of all was Miss Mabel. The hen was past her egg laying years by now, but Nellie claimed she was still useful because she was the most attentive to her nest. Ma didn't have the heart to consign Nellie's pet bird to the stew pot, so she didn't dispute it. Any stray eggs that a neglectful hen might abandon found their way under Miss Maybel. Was she grateful? Not on your life. She would defend her eggs vigorously against all comers. I think even Dillon was afraid of the vengeful bird.

Miss Maybel squawked mightily as Nellie displaced her from her nesting box and quickly emptied it of straw. Placing our three overlarge eggs within, she packed fresh straw around them and covered them back up. Finally, she coaxed Miss Maybel back atop the pile, and we watched her settle in. I once heard the name 'Maybel' means 'lovable', but the hen was anything but. The eggs should rest safe with her.

"Are you feeling all right, Drew?" Nellie asked.

The boy was looking a little peaked. And though it was hot and stuffy in the henhouse, I thought his cheeks and nose looked a little too flushed.

"I'm right as rain now that our eggs are well hid," he declared.

It turned out that he was only as right as rain was indoors, for the following morning both he and Nellie came down with the cow pox.

***

It just wasn't fair.

It was Drew and Nellie that had gotten sick. But instead of keeping me safe, Ma had insisted I share a bed with both of them specifically so I could catch it too. When morning first came, Ma had poked her head in my and Nellie's room, cheerful as always.

"Rise and shine, sleepyheads," she sang. "It's the early bird that catches the worm!"

I had heard that so many times it rankled. I didn't answer back. Ma hadn't liked it when once I had pulled the covers over my head and asked her: 'Yeah? What does the early worm get?' Ma has a powerful grip. I think it came from churning all that butter. Whatever the cause, I can tell you personally that it doesn't do your ear much good when she uses it to drag your lazy bones out of bed.

So I sat up and stretched and started making ready for the day. Nellie only moaned. Snatching back her covers, Ma had declared: 'Stars above but this child has the pox!'

I was full awake now. A case of the pox was nothing to sneeze at. Lucky for us, it was just the cowpox, and it turned out Drew had it too. Since I was still hale, Ma had put me straight to work. The cows still needed to be milked, though we had to pour it all out. No one should be drinking poxy milk.

"I'll collect the eggs," said ma.

"No, ma," I quickly supplied. "I can do it after the milking. You stay and tend the brats."

160

Ma smiled. Like everything else about her, it was a pretty smile, and I wished I had earned it honestly.

After a hard day of double chores made useless by pouring out the pails, I sat down and thought. Somebody once said there was no use crying over spilt milk. But that person hadn't seen Papa's face when it came to him there'd be no deliveries today. Nor could he risk such for another couple weeks. He spent the day mending fences and cursing our misfortune. At least he had the baron's buying of Bessie to console him.

That night, Papa had pushed my and Nellie's beds together and brought Drew in to join us as well. 'Best to get it all over with in one go,' he had said. It was easy for him to say. He and Ma had already had the cowpox. The brats looked gruesome with those blisters breaking out on their hands and faces.

"How're the eggs?" Drew whispered through his sore throat. "Did you check on them?"

"Yep," I answered, "and I've got the marks to prove it. They seem fine. Ma doesn't suspect."

"I was thinking," Nellie said, "pa checks the chicken eggs by candling them. To see if there's a chick inside. We should try to candle Drew's eagles."

"*Our* eagles, you mean," I corrected. "But I don't think you could see through those great thick shells with a candle."

"Unless we use the biggest candle there is," she said.

As Nellie was explaining her plan, I felt a sudden tickle on my leg and screamed. I couldn't help it. Scrabbling up my leg was that crazy ferret, Dillon. The mad thing crawled up beneath the blankets to poke his nose out between Drew and me. His tongue lolled out from his sharply pointed muzzle, and he squirmed as he launched himself to land upon my brother's chest. I don't know how big Charlie had stood it. Add to that, the filthy thing stank.

You see, after all his other deliveries, Papa went to the town tavern. They would always take any extra milk he couldn't sell. Although they didn't pay in good coin, they would let Papa take it out in trade. We all knew if Papa came home late, it'd be with a near empty cart and a wobbly walk. This wasn't very often the case, though, as Papa really did work very hard to sell his product.

One day, Papa had come home very late indeed, but he surprised us all by being quite sober and bringing us the tale of Dillon. It seemed that a stranger had come to the tavern with a caged ferret. He was offering a wager. If a man could withstand Dillon's attentions for a full two minutes, he would win one shilling and five pence. It cost only two pence to play. A man's trousers were tucked firmly into his boots. When Dillon was dropped into his breeches, a rope was tightened around his waist trapping the squirming, biting ferret within. If a man freed the ferret or lost his feet, he would lose. Ferret legging, he called it.

Several men had tried it and lost their coin long before the timer ran out. But the stranger hadn't counted on big Charlie. Third up, the strapping glassblower stood in stony silence for the required time without so much as cracking a smile. It turned out that the stranger was a cheat and hadn't the funds to cover the wager. Outraged, the men of the tavern threw him out into the street and claimed Dillon as due recompense for Charlie. Papa quietly approached the man.

"What are your plans for the ferret, Charlie?" he had asked.

"I dunno, Andrew. Probably I'll wring his filthy neck for the harm he done my manhood."

"Would you take a shilling and two pence for him?" Papa asked. "It's all I've got, but my boy could make good use of him, I'm thinking."

And so, Dillon came into our lives.

Originally, I thought the cats might eat him. Several days later, they all ran at his approach. Fearless, he was. Drew taught him to hunt. First my brother would set snare nets covering every entrance to a rabbit warren. Then he would release Dillon into its tunnels. Soon the frightened hares would emerge, get caught in a snare and be bitten to death by Dillon. In the past year alone, Dillon had saved us far more that a shilling on meals. My brother also skinned a decent number of rabbit pelts each week, which Papa sold to the furrier in town.

I still loathed the little rascal.

Being as I still wasn't showing any pox when morning came, it fell on me to candle the eggs. I didn't want to admit it, but Nellie was always full of good ideas. Papa had gone to town on errands, and I told Ma I could look after the brats so she could run over to the Henderson's. Goody Henderson was expecting and really starting to show. When Ma was well gone, I went to my parents' room and helped myself to Ma's large makeup mirror on her dresser.

Behind the henhouse, I pried loose a board, then set the mirror to shine a sunbeam within.

On entering the coop, I found the broody hens all aroused by the light within it. Miss Mabel hissed and threatened me as I approached, but this time I'd come prepared. With a shovel, I scooped her as gently as I could from off the nesting box and shooed her out the door. Then, lifting the first egg up into the light, I peered within.

A soft orange glow showed a pattern of red veins spread within it and a pulsing, crimson heart. All was right with this one. The other two eggs were the same. Shoving everything back together, I nailed the board back, returned ma's mirror to its place and reported back to my sibs. I remembered to collect the regular eggs before I left and put them on the kitchen table.

"Good job, sis," said Drew weakly from his puckered red face.

It had splotches I knew I'd be seeing from a mirror before too long. I got him a cool towel for his forehead. I didn't even begrudge him his ferret. When Ma came back home, she found me milking in the barn. Although we had to pour it all out, that was no reason to let their udders get overfull. Mastitis was a painful affliction I'd not wish on even a goblin's cow.

Before long, Ma would have to do it and even Papa might need to pitch in. A week later, it turned out I was right on both counts. By the day I felt the sickness take hold, Drew and Nellie weren't quite better yet. Their sores had opened up and were oozing, crusting over and doing things I wished I hadn't seen. They would soon get over it, but mine was just starting.

That was the day Phillip came to our farm. He rang his harker's bell until Papa went out to talk to him.

"Sweetheart," Papa said to me when he came back in, "you need to go with the harker to the baron's castle. Her ladyship, the baroness, would like you to stay with them for a week or so."

"Can't you tell her I'm sick?" I asked, confused.

"It's *because* you're sick that they want you to go," he answered. "Her ladyship would like to catch your cowpox. It'll only be for a little while, my Marjery. And just think, you'll get to stay at the castle."

Who would want this dire affliction? Some adults were just as crazy as a ferret.

***

I'd heard that misery loves company, and I guess it must be true. But as I lay too hot with my skin all itchy I resented the old woman who lay next to me. The baroness was too familiar, insisting I lie close to her and making me feel hotter still.

Her bed, however, was a fine thing indeed. All soft, it was. The bedspread I kept trying to shift loose from was pretty and stitched together with a thread so fine that it never poked at a person.

"Stop squirming, child," said her ladyship.

The baroness talked funny. She made big, tall 'Ohs' like her mouth wouldn't go no wider and ended each word with a crisp sound that did little to improve my disposition.

"What's that you're doing, milady?" I asked in my best manners.

"I'm reading a book," she said.

Ma had taught me my letters. I could name most of them on sight. But I'd never seen the appeal of doing it over and over again.

"Why are all the letters out of their proper order, milady?" I politely asked.

The baroness really looked at me for the first time. She seemed questioning of something, and she set her book aside.

164

"Firstly," said she, "you may call me Lady Chamille. Not in public, mind you. But since at my request, we seem to be strange bedfellows, I would lief as hear the sound of my own name for a change. It seems only proper that you be granted this privilege to comfort you in your illness."

Lady Chamille was like that. She never spoke plainly, but bunched up her words to make what she said seem bigger. I got the idea, though.

"And secondly," she continued, "I would inquire as to the status of your education. Can you not read, child?"

"Seeing as we're bedmates as you say, you can just call me Marjery," I said, trying to imitate her tall Ohs. "And yes; I know almost all my letters and even some of the sounds they make."

The baroness smiled at this and reached over to the night stand to fetch a fancy place-mat she had under the lantern.

"Show me," she said with a smile. "What's this one, then."

On her mat, Lady Chamille had all the letters, big and small, stitched in colored thread. She was pointing to the letter 'M', and I told her so. And these letters did seem to be fit together right.

"This is the embroidery primer I first used to teach Megan her letters," the lady said, getting a distant look when she said it. "'M' is quite correct Marjery. And what do you think is the second letter of your name?"

This game went on for some time, and Chamille got happier each time I was right. I nearly forgot my uncomfortableness as my new friend showed me how the letters could fit together to make all different words. It was gratifying to finally see the use of it.

In the morning, the baroness' servants helped me to get dressed. I didn't have the heart to tell them I was old enough to do it on my own. I remembered to call her milady in front of them.

I don't think my clothes had ever been so clean, and they smelled just like flowers as did the whole room. When I'd first gotten to the castle, I didn't think I would like it. The dead griffin lay splayed out and gutted on the terrace they called their 'inner ward.' The thing smelled to high heaven. But in here, it wasn't so bad.

"Agatha," said the lady, "as we discussed, Marjery, here is to infect all my ladies with cowpox. Please take her to the sitting parlor and have her handle all the sewing needles and threads to be used for today's projects. Also have the child sit among them. Pray, give her some makework to pass the time."

With that, I was handed over to milady's old maid servant who took me by the hand and led me off. She took me to another room where a bunch of other old ladies sat about stitching on clothing and other things. They weren't mending them like I thought at first. Instead, they were making pictures on them and sometimes even letters like on Chamille's 'primer.' I was made to touch all of their things and rub my arms and face on their cloth. Then I was sat down in a corner.

"My lady instructed me to give you work to help pass the time. Having seen what we are about, is there some suitable project you would prefer?"

She had a nice face. The lines on it weren't stern, and they crinkled around her eyes like she smiled a lot. I thought about what she was asking. It only made sense I should work for my supper.

"If we're making pictures on stuff," I started. "Then I'd like to make something for Sir Trenton. He did us a great favor when he killed that monster that murdered Bessie."

Apparently, this was the right answer. All the ladies stopped what they were doing to look up and smile kindly at me. Some looked sad until I explained that Bessie was a cow.

"In that case," said Agatha, "I would suggest that you start small. A handkerchief, perhaps?"

With that, she handed me a white square of linen and enough colored thread to get started. What should I make? A griffin, of course. As I began to stitch, the ladies soon forgot me and began talking among themselves. They spoke of all kinds of things and the goings on in the barony and even other parts of the kingdom. A girl could learn a lot just sitting here and listening.

"I hear that awful boy from the mill has been exiled to a sheep ranch in Arborvale," one lady remarked.

"He wasn't so bad," said another. "I hear his father is at death's door. His aunt and uncle are going to help run the mill."

"I should hope so. Else where would we get our bread."

"The baron's happy about the griffin incident; I hear he's preparing to see his son knighted for the deed before the winter's end."

"Have you heard the latest from Barony Stein? I hear the Lady Stein is with child!"

"I doubt you heard correctly," said Agatha. "I once worked for the Lord and Lady Stein, back in the day. They were most distraught to find her ladyship couldn't bring a second child to term, given the problem with their first."

"Do tell us, Madam Grimbley. What was the matter with the first?"

"Well, I was their midwife before I came here. Perhaps I shouldn't say as it would violate their privacy."

"Oh, you're a heartless one! Better you tell us than we spread rumors that be wrong. Tis common knowledge what was amiss with their first lad anyway."

"All right then," returned Agatha with unhappy eyes. "But this stays within our circle and is not to be bandied about. As you probably know, their first son and heir was found to have the gift."

"No!" burst from a few of the ladies who sat hanging on her every word.

"He did. Once this was discovered, he became ineligible to become the heir of Stein and was commanded to report to Conclave. He is presently studying to become a mage. Although disappointed, Lord Leopold and his lady wife thought to try again. Most regrettably, the Steins soon found that they were afflicted by a most perfidious and little known curse. Although they could conceive, a second child could not be brought fully to term."

"That's ghastly," said a younger maid looking stricken. "Whatever did they do?"

"Some counseled Leopold to set her aside and remarry," continued Agatha with a grimace. "Such is sometimes the way of nobles in such important matters of succession. But the good lord wouldn't hear of it. 'She is my one true love,' said he, 'and the only woman fit to wear the title of Lady Stein.' And so, for his lordship's sake, Wilhelmine tried again and again until the bitter end. Each time she caught, it was the same thing. I'd see the glow of optimism shine forth for a time only to once again see the hope die in her eyes."

"That's so sad."

"At least from the sounds of it, it was no fault of the bull," said one maid indifferently. "That should be some comfort to Leopold, I should think. No gomer he."

I knew that one. If a bull was castrated when young, he became a steer and had no interest in cows. If he was castrated *after* he'd matured, he became a gomer bull. He still had the inclination, but could no longer get a cow with calf. The Cains had a gomer bull. They were plumb useful. The Cains didn't want to get their herd all inbred. They let him roam around keeping the cows happy with a marker ball affixed to his belly full of blue chalk. When a cow had a blue spot on her back, they knew she was in season and would march her straightaway to our farm to breed with our prize bull, Toro.

"Tis a cold comfort indeed," said another "as he remains heirless. "Twere best he find a better cow."

I decided to speak up.

"If it pleases my ladies, I'm a dairy maid. My father noted a similar problem in our herd. These matters sometimes just arise and are the fault of neither the bull nor the cow. I think it was brave and fitting that Leopold kept to his vows. Ma says, 'a man shall cleave unto his wife.' I should hope for such faithfulness when *I* one day marry."

Startled, all looked over at me.

"Delightful child," Agatha praised. "You are exactly right. Tis no fault of either the bull or the cow. Rather it's some incompatibility betwixt the two. Out of the mouths of babes. And the baron's fidelity is now well rewarded. Though denying him an heir, providence provided him instead with a faithful woman who does him honor in his final years."

"But I thought Lord Leopold was forty-seven. That's hardly ancient!"

"It was not so many years ago that Lord Leopold was a vigorous force to be reckoned with," said Agatha. "When I knew him, he was overturning all that was known of modern agriculture and leading the way to a brighter future. Lord Downham will never forgive the man for dropping the bottom out of the corn market just when he sought to dominate it. One could almost hear the screeching of that nasty old crow from all the way across the Danstonshire. It was bandied about that Stein had the king's notice and was assuredly to be the next Duke of Northford. Alas, Leopold is but a shadow of that man today."

"What happened to him then, pray tell."

Agatha looked glum, and she worked at her stitching a bit before continuing her story.

"As sometimes happens to older gentlemen, his wits are failing him. It began with a few simple things. He would forget an appointment or misplace something. But then it grew more severe. He would fail to recognize a well-known friend, or be found wandering about the castle with no clue as to where he was going. Such is the sad fate of very elderly people, but it was happening to the good lord right in his prime. And it is getting steadily worse. When I left bound for Westarbor, he happily told me to give his regards to Sir Nicholas, a deceased friend from his youth."

That poor man, I thought. I wished someone could help him. But just like providence had given old Leo what he really needed, it was about to play me a trick as well. For before the year was out, it would be me needing *that* old man's help instead.

***

Over the following couple of nights, milady kept teaching me my letters. She had fetched some books from the baron's library. I now knew about all kinds of flowers and how to sound out their names. I finished my handkerchief for Sir Trenton, but I hadn't given it to him yet. Agatha had tried putting on a good face when I showed it to her, but I knew it looked more like an ugly duck with a cat tacked on than a proper griffin.

Though I was free to wander about in the daytime, most people avoided me in the halls, seeing as my spots were showing something fierce by now. So after my morning stitching, I decided to visit the Lawsons. I'd heard they lived at the top of the east tower, looking over the baron's birds. And it was birds, not flowers, I truly hankered to learn something of.

You see, I had not forgotten the special eggs in our henhouse. When they hatched one day, the eagle chicks would need special care. And no one knew more about birds than Goody Lawson. It might also give me a chance to see Peter and his younger brother and sisters. We could catch up, and I could see how they were getting on.

On my way there, I was happy to see the gory griffin was gone. There was still some smell, but the courtyard was clear of the mangy beast, and the knights were gathering about.

"Finally," said Sir Fletcher, "practice may resume. I trust the discontinuity of our morning drills, and the loss of your squire haven't softened your sword arm, Sir London."

"Never," replied the other knight. "Myles Nieves wasn't proper knight material. His discourtesy to the first heir at the feast was merely the final straw. Sean Henry here is more than an adequate replacement. As a Baldwin, he undoubtedly possesses the heart of a lion. And should you believe my sword arm 'soft,' I would invite you to test that theory. Shall we enjoy the first bout of the day?"

The two men faced off in the square and had at it most fiercely. I could barely keep up with the ringing exchange of blows that followed. It was bigger than the donny brook I'd once seen break out at the fall harvest festival. Yet when the two were done, they came out laughing about it and complimenting each other in happy tones. The other knights milling about were starting to pair off and wait for their turn to do the same.

I spotted Sir Trenton with them. So I walked over to thank him once again for saving our farm. I fished about for the gift I'd made him. As I was walking over, the men all shuffled about to make way and looked curiously at me.

"Can we help you, miss?" asked Jay Harvey.

He was that squire that was always running about with Sir Nolan. He was kind of handsome. He seemed almost like one of the knights himself, but I knew he wasn't any older than me. Maybe it was the armor he wore that made him seem larger.

"If it pleases m'lords," said I with my finest curtsy, "I am here to see Sir Trenton. I'd like to gift him this handkerchief I made in thanks for killing that beast. If he hadn't done it, our herd would've been scattered and who knows what would've become of us."

"It would seem you have an admirer, Sir Trenton," said his knight, pushing him to the fore.

Trenton reached out and took the cloth I was offering. When he held it up, all of those knights took to laughing like there was no tomorrow. I knew they were laughing at me and my efforts, but I didn't care.

"It's a griffin," I said in case he couldn't make it out.

This caused louder laughs from the men, but Sir Trenton squinted at it and turned it up to its proper side. He then hung it out from his collar and looked on me again.

"Thank you, miss," said he. "I shall wear it with pride."

Turning about to face the others, he said: 'Know that Trenton Arenson shall never be one to spurn a lady's favor. Even so humble a gift is worth a thousand more extravagant honors when offered in earnest friendship by a heart as pure as this. I shall treasure it.'

It was that very moment I knew for certain I was looking at a knight.

I stepped into the east tower. I could still hear the knights at their drilling, but it got all muffled by the thick stone walls. Inside, it was like the sun shooting down through the leaves in the forest because the walls were pierced everywhere with holes. The holes were shaped like funny little crosses. I was told later this was so archers could use them to let out their arrows should this be needful.

Peter stood across the big circle bent over a bunch of cages collecting eggs into a basket. I tried keeping the girlish glee from my voice because I knew boys didn't favor such. I decided on a cooler greeting.

"Peter Lawson," I said. "I see you're still tending your ma's birds. It seems like she's added quite a few more, though."

Turning, he held up a hand to block the light from his eyes and spotted me.

"Marjery? Marjery Cunningham?" he said with surprise.

Setting his eggs aside, he started over. But then he paused.

"What are all those spots on your face? Have your freckles decided to get even bigger?"

"Cowpox," I answered. "I caught them at the dairy, and the baroness wanted me to get her sick too."

"That's daft!" he declared. "Keep well away from *me* then. And don't be *touching* anything in here."

"That's what I said," I returned. "But she said cowpox was better than smallpox and she'd 'prefer to avoid the latter.' I guess 'the ladder' has something to do with dying."

"Well why'd you bring your poxy self here, anyway?" he asked with a mean face.

"I just wanted to say hello while I was here and..."

"Hello and goodbye," he said while pointing at the door.

"Is your ma here? I have some questions about caring for hunting birds and ..."

"Mother's sitting in council with the baron. And she doesn't have no truck with hunting birds. Pigeons and geese are her specialty - and chickens, of course. I'll say it again, Marjery.

Take your sickness out of the dovecote. People *eat* these birds, you know."

And so I fled the tower and walked over toward the side of the castle. Peter used to be nice. I'd had a crush on him as big as *life* when the Lawsons lived on the next farm over. Even then he'd been indifferent to me, always choosing me last for the games we played. I think he favored Nellie, and that had just tore at my heart.

I found a place to sit down. The baron's garden was pretty with its flowers all in a row and its neatly trimmed hedges. Some of them were even shaped like things: animals, castle battlements, or just shapes like balls or squares. Why didn't Peter like me? Was it the freckles?

"Hey!" came a fearsome growl. "You kid's should Kn-n-n-ow better than to be s-s-s-ittn' on me g-g-grounds!

The man who had suddenly sprung up was frightening. He was bigger than most and had a sharp pair of sheers in hand. His upper lip was split in the middle, making his lips hang down on each side like a dog. His crazy eyes didn't track right and made you think he might just do anything.

"I'm s-s-sorry, mister," I said in a small voice, turning my sobbing, pimply face up to his. "I didn't know."

The man stopped in his tracks and seemed to shrink some. He stopped looming over me and crouched down with his big hands on his knees.

"Here now, m-m-miss," he said. A p... a p-p-purdy little thing like you oughtn't to cry. W-w-what's wrong?"

I doubted he thought me pretty. I was a mess. But maybe he was reckoning it with a different eye. Especially as he only had one on me at the time. My story came out in a rush. Maybe because he didn't talk so easily, he was a good listener instead. He sat down by my side while I went on about everything.

When I was done and my cheeks had gone dry, he gave me some comforting advice and also a few good ideas. He told me the nobles had a library that was full of books. In these could be found all kinds of stuff. One time, the baron had read him one on gardening that was chock full of new ideas. If I wanted to know about hunting birds, he said, it was a sure bet the baron could dig up a few books on the topic.

He said that Peter should be nicer and offered to have a talk with his ma. I told him not to bother. Peter had made his feelings plain. 'It is what it is' I told him. He then used his sheers to cut down a whole row of white flowers. He said they were called 'Edelweiss.' He asked me to take them to the baroness because she treats folks right and he knew she favored them.

"You know, you're actually very nice, mister Grek." I told him.

"The b-b-baron once t-t-told me: 'You j-j-judge a b-b-book by what's in its p-p-pages.'"

Later that day, I went to the library. The baron was in there and so was Sir Declan, Trenton's knight. I didn't want to disturb them, so I hung back. Sir Declan was saying how the boy was now ready. This made the baron happy as a cat in a bucket of cream. He asked if the knight was certain, saying there wasn't any rush. But the knight then told him as to how he'd just seen a 'remarkable display of chivalry and empathy.' Adding this to his 'restraint at the feast' had shown the boy was worthy.

When the knight was making to leave, I knocked on the door. The baron told me to enter, but soon shied back from my blistering face. He soon worked out I was the girl his wife had sent for and told me he didn't cotton to his lady's half-baked notions on 'immunization.' I could come in, but had to stand well back from his lordship. When I explained my need, he took me most seriously. He was quick to fetch several thick books on falconry and a few shallower ones on birds in general. I thanked him kindly and made my way back to milady's room.

Lady Chamille was nice enough to help me study up. It was slow-go at first because these were serious books and not the simple ones like we were using before. But I stuck at it, having a stake in the matter.

"I find myself impressed by your diligence, Marjery," said the lady. "It is rare to find in one so young. I believe you may have found a topic that intrigues you. For Megan, it was flowers.

It is my firmly held belief that everyone, and especially young ladies, should be free to explore their passions, the better to find their eventual niche and thus live happy lives. I've half a mind to let you borrow these books, for you shall soon return to your farm."

The baroness wasn't looking too well. Her face had reddened, and she was coughing from time to time. I looked on in sadness because we both knew what would come next.

"Well," said I, "if milady ever has that thought with her whole mind, let me know it because I'd be very happy to borrow them for a while. I'd promise to return them just as clean and sharp as the day they left the shelf.

That was my last night with the baroness. She and half her ladies had been brought low by the cowpox. And though I still thought her a bit mad for wanting it in the first place, I wouldn't have missed my time at the castle for all the bacon in Master Verney's smokehouse. I returned home to Papa and Ma feeling better and with a clutch of books under my arm. I hoped Nellie and Drew had kept our eggs safe. I'd even be glad to look in on Miss Mabel again.

CHAPTER SEVEN

The Hunter

"Ideas are like rabbits. You get a couple and learn how to handle them, and pretty soon you have a dozen."

~ John Steinbeck ~

Back home, things were getting more normal. Nellie and Drew were up and about, and Papa was selling his milk once again. In my absence, Nellie was given the milking chore, and Drew was gathering the eggs. Everyone seemed happy but me. Things were happening again, but here *I* was stuck in my bed. Still showing signs of the sickness, I wasn't allowed to leave my room, much less go anywhere *near* the cows. Even worse, my sores had broken open and were itching to beat the band. Ma made me wear socks over my hands so I wouldn't scratch at them in my sleep. I was glad at least that the baroness wouldn't have to look on and see what was in store for her and her ladies.

I was comforted to know that our special project was still on track. Drew had snuck into my room to tell me Miss Mabel was still on the job. I showed him the books I'd gotten from the baron, and he seemed mightily impressed. I decided I'd use my time while I was laid up to read them properly.

Without milady's help, the baron's thick books proved a tough chew. I had to skip over many words I couldn't make out and come back to them knowing what the other words around them said. Milady had called this 'context' and insisted that reading more could teach you to read. I suppose this made sense as milking more would soon make you a better milker. So I read on, slowly puzzling out what I could.

I learned that with hunting birds. It was important to feed them only from their master's hand. In that way, they wouldn't know they could kill their own food. They'd still hunt, but they'd leave you the kill. I guessed this was like the cows letting us have their milk when their calves were taken away. Another funny thing I learned was that such birds hunted in the daytime and slept when the sun was down. Because of this, you could put a hood over their heads and trick them into believing it was time for a nap. Cows must be much smarter than birds. You'd never trick a cow to sleep in such a way.

As the days passed, I learned many such things. It was much slower than just having someone explain it to you. But I could see if such a knowing person wasn't around, this was a way you might still find out what was needful. The baron's great cache of books was like having a whole group of experts ready with the answers to his questions. If everyone could read like the baron seemed to want, his people could do *anything*. Well, knowing and doing were two different things, I supposed. But the thought of it was still ringing in my head when Ma entered my room with a tray of food.

"How's my little bookworm today?" she asked, placing her hand on my forehead.

"Much better, Ma."

"We'll see," she said, turning my face up to the light. "Your fever's gone, and those blisters are all on the mend. I don't think you'll have any scarring if you can leave off scratching at them. I believe you can go outside today if you feel up to it."

I was out of the bed like a shot from a bow. Shucking my nightgown, I grabbed up a blouse and skirt. Ma was grinning as I quickly made ready to taste freedom.

"And wear your bonnet," Ma reminded me. "Even the winter sun wrecks havoc on that freckled skin of yours, sores or no."

I wasn't partial to this reminder. Papa wore a hat. Drew wore a hat. Only Ma and Nellie were spared the need, and it was irksome. But I ran back and gave Ma a hug anyway for looking out for me.

Outside, I most wanted to go check on the eggs, but it would be suspicious if that was the first thing I did. The snow crunched under my boots as I made my way over to the barn. Papa was there, just returned from his trip to town. It was hard for him to clean the empty jugs because the dregs of the milk inside them had all frozen stiff. Ma had to melt snow in the kitchen and tote it out to him to wash them with.

"Good. You're up," he said. "Now you can help your sister keep up with the daily milking. She's new to her bonnet and not used to the rigors. Her little arms have been aching for days. I've been having to milk half the herd myself."

Good to know I'm useful. I love you too, Papa. The open-sided milking barn didn't provide full shelter from the chill. So Nellie was likely over at the big barn where we wintered the herd.

"I've got some disappointing news for you as well, darling. I know we'd hoped to go as a family on the solstice. But some of the folks in town don't want anyone with pox to attend, recovered or not."

The *knighting* ceremony. *Please* tell me this wasn't heading where I thought it was.

"The townsfolk are already celebrating. It's a five day affair. But I was hoping to take at least your mother. She doesn't get out much, and she was, after all, the one who gave Sir Trenton the come hither that day. Do you feel well enough to manage things here while we're away?"

"Of course, Papa. You and Ma should go. When will you be leaving?"

"That's the thing, darling. Helen and I were invited by the baron to stay in his guest quarters at the castle, seeing as how we could speak of Trenton's amazing battle here in our barn. Now I'm not much of a speaker, but I figure we owe the lad that much. We've been holding off up to now due to your illness, but the baron would like us to come right away. We'd leave tonight if you can be trusted on your own for a couple of days, three at most."

And there was that providence again. Taking something bad and making a good come out of it. For no sooner had my folks set off for town than Drew came running up to me.

"Marjery, something's happening with the *eggs!*"

"What's happening?"

"I'm hearing peeps and tapping from one of them. I think they're gonna *hatch!*"

"Go get Nellie," I told him. "I'll meet you there."

After we'd chased out Miss Maybel and some of the other broody hens, we pulled the eggs up out of the straw. I thought it might be a little too cold in the henhouse. So Nellie and I cradled them gently in our aprons and carried them to the big barn. I told Drew to run and fetch us some of Papa's socks. We might want to hood them right away.

I have to hand it to my sister. Calm as anything I've ever seen, she made Skye get up from where she lay and built a little nest for the eggs on the warm spot, covering it with fresh straw. She put the lie to the saying: 'nervous Nellie.' She led Skye over to share a stall with her sister, Sarah. Both young cows had been bred this past autumn by our prized bull, Toro. When they dropped calves in the spring, we'd have two more to milk. My arms ached just thinking about it. Toro snorted and stood watching from over in his corner stall.

One egg wiggled about and we could hear peeps and tapping from it. I'd once watched a clutch of chickens hatching, so I knew it wasn't a quick process. I clamped down on the urge to help it along. Papa said it was best they get out on their own. Sooner or later, a crack would appear, and things would start getting serious.

Nellie and Drew looked on with fascination, and Drew yelped and pointed when a second egg began to quiver. Roused by the peeping of the first egg, the others were starting to stir. I knew from my books the baby eagles would be hungry. But were they eagles? For chickens, we'd give them corn meal to get started on. From my reading, I knew baby hawks ate anything their ma could get her claws on. Meat was their preference, but they'd eat bugs and the like. Also, snakes, lizards, frogs and toads weren't out of line.

I explained this to my sibs and asked Drew to run to the house and fetch us something.

"When did you get so smart, sis?" he asked. "I'm sure glad I shared this with you and Nellie."

"Best you don't forget that, little brother," I told him. "As the oldest, I get the first one to hatch."

He looked like he wanted to argue, but he knew better than to cross me when my back was up.

"And Nellie's second," I added to his retreating back.

He came back with some skinned rabbits with Dillon at his heels. He'd even brought Ma's cutting board and a sharp knife. While he set to work chopping the bunnies to bits. The first big crack appeared. We'd be ready when the birds came out.

Then I saw its head.

"Eee-oooo!" she called, still struggling to be shed of her egg.

The other two eggs took to shaking more vigorously, cheered on by the first bird's success.

"Awwww," Nellie gushed. "She's so *cute*. Look how her little eyes are blinking in the light."

"I've got the perfect name for her," I said. "I'm going to call her Wynken."

"How do you know it's a *girl* bird?" asked Drew. "Maybe it's a *rooster* eagle."

"I know how to check for such. It's in my books. But let's get 'em hatched first."

The second egg split and the head came poking out. This one too was blinking in the light of the lantern in our barn. Wynken had a wing free by then.

"Not to steal your thunder," said Nellie, "but I want to call her Blynken. Would that be alright?"

"It suits her," I said.

Ma used to tell us bedtime stories when we were younger. One of Nellie's favorites was a poem she used to recite to put us to sleep.

Wynken and Blynken are two little eyes,
And Nod is a little head,
And the wooden shoe that sailed the skies
Is a wee one's trundle-bed;
So shut your eyes while Mother sings
Of wonderful sights that be,
And you shall see the beautiful things
As you rock in the misty sea

The third egg went still.

After a few minutes, Drew got impatient and started tapping on it. Our two birds were nearly out, but were still moving about strangely.

Finally, Drew hauled back and struck his egg hard enough to crack it. Out came the little head, blinking like the others. But it was also bobbing up and down.

"Todd," declared Drew. "I'm gonna name him Todd."

"I think you mean 'Nod,'" said Nellie with a bothered look.

"What kind of a name is 'Nod' for an eagle?" the boy asked hotly. "You got to name yours. So I'm calling him Todd."

But just then, Wynkin crawled the rest of the way out of her egg and toward me where I sat. I was aghast to see that out from her back was the body of a kitten, tail and all. I wanted to scream. It was no eagle blinking up at me, but spawn of that mama griffin that had killed poor Bessie and nearly had my head as well.

"Eee-oooo!" cried Wynken as she looked up at me and blinked her little eyes.

I knew the proper thing to do would be to drown them in the stream, and I said so.

"You *can't!*" shouted Nellie, nearly bursting into tears on the spot. "They're helpless! Marjery Cunningham, if you can be so mean as to do that, I'll never speak to you again."

Drew was already feeding bits of the rabbit to his, and Nellie was hovering protectively over 'her bird.'

I knew in my heart we couldn't keep the things. They'd grow up to be a danger to folks and their livestock. I tried to harden my heart. But when Wynken climbed up into my lap and commenced purring, I knew we had to find some other way.

I had read a curious thing about birds. When they were first hatched, they didn't know what to be. They would 'visually imprint' on the first thing they saw. Thereafter, they would go on thinking that creature was its mama and 'identify with that species' for the rest of their lives. It was why baby ducks would follow a person around until you shooed them back to the pond. If my reading was right, we might've just spoiled these critters from ever being able to live in the wild. But maybe it wasn't too late.

"We can't keep them here," I declared over my sibs' objections. "You know what Papa would advise. How about this, then? We can take them back to the nest Drew found and sneak them some food until they're fledged. Then they can fly off and find some better place to carry on.

I suspected the cute little creatures might not survive the cold without a mother's warmth. Much less could they fend for themselves against forest predators without her protection. They would probably die. I thought that might be for the best as we took them there, set up a pile of soft straw, and placed food nearby.

Against all odds it turned out we had called it exactly right. When I had sexed them, it turned out that Todd was a boy griffin, and the other two were girls. The three griffin fledglings (kittens?) crawled into a pile under the straw and promptly fell asleep. But in thinking they might die out here, I hadn't reckoned on my brother's stubbornness. He and Dillon refused to leave the spot for the next couple days. Ma and Papa were gonna be in town for a while, and I wondered how things would be when they came back.

Nellie and I visited after attending to milking and other chores. It turns out that baby griffins are right playful. Dillon had found three new playmates as fearless as he. It was still cute how they'd raise their little heads with beaks open wide waiting for the bits of rabbit and other stuff we'd feed them. Drew kept a small, smokeless fire going at his camp in the briers, and would on occasion trap a few rabbits.

By the time our folks did return, all seemed normal. Nellie and I made sure all was right with the herd, and Drew returned. He even brought a brace of rabbits to help explain his absence. But the days ahead would get interesting and my plan to free the fledglings was not to come about.

***

The days flew by as the winter wore on. It turned out the fledglings were fierce enough to fend off anything that might want to make a meal of them. Drew was gone a lot, but Papa just said that he was proud the boy was learning to make his own way as a hunter. Though he was gone a lot more, Drew brought fewer rabbits home each week. Nellie and I knew our brother was hunting ever more to feed the fledgling's growing appetites. One day, Papa even took him to task for it.

"Gone all day, and you only got a single rabbit?" he chided. I think you and your pet must be loafing. Perhaps I should find you some chores around the farm. The fencing needs attention around the north pasture."

"I'll do better Pop," said Drew looking crestfallen.

"See that you do," Papa said. "Your sisters are working very hard to help keep us afloat, and I won't have you laying about."

"Eee-oooo!" we heard from off in the distance.

"I gotta go, Pop" said Drew. "Dillon and I found a new rabbit's warren just north of the Henderson place. I think there're a bunch of fat hares in there just waiting to meet Dillon's teeth."

"I hope you're right," said Papa with a grin, "Best you get a move on lest those hawks beat you to them. The pelts you've gathered thus far have made a nice addition to the family finances. I sell them to the Tillerson boy. His fur-lined boots have been all the rage in Meadowfork this winter. There's nothing quite so soft and warm as rabbit skin. Carry on, then."

Drew had a problem. When he fed the fledglings, he couldn't even bring the rabbit pelts home lest our parents should wonder where the meat had gone. He had expanded his camp in the brier patch and was drying and curing the extra pelts before his low fire there. But he dared not bring them home. The problem was soon solved in a most unexpected way.

One day when Nellie and I were visiting 'Camp Griffinbrier', Blynken came prowling back lugging a fat hare in her beak. This she promptly dropped before my startled brother sitting at the fire.

"Good girl!" Nellie praised, as she scratched the fledgling behind her neck. "*Who's* a clever griffin."

It happened there *was* a rabbit warren nearby. The fledglings, on discovering it, had set about laying in wait near its openings. When they saw a rabbit coming or going, they would pounce on it and peck it to death. They thought it was great fun, but they didn't know what to do with the dead hares afterward. Like cats, they would bring these prizes home to share with their 'family,' and Drew would praise them and feed them. Soon Drew had many more rabbits than he needed to feed the griffins. So he proudly brought them home to Papa, who would praise him and feed him.

Having more than enough rabbits for our family dinner, Papa carted the excess into town for sale to Master Verney. He would smoke the meat as a nice change from his hogs and mutton. At this point, Drew had no problem sneaking a few extra skins onto the cart.

Winter finally gave way to spring, and the cows could again be set out to graze. There was some excitement when the knights set out down the road on a quest to 'purge the Mygaloms,' whatever that might mean. More weeks passed, and the knights came home. They were sad because they'd lost two men. I cried when I heard of the battle at their ceremony up on the hill. Not long after that, Papa gave Skye and Sarah to the Tillersons to replace an ox they'd lost. He claimed this squared him with the baron for Trenton's help last fall. And summer arrived.

Once again I found myself overlooked in favor of Nellie. It started when we were sitting on the fence one day waiting for the Cain's cow. Toro had been placed out in a fenced pasture waiting to do his duty. Rupert Cain came down the lane leading a cow to be bred. She bore the blue mark on her back that declared her to be in heat. We let her into the pasture, and Toro took an interest at once. Rupert leaned on the fence nearby to watch the proceedings.

The Cains were a funny lot. They rarely had anything to do with other folks, but seemed courteous enough when they did. When we'd had our barn raising for the big barn, the men of their clan had been the first to arrive. In truth, they had the job half done before other neighbors started arriving and joining in. But none of their women showed up with dishes for the picnic to follow. Rumor was, the Cain men kept them locked up behind a spite fence. And after the roof was on proper, all the Cains stepped off back home, foregoing the drinking and dancing that went on into the night. Like I said, they were a strange lot, but good neighbors on balance.

The bull started nuzzling the cow in preparation to mount her. Glancing sideways toward the woodshed, Rupert drawled: 'I sure wouldn't mind getting some of what *he's* having, Miss Nellie.' My sister puzzled on this for a moment, then smiled at him.

"I don't see why not," she said with an inviting grin and a wave of her hand toward the pasture. "She's your cow, after all."

Yup. Nellie always got all the attention. It was like *I* wasn't even there. It was true the boy was no charmer, but didn't he know how it stung to make a play for the younger sister?

The boy was soon crouched down by a strange plant growing at the pasture's edge.

"Don't let 'em graze on this, Miss Nellie" he said. "It gives our cattle the flux somethin' fierce."

Having so declared, he then uprooted the weed and collected it into his shoulder bag. The Cains are strange folks.

I remember it so well because that was the day the harker rode up, hollering and ringing his bell. 'The goblins are coming to threaten all,' he decried. When Papa and Ma came out from the house, he launched into a drawn-out speech telling us what to do. We were to collect all our things and gather our herd and drive them to the keep. We'd all be made safe behind the baron's walls. We were to bring such food and supplies as we could carry and ruin everything else so the goblins couldn't use it.

Rupert rushed off home with his cow to see what his kin would make of it.

"Hey Rupert!" I shouted at his back. "Maybe you'd best head straight into town. You can meet up with your folks when they get there."

"Can't," the boy hollered back, squinting at me. "There's no moon tonight!"

***

We rushed to gather up anything we thought was needful. Ma was in a tizzy as Papa kept rejecting things from the pile she was laying out.

"Look," he finally said, "I've got to drive the cattle to town. You load the pushcart with only the things were going to need. Leave this other frippery. It ain't worth your life, woman."

Sobbing, Ma agreed, but then she jumped up like a dragon had just flown over her grave.

"The Hendersons," she exclaimed. "Poor Annabel must be at her wit's end. I should go over there and help. She only just gave birth a week ago; I doubt she's back on her feet yet. Grant'll be gathering up their animals. You can help him herd them into town."

"Nellie and Drew and I can manage the pushcart, Ma," I offered.

So, as Ma stalked off toward the neighbors and Papa headed to the pasture, I turned to my sibs.

"What about the fledglings?" Drew asked with a worried look. "They don't even know how to feed themselves. And I'd hate to think what goblins might do if they found them. We can't just leave them out there, Marjery."

"We won't," I decided. "We're the ones that spoiled them, so it falls to us to keep them safe. Drew. Go get them and lead them to the roadside. I'll meet you there with the cart. Nellie. Start hiding all of Ma's stuff. Keep only some food and a few tools that might prove useful and meet us out there."

Following my lead, the sibs got right to work. I lined the cart with a bit of soft straw and pushed it across the road to the trailhead. When Drew got there, he was leading the griffins through the underbrush. The trio had grown a mite and barely fit in the cart. They quit trying to get loose once I put socks over their heads to convince them it was night. I then covered the lot of them with a tablecloth I'd looted from Ma's supplies. Nellie soon joined us, and we scattered her offerings on top so the cart would look stocked.

Some days, when you're of a like mind, it wasn't so bad to have sibs.

We could never bring the griffins to the keep, but we headed out that way at least until we were out of Papa's sight. Papa's cart and its three passengers were heavy, but helping each other, we managed. When we sighted Meadowfork ahead, we turned aside to the east road.

"Where are we going, Marjery?" asked Nellie.

"I'm not entirely sure as yet," I answered. "But I thought we might stash the fledglings at the edge of the Danstonshire with Drew to watch over them. Then Nellie and I could circle back and see what's what."

Drew had most of his camping gear and could like as not make do for a while. I was surprised there was no arguing as I took charge. Even Dillon was being well-mannered.

When Nellie and I looked in on the doings, we saw the baron's head clerk ordering men about. They were laying out new fencing and building a ramp up to a barn at the edge of town. Master Verney, the swineherd, and his men were setting up shop at that barn. There was some godawful squealing when they began killing the animals that were marched up the ramp. Some wagons came rolling up to Master Keaton, who was looking in them and deciding what was needful. I was glad we hadn't brought any of Ma's 'frippery,' because such belongings were being tossed aside in a pile beside the road.

We saw Papa arrive with our herd, mister Henderson and a few of *his* animals. We didn't make ourselves known as we watched the animals being driven into the new pens to await their turn under the butcher's ax. I knew what we had to do.

"Nellie," I said "I know that fibbing is wrong, but don't call me on it if you want to help the fledglings."

We went back and found where my brother had set up a little way into the woods. I filled him in on my plan, and he agreed. For the next couple of days, we were all busy. Nellie and I went back to Meadowfork and found Ma. When she asked where Drew had gotten, one or the other of us would say we had just seen him. Or we'd say he'd been called to help with this or that.

Meanwhile, Drew would wait till after dark and sneak over to the pile of goods the clerk had shucked aside. He collected up small valuables and things we could carry stuff in. By day, he joined the men helping out at the slaughterhouse, and no one questioned it. He made off with many buckets of sheep guts and other animal parts they were throwing away. These he gave to Wynken, Blynken and Todd as they weren't too particular about what they'd eat.

One day, the Cains rolled by into the Danstonshire. The whole clan was making for the east in four great wagons. Crouching down, my brother watched them pass by. Then things got tougher when we were all herded into the castle and down to some big, dark stone rooms underneath. Papa and Grant Henderson had been tapped to hide out in the woods to the west. Peter Lawson gave them each a cage of messenger birds and they were ordered to stay hid and let us know when the goblins were coming. I hoped Papa would be okay. Ma was still distracted helping Goodwife Henderson whose babe wouldn't stop crying. There was water and some food, but folks were scared and angry. And our fibs about Drew were starting to wear thin.

We were let out once to see the knights come home. We let out a big cheer because we had been worried for them and also because they were a fine sight to see. It was then that Ma came to us all teary eyed.

"Girls," she said, "the baron is setting up an escort for some of the women and children. A lucky few will be sent east to be hosted by the ladies of the eastern estates while their knights help us defend the keep. I want *you* to go. I have given up *my* place so I can stay and assist Annabel with her little Polly. The child is too small and ill to make the journey, and Anna is all alone. Know that whatever happens, I love you both; and pray for your father that he may stay safe. Where is your brother? He must go as well."

"Drew has been helping, Ma," I said. "More ways than you can know. And you should be right proud of him. I promise you that I'll see he heads east with us. Help your friend and rest easy knowing that your children can look after themselves."

Nellie and I hugged her tight. And Ma smiled. It was still a pretty smile, and this time I felt I *had* earned it.

An escort was hastily drawn from such men as the baron could spare. There were elderly and wounded soldiers and a few boys nearly as young as Nellie or me. They had to manage a bunch of pack animals and lesser horses. And the group of unruly brats and maids were too many for a quick head count. I made sure Nellie and I were right at the rear as we headed up the eastern road. We weren't twenty feet into the forest of Danstonshire when I tugged my sister aside and we lost ourselves in a thicket. It'd be quite a while before they missed us, if they ever did.

When they were well gone Nellie and I made for my brother's camp. The hand cart was fully loaded with griffin provisions and items of trade. We rested half the day to give that other group a proper head start, then we *too* set off down the road to the east. If they'd been purely cats, they might have wandered about indifferent to our wants. But our noble birds proved to be loyal types. The fledglings followed.

It was getting dark when we came upon the side trail. Its marker read 'Lakethroat.' This was to be our haven. We weren't safe here in the forest. Also, from my readings I knew that eagles ate fish. From life on the farm, I already knew that tomcats also favored fish and would yowl annoyingly until you gave them some. Because of this I reckoned that fish was the perfect food for griffins. And Lakethroat was known as a place to get loads of fish.

We headed up this new trail till it was full on dark. Then we made camp. It was a good thing that Drew was so fond of camping out. He showed us things I'd have never considered. First off, he chucked all the griffin food far beyond our campsite, after letting the fledglings eat their fill. It seemed an awful waste, but he claimed it might draw other creatures. These ranged from just pesky to plain dangerous. Also, the stuff was putting out a terrible stink. Tomorrow, we'd have to get them something fresher if my fish idea didn't work out.

Drew told us our small fire would keep away most of the night hunters, being as they were unaccustomed to the light and smoke. We huddled together through the night, always with one of us keeping an eye peeled. When morning came, we set out again. I knew we'd reach the little fishing town before nightfall, but that was as far as I'd gotten in my planning. What would we find there? Would the folks take us in? I wondered if I was too reckless and what it might cost us in the end. But I knew one thing sure as the sun came up when roosters crowed. It beat fighting goblins.

CHAPTER EIGHT

The Fisherman

"It is not down in any map; true places never are."

~ *Herman Melville* ~

Before we reached Lakethroat Village, we needed to hide the griffins again. We emptied the cart and got all the small items my brother had filched into makeshift sacs we had made from pillow cases and our bonnets. The griffins seemed larger but had fit inside it only a short week ago. If you've ever seen a pile of cats, you would know that cats can curl into almost any space. And I'd known birds could enter the tiniest of holes and cracks for their nesting. We soon found that this was true only when the cat's claws weren't splayed out across an opening, and their wings weren't beating furiously in your face. It took three of Papa's best socks and a few minutes of soothing to lure them back into the stuffy old cart and get them settled.

During this time, Nellie swore she had spotted a cloaked figure in the woods watching us. When Drew and I checked, there was no sign of such. So we set off once more with the calls of seagulls leading us on.

We came out of the forest to discover the houses of Lakethroat. Our clothes had seen better days. By this time, our bodice dresses lacked the clean, sharp lines Ma starched into them when she did the laundry. Our rumpled look was made even more plain by the dirty aprons that hung shamefully from our soot stained selves. At least Drew had an excuse; he was a boy. We nonetheless took ourselves down the street toward the lake.

The people of this village proved to be a mite tetchy. Rumors of the goblin invasion had like as not spread to out here, and they were worried. I waved, but few waved back as we trundled our cart down the narrow street. Most just cast us dark looks and muttered to their fellows behind their hands. I didn't see where they had cause to be so standoffish. The little shanties we passed certainly weren't much to brag on.

It stood to reason the place to find fish would be over by the lake. They likely had a fish market or some such over that way. On cresting a rise, we made a discovery. The lake was big! There was water, water everywhere. The street ended at another street running crosswise to it that was made of wood planks. I would learn later they called it the boardwalk, which made perfect sense. Out from this were several long bridges to nowhere the villagers called piers. Tied to these were all manner of little boats bobbing on the water. Seagulls flew above all of this, calling out like crows that had just found your cornfield. And the lake just kept going out beyond. As far as the eye could see, there was no firm ground to be found.

I spied the vendors I had suspected a ways down on this 'board walk,' and conferred with my sibs about what we had to trade.

"There he is again," said Nellie, pointing back up the way we came.

This time we all saw him. The man had a big cloak clasped together at the neck. Its hem flapped about in the breeze that came off the lake. This was a little unusual outside of wintertime. It was the large hood covering his head that really seemed strange. It was pulled far forward and shaded his face to the point where you couldn't even make out his eyes.

The man was bigger than most, and if I wasn't mistaken, he was stepping toward us with a purpose. Drew made to step up in front, but I shoved him back. He was the youngest, after all. The man stopped before us with his beard jutting out from his hood like a gopher peeking out from its hole.

"You're a long way from your farm, children," he said, "and your cargo is more than a mite suspect. Why'd you come here and what are you meaning to do?"

"We just came to buy some fish, mister," I began. "I'm Marjery, and this is..."

"Nellie, Drew, and Dillon," he completed. "I know."

"Is that you, Caleb?" spouted Drew. "I think I recognize that hen's nest of a beard, and your voice marks you as a Cain."

At this, the man drew back his hood, and I realized he was indeed the Cains' second oldest.

"You've got the right of it, Drew Cunningham," he said, "but my questions stand. What are you kids doing out so far, and what do you intend with those things in your cart?"

And I knew we were caught out.

"We hatched them from their eggs after the baron's son killed their ma. We're trying to take them someplace safe from the goblins. We were hoping to get them some fish."

He looked amazed for a minute, then he started puzzling on what to do. Finally, after stroking on his beard for a bit, he shared his decision.

"You'd best come with me, then. I'd like to hear more, but not here. I can take you somewhere with *plenty* of fish that's safe from prying eyes. Follow me."

"Then you'll help us?" I asked as I trotted after. "Just like that?"

Nellie and Drew began hauling the cart behind us toward the longest pier.

"Just like that," Caleb confirmed with a nod. "We *monsters* gotta stick together. My boat is out near the end."

Approaching the long pier's end, I spied a grand vessel moored to the pylons. It was more like two boats joined together by a platform that stretched between. It had oarlocks, but also a set of masts that must be for its sails. It had sleek lines that set it apart from the other old tubs bobbing about nearby. It was a pretty thing, even with its sails missing. I imagined it would be a lovely sight out on the lake and said so.

"That?" said Caleb, "No. That's Sir Harrison's catamaran, fresh out from dry-dock. The villagers try keeping it in Bristol fashion. He pays good coin. The good knight is usually out on it come spring. But seeing as the summer's half over and he's defending the keep right now, I doubt he'll be needing it this season. No. *That's my* boat, Callisto, yonder."

As we passed Sir Harrison's beautiful boat, a smaller skiff came into view. It was very near the pier's end, next to a broad beam of wood on a swivel. The skiff had weather-beaten planks of gray wood for its hull and looked none too reliable as the waves washed against its sides. It kind of made me consider what our henhouse might resemble if someone set it afloat.

"Hop aboard, ladies and gent. I'll see to your precious cargo in a moment."

"Where are we going?" asked Nellie.

"Someplace we can stretch out in safety," Caleb replied as my brother stepped aboard.

Not trusting the swaying, Nellie gingerly stepped across, gathering up her skirts to avoid catching on the metal hooks to which the skiff was lashed. I did likewise on seeing her success. Caleb stepped over to the swivel-mounted beam he called a hoist. From its top hung a length of rope ending in a net woven of other thick ropes. This he spread open on the peer before wheeling our cart onto it. Then he raised the hoist using a crank set on its side and swung it over to dangle just above the deck.

I must confess I was worried for the little griffins. This called to mind that 'Rock-A-Bye-Baby' song that Ma used to sing. And that hadn't ended too well, as I recall. But Caleb lowered the boom gentle as a feather while Drew steadied it, as he stood the closest. The netting was flattened out, and Drew moved the cart off it and set the wheel lock lest it roll over the railing. Then Caleb set to unlashing the skiff from its moorings and hopped across pretty as you please before the skiff could drift too far out. I didn't know all these seafaring words at the time, but was to learn them later as the summer wore on.

"Eee-oooo!" we heard from inside the cart.

The rocking and swaying were new to the fledglings. And they were sounding off about it in spite of being well-hooded.

"Hush darlings," I soothed as I reached in and gently addressed their complaints.

Caleb tied the cart firmly to the single mast. Though our skiff was small and wasn't sporting any sail, it seemed to be equipped for such. Our cart wasn't the only thing Caleb was carrying. In the back was a cargo net full of cantaloupe melons. Caleb set himself down and started rowing. 'Maybe one of you would like to help,' he suggested. So I grabbed up a second set of oars, set down and set to paddling myself.

"I was thinking more of your brother, Miss Marjery."

"Mister," I answered, "have you ever milked twenty-three cows?"

"I've done my share of the milking, but mostly its our women that do such."

"Well I milk every morning and nary a day passes that I don't," I told him as I continued to row. "And sometimes I churn afterwords. Drew here may be coming into his manhood, but he wouldn't be able to lift his arms up for a week if he did the same."

"I guess I never gave it much thought. The oars are yours."

"How do you know which way to go?" Nellie asked as the shore shrank into the distance.

"I use dead reckoning."

"That doesn't sound too promising," Drew put forth.

Soon even the shore was lost to our view. Despite all my bragging, I found that milking cows hadn't prepared me fully for the strain on my back and shoulders. But I was bound and determined not to give Caleb a reason to undervalue us women. I breathed deep and tried not to grunt as I pulled on the oars.

"I'm thinking we must be turned around," said my brother in a panicky voice. "You can't even see the sun with all those clouds overhead."

"Just keep your eyes front, lad. You'll make it out soon."

And he was right. Drew soon spotted an island off in the distance. I paused in my rowing to peer back over my shoulder. There was just a tiny speck of green off in the distance. It didn't do my back any good to know there was still that far to go, but it was comforting to look upon, anyway.

Just then, I heard a bump, and our skiff lurched to one side. Nellie squealed and grabbed tightly onto the mast where she was soothing our griffins. They took to sounding off as well. The water around our skiff had been mostly level, but now it was churning up choppy whitecaps and I could make out a darker shape against the pale blue-green waters.

Caleb just laughed and hollered: 'I'm ready for you this time, Tessie. I've brought the proper tribute.' At this, he hauled himself up and staggered across the rolling deck to the melons netted in the back. Taking up one of these, he flung it out far to the side where it landed with a mighty splash. Immediately after it bobbed back to the surface, the churning waters under our boat let up. But I could feel a surge of current tugging us to that side and the whole skiff tilted some more.

Then I saw the most frightening and amazing sight I'd ever set eyes on. It was right up there with watching a grown griffin plow into a cow. From the deep waters of the lake, there came a reptile head the size of a wagon. When it breeched the surface with its beak open wide, it took in that fruit like it was a pebble. Its scaly neck was as big around as a bull is long, with each scale the size of a shovel head.

"Drew," said Caleb laughingly, "come and throw her some more while your sister and I get back to rowing."

At this, the man sat back down. Drew complied nervously, but soon was awed by the wonder of it. Again and again, the monster went to the melons Drew was tossing out like a dog fetches a stick. But it never bothered our boat again. Soon it let off entirely. Caleb explained the water got too shallow for Tessie as we neared the island ahead. She only came up on land two or three times a season to lay her eggs.

The Cains had discovered years ago that the enormous sea turtle was playful and favored the melons that grew near the shore. The island ahead was a safe place the Cains could go in times of trouble. They spread the rumor that ships were lost to the 'monster' of the loch. Tessie helped in this by bothering boats that came out here. Her hearing was sharp, but her eyesight was none too keen according to Cain family lore. From below the water, a paddling boat looked to her enough like a rival come into her territory to swim up and give it a nudge.

So the Cain's secret island got few visitors. One time last season, Sir Harrison's catamaran had come out exploring almost to the island itself. Gideon and Francine Cain and their children had been taking a holiday here at the time. They hid in the trees by the shore where they marked Tessie 'playing' with the great craft. The *Lester's Pride*, with its grand yellow cinquefoil sails, had hightailed it back toward the mainland and hadn't been seen in these waters since. This had my brother laughing so hard that he nearly lost his feet when we bumped up onto the beach.

"Welcome to the House of Straw," declared Caleb as he leaped down and started dragging us further up onto the sand.

***

We were met with strange looks as a dozen or more Cains, men and women alike, came down to help tow our skiff the rest of the way up on the beach. Setting a board over the side, Caleb set to wrestling our cart up onto it and over the rail. Loosing the wheel locks, he rolled it down this gangplank while his kinsmen stood about muttering.

"Why in tarnation did you bring townies out here?" Rupert said at last.

The others all looked at Caleb, seeking the same answer.

"It wasn't safe for them back at the village," Caleb replied. "You'll soon see why. I judged it needful. Whatever may come of it, its on *my* head."

The secret was out now, so I decided we might as well let the cats out of the cart. Peeling back its covering revealed our wriggling pile of winged cats. I pulled the sock off Wynken's head when she obligingly poked it out. Scrabbling at the cart's edge with her claws, she hefted herself over its edge to alight on the sand in a flutter of wings. The Cains all stood amazed as she did her duty right there in the biggest sandbox she'd ever seen.

"Grandpa must hear of this right away," said Rupert as he turned and ran off.

By this time, Blynken and Todd had come out as well and Wynken was showing the good grace to bury her doings.

"They're cute," supplied one of the younger girls. "Can we pet them?"

"Likely so," said another to the waif. "But best you wait and see how Bethiah rules it, Lisbeth."

"Follow me," said Caleb. "The compound is just over this way."

At that, he headed us up the beach toward the path from where the other Cains had first come. I led my sibs, and the fledglings followed dutifully. The gaggle of Cains came behind us still marveling at our pets. We arrived to find a set of small huts that the Cains called their bungalows. They were roofed with thatch and stood on long legs that held them slightly above the ground. The sand had given way to more normal soil by this point, but I could still feel the gritty stuff where it had worked into my shoes.

In front of the huts hung a canvass hammock. Reclining on this, a shirtless, bearded old man lay sunning himself. He was facing away from us, and his eyes were closed.

"Is that you, Caleb?" he asked "Did you get the wagons settled, then?"

"The wagons are fine, Grandpa," Caleb replied. "The harbor master agreed to our price and put them up in his boathouse once he cleared *Lester's Pride* out of drydock.

"Rupert just brought me a wild tale, but I didn't credit it much. Tell me, has the boy been sipping at the hooch again, or have you something else to report?"

"He probably told it true, Grandpa. The baron's escort passed through the Danstonshire, but I had to rescue three stragglers who found their way up to the village."

At this, the old man sat up, and the hammock swayed alarmingly before he got his feet firmly planted. Rubbing at his eyes with his fists, the old man turned to give us a gander. The others stayed quiet to see what he'd make of us. His eyes got wild when they took us in and fell on the fledglings. He tugged at his beard and pondered it a bit before speaking.

"Well, if it isn't little Marjery and the other Cunningham youngsters," he declared. "And what in tarnation happened to their cats?"

I stayed silent as Caleb related the tale.

"And you thought it right to bring them here?" the man scolded. "Once our secret's out, we'll have no peace here either."

"They're neighbors, Grandpa," Caleb returned. "They were in danger, and they have secrets of their own. I figured they could stay with the women. It's no different from those ranchers you took in last week."

"That was a *temporary* arrangement," the man shot back.

But then the old man's shoulders sagged, and the wind seemed to go out of him.

"Well, done is done, I suppose," the man muttered. "I'll tell you what. Recent events have had me thinking hard on succession. I thought Gregor might be the one, but *that* lad seems keen on making a life for himself *outside* of our clan. While we're all gathered anyway, maybe it's time to speak on such matters."

Uriah Cain stood.

"Since you took it on yourself to decide for the whole clan, we'll give it a try. I've been watching you, Caleb Cain. You have a good head for most things and aren't too shy to make the tough decisions. While we're here, I'll pass you the mantle of patriarch. If you do a good enough job of it, we'll see whether that becomes permanent. Then I can rest my bones knowing the clan is in good hands. You can start by deciding what's to be done with *this* flotsam."

Caleb looked stunned, and the others gazed with wide-eyed amazement between him and his grandfather. The old man grabbed up a clay jug that rested near his hammock. After uncorking it and taking a long swallow from its mouth, he lay back down.

"Now go away and let retired folks rest."

"They were right helpful with Tessie," Caleb added as Uriah closed his eyes and settled back.

"It never ceases tickling my fancy," the old man giggled, "how I named her after Bethiah's ma. She was a stern old matron. That creatures beak put me in mind of her fearsome overbite."

And that was all there was to the Cain's ceremony that shifted leadership in their clan. As the days wore on. Caleb took charge. No one argued or talked back to him. We were given space in the ladies' hut and came to know all the members of family Cain. Life wasn't so restrictive as we'd feared. Although we were made to work for our supper, the Cains were pretty much free to do as they liked once their chores were done. I didn't understand why they failed to mix much with neighbors. Knowledge of such was to come soon enough.

Our clothing was soon naught but tatters and rags. But the summer had come full on, and in the privacy of the little island, we didn't mind being shed of the bulkier garments. The boys didn't gawk overmuch at us. They'd seen their sisters running about in less. Drew and I had to stay in the shade because of our sensitive skin. But this was mostly solved by Bethiah.

Such was her knowledge of herbals and folk remedies, that she was soon able to make us an ointment to protect us from that mean old summer sun. I tried attending her when she was crushing and mixing bean hulls, sorghum, rhubarb and whatnot into a paste that worked this wonder. I soon got lost in the details. I thought it would prove useful to write it all down and said so. Sadly, none of the Cains could even read, much less write. Only Gregor could make out some markings from his time at the mill. I decided then and there I would collect what was needful and learn to write when next I had the chance.

We fished a lot. The Cains showed us how to bait a line and drop a hook and all the best spots to do such. The Cains had a mighty store of grains and other supplies they had laid up in a cave. Fresh meat was a bit scarce, but we sometimes brought down a wild bird or killed one of the Cains chickens. This was a rare event because we favored them more for their eggs.

The griffins were well fed on all the fish. So much so, that they were growing by the day. Based on the size of their ma, we guessed they'd get much bigger still. Feeding Dillon was more of a bother. He didn't cotton to fish. Though he didn't eat much, he needed meat every day. We caught snakes and lizards and he'd hunt other vermin. Once in a while, the Cains would let a few eggs hatch, and he'd get a fresh chick.

On occasion, the Callisto was run back over to the village on the mainland. We'd get news of how the war was progressing. We always sent it off with plenty of the melons that grew on the island's north side, and Tessie was appreciative. Gregor returned from the first trip out. He brought some wild tales about the grisly murder at the mill and his time in the baron's prison. He was very surprised to find Caleb in charge, but knuckled right under to his cousin's command.

Caleb sent several of the men on one trip to hunt some game in the Danstonshire. Drew wanted to go with them, but Caleb thought better of it. They returned from that trip with a deer Gregor had felled with his new crossbow. Word soon came back the goblins had finally appeared. After clashing with the baron's men, it'd become a stand-off. The goblins camped up on a hill by the mill and wouldn't give way.

Then came a time of summer storms. As the lightning flashed and thunder boomed, we women all huddled close in the dry cave where the Cains stored their gear. Wynken, Blynken, and Todd staid with us there. They didn't favor the downpour, and despite their size, the Cain women had grown to trust in their gentle nature and peaceful ways. The men, with Drew among them, stayed in the huts and tried to patch up the leaking roofs as best they could.

"It's time, girls, that we share something with you," said Bethiah as we shivered there in the dark. "It's about our men."

Lighting an old lantern, she set it on the floor. By its flickering glow, I could see her ladies and their girls staring moon-eyed at us, anticipating the tale.

"This is a close-held secret of our clan," remarked Silas' wife Amoreth. "Up till now, we've kept quiet, but the time is drawing nigh that you will need to know."

"Long ago," continued Bethiah, "our clan worked for the witch of the western wild, Abigale Wagge. We lived in her castle, the same one your baron claims now. But when she was getting on in years, things changed. We became affrighted by the way she began to carry on and decided to leave her service. When we did, she called down a curse upon us."

Just then, a peal of thunder split the night. I felt Nellie's hand seek my own. So I took it and gave it a squeeze. The old woman pursed her lips and stared into the lantern for a long moment.

"Tell it, Gramma," urged the small voice of Lisbeth, Francine's youngest.

Taking in a shaky breath, the old woman spoke on.

"Our men seem nice and gentle, and for the most part, they are. But once a month, by the dark of the moon, they change. They turn savage and ignorant of the harm they might do others. They rage about and destroy everything in their sight all through the long night."

"Folks are right to fear the Cains on such a night," remarked Mercy as she stroked the soft fur on Blynken's back. "I suspect they'd fear your griffins just as much, though they don't have any cause to with these purdy angels."

Blynken leaned into the girl and purred her affection. Not to be left out, Lisbeth approached Wynken and started petting her as well. She leaned hard against her and hugged her around the neck. Then, unexpectedly, the girl hopped up and straddled the beast. Wynken was startled and stood to her feet. She looked fit to be tied and poised to run off, but then she settled and walked smoothly forward while the waif held her wings to steady herself. We all watched in wonder as the girl rode the griffin. Wynken paced to the caves far end then promptly sat down, dumping a laughing Lisbeth to the stone floor.

"Drew must not hear of this," I said, turning to my sister.

"He'd break poor Todd's back trying it," Nellie agreed. "Let's keep it our secret for now."

I had no cause to doubt Bethiah, but some things about this curse didn't make any sense to me.

"Speaking of secrets," I said, turning back to Bethiah. "We'll surely keep yours, but do you know why it only happens on the dark of the moon?"

"Uriah once asked your baron's artificer, that Javier fellow. He reckons that it's the sun's rays keeping the witch's curse at bay. The sun shines light down on us all through the day. He claims it also shines out 'invisible light' and it's this that causes your skin to redden."

"What about at night?" Nellie quickly asked.

"He told us the moon don't have any light of his own. Instead, old man moon is just reflecting the sun's light from wherever he gets to at night. It's only when the moon hides his face that we've got a problem."

"That's crazy," I said. "What about when the sun sets and the moon ain't up yet?"

"Well, it was just his guess. The man admits he doesn't know squat about magic, and many are the folk that claim he's touched in the head. All we know is our men change at the dark of the moon. On that day, you and your sister, and your brother too, better join us here when we block ourselves in."

"Can't you go to this witch and force her to make it right?" I asked, not willing to let it go.

"That's just the thing, missy," said Amoreth. "We thought she died when the baron took her castle from her. But our continuing sorry state tells a different tale."

And so we made our peace with it, and soon the storm had quieted. The rain never let up, however. It continued off and on over the next couple of weeks, making life generally miserable. Fishing in the rain wasn't nearly as fun as from a sunny beach. The griffins claimed the cave, and no one had the heart to dislodge them.

***

The egret stood patiently on the shore's edge. Her neck was shaped like the letter 'S'. She was still as a statue. The griffin crept up with her belly to the sand. She too was mostly still and moved in fits and starts. But being young and eager, her tail twitched nervously. I'd seen cats do it a hundred times. When cats stalked, their shoulders bunched up. The griffin equivalent seemed to be spreading her wings open a little with their tips pointing backwards. As my cork bobbed on the water I thought about the chain of life and my place in it.

Suddenly, the beak shot down and pulled up a flapping fish. Distracted thus, the egret nearly became dinner herself as Wynken pounced. Instead, she lifted into the air as my friend passed under, claws aflailing to splash directly into an onrushing wave. What a shame. Not only are you wet now, but that could have been a two-fer.

Griffins came with a few special problems I hadn't had cause to consider before. A bird might ruffle out her feathers and shake. And she did. A cat might drag her sorry self someplace dry and lick herself. And she couldn't. Instead, she just stalked off up the beach, dragging her wet tail behind her and chuffing out a bunch of shrill 'chwirk' noises.

I decided to reel in my line and call it quits for the day. The nearby disturbance had like as not scared away any fish, and it was getting to be time for supper. As I followed Wynken up the strand and came up on the bungalows, a strange, blinking light caught my eye. Every few seconds it would wink forth to dazzle me from on top of one of the huts. Clustered about were a bunch of the Cain men and a gaggle of the girls busting out in laughter and slapping their knees every now and then.

I moved closer and saw it was Mercy Cain on top of the hut. I wasn't sure how I felt about Mercy. She seemed friendly enough, but she was also what Papa would call an 'attention hound.' If something wasn't about her to begin with, it soon would be. Also, she had set her cap for Drew. I couldn't blame the girl. With only her brother and cousins to choose among otherwise, it only made sense that my brother was the one to make eyes at. The problem was Drew didn't know aught of girls and our ways, and I didn't reckon Mercy was a good one to teach him of such.

Then I saw Todd. He had his wings half spread and his beak open wide. He was dancing around in the circle of folks with his feathers ruffled out and his back up making frustrated hunting cries. Mercy had a hand mirror and was playing it about so a spot of light would wiggle around on the ground or up the side of a hut. Todd was bound and determined to catch it. He'd pounce and tear at the ground only to see it flit away again. And each time, the Cains would laugh and call out their encouragement. It surprised me that no one had gotten hurt yet. The griffins outweighed even some of the bigger Cains by now, and I could attest to the sharpness of their claws.

It looked like it had been going on too long, and Todd seemed worn out. Drew stood by looking unhappy, but he daren't speak out against his new belle. Well, if Drew wouldn't stick up for his bird, then it was clear I'd have to do it. I stalked into the girls hut and came back out with Mercy's boxwood comb. Sitting in plain view of all, I began using it to comb out the wet sand from Wynken's back, sides and tail. Recognizing her comb and forsaking her game, Mercy scowled down at me. The others paused to watch.

"Stop that this instant, Marjery Cunningham!" she hollered down.

"Why don't you come down here and make me, Mercy Cain," I said as I worked the wooden comb through the tangled hair of Wynken's backside.

"Pa gave me that comb, miss freckles. And I won't see it used on a cat's arse," she sobbed.

"Then stop teasing poor Todd and come down so it can be used on a proper horse's arse."

I'll never know what the girl meant to do, because when she jumped down and came at me, her cousins grabbed her and held her back. Caleb showed up to see what had everyone riled. When the story came out, he judged that I should get swats to teach me not to trifle with other folks' belongings. He applied the stick himself while Mercy watched on triumphant. He didn't hold back any. And though I cried, I took comfort in Todd's more restful manner and Wynken's glossy coat.

As you can see, life wasn't all sunshine and roses at the House of Straw, but we had our happy times even as we worried for the folks back in Meadowfork. I prayed every night that Papa and Ma would stay safe, and that all the good folks would run the goblins off to wherever they belonged.

***

"Come see!" shouted Drew.

We rushed outside. The boy was pointing up, so I cast a look that way. Up on the rooftop of the supply hut right where Mercy Cain had stood the day before was Todd. He was perched on the center pole, which sagged under his weight with his cat feet splayed out on the roof behind him. As a fairly *big* lion, I was pretty sure he could jump up to the edge of the roof, but I was likewise of a mind that the grass thatch wouldn't support his weight if he did. To get where he was in one jump would be the amazing feat of a cat more agile than Todd.

"How'd he get up there?" I asked, knowing the answer already.

"He flew, of course. It was brilliant, sis! The last to hatch but the first to fly," said my brother with pride.

Just then, the pole snapped, and the roof fell in. I was glad no one was inside. The horrified look on Drew's face reminded me of a saying of which Ma was fond: 'Pride goeth before the fall.' I knew there'd be heck to pay when Caleb found out, but it was still a glorious sight. Nellie and I hadn't mentioned to Drew how easy it was to ride on the griffins' backs. But I suspected his thoughts were headed that direction anyway. It was time to share and maybe to lay down some rules.

Though we planned to take it up, pretty soon we got distracted. The Callisto came back that day with Gregor at its rudder. He bore exciting news. The goblins were on the run following an almighty great fracas at the keep. There were arrows whizzing about and great thumping stones tossed by big stone throwers. Magic was flying back and forth with fire and earth shaking. There were plagues of insects like it was the final days, and the mill wheel rolled over a bunch of buildings. Apparently, the goblins took the worst of it and were now hightailing it back west.

I was sure it couldn't have been so dire. I knew such tales tended to grow with each teller. Still, we all turned to Caleb to see how he'd judge it. After scratching at his tangled beard for a bit, the patriarch in training shared his thoughts on the matter. From the sounds of it, we could all be going home soon, but there was no great rush. With the dark of the moon soon to come on us, we would stay here, and we women would weather it out in the caves.

That was all fine for the Cains, but what would happen to the griffins when we left here?

Before long, it was time to seal ourselves in. I'd only half believed Bethiah's wild tales about the curse. But all the girls had seen the men change into walking, talking boars, growing fur and sprouting tusks. On the prior night, it didn't seem so dire as they described. Though they'd stay well-mannered, the men took themselves off to the island's far side and hadn't returned till morning. The Cains assured us they'd completely lose their minds on the full night of the dark moon. As beasts, they'd likely gut anything that wasn't one of them with their angry, sharp tusks.

As before during the storms, the griffins were allowed to join us in the cave. Unlike before, it was a snug fit. The beasts had grown a considerable bit since then and now could almost meet your eyes as an equal.

It seemed laughable to me that such monsters would be hiding from the Cain men, but here they were. The three were laying just as peaceful as sleeping cats in the back of the cave. The younger girls were even using them as furniture. Amoriah and Lisbeth were laying against Wynken and Blynken, and the griffins covered them with their wings. Todd lay alone. Although he'd let Drew pet him, he didn't have any truck with the others. He'd screech and threaten when others came too close. It must be a boy thing.

"Gramma, tell us a story," the youngest girl pleaded.

"What story would you like, sweetheart?" said Bethiah.

"The Three Little Pigs."

"Oh. That one. Maybe you'd best choose another." Bethiah suggested.

"The Three Little Pigs," the girl insisted.

In the soft glow of her lantern, Bethiah sighed.

"After they had fled the witch's castle, Otis, Silas, and Gideon started looking for a new place where the clan could live. So each took his purdy wife and set out into Arbordell forest. Loretta, already heavy with child, told Otis to head east. From the banks of Lake Ganymede, she had once seen an island, and she thought it might be a nice place to stay. They built a raft and found it. They were lucky enough not to rile the great turtle on that trip. They took to fishing, and Gregor was born at that time."

"What about my Pa?" asked Charity.

"Gideon and his purdy wife, Francine, went back to the spot we mostly live now. It was the original farm Uriah had founded in Arbordel. It lay in the middle of the valley, and they hoped the witch might have forgot about it. They fixed it up and fenced it in and built a great barn to keep safe all their belongings while they farmed the land. They called it the House of Sticks."

"And my Pa. Speak of Silas" said Amariah, shifting under Blynken's wink.

"Amoreth and Silas were adventuresome sorts. Farther west they would go. Across the valley and all the way to the western mountains, their journey took them. They met the goblins of the west at the mouth of the pass, but that's a story for another day. They founded the 'House of Stone' and tended wild goats."

"Tell us of who lives there now, Gramma," said Comfort with a sidelong glance at Bethiah.

"We don't speak of *them*, and you know it, girl. It has to do with how the curse took up and is no proper story for a night such as this."

"But one day we might *meet* them," insisted the girl with her sister, Mercy, nodding along by her side.

"My husband's brother, Zebediah, may be a Cain, but he's no longer a part of this clan. He has no proper place in our stories. As to Deliverance, you may well meet her someday, but I hope for your sakes you don't. Now go to sleep."

I certainly couldn't sleep after *that*. But it seemed to have done the trick for the younger girls. The cave was over warm from all of us crowded within it, and it was stuffy from the stones piled up over its entrance. Bethiah snuffed her lantern. It struck me that someone ought to write her stories down. Elsewise, who would remember them all when they one day laid her old bones to rest. Could Lisbeth keep it all straight?

It was in the darkest part of the night when we heard the sounds. There was a babble of men's voices approaching and then the scraping sounds of rocks being flung loose. Comfort Cain was waking all the girls and herding us toward the back of the cave. Bethiah lit her lantern and took up a long staff she had leaned on the wall nearby her bedding.

"Womenfolk, we're coming in," announced Uriah.

"Not if there's hair on your chinny chin chin!" Bethiah declared.

"That ain't a reliable measure no more," he replied, sliding back another stone to reveal his face. "You know I've sported this beard for years now, woman."

Bethiah watched in fascination as the men cleared all the rocks from the entrance to our cave. She looked on sharply when her husband entered, dropped her stick, and flung her arms about him.

"Dare we to hope, husband?" she said, hugging him tight. "Could our monthly curse be over at last?"

"Well," he laughingly replied, "for the men at least ... and some of you older ladies, I suppose ..."

I once overheard Papa telling Drew that if women knew exactly what men were thinking all the time, we'd never stop slapping them. And I guess it must be true. I swear Uriah wore that red mark across his cheek as a badge of honor while we celebrated into the night and half of the next day.

CHAPTER NINE

The Wrangler

"Two such as you with such a master speed,
cannot be parted nor be swept away,
from one another once you are agreed,
that life is only life forevermore,
together wing to wing and oar to oar."

~ Robert Frost ~

That night, we gathered around a driftwood fire on the beach. We told Drew of how easily Blynken had let Lisbeth ride on her back during the storms. Drew's eyes got round, but I suspected he was only making a show.

"So I was thinking, now that they're bigger, we should get them *used* to the idea."

"Do you think someday we could fly on them, sis?"

"That would be the goal, Drew," said Nellie. "But who knows whether they can get off the ground with a person's weight on their backs. I never heard of it being done. I imagine it would be fun even just to ride them, though."

"Well, *I* imagine we'll need some kind of saddle or something. We can't just hold onto their wings like the handlebars of Papa's cart, not and expect them to maybe fly. I confess I don't know the first thing about riding, but I know someone who does."

We were all thinking it. Rupert Cain was a really skilled rider, and he even made leather equipment and such. Back at the Cain stead, he'd been the chief wrangler for their herd.

The other Cains had pulled out all the stops and were celebrating their new freedom from the curse. The witch must be finally dead. A big stewpot stood simmering over Loretta's cook fire. Earlier, the children had raked up a mess of clams in the shallows of the bay. So near the dark of the moon, the low tide was at its lowest, allowing this extravagance. Her kids had the task of shucking and cleaning them while an old pelican had looked on with interest.

Mister Otis told us that the lake, being fresh water, wasn't truly subject to tides. Instead, it was a 'seiche', caused by the winds coming off of or going out to the lake. But this distinction made no nevermind to me. Tide was tide, and it went out every seven hours.

The stars were out and brighter than I'd seen in a long while. Above, the grinning moon was just a tiny waxing sliver. Silas had brought out his vielle and stood bowing at it while the other Cains danced on the beach. I envied his kinship with his fiddle. There was something *else* you couldn't learn from books. Uriah joined in, blowing notes across his jug. At first they didn't blend in right, but he happily hoisted it up and drank until they did.

I walked toward a lonely figure sitting on a rock and staring out on the lake.

"Two pence for your thoughts, Rupert," I said on the approach.

"Lemme see the coin and I'll consider it," he replied.

I fished in my apron pocket and brought out a sand dollar. Mister Otis had marveled that I'd found one, claiming they should only be found in salt water. Yet one had washed up here.

I'd asked Mister Otis how he came by so many facts about the sea. He told me that Loretta's uncle had been a sailor in the king's navy, and he'd told them a lot of stories about it before he passed.

"You can have this," I said, "but I'll be expecting my change."

He smiled, weighing it in his hand.

"I've been thinking about what I can get for your sister. I think she's purdier than a plum pit, but I don't know how to spend more time with her. I get all tongue tied around her and can only think of stupid things to say."

This again; I sighed. Then an idea struck. We wanted Rupert's help on a matter, and though I wouldn't whore out my sister to get it, maybe he'd be happy just to spend more time with us.

"Nellie already admires you, Rupert," I said. "We all do."

"She does?"

"She was just remarking on how proud you ride a horse. We were hoping to learn how to ride our griffins. We judge they're big enough now. But we don't know a whit about it. I bet you could spend a lot more time with Nellie if you were to help school us in it."

"I'll consider it," he replied, "but I wasn't hatched yesterday. I can see you'd like to pay for such lessons with flattery. Tempting though it is, I might be wanting something *else* for such efforts when all's said and done."

Maybe Rupert was smarter than I'd thought.

"Would you care to dance, Miss Marjery?" he asked out of the blue, or I guess black seeing as it was night.

"I'd be honored, Mister Cain," said I. "I'm not much of a dancer, but I've tread the floor with Nellie at a few hoedowns. If you take it slow, maybe I could follow your lead."

He took my hand and towed me back toward the others. In the light of the bonfire, I danced with Rupert. He swayed me about to the lively fiddling and we laughed at my clumsy steps.

When Silas struck up a slower tune, Rupert led me in a three step that I marked Mercy was showing Drew as well. Locking my right hand in his, he took me about the waist, and we made circles in the sand to the 'Westarbor Waltz.' It was a tune with which all the Cains seemed familiar. Silas had invented it himself some years back.

As the song came to a close, Uriah, standing tall upon a rock before the fire, started beating on a frying pan with a wooden soup-dipper. The noise this rendered caused all to stop and attend him.

"We had a lot of exciting news over the past week," he began, "The goblins are skedaddling, so it might be safe to return home. What's more, the curse seems to have lifted at long last, so we might even be able to mix better with other folks!"

The Cains all shouted and whistled their favor for such news.

"Now as you all know, we've been trying Caleb out in the role of patriarch. I judge he's done a fit job. And talking it over, everyone seems to agree he's a man the clan can follow. So I hereby pass the torch to Silas' eldest and shed the mantel of patriarch. He'll now step up and say a few words, and the clan will heed him."

At that, the old codger hopped down to chants of 'Ca-leb!, Ca-leb!'. The young man arose to the rock and looked about as they stilled, stroking on his beard.

"Word has come that the goblins are running, though they ain't fully gone as yet. The lord's men are chasing them down even while we speak. I say, with the dark moon off our minds, let's start a new era for our clan. Though it ain't fully safe yet at the House of Sticks, the clan can go to Meadowfork and help clean up this mess. We can bury the dead and console the widows. We can help them rebuild or whatever else they might need. We didn't seek out the lord's protection, yet we had it anyway when he broke the back of that goblin army. Let's show them the Cains now have something to offer and that the clan stands on the right side of our neighbors."

The other Cain's milled around for a second waiting to see if he was done, then broke out in loud applause. 'You tell it, Caleb!' someone shouted, and another chant broke out: 'clan Cain! clan Cain! clan Cain! '

Drew, Nellie and I got sucked into it as well. It was that kind of night.

***

The following day, I tracked down Caleb for a private chat. I found him working with Uriah to ready the Callisto for its next trip out.

"Melons are nearly out of season by now. These are the last of them. Will they be enough?"

"I hope so," said Caleb. "I figure at least four round trips, maybe five. Hello Miss Marjery, what can we do for you?"

"When are you leaving?" I asked them.

"We won't set out for Meadowfork until the day after tomorrow, but we'll start ferrying folks over to the village as soon as we're ship shape. Then we'll collect our wagons and be off."

"I was thinking that Nellie and Drew and I should stay a while longer. The griffins might be a bit much for folks to take in, so close to the occupation and all."

"We were thinking the same," Caleb supplied. "I'm certain your folks are praying for you. If you don't come back with the group that headed east, they might go plumb out of their minds with worry. So I was thinking we could leave someone here to manage the skiff, then I'll have a quiet word with your folks and let them know you're all right."

"Better still," Uriah pitched in, "we can tell the baron about these overgrown hatchlings of yours. Let him know they're peaceful. Give him a chance to get used to the idea. Normally, I don't expect much from nobles, but this baron is different. He's been understanding of strange things in times past."

I was relieved to hear this, and I said so.

"Who's the one that'll be staying behind here with us?"

"Rupert volunteered for it," Caleb replied.

217

"Rupert never volunteers for anything," Uriah added, staring at me sharply. "He must have been offered some powerful persuasion."

"I paid him a whole sand dollar," I chortled.

"I'd heard you found one of those. Uncle Otis was pleased as a pickle to hear of your find. It lends support to one of his ponderings on the nature of things."

It was said that the northern reaches of Lake Ganymede poked out into the 'Unchartable Lands.' There, the waterways ran contrariwise to logic and no one who'd come back could trace their channels. Mister Otis suspected they might in some way connect to a distant sea, and that once in a while flotsam from there might wash up here. Maybe even Tessie had come from there as a baby turtle, no bigger than a wagon.

As each Cain family sailed off, we said our goodbyes and saw them off from the beach. When Mister Otis' lot were ready to light out, Mercy hung back. She gave my brother a squeeze so big and long that it colored his cheeks bright orange. You couldn't even make out his freckles. She only let up when Dillon climbed up to his shoulder and tried to bite her nose. As she passed me by, she made an unexpected parting gift. She handed me her boxwood comb.

"It's for your cat thing," she said. "Leastways, I'm pretty sure it couldn't sort out that nest of red hair *you've* got. I can get another one in town."

It was kind of lukewarm as apologies went, but I hugged her just the same. We women might be catty at times, but we knew enough to let 'bye-gones' be bygones.

From the last trip out, only Rupert returned, and the island felt kind of empty with nobody here but the griffins and them as rides them.

And so began lessons. Not just for us, but for Wynken, Blynken and Todd. There were embarrassing incidents, moments of glory, and of shame. Rupert soon remarked on how easy the griffins were to break to the weight of a rider. 'It's like they were born for it,' he said. But though each griffin would bear the weight of its own rider, no other would be tolerated. Wynken would beat her wings and roll in the sand if Drew tried sitting on her. Likewise, Todd would show his temper if Nellie tried to mount. Griffins, it seemed, were loyal only to one owner. I wondered why Wynken had let Lisbeth on her back in the cave that night. Maybe female griffins have a soft spot for children. It must be a girl thing.

Whatever the cause, it made it hard for Rupert to show us things that he couldn't sit a griffin himself. Rupert tried to make bit and bridle, but the griffins flat out refused to cooperate with these efforts. The best he could come up with was a kind of saddle horn we could hold on to as we rode.

Griffins were strange beasts. Lacking the instincts of a proper four-legged critter, the lion paws would pace as normal, but the bird feet in front would kind of hop along to keep up. It was awkward and would bounce you worse than a trotting horse. That seemed to be the top speed they could sustain, too, with one notable exception.

Having the muscled back legs of a great lion sized up to nearly as big as a horse, the griffins could make sudden, incredible leaps forward and add to that distance by opening their wings a little for added glide. The problem was, they'd usually leave their rider behind when they did so. We only had one proper 'saddle' among us. Rupert called it the 'catbird seat.' It was made from stitched-together rabbit pelts that we'd originally brought with us on Papa's cart and some odds and ends of leather Rupert had laying around. To this, Rupert added sleeves for our legs that laced up the sides. Papa was right. There's nothing quite so soft and warm as rabbit skin.

It still wasn't enough to save you from that great leap forward unless you were braced for it. Rupert kept hammering home how we needed to be 'one with' the animal and expecting her movements. And, over time, this came to be the case. I could guide Wynken just with my feet or by strokes on her neck to one side or the other. I would lean in hard for the long jump and praise her when she did right. Wynken seemed to like the sound of my voice, so I took to talking to her gently as we rode. We were getting better.

The next time Rupert sailed to Lakethroat, we took the day off. The griffins were flying more often. I watched them chase seagulls or just glide along the shore. I laughed when Blynken dove at her own shadow on the water with her piercing hunting cry only to end up wet and discouraged. I lent Nellie my comb to console her.

Rupert brought back some distressing news. Though Ma and Papa were alright, Grant Henderson was missing and presumed dead. Anabelle Henderson and her new babe had caught smallpox during the siege, and Ma's friend had died as well. The newborn had lived - saved by the baroness, and I liked to think I'd helped. The baroness couldn't catch the smallpox because she'd had my cowpox last winter. With no parents, baby Pollyanna was adopted by Sir Declan and his lady wife. She was to be taken to his new fiefdom and raised as his ward. The poor little thing might forever bear scars from the disease. Already, the castle maids were calling her 'Poxie Polly.'

Regarding us, the baron said we were to 'sit tight.' His people weren't yet ready for another shock so soon after the siege. And so we rode, and we fished, and we laughed and we cried as the summer wore on into autumn.

***

When the first flight happened, it was no surprise. It came about as a natural outcome of what we'd been doing already. It was Drew's turn with the good saddle. And one time when he was leaping an obstacle that Rupert had dragged down onto the beach, he just kept going. Up and up he and Todd rose to then circle back over the bay.

"Eee-oooo!" said Todd, looking down on us from above.

"Whoo-hooo!" said Drew durn near as loud. "Last to hatch is the first to fly!"

Unlike Todd's first awkward flight, this one ended in a smooth landing on the beach. The pride didn't goeth before a fall. Instead, it went-eth before a long evening of crowing and rubbing it in. We didn't mind. We now knew it was possible and looked forward to *our* turns coming about. Rupert had no such consolation. Though he seemed happy enough, I couldn't help but notice the envious glances he sometimes cast at our birds.

The fish were getting scarce in our usual spots. As the season turned chill, the perch moved out to deeper waters, and the dace quit coming up as close to the surface. And I hadn't seen a catfish for weeks. To keep up with the griffins' mighty appetites, we had to leave off training for a few days just when it'd gotten the most exciting. Rupert took us out on the lake in the Callisto. He showed us how and where to drop weighted nets to best effect. We stocked up some barrels in the cave. The colder air did have one benefit. The fish wouldn't spoil as fast so we could keep them for longer.

That night as I lay down in our hut, Nellie asked me: 'Marjery, do you think Rupert is handsome?'

Rupert had come a long way from the boy she'd told to pleasure his own cow. Since we started living with his clan day in and day out, he'd learned to relax more around us. He hadn't said anything stupid in weeks. I knew he'd been making moon eyes at Nellie, but since coming to know him, I liked to think we'd all become friends as well. And he was a friend worth knowing. He had his wisdom and things he was partial to, and the only bad habits I'd marked was he was a mite over quiet. He was easy on the ears. He wasn't the best looking man I'd seen, but I didn't want to knock him down out of turn.

"The baron says you judge a book by what's in its pages," I answered her.

"That baron is a smart man," she said. "G'nite."

On the following day, Rupert set out for the village once again. We had enough fish stocked, and he was to meet one of his cousins in Lakethroat to get news. As a cold-blooded critter, Tessie got a lot less feisty in the wintertime. Fishing would only get tougher from here on out. In winter, the lake was known to freeze over for a time. Some of the villagers were partial to ice fishing, but Rupert told us we weren't equipped for that. It was a far cry from wintering at the farm.

We kept at our lessons while he was gone, but nothing exciting happened for Nellie and me. Drew could now get Todd to fly on command and never seemed to get his fill of it.

When Rupert returned, he brought all kinds of news and also a letter from our folks. The baron had his scribe write down their words for them, and Lady Chamille assured them that 'little Marjery' could make it out. He also brought a couple of the baron's pigeons so we could reply, ink and quills and all. I'd seen it done, but I'd never wrote anything myself. I sounded out the letter from Papa and Ma for Drew and Nellie. Nellie cried when they spoke of their worry for us.

I dipped the quill in the inkpot and made my first mark on the tiny paper. It made me nervous to have three other sets of eyes intent on what I was doing. Four if you counted Dillon. Now even Drew wanted to know his letters, so I had to recite them for him as I scratched out our reply.

"Love you. Be home soon. Marjery Nellie and Drew."

It would have to do. I couldn't write any smaller. Rupert attached it to the baron's bird as he'd been shown and sent it off into the sky.

The baron planned to tell all the folks that griffins were coming to his keep, but first he had to host a trade caravan. And he didn't want anything to mess that up. We were to lie low for just another couple weeks, and he'd send for us. I pictured us riding through the gates on our proud animals and all the folks cheering. Papa and Ma would be there, and everything would be grand and fine. But providence had something else in mind for Wynken and me.

***

Then it finally happened. As we were clearing a jump, Wynken suddenly took a mind to keep on going. I was pressed down hard into the riding saddle as Wynken spread her wings wide and pumped them down. She did this again and again as the ground below shrank back from my sight. The cold wind on my face kept my eyes squinted near shut, but what I could see through them nearly stopped my heart. The gulls scattered before us as the wings stopped beating and Wynken started a smooth, silent glide that felt like freedom itself.

She banked, and my sight turned out to sea where the waves made tiny by our height rippled on and on to the edge of the world. Then she let out her cry, and I caught the joy of it.

"Kee-eeeee-arr!" she cried, telling the world to watch out.

I leaned forward and remembered to praise her, lest she find me ungrateful. I stroked her neck in the way that told her to turn to the left. She banked again, pretty as you please. With my other hand, I was gripping the saddlebow till my knuckles were white. I didn't fancy a dunk in the cold waters of Lake Ganymede below. But it wasn't needful. My rabbit skin leggings were laced up proper and kept me snug in my seat. Besides, between Rupert's coaching and all my practice, Wynken and I now moved as one. She responded to the slightest touch of my boot or my hand, and I leaned this way and that to help in her efforts.

I could grasp why Drew never got his fill of this. For my first time up, I'd best keep it short, in spite of my longing for it to go on. I signaled for another turn. With powerful strokes of her beautiful wings, we turned and headed back toward the shore.

I wanted to say something momentous such as 'First to hatch ain't last to fly,' but I thought better of it. I didn't want to hurt Nellie's feelings, and I couldn't come up with anything better on the fly. So I just smiled and accepted the gladsome praise my sibs heaped on me. I was gratified I'd held my tongue when Nellie and Blynken took to the sky later on that very same day. It wasn't a feeling you could convey with mere words. It was a glow of knowing that sprang up from deep inside. But now my sister, Drew and I shared in it, and naught else need be said.

That night as we were drifting toward sleep, I asked my sister whether she had set her heart on Rupert Cain.

"I thought about it," she said. "He's nice, and his folks are nice. He's helped us out for months and he's a lot smarter and more wise than I used to think."

"If you end up marrying the man, you should take care in naming your brats. Avoid names like 'Candice' or 'Sugar' for your daughters."

"Why," she giggled, "Candy Cain has a festive ring to it. And what if it's a boy?"

"Harry," I replied stone-faced. "It's the best I could come up with."

"I can see someone else has been thinking on this a lot," she said. "So, it's okay then? You wouldn't feel jealous if I gave him the come hither?"

My sister was fourteen. I judged she could look out for any improper advances. Because of her looks, she'd been fending off boys ever since she'd started getting top heavy. And Rupert seemed an honorable sort now that I knew him better.

"Just be careful, sis," I said. "And don't do anything Ma would reckon as unsavory. Dairy maids are the butt of enough vulgar talk at the tavern as it is. Don't make it worse for the rest of us."

"G'nite, Marjery."

The next morning, I met Drew and Todd and Dillon on the beach.

"Where's Nellie and Rupert?" I asked.

"They went back in the thicket," he smirked. "And they were holding hands! They said they'd be back in no more'n fifteen minutes."

I waited impatiently. My sister was a fast worker, it would seem.

When Rupert came out to join us, he was grinning ear to ear. But as he stepped up near me, his face got more serious.

"Marjery," he said, "remember when I told you I might be wanting something *else* for helping to train you to ride?"

I told him I did.

"Well I'm ready to say what it is. I just spoke with your sister, and she's agreeable. She said the rest was up to you."

"Up to me?"

"I want to start whelping cubs right away, and you and your sister can both learn how to do it."

I saw red.

"Rupert Cain, I don't know how things are done at the Cain Stead, and from the sounds of it maybe I don't ever want to know. On our farm, you don't trifle with a girls heart. There's courting and sweetness and manners your folks seem to lack! We'll find some way to pay you that don't involve adulterous harlotry!"

"Courting? I don't see how it's any different from breeding our cows to your Toro."

Drew started to laugh. Traitor.

"It's true mating brother to sisters ain't ideal," Rupert continued, "but they're all we've got to work with. If we breed Todd to Wynken and Blynken, we double our chances of fertile eggs. And for my payment, I want the first one to hatch. It's only right, Marjery Cunningham, after all the work I've done. Before you go hatching plans with the baron, I want to make my claim known. I want a griffin of my own. One day, I want to fly like you do!"

Drew's face was so red it nearly matched his flaming hair. As he was only sitting one of the walking saddles, he fell off it to the sand laughing out loud. He scrambled to his feet and ran off in the direction of the huts, and Todd went galumphing after.

I was mortified. To save face, I answered in a small voice.

"Alright then, Rupert, but in spite of her size, Wynken's young yet. See it's done gentle."

Relief washed over the man's face, and his smile returned. It went all the way up his face to shine out from his eyes. And in this light, he did approach handsome. I reckoned Nellie could do worse.

***

We hadn't gotten very far in our plans to breed the griffins. So far it was all talk. We weren't precisely certain how griffins set about their courting, but they seemed to have the right equipment for such. As Nellie and I sat discussing the matter with Rupert, Drew came running up.

"Sails," he hollered. "I sighted sails out on the lake!"

We hurried to the beach. And there on the water, big as life, was a set of white sails sporting big yellow flowers.

"It's the *Lester's Pride*," said Rupert. "Best we hide ourselves and get the griffins off the beach."

And so we did. Being as it was winter, many of the bushes had lost their leaves. But we found a stand of black spruce nearby with branches low enough to give us cover as the catamaran drew nigh. It was making directly for our cove. If it landed there, our tracks in the sand would be plain enough to betray us. There was nothing for it but to watch.

When the boat touched ground, two men jumped out and hauled it free of the lapping waters of the lake. It came to rest firmly on our beach even as its sails were furled. Then down stepped the knight. I knew he was such a man as he wore fine clothing under his flapping cloak trimmed with fur. The first thing he did was draw his sword and plunge it straight down into the sand of our beach. Before it, he knelt down and lowered his head. The hilt of his sword resembled a cross. Was he praying? When he stood, he cupped his hands beside his mouth and shouted.

"I seek Rupert Cain and the children of Andrew and Helen Cunningham," he yelled into the wind. "In the name of his lordship the good Baron Westarbor, you are commanded to present yourselves forthwith!"

And that is how we first met Sir Harrison Lester. I'd seen him once before when the knights all rode into the keep before the siege. I hadn't marked him at the time because there was so much else going on. We all came out and introduced ourselves while he marveled at the griffins. But he soon shook himself loose from his startlement and asked.

"Is it true you can fly on these?"

"It is," I replied.

"I have many questions regarding your unusual mounts and many more about this strange island. But be that as it may, I shall forego the quenching of such idle curiosity in favor of expediency. For my lord's need is urgent, and it is my sworn duty to serve him in this matter with alacrity."

"So you're in a hurry?" said Nellie.

"Indeed," replied the knight, looking shamed. "I'm not well-versed in brevity; I must confess. The long and the short of it are thus. Lord Westarbor urgently requires someone who can swiftly bear a message four dozen leagues to the east and south. Can yon gryphons manage such a feat or no?"

I looked over at Rupert, who was rubbing at his chin.

"They've only flown around the island so far, Sir," he said, "I expect they could do much more, as it doesn't seem to tire them much. How far is a league?"

"It's nearly six leagues from here to Westarbor Keep. The full journey to follow would be over eight times that. Can they do it?"

"I'll be jiggered if I know, Sir," Rupert shrugged his reply.

"You say it's important?" I asked.

The knight glanced impatiently at me as if I'd rudely interrupted.

"Yes," he said. "It is a matter of extreme import. Lives may be lost should this matter remain unsolved."

"Then I'll attempt it."

The baron and his wife had been good to me when I stayed there. He and his knights kept us safe. So if there was something I could do to help them in return, then I should do it. And if it involved flying, all the better.

"We can all go," said Drew.

"I don't think so, Drew," I said. "We've only got the one flying harness among us."

"This is a dangerous task. Surely, Rupert here would be more suited for such?" the knight suggested.

"Don't I just wish," Rupert said. "It turns out griffins only permit a single, specific rider to mount them, Sir. I understand time is precious, so wait here while I run and get some supplies. Marjery can catch you up."

At that, the man jogged off toward the supply cave.

"What were you praying for on the beach when you landed, Sir Harrison?" I asked.

"Ah. That. I was giving thanks for our safe deliverance from the dragon that guards these shores."

"You mean Tessie? She's laying at the bottom this time of the season."

"Tessie! You call it Tessie?!" exclaimed the knight in an offended tone. "I should think a beast so dire should merit a far grander appellation."

"Well, she is big, Sir," I granted, "but she's only a turtle, after all."

"A turtle, you say?" the knight muttered darkly. "I shall have some stern words for that Uriah Cain. When I expressed my concerns regarding the monster of the loch, he informed me that the 'dragon' was sleeping."

I was spared from comment when Rupert came stalking up. He handed me a large, hooded cloak like Caleb was wearing when we'd first met him. The Cain men had always worn such on nights just before or after the dark of the moon. They found them sufficient to hide their bestial arms and faces from unsuspecting watchers. Of course, they didn't need them any longer.

"It was Grindal's," said Rupert. "He's about your size. It should protect you some from the cold. Go west and overfly Lakethroat, then just keep going west until you see the road. You should be able to make out Meadowfork and the keep a little ways farther on."

He walked over to Wynken, stroked her neck, and slung a strange belt over her saddled back.

"What's that?" I asked.

"Something I've been working on. I was going to surprise you with it. It's sort of a griffin version of saddle bags. They don't hold as much, but it beats an empty nest. For now, I just put some extra fish in it. Make them last."

"What do the rest of us do?" asked Nellie.

Sir Harrison eyed the fierce griffins and their small riders and came to a decision.

"I would offer you the services of *Lester's Pride* if your steeds are well behaved. It would honor my vessel to host such noble birds and convey you safely back."

"We thank you, Sir," my sister replied with the curtsy Ma had insisted we practice.

Though grubby and unkempt, Nellie could still carry herself with the dignity of a maid. Drew, on the other hand, let out a whoop and ran to explore the catamaran. He dodged past Sir Harrison's men with a playful, four-hundred pound griffin at his heels.

"And don't forget about our bargain, Marjery Cunningham!" shouted Rupert.

That was the last time I saw them. I swung up onto Wynken, urged her up to speed, and we launched ourselves into the sky.

We had flown out over the bay before, but never had we gone beyond the sight of land. The water below us was all of one color and stretched all around us. The last time I was out here, I'd been rowing hard and counting on Caleb to know where we were going. So I hadn't noticed how it felt like we were in the bottom of a big, blue bowl that curved up in every direction. There was nothing to mark our progress against after the island had shrunk away at our rear.

My hood wouldn't stay up, so my red hair fluttered out behind like a banner. Six months away from Ma's scissors had left it hanging lower than my shoulders. It now took a spell each morning with Mercy's comb to set it to anything like dignified. I was starting to feel the cold. The gray clouds above hid the sun from view and only a faint difference in light gave any clue where to go. It was morning, and the sun rose in the east. That should place it at my back, so Wynken and I kept heading for the darkest sky we could make out.

I could see why Caleb had called it 'dead reckoning,' because if we were heading farther out to sea...

There! Ahead! Shore. The sight of it made me want to stick a sword in it and pray my thanks. It had only been a few minutes, I bet. That was really fast. I never had a head for numbers, but at this rate, Wynken and I might beat the midday sun to the keep.

Also, Wynken had been silently gliding most of this time so far. At the start, she'd pumped her wings to gain some height, but after that it had been mostly like sailing along. Rupert had said he'd watched hawks most of his life. They seemed to know in their bones how to best use the winds. Maybe griffins were the same. This gave me hope that Wynken and I might succeed at the baron's chore.

I saw the buildings of Lakethroat. From this height, they looked like toys. They were a bit off to the left, so we hadn't gone straight west after all. I decided we should keep flying straight ahead so as not to scare the villagers. They had seemed a suspicious and unwelcoming lot when we'd last passed through, and I doubted they'd take a griffin flying over as a favourable omen.

Wynken let out her cry and started swooping down toward the inviting beach below. I stroked her neck with our new signal for 'up' and shifted my weight back. She cried out again in protest, but heeded and leveled off. A few more beats of her wings and we were soaring above the forest of Danstonshire. From up here, what I knew to be brambly thickets that caught at your clothes and pine boughs that would poke at your eyes looked like soft puffs of green wool. Even the skeletal trees that had lost their leaves looked a lot less sinister.

Outbound, it had taken Drew, Nellie and me at least a day and a half to push Papa's cart through the trails and make our way to Lakethroat. I reckon Wynken and I made the same trip in just over an hour. In the baron's books, I'd read that a hawk usually flew at about half the speed of a galloping horse and could likely do more if they wanted to. They could keep it up most of a whole day when they were going from place to place (migranating, I believed they styled it). Now a griffin is much bigger than a hawk, so would that make it faster or slow it down? And would Wynken be able to keep at it for as long while dragging her cat body and with me on her back? I supposed we would just have to find out.

As we burst out from over the treetops, I spied a straight, brown line dividing the fields which must be the eastern road. It was far off to our right. We must have drifted again.

"Kee-eeeee-arr!" Wynken said.

"A little to the right," I replied, stroking her neck gently.

The cold was bothering me more. It was like on those frosty winter days when you came back from milking in the barn and the wind was blowing fiercely in your face. Before long, you couldn't feel your nose, and the metal handle of the pail was biting into your palm. I hunched down more in my seat to use the wind break of Wynken's beak and tilted my head forward. It was in this prayerful pose that I saw the keep.

CHAPTER TEN

The Harker

A shape in the moonlight, a bulk in the dark,
And beneath from the pebbles, in passing, a spark
Struck out by a steed that flies fearless and fleet:
That was all! And yet, through the gloom and the light,
The fate of a nation was riding that night;

~ Henry Wadsworth Longfellow ~
(from: Paul Revere's Ride)

On the rise ahead stood the hamlet of Meadowfork. It had seemed so big when I'd only gotten to visit on special occasions from my farm. Now it looked small, like I could reach out and pick it up in my hands. Next to the town was the keep. It stood on a hill of its own with long, pointed banners flapping from on top of its tall towers and the regular stone blocks on its walls lined up like teeth. My own teeth were chattering from cold as I steered Wynken toward it.

As we came in lower, I could make out people down its streets stopping to stare up. It was clear where we were meant to land. Knights lined the walls of the keep, but a space was clear on top of the gatehouse. And in that space was a large, red letter 'X,' just like in a pirate map in the stories. I guided Wynken toward the clear space. She resisted at first, not being used to landing on top of things, but she soon got the right idea. With a flutter of wings, we thumped down. Wynken's wings were each twice as long as a man was tall when they were fully spread out, and the people shied back from our landing.

The knights had their bows out, but none were drawn back. Some in front had swords drawn. Given the nature of my beast, it seemed a fair precaution. The baron shouldered out from among them and opened his mouth to speak.

"Kee-eeeee-arr!" Wynken greeted him.

I was busy working loose the straps and lacings on my leggings. Grindal's cloak was interfering, so I shucked loose of it. As the rabbit skins fell back, and I was finally able to shift my aching backside, I looked up. The eyes of every knight were on me and unblinking. I knew I was never much to look upon and was used to being ignored. It seemed that the way to get a man's attention was to arrive straddling a giant monster scantily dressed with long, red hair beaten into submission by the wind. I felt no shame as I swung down, and I defied any man to recommend I go side-saddle.

"On this momentous day, I greet..."

"Chwirk," Wynken interrupted. "Chwirk, chwirk."

"One moment, your lordship," I said as I fished about in the saddle bags. "Wynken's been flying all morning, and she's hungry. Besides, she did a good job, and I need to reward her straight away so she'll heed me the next time."

Fascinated, the baron wandered near as I tossed Wynken a fish Rupert had provided.

"I see you've made good use of the books I lent you," he said more quietly. "Still, the people need some sort of a ceremony. May I toss her one?"

And so the ceremony to welcome a griffin that arrived at your castle was begun.

When the ceremony was done, the baron told his knights to step off. Wynken clearly wasn't any threat. A few stayed with us and moved closer to huddle around the baron. I saw Sir Trenton among them, still wearing my handkerchief.

"How long?" asked the baron after most had gone. "How long did it take you to fly here from the House of Straw?"

"Sir Harrison came to us about two hours after dawn," I said with my teeth still chattering from the cold. "We lifted off soon after that."

Sir Trenton scooped up my hooded cloak and set it over my shoulders as the baron stared distractedly at the sundial. As the sky was overcast, this did him little good. On the other side of the bell that marked the hours stood a curious contraption. It had a round face like the sundial, but it stood upright instead of flat. Two arrows sprang out from its center, both pointing mostly up, and a little brass ball hung beneath it swinging back and forth. The baron came around to peer at the strange device and finally shook his head.

"I shall have to make Javier mark the proper hours on his hickory-dickery," he said. "But from what I can determine, we should still have sufficient time. Escort her to Megan. Get the girl some food and proper clothes and whatever else she might need, and have her brought to the map room by the noon bell."

"I shall see to it, sire," said Sir Trenton.

Turning to me, the baron said, "I trust 'Wynken' will cause no mischief if you take her down to the inner ward?"

"She follows her own mind, milord, but she usually stays close if you feed her. She won't bite a person, but she might take after a chicken if she sees one."

Then Sir Trenton held up his elbow at me.

I took it like I'd seen fine ladies do, and he led me toward the stairway down. Wynken followed meekly, but soon gave up on figuring out the stairs. She leaped from the wall, spread her wings a bit and landed softly thirty feet below. As we crossed the inner ward, many people were staring, and I spied Peter looking out from his dovecote's door.

***

It started when Sir Trenton knocked on the door and introduced me to his sister, Megan. She had two other ladies staying with her. It was fitting for such a large set of rooms. Nellie and I shared a room that would have fit into any one of theirs. Still, I didn't remark on it. It must cost a lot to keep such a large castle running. If the baron saw fit to take on boarders to make ends meet, who was I to judge? The other ladies were Constance and Lynette, but Megan was the obvious leader.

Instead of leaving when I was invited in, Trenton took a seat on a soft-looking bench across the hall. He told Megan he needed to run me down to the map room by the noon bell. On the way in, he'd told a guardsman to run and fetch us some food, and would let us know when it came.

It didn't start well.

"So this is the urchin who infected us all with the *pox* last spring," said Constance with a frown.

"She just flew in on a gryphon, and *that's* your first concern?" remarked Megan. "Let it go, Constance. It was at mother's behest and for your own good, after all."

"As my lady wishes," said Constance, taking up a hairbrush and approaching me. "I suppose we should start with *this* tangle."

"Don't you *dare*, Constance Baldwin," said the other girl, Lynette. "Don't you see it? Those aren't tangles; they're a *style*, a new style. However did you get your hair to do that, Marjery, is it?"

"Well," I replied grumpily, "you fly into a biting cold winter headwind while it flaps about behind you for about two hours."

"That's enough, ladies," said Megan, "The poor girl has been through an awful ordeal. And since there's no time for a proper hot bath, we shall begin with a bit of freshening up. I hope you won't mind, Marjery, if we help get you more presentable as my father instructed me?"

The girl spoke softly, but from a place of confidence. The other two followed her directions straight away. And the gentle way she seemed to ask me without asking made me want to go along as well. The reminder that this was what the baron wanted hadn't hurt either. I noted those blue eyes could hold you like a snake numbs its prey. But I doubt she could fox me long with such if I didn't allow it. The Cunninghams are known for having a stubborn streak a mile long.

They led me over to a wash basin where I shucked my dirty clothes, and they scrubbed my face and hands. They were quick and thorough. They had a bunch of different brushes and cloths for each task. When they were done, there wasn't even a speck of dirt underneath my nails. And even these were rendered smooth by Lynette's tiny metal file while Constance kneaded scented oils into my cheeks, neck and forehead.

As I mentioned before, I'd lived for months on an island with few outfits to wear. The remnants of my dairy maid attire had long ago been consigned to use as rags. They'd been replaced by makeshift garments made from the rough cloth the Cain women spun. Constance called them a total loss and went to fetch something better. I was afraid she'd bring some froufrou outfit like they were wearing, but the girl surprised me.

"This is a riding outfit worn by the men of my family."

"It's so soft," I said, taking it up. "It looks warm too."

"Of course," she said, stiffly. "It's my winter outfit. Though pants are generally deemed unsuitable for a young lady, any *serious* rider must make this exception. I don them only for private rides about the countryside; one of my few indulgences. Given the nature of your task, I thought they might be fitting. Take them. A gift."

"They're lovely," I mumbled. "I think with these I should be able to fly the leagues needed and have *you* to thank for it!"

Sometimes words weren't enough. I hugged the girl. She grew tense for a moment, then hugged me back. When I started to dress, she held me back from my nether garments, supplying a different set she got from Lynette. These *were* a mite froufrou but softer than anything I'd ever felt, including rabbit fur. No one would see. I put them on. The riding clothes were a bit baggy, but it didn't seem grateful or kind to remark on such. At least the boots fit.

"It needs a splash of color and a little something to bring it in at the waist," said Lynette. "Here. Try this."

She threw a green sash about my middle and tugged it a mite tighter than apron strings. This gathered in the excess of tan-colored cloth and kept it from shifting on me as much. After inspecting me all around, Lynette hauled me over by a table where she began to select different colored powders and sponges.

"Sit down," she said.

"I don't need any of *that*. Ma doesn't favor face paint. She says painted ladies are prone to sin."

"Nonsense," said Lynette, steering me into the chair. "This is nothing like *that*. You just need a touch of blush to accentuate those mysterious green eyes. Press your lips together on this."

There was a knock on the door.

"Food's here," said Trenton's voice from the hall.

"Give us just another minute, brother dear," Megan replied.

"Well hurry up," he said, "It's almost time."

While this was going on, Lynette came at my eyes with some pointy-looking brushes. I couldn't help but flinch back. When she'd finally had her way and I sat all powdered and perfumed, she took me over to a mirror as tall as myself. It put Ma's big makeup mirror to shame.

"And *viola*," said Lynette as she faced me off with my new self.

I didn't know what 'wah-lah' meant, but the way she said it put me in mind of the whoops Drew had made when he'd first flown on Todd. I stared in puzzlement at a total stranger. Was that me? It didn't look like a Cunningham. It looked like one of *these* three girls, only a mite more exotic. I'd swear I was looking at a barbarian queen.

"Time's up, dear sister. Let me in, or the girl shall have to make her long journey with an empty stomach."

"Enter," Megan said.

Trenton strode in like he owned the castle, toting a platter heaped with food. Setting it down, he looked up and froze.

"Astonishing," he said from his bowed-down position.

Then he shook himself and sat down.

"Eat up, ladies," he said, taking up a chicken leg. "We've only a short time before the noon bell sounds."

He took a bite while I surveyed the table. I liked fish as a general rule, but six months of meals heavily favoring it had left me aching for what was on that platter. I took my seat at the small table, as did the others. I lowered my head to give thanks. The ladies were setting napkins in their laps and taking up bread and the like, but Constance paused.

"My father always insisted we give thanks before each meal," she said. "I know that customs differ, but it would please me greatly to hear what prayers are offered at the Cunningham household. Will you say grace, Marjery?"

Since the others were all staring at me by this point, I didn't want to keep them waiting.

"Creator above, we thank you for the gifts and the blessings you have given us. On this day, like every other, we think on the goodness you shine down. And we pray those who have passed before us will rest easy knowing we remember them and carry on your work in their honor."

"Amen," Megan said.

The others quickly chimed in as well. It was a simple thing, but it always quieted my spirit to know that one day the folks that came after me might pause and reflect. And if I were in a position to hear them, I'd know their lives would be better for having done it.

I lit into my food with relish. It was no time for ladylike bites. I'd soon have to fly to perdition and back if Sir Harrison's reckoning was right. I hoped the baron would soon explain the need. On finishing, no one stacked the plates. We just got up, and they hustled me toward the door.

"And bring some oathbloom," said Sir Trenton, again taking up my arm in his. "We may need it."

***

The baron's map room was a big place with a sturdy table at its center. Men clustered about, muttering to one another in low tones. Shelves lined the walls with many rolls of parchment stacked upon them, and the place had a musky smell the same as in the baron's library. When Trenton and I entered, all stopped dumbstruck to stare. If this was what a brief session with Megan's ladies could achieve, I'd like to see what they could do with Nellie.

"Ah. You're here," said the baron. "And what a remarkable transformation my daughter has wrought. Come and join us. This is a map of Northford Duchy. It's a tad dated, but serviceable enough."

Spread out on the table was the map he was indicating. Men made way when I walked up to give it a proper look. It was bigger than most maps, and I could see where sections of parchment had been stitched together to form it. Drawn all across it was pictures of tiny castles, woodlands, waterways and the like. An older gentleman with graying sideburns was leaned over it fussing with a small round thing with an arrow while the baron went on with his talk.

"The king's cartographers used the utmost care to render it as accurately as possible. Javier here is aligning it to true north."

"It's ready, my liege," said this Javier.

"Good," said the baron. "Now *we* are here," he said, pointing at one of the castles.

"And Castle Stein is down *here*, about forty-eight leagues to the south and east of us."

He moved his hand to point at another of the castles on the map. He told Javier to 'take a reading.' And the man placed the round thing down on 'our' castle and sighted along it toward the other. He then stretched a tailor's tape between the two and marked how many inches they were apart. His bushy eyebrows seemed to move on their own as he took the measure.

"It is almost exactly due South by Southeast, and according to the legend, the distance is approximately forty-five and three quarter leagues, my lord."

I wondered what language the man was speaking. Then my eyes fell upon a large blue spot in the middle of a green area somewhere between the two and it all made sense. I pointed excitedly at it.

"And this is the House of Straw as seen from up above," I exclaimed.

"Precisely, Marjery," said the baron. "We need you and Wynken to carry a letter to Leopold's castle. Gerrard is drafting it even now. You see, a caravan soon to pass into the Stein Barony is imperiled. A group of bandits seek to waylay them and steal their cargo. Lives may be lost unless Leopold can be made aware of this contemptible scheme."

He produced a chess knight from his pocket and placed it on the map.

"We think the caravan is somewhere near *here* on route from Downham. You'll need to fly in as direct a manner as you dare without getting lost. Perhaps it were best if you follow the roads as much as possible. But whatever you do, avoid *this* place."

He pointed at another castle across what I now recognized as the forest of Danstonshire.

"In fact, give her that magnetic compass thing, Javier. She may need it to take her bearings along the way."

"This one was presented to me by the king himself, your lordship, upon completion of the fortifications to his castle. It's wrought from solid gold. I shall make her another. It should take me only an hour's time to craft and calibrate in my workshop."

"We've not that hour to spare, Javier. Lives are more precious than gold. Give it up, I say."

As the man handed me the precious bauble, I thanked him and told him I'd see it found its way back to him. Meanwhile, the baron had found and rolled up a smaller map of the area. He presented it to me.

"She'll need livery, so Leopold's men will know she's from me. Also a harker's bell. Give her yours, Phillip."

The baron's page, Ronnie Turner, stripped off his tabard. It was blue and sported the image of a dove carrying an olive branch in its beak. Some said it lacked fierceness. Papa had once explained it to me. Even though the baron was known as a fearsome warrior, he saw his role more as spreading peace and stability. I'd be proud to wear such a symbol in his service and let Wynken speak to the fierceness.

"Am I overlooking anything? Are we ready?

"Your lordship," said Phillip, after clearing his throat. "A minor matter of protocol. If she's to deliver that for you, shouldn't she be bound by the oath?"

"Ah yes," replied the baron. "It were best to do this properly. Kneel Phillip."

"*Me*, your lordship?"

"Yes, you Philip Finley of Mountanbrook. As chief among my harkers, I deem you worthy of greater responsibilities. If you accept, I would name you my minister of transport. This position will bear the title of Martial. Henceforth, you would be responsible not only for all my other harkers but also the following. The stable overseen by my Master of the Horse, Alexander Hart. The dovecote as overseen by its postmaster, Peter Lawson. Special events such as the welcoming of inbound caravans. And lastly, direct oversight of this new breed of harker, my gryphon riders. Do you accept?"

Phillip knelt.

"I do," he said once his jaw would work proper.

Megan's maids stepped in from the hallway carrying a large urn between them filled with bright orange blooms and set it in front of the man. The baron drew his sword and brought it down twice, touching the man with its flat on each of his shoulders.

"Arise, Martial Phillip, Westarbor's minister of transport. Your first task will be to administer the harker's oath to Marjery Cunningham, that she may bear my word to Castle Stein."

Phillip stood and turned to me.

"Kneel before our good lord, Marjery Cunningham, and if you agree, repeat the words as I give them to you."

Megan smiled encouragingly at me as I considered. I soon did as the man asked. I'd thought about what it would mean. No more would I be a simple milkmaid. And Wynken and I would have to do whatever the baron said. That was a lot of trust. Providence had led me up to this point, step by stumbling step.

And now it was pointing me to a new life. What sealed the deal was I now knew I'd be working for a man who believed that lives are more precious than gold. So I said the words, changing them only a bit.

"Neither snow nor rain nor heat nor gloom of night shall stay this courier from the swift completion of her appointed rounds."

***

When I stepped into the inner ward where I'd left Wynken, I found a man laughing and throwing out fish to her. The baron said it was Alexander Hart, that Master of the Horse fellow he'd mentioned earlier. Wynken was prancing all about to catch them because the man wasn't pitching them straight. I hoped this hadn't been going on for long. If Wynken was worn out from this frolic, she'd not be ready to go. And if she'd had too many, she mightn't even be able to get off the ground.

When I approached her, Wynken gave me a blank look like she didn't know me. My clothes were different, and I smelled like a field of flowers had grown out from my back, but I'd have thought the hair at least should be a dead giveaway.

"It's just me, Wynken," I soothed, stepping closer.

At the sound of my voice, she ran over and lowered her head for a scratch. I was happy to oblige her.

"Tell me what you see there, Gerrard," said the baron to his head clerk.

"I see a dangerous beast, sire," the man replied.

The baron smiled.

"*I* see a *game changer*," he said. "Should this flight prove successful, it will transform commerce throughout the kingdom. The air navy of Westarbor or whatever Phillip names it will leave others grubbing in the dirt. With such a creature, and with two more on the way, we'll have achieved air superiority over our rivals. Henceforth, smaller, more valuable shipments can pass straight over Downham Barony. Its greedy lord can lay tariffs only upon the bulkier goods, which must still travel by caravan, to feed his avarice."

"I have previously discussed with my lord the advisability of counting one's chickens early," said the man with a cautious smile. "But I *do* appreciate the potential, as will the *king*."

The baron frowned.

"I fear you're right, Gerrard. For just as his majesty has proclaimed gyr falcons and mages to be solely in the royal family's purview, he might soon add gryphons to the list of items so proscribed. If he can deny us the color purple, of all things, then he certainly might try to deny us our gryphons. We must begin establishing the priority of our claim at once. Tis most useful that such beasts will heed only a single master. And we shall have sworn the only three known to exist. If the king wants an egg, we shall have a great deal of leverage at the bargaining table."

"Speaking of *eggs*, milord," I said as I mounted and began lacing up my leggings. "Now might be a good time to mention that the first one is already promised."

The baron looked thunderstruck.

"To whom?" he asked.

"Rupert Cain," I replied, "We can talk about it later, milord. Lives are in danger."

"Remember. You will know you're at the proper castle by its banners. Leopold's color is gray, and his symbol is the wolf."

Between the riding outfit and the tabard I was plenty warm, but remembering the cold winds higher up, I pulled on Grindal's hooded cloak as well. I left the hood down as it wouldn't stay up for long anyway. With a great leap and a sweep of wings, we took to the sky.

***

It was much easier the second time...at the beginning. We simply headed for the trees to the east. The eastern road pointed the way until we reached the trees themselves. Then it was hidden. I retrieved Javier's compass, careful not to drop it, and turned it until the red arrow pointed to 'N'. Then I just kept us going 'E'. It may have been quicker going 'SSE' the whole way, but I didn't want to lose sight of the roads for long.

Before long I could see Lake Ganymede stretching out on our left. The eastern road through the Danstonshire ran next to the lake for a time. In an hour we had cleared the trees and were flying over flat farmland. From up here, the fields below looked like the patchwork quilt Ma had made for our bed. The gray skies above were unnerving. If snow began to fall, I wouldn't like our chances of finding our way.

Up ahead, the eastern road met another, greater road. Where they crossed was a statue of a man on a horse. I was to continue east and then turn south when I sighted that other castle in the distance. Already, I felt the cold creeping in. Had I thought of it, maybe I should have worn the hooded cloak backwards and cut eyeholes in the hood. Something to think about for next time.

We went for a time more, and my mind began to drift. The boring flat land below and the wing beats now and then started to wear on me. I shook myself and tried to think of something stirring. Then I saw it way up ahead. Another little town with a castle sticking up. I knew I should turn south, but my eyes wanted something more interesting to lie on for a bit. I decided a little closer couldn't hurt. That decision proved to be a foolish one.

As I came closer to the castle at Downbury, I saw its big iron gate was laying flat upon the ground. Scores of tiny men were beating at it with hammers. Curious, I drew nearer still. Then something passed by just in front of Wynken's beak.

"Kee-eeeee-arr!" she cried as she veered sharply right.

Only my leggings kept me on my bird as we dove, and I nearly lost the compass. Looking down, I saw the road south. Looking back over my shoulder, I saw a great wooden crossbow atop the wall lining up for another shot at us. I was later to learn these gigantic crossbows were called 'ballistae' and threw great spears with such force they could pierce a tree right through. I nudged Wynken to the right and kept us going away from the keep and its wicked spears.

But we'd been spotted. We had a fair head start, and the keep was gone in the distance behind us before I heard a thundering sound to our rear. Did I mention before that hawks glided along at about half the speed of a galloping horse? Well, griffins must as well because knights were soon riding underneath us, pointing up and gathering their bows. It was lucky for us that a man shooting a bow from a galloping horse was unlikely to hit his mark. I urged Wynken up higher to make us a smaller target.

This was all my fault. I felt like Lot's wife must have when she'd looked back on Sodom. Curiosity had gotten the better of me, and now we were paying a price. A wicked part of me noted that a pillar of salt might be an easier way to go. At least it might be warmer than freezing solid up here. Worse still, this was near where the baron said the caravan should be by now. And here I was bringing all those wicked knights down on their necks.

Then I suddenly saw sense. I swung Wynken over far to the left until the road was nearly out of sight. I bet those knights couldn't gallop along so fast through the fields and thickets. Some tried, but they soon left off their pursuit. I drew out the compass. I had to handle it with extra care because my fingers were getting stiff from the cold. Wynken was making like she wanted to land, but I kept giving her the signal for up and words of encouragement.

I kept us going toward 'S' and swung closer to the road once it was clear of knights. There. Up ahead. I saw a line of wagons heading down the road. I stayed well clear of them so as not to give them a scare. My business was with Lord Leopold. Passing farther south, I came to a fork in the road. The sky was darkening, and I felt the bite of snowflakes striking my face. The fork that went east looked less traveled, so despite my spirit of adventure, I swung right.

I tried telling Wynken to get more height, but she was tiring. When I saw the light of fires on a ridge to our left, I wanted nothing more than to set down there and rest a bit and get warm. Maybe it was Leopold's soldiers, and I could tell them about the ambush. I was fixing to do just that when I remembered my oath. I had promised to get this letter to Castle Stein, and neither snow nor gloom of night was going to stay me from doing it. Oaths were sworn for a reason.

We flew by that ridge and kept to the road. Soon we were rewarded. I sighted the castle up ahead, and it was a big one.

Snow stung my eyes, coming down harder than before, and Wynken's cry came out all sad.

"Kee-uuuuu-urr." she wailed as we closed the final distance.

"Almost there, dear heart" I told her. "Then we can rest."

We barely made it to the top of the wall and plunked down. Too late, I remembered to ring my bell. As I fished it out with frozen fingers a bigger bell nearby started tolling a warning so loud it could've woken the dead. I rang mine, but it could barely be heard. I couldn't tell if the pennants were gray, because it had gotten so dark that everything seemed shades of that hue.

Then signal fires flared to life nearby and men shouted and pulled out weapons. I threw off my cloak, so they could see the colors I wore, even while Wynken lay down and hung her head in exhaustion. Archers leveled their bows at us. Then a door burst open from a tower that connected to the battlement. A man sprang out, waving his arms around excitedly. He was tall and handsome in the way of older gentlemen. He wore fine clothes, and on his chest was rendered the head of a wolf. His eyes were wide open, and his mouth was a rictus of mad glee.

"Stand down men, stand down I say. Tis the red-haired angel of death come for me at last. I'm coming to join you, Sir Nicolas! Well? Have you aught to say to me before you snatch me from this life?"

The man looked unsteady. From the cut of his clothing, I knew he must be a knight at the very least. I suspected I was looking on Lord Leopold himself. If so, I'd heard of his troubles and feared upsetting him. I stared around, looking for something to say that might bring about calm. Only one foolish thought came to mind.

"My," said I, "such big towers you have, milord."

The light of reason returned to his eyes, and he smiled at me sheepishly.

"The better to greet you with, my dear."

PART III

A Necromancer's Tale

(Journey's End)

CHAPTER ELEVEN

The Wainwright

"Unhappy man! Do you share my madness? Have you drunk also of the intoxicating draught? Hear me; let me reveal my tale, and you will dash the cup from your lips!"

~ Mary Shelley ~

The harker paused for a drink from the waterskin we'd been passing around. After she was done with it, she leaned forward to warm her hands over the fire. It had burned down lower as the night had progressed. The sky was brightening to the east, and I could hear a blackbird take up his morning song. The robins and wrens and others would soon join in the chorus that greeted the new day.

Lucas sat beside me, enthralled by the harker's tale and eager for more. As usual, my cousin was the first to fill the silence.

"So what happened next?" he asked, though the answer should be obvious.

"Yes miss, don't leave us hanging," prompted Jeremiah.

The little redhead shrugged.

"I delivered the letter. Then we rested a bit while the Steins rallied their knights. I told them about the men up on the ridge and they rode out swearing to round them all up."

"And after all that, you took it on yourself to come and bring us word," said Cameron. "I must say, we appreciate it, miss."

I remembered Marjery from my time growing up on the Wagge farm. Like most farms that outlay Meadowfork, we had a couple milk cows of our own. But we sometimes had occasion to buy our butter from the Cunninghams. Andrew was a good neighbor. He would drop everything to come and help if one of our cows got blackfoot or had the bloat.

Marjery was different now from the little maid I'd seen when father and I stopped by their place. The woman I was seeing now had a much stronger aura than I remembered. Her feelings were bright and clear and possessed of a self-honesty most people sorely lacked. Even my cousin, who remained humbler than most, despite the gifts that set him apart, held notions about himself that didn't fully fit the facts.

I too was much transformed from how I'd been in those days. The droning in my head had ceased to dominate my thoughts. This was thanks in large part to my apprenticeship of the prior year. The hive still called to me and tried to lure me into its welcoming commune, but I had learned to strike a balance. I now lived with one foot in the world without and was much better for it.

Perhaps at Conclave I might find others like myself and could commune with them as an equal, finally free of the alienation that had haunted me all my days. Failing that, I planned to create a social facade that would at least fend off the pity and derision that others always seemed to direct my way. It would start with speaking up more.

"That was a wonderful story, Marjery," I praised. "We thank you for it, and for all you have done on our behalf."

I made sure to meet her gaze squarely as she smiled. It wasn't so hard when I was braced for it. The joyous feelings that flowed out from her were untainted by surprise that I had spoken. Some of the others glanced over sharply at me, but I carefully avoided the sorrowful compassion from *those* eyes.

"It was our pleasure, Roy," she returned. "Besides, I had one more delivery to make. Which one of you is Lucas Harper?"

"That would be *me*," my cousin chimed in with surprise.

The girl reached into her pocket and withdrew from it a letter.

"The lady Megan sends her regards and would have me and Wynken wait for your answer."

"Will you be staying long?" asked my cousin. "It could take me some time to decipher that and encode a suitable reply."

As she handed him the envelope, the girl looked on in sympathy and her voice dripped with encouragement. I grinned ear to ear as Lucas received a taste of the condescension on which I was regularly forced to dine.

"It's okay, mister. *I* understand. It sometimes takes me quite a while too. But if you keep at it, you'll learn to read faster; I've been told. Patience is the key."

"Hey, where *is* Wynken?" Harold asked. "I was so wrapped up in the story I didn't see her leave."

I had. The gryphon had quietly gotten up and stalked off into the forest an hour or so after Taylor had returned to the fire. Another might have mentioned it, but such wasn't my way. I was used to noticing things others missed. It rarely made them happy when I remarked on such unless it was noteworthy.

"She'll be back, mister," said Marjery. "She never wanders far; she'll come directly if I whistle."

A lot of useless banter and chatter followed. When people were together, they seemed to feel the need to fill the silence with their voices rather than their thoughts. It was challenging to ponder things properly when I was near others. Still, I had best practice joining in if my plan was to succeed. The snow fell thicker about us. We huddled closer to the fire as the light of dawn painted the camp. I provided words of little meaning with which to help fill the silence, like the sticks being added to our fire. They would burn for a time and shed their warmth among us only to crumble to ashes and be replaced by others. I would add my share of them.

This went on for some time before the gryphon returned from her hunt.

From her beak dangled the carcass of a baby deer, not even a yearling by the look of it. She approached her rider where she sat by the fire. As the others scrambled back, Marjery praised her and stroked her neck. Despite their initial caution, it was remarkable how quickly the others accepted the monster into our company. After the harker's tale, all knew Wynken and afforded her some measure of trust. As Harold Hunt set about field dressing and butchering the deer, some others approached well within reach of that cruel beak to add their praise as well. The creature responded to her name and allowed them to scratch her head or pat her on the neck. I ached to do the same but felt we shouldn't crowd the beast.

While Wynken was given the lion's share of the meat, the cook set several haunches over the fire to sizzle and pop on makeshift skewers. Their savory aroma did much to overcome the lingering aftertaste of pickled cabbage as we salivated in anticipation.

And that was how the knights of Stein found us. Huddled about the coals, we were sharing legs of venison and sipping warm mugs of tea Addy Blessings had brewed in a kettle over the open fire. Our sentries had spotted them coming. Rather than joining us as we had offered, they bade us to collect our wagons and follow them to Castle Stein. The wind was whipping up, and the sky had failed to brighten as thick, black clouds began to disgorge the heavy snowfall they had thus far held in abeyance.

"Her ladyship will know what to do with them," I overheard one soldier to remark as we gathered our belongings.

It was interesting that he had not referenced Leopold. From other such remarks, I was beginning to assemble a picture of the state of affairs at Castle Stein. It appeared the knights and their attendants loved their lord well, but had little respect for his current mental abilities. They seemed overly protective of their 'addled' lord and wanted to spare him embarrassment or undue strain. I heard things like: 'he's more lucid today; recent events seem to have brought him more to himself'. From other things I heard, I gathered that Leopold was in his audience chamber 'demanding to see the mages.' I would take a cautious approach when introduced.

My cousin had a problem. To get the wagons out, he had to lead the way, repairing all the damage he had done to the trail on the way in. Unfortunately, what greenery there had been lay shriveled and blackened underneath an inch of snow. As he trod tiredly on, I could see his inner hill diminishing with every furlong. By the time we gained the main road, his magic center lay flat and spent. Lucas stood swaying on his feet, having expended all the energy he'd gathered the previous evening. I wished I could have helped, but my hive mites weren't nearly so facile at earth shaping.

I steered him back to our coach and helped settle him within it as the day's journey southward commenced. I covered his shivering form with the heavy saddle blanket I'd borrowed from Ollie Reed. The mules didn't care for hauling in the snow into the teeth of a biting wind. We found, however, that their reticence was expressed far less frequently when the gryphon stalked at the caravan's tail.

"Kee-eeeee-arr!" Wynken sang into the wind, causing the mules once again to pick up their pace.

Sometimes, threat of the stick was more effective than the promise of the carrot.

By day's end, we reached Castle Stein. The massive stone structure stood atop a rise with its flapping gray pennants all but invisible against the backdrop of the gray clouds above. The snow covering the roadway was by now three inches deep and lay in drifts much deeper where blown to one side. The bell atop the gatehouse could be heard. It was a welcome sound that heralded our arrival and bade us enter.

In keeping with my promise to be more outgoing, I shook my cousin awake.

"We've arrived, Lucas," I said. "It won't be long now before we're safe and warm."

Lucas sat up too quickly, and terror shone out from his eyes as he swung them up to bludgeon mine. I shifted my eyes aside, only partially blunting the assault as waves of disgust and fright continued to emanate from my cousin. My stomach clenched and twisted, and the sour taste of bile rose at the back of my throat.

I knew I was witnessing the trailing end of a nightmare. Lucas had confided in me that horrors stalked his sleep. Visions of his grandmother and her ill-spent life would assail his dreams and lock him in the throes of dread as scenes of her wretched past paraded through his sleeping mind. Even second-hand, the emotions this elicited from my cousin were uncomfortable to me. This was the first time I had looked upon one directly and I was aghast.

Words came unbidden to my lips, the silent words that gave comfort. Only it was a *lie*. The hive mites swirled up from the deep recesses of my magic center. As they enshrouded my offended perceptions, they brought naught but the cold comfort of oblivion. Screened thus from the world without by their humming chorus, I ceased to feel anything but the rapture of their patterned weaving about. My sense of self dissolved to be replaced by the restful allure of nothingness.

The worst part was not knowing whether it was safe to come out. Lucas was awakening and would soon find himself. But I was loath to stare again into the face of nightmare. I was ashamed at having lapsed into this behavior. I had promised myself I would stop doing so. My plan would fail utterly should a new acquaintance even once glimpsed me in such a state. And the cycle of pity would begin anew. Bracing myself, I stilled my lips and banished the haze. My cousin's sad face swam back into view.

"I'm sorry, Roy," said the boy. "I was having a bad dream."

As if I didn't know it already. It was my own fault. When I had settled Lucas into the carriage, I had neglected to remind him to sip of the green elixir that smothered the sendings of his vengeful hag. The patronizing sorrow that edged his voice was almost too much to bear. How would an amiable friend respond?

"It's alright, Lucas," I said with false equanimity. "We've arrived at the castle. What was this one about?"

He tightened his lips and cast his gaze downward. Good. I was tired of meeting the intolerable compassion in those eyes.

"They took her to Conclave and apprenticed her to a man she despised," he said. "There's really too much to go into just now, and it's still too raw. If we've arrived, we should make ready. I'll tell you the rest later."

So as the young man laced up his boots, I did likewise and organized my belongings, preparing to disembark.

***

Freshly bathed and wearing our finest, we approached the old man on the dais. Seated to his left was the baroness. Our entourage included Lucas and me, Cameron, Taylor, and strangely, Maestros Bok, Gordon, and Farrell. I could understand the inclusion of the caravan's master and Taylor as our attendant, but why entertainers had been invited remained a mystery.

Marjery had opted to remain in the carriage house to keep Wynken out of mischief. The beast couldn't be left out in the cold, and the other animals in the stables would never accept her presence there. After letting our wagons into the keep, the other members of our troupe had been given shelter from the storm in some of the castle's many empty rooms. Though the grandeur of its furnishings spoke of a glorious past, Castle Stein seemed but poorly occupied and maintained.

I also wondered where Manny had gone. No one had seen him since last night at the logging camp. Aaron Reynolds had to drive his wagon, and Ollie Reed reported one of the mules was missing. I had long suspected the man had secrets and depths that the others failed to plumb. In a corner directly beyond Leopold's great chair stood a large harp. Leaning nearby it rested a long wooden horn.

"Approach, Cameron Ross," said the baroness, speaking uncustomarily first.

We had been informed by Sir Christopher that Lord Leopold was in poor health and asked not to tire him overmuch lest our interview be cut short. The baron was attended by his page and an elderly gentleman who was standing to his right and whispering into his lordship's ear. With my talent, I sensed tension from the chamberlain whenever his gaze flitted our way. Cameron stepped forward from among us and bowed low.

"Your lordship and your ladyship," said Master Ross dutifully.

"Do you find the accommodations suitable?" she asked. "We have not entertained for quite a while, but circumstances dictate we host you here for a time. At least until the roads have cleared sufficiently. I fear the sun may be on French leave for some time yet to come. But know that the hospitality of Barony Stein shall be yours to enjoy until he returns."

"Your ladyship is most gracious," said Cameron, "I have arranged for the bulk of my fellows to be hosteled indefinitely at the Sojourner's Thrifty Inne here at Ingolnook. We had hoped to make the caravansary to the south before this inclement condition fell upon us. But I fear we were too reckless, traveling north this late in the season."

"Nonsense, young man," said the baron, piping up for the first time. "The young mages, at least, must stay here. And you as well if you enjoy a good game of Karnöffel."

"I've been known to play a few hands..."

"Then it's settled. Mason. See that our guests here are assigned proper quarters. The musicians too."

The man to the baron's right looked helplessly over at the baroness, who promptly nodded at the lady maid to her left. The lady curtsied and smoothly glided away.

"In case you were wondering," Leopold continued, "the minstrels are here at my special request. It has to do with me and my Willie."

The baroness remained motionless, but her eyes flitted over to her husband before returning to us.

"Your... willey, my lord?"

"Yes, my Wilhelmine, the Baroness Stein," he said with a flicker of annoyance. "You see, I'm quite proud of my Willie. She is quite an able administrator. Not to brag, but my Willie stands firmly in charge of all the ladies in my castle."

Cameron stood aghast, and the baroness lowered her head and placed a hand to her forehead. Lord Stein looked at the man with a level, stern-faced glare that all but shouted he was an idiot. But though his face was set in grim lines, his eyes couldn't lie to mine. Inside, the baron was laughing.

"Despite many proud achievements, my Willie and I share a notable flaw. We are not musically gifted. I hoped your musicians might help straighten us out."

"Straighten you out, your lordship?" asked Liam, his face slightly reddening.

"My wife practices daily at her harp. And I do my best to accompany her on my shawm," he said while indicating the wooden horn. "We're not very good as yet. But on the odd occasion when no one else is around, I like to play with my Willie right here in my audience chamber. I'm still too shy to do it in front of others."

Ben Farrell coughed oddly and stamped his foot, and Liam was bent nearly double and clutching his ribs. Master Ross had his lips pursed in a great frown, and odd snorts were emerging from his nose. I flung back my head and laughed out loud. It was a sound I only rarely made, but I did so gladly. It rang out to echo all about the chamber. The others looked at me in horror, still ignorant of the truth. Leopold was just having them on. I wasn't laughing at the baron. I was laughing *with* the baron - at them.

Tired of being patronized and talked about, the baron was using his authority to make others uncomfortable. Though distressing to his minders, it was the old wolf's prerogative, and he was abusing it shamelessly.

"This one gets it," said the old man, staring at me. "What is your name, young man?"

"Royland Wagge, your lordship," I replied. "It is a pleasure to meet you. I'm somewhat of a musician myself. I play the drum. If it would please your lordship, I would be happy to sit in sometime and play with you and your... lady wife... while we are snowbound here."

The others were now staring at us both in confusion, sensing that something beyond their ken was being discussed. I ignored them and met the baron's gaze as a ghost of a smile played about his lips.

***

"Teufel," I said, tossing down the two of trumps and scooping up the trick.

Taylor groaned and tossed in his hand as this was our third trick. My cousin sat across from me with a spreading grin as though he had contributed to our win. In point of fact, he was my handicap. The lord and lady Stein were a well-coordinated team and long-time savants of the game. Initially, they had gained a commanding lead. Taylor and Cameron also possessed a good grasp of the game but were still working out their teamwork. Though I had never played Karnöffel before, I had enjoyed many such games with my mother and father back on the Wagge farm. Add to that; I had the unnatural advantage bestowed by my talent. No one could succeed at bluffing me if they met my eyes.

Lucas was intelligent and quickly grasped the rules. However, he may as well play the game with all of his cards showing. If he possessed a king-beater or turned up a trump he favored, his face would declare such to the entire room even before the bidding began. This had radically altered my strategy from how I would have preferred to play.

The deal passed to me, and I shuffled. Once, when I was a boy, I had become fascinated with cards. I had played with them for weeks until I could practically make them stand up and dance. My father had said I should slow down lest I wear the faces off them. My long, skinny fingers could still flip them about and fold them together with a smooth precision unusual to most dealers. Cameron Ross had groaned when I'd first exhibited this skill and thanked the stars we weren't playing for coin. Leopold and Wilhelmine had merely grinned, sensing a challenge. All were thankful I'd been partnered with Lucas.

We had retired to a cozy parlor deep in the recesses of Castle Stein where a grand hearth burned brightly to reflect off a polished wooden table. It was the second day of heavy snowfall, and the wind gusted and moaned. An occasional chill breeze could be felt stirring in the drafty castle, causing the thick tapestries to flap about as though moved by some ghostly hand. Strange creaks and groans could be heard nurturing the notion that the place was haunted.

Whereas Westarbor was a relatively new barony, Castle Stein had been occupied for centuries. This was reflected in its decor. There were antique suits of armor from earlier times standing about. On the walls, faded tapestries depicted scenes from events long gone. Some of these were barely discernible. And though clean of such, one could almost imagine cobwebs hanging down in each darkened corner of the room. I dealt each a face-up card, the lowest of which was a *deuce die sau*. This made bells the trump.

"I understand that discovery of your gift was somewhat unusual, Lucas," said the baron.

"Indeed it was, your lordship," my cousin replied.

"If it isn't too personal, I would hear it from you directly," he said while assessing the hand I had dealt him. "What is your magic center?"

While my cousin explained, Taylor proposed an increase to seven points.

"Interesting. Vines, you say?" noted Leopold as he reordered his cards. "We accept the increase."

Cameron looked sharply between the two, then proposed an increase to ten points. I had heard that the Stein's firstborn was also a mage who had apprenticed at Conclave. In keeping with my new outgoing facade, I decided to ask them about it.

"Too rich for my digestion, we surrender," said I, tossing my cards into the middle.

Sometimes, prudence was the better part of wisdom. Besides, Lucas had nothing.

"If the question isn't too indelicate," I continued, turning to the baron, "I understand your son is at Conclave. How did he discover *his* gift, and what does his magic's source resemble?"

The Steins' eyes met over the table, and I felt waves of woe rippling out from them. Perchance, I had overstepped. I would withdraw the question if I were able. But then an understanding seemed to pass between the two, and while Leopold directed his saddened gaze downward, Wilhelmine prepared to respond.

"We don't speak of it often, for it is in truth a rather tragic tale. But seeing as you will likely encounter him soon, it were best you be forewarned."

The others at the table rested their hands and grew more attentive. Who could focus on a mere game with a beginning like that?

"It was just after his twelfth birthday that our son's gift was revealed. He was distraught that his old cat, Fritz, had died, and naught we did could console him. He stayed in the tower he had claimed as a bastion of sorts and came out not even for his meals that day. It was during a storm that I sat in our audience chamber wondering what was to be done and plucking at my harp when..."

The lady winced and turned her face aside. The baron arose and reached across the table to offer a handkerchief. I was hard pressed to deny the inviting hum of oblivion that swirled up to drag me into a stupor when faced with the distressing anguish that lanced out from her eyes.

"There there, dearest," mumbled Leopold. "You needn't go on. I can face it now."

"Into the chamber walked Fritz. He was a bit stiff-legged, and his fur was unkempt. He tottered up and sat before us, reeking of the grave. 'It's alive!' I cried just as the ghoulish grimalkin, back-lighted by the storm's fury, fell over on its side. Then in came our sobbing son, our little Franklin. He scooped up the beast and cradled it to his bosom."

"No," said he "not alive. I tried, father, but Fritzie keeps getting worse and worse."

The Steins went on to explain their son had a rare magic center involving death and the reanimation of the dead. Such mages were called necromancers and weren't favorably regarded. Nonetheless, the law required him to become a mage in the king's service and barred him from holding a noble title apart from 'Master Wizard.'

The card game was forgotten. It was clear to me the Stein's would have won, regardless. Since we had already intruded upon the couple's private grief, the Steins were very forthcoming with further details. Franklin had gone to Conclave five years ago to begin his apprenticeship. About six months in, he had quit writing. The baron and his wife urged Lucas and I to seek him out and discover how he was getting on. They'd had reports from others there that Franklin had yet to be selected by any of the masters as a journeyman. Undoubtedly, the nature of his gift had something to do with this, and the lad was bitter.

Franklin would be seventeen now, and a journeyman aspirant just as we were, albeit a more experienced one. Perhaps he could help us acclimate to the place, and we could become his friends. Taylor offered to convey a bevy of the Stein's gray-banded pigeons to Conclave so we might update the good lord and her ladyship regarding his status. Lord Leopold put aside the Karnöffel deck and ordered that strong drink be served. I sipped at mine to be sociable. Lucas wrinkled up his nose at the first sip and set it aside. He wasn't being rude; it was just Lucas.

Not much else was said as the fire burned lower and the castle continued to creak and moan. We had become a morose company. The ensuing silence was refreshing to me even as it failed to offer comfort to the others. Even Lucas had no chipper chatter with which to shatter our bleak laconism.

It was then a muffled thumping was heard. Only by its insistence did it fail to be dismissed as a loose shutter blown by the wind. The baron and his lady arose to see who would disturb the peace of their castle at so late an hour. Curious, we followed as well. When we arrived at the entrance hall, we found the baron's servants clustered about two men. One was Aaron Reynolds, our wainwright. At his feet lay his brother, Noah. A chill greeted us as we entered the room, and melting snow was puddling about the two men.

Twisting his hat in his hands, Aaron turned to the baron as he approached.

"I beg your lordship's pardon, but my brother is bad off," said the man. "I heard you had a proper physic here at the castle and prayed you might ask him to have a look at Noah."

"What happened?" asked the baroness, nodding to a servant and pointing toward a hall.

"Well, that's the thing, mum... milady. My brother done fell off the wagon again."

For once, my cousin respectfully held his tongue. From the way his eyes popped, I was certain he had many questions like 'which wagon?' or 'what did he fall on?'

"I should've been looking after him closer. But he'd sworn off the drink years ago, knowing it would end him if he kept at it. Not a dram has passed his lips in all that time and I'd nearly forgot he *had* a problem. One drink would always lead to another, and before I knew it, he'd be passed out. There at that inne, everyone got to celebrating and making merry and I guess he just couldn't help himself. This time seems worse, though. He's barely breathing. Please help my brother."

The physic soon arrived with several other servants and conveyed Noah off on a stretcher. Our sour mood had gotten even grimmer as we saw our friend hauled away. As the snow continued to fall, borne by the howling wind, we retired to our rooms to await news of his fate. The wainwright would have our prayers this night. We all implored the creator above that Noah would still be among us to greet the dawn.

***

Several days passed, and the snows piled up before the clouds parted and the sun shone down once more. Noah had survived the night but was in no fit shape to do aught but lie abed until this morning. We were all thankful to the Steins for granting us shelter from the blizzard. The like hadn't been seen in years. Though the day was bright, the caravan couldn't be on its way until the snow cleared. And by the looks of it, that could take weeks. The wagons all sat buried under drifts in the keep's inner ward while the mules were snuggled safe in Leopold's more than adequate stables.

Though the Tomcats were snowbound, the same couldn't be said for the harker. She and Wynken set off for Westarbor amid cheers and fanfare. The snow blanketing the land would deprive her of landmarks, but she was certain they could find their way home. All of Westarbor would be waiting to receive her, as Taylor had expended one of his birds to send ahead the joyous news of her success. Lord Leopold had lapsed once again into a befuddled state. He nonetheless stood among us, smiling and waving her off.

The Tomcats emerged from the inne at Ingolnook Village and shoveled clear a path up to the gates of the keep. Tired of lazing about, they helped the servants to clean away the snow from the inner ward. Aaron Reynolds took up station in the carriage house and brought his recovering brother there to begin overhauling the wagons one by one, starting with their own. We all set out to take what enjoyment we could from the windless winter landscape. All save for one, that is.

Yesterday, Trader Sam had been brought before the baron in chains. Taylor and others spoke at length of the man's perfidies in siding with Leopold's adversaries to work harm upon the baron's reputation. Curiously, this was considered a higher crime than merely plotting the deaths of his fellows. The cloth merchant denied it, trying to cast blame on the missing jester, but Leopold was unmoved by his plea of innocence. *I* could tell the man was lying, of course, but magery hardly constituted proof of misdeeds. Fortunately, my testimony proved unnecessary.

"Your goods and your wagon are forfeit to the caravan you sought to harm," announced the baron's chamberlain. "Several of your bandit confederates have already named you in a plea for leniency. You will rejoin them in a cell. But such is our lord's mercy that you shall be kept separate from these desperate men. You will be granted meals twice each day and such sacraments as you would have from our chaplain once a week. I would recommend you avail yourself of the confessional at the very least. After the spring thaw we shall review your case again."

This sentence seemed to please the baron's hunchbacked gaolor. I'd heard there'd been no prisoners in his dungeon for over a year, and the man had been lonely.

"You heard the man, Igor," observed the baroness. "Return him to his cell."

And that was the last we saw of Sam Robinson. He was weeping openly as they hauled him off.

This morning, my cousin proposed we should have some fun in the snow. We had often enjoyed such as boys. I feared that at nineteen, I might be getting a bit too old for these antics. I decided instead to visit the inne. The maestros had gone down there with the thought of earning a few coins, and I had a standing invitation to sit in whenever my other duties allowed it. There might even be some lovely maids down there.

I had been over-sheltered on the Wagge farm. As a younger man, such women as I met were already spoiled by rumors of my 'strangeness.' They looked on me with pity or derision. I wasn't sure which had been worse, but I certainly felt no urge to take up with them. It wasn't until I met Prissy that I'd discovered how nice women could be. She'd seen me as odd, but kind of wonderful. It was a heady feeling holding her in my arms and swimming in the nice feelings we shared.

As long as I took care to meet their eyes and did nothing weird, I'd found some women looked on me with desire. Some others were more calculating, weighing what kind of life I could give them were they to wed me. I avoided that type and gravitated toward those seeking only to share some pleasant company.

Since joining the caravan, I'd become familiar with many words that I'd never encountered in books. Or, if I did, they'd acquired a whole different meaning. Take, for instance, 'mutton monger.' On its face, I would think it suggested someone who sold or managed sheep or was, perhaps, a specialty butcher. But the way Taylor and the others used it, it meant someone who was addicted to having dalliances with women. Taylor was an ass to refer to me in that way. By that definition, almost every man was a mutton monger. What I did hurt no one. And I could always tell I wasn't falsely preying on a gal's expectations. That was more than could be said of most.

Approaching the inne, I spotted a long row of snow angels decorating the ground beside the shoveled-out path. Up by the keep earlier, I'd noted Jeremiah's children making them. As with those, I reached for my gift and made the snow dimple into perfect halos above the head of each. Such details shouldn't be neglected.

The Sojourner's Thrifty Inne was at its heart a tavern. I could see why Noah Reynolds had fallen from grace here. The room was lively and the tavern maids flitted about bearing alcoholic beverages like a swarm of gnats over a pond. Moreover, proper tankards weren't available. The drinks were all served in firkins. These vessels had a pointed bottom, so they couldn't be set aside or rested on a table. The patrons were thus required to wander around, drink in hand, until they'd finished it before setting it down. It was a clever ruse to separate a man from more of his coin.

I could see my fellows performing over by the far wall. Liam smiled and signaled me over on sighting me. I had carefully cultivated our friendship as a test to see whether I could overcome the perception that I was weird. It had worked surprisingly well. I sashayed across the room, bobbing my head to the rhythm of the music and stepped up to be seated before my drum. It helped that they were fellow musicians and understood the hyper-focus that went into my performance. They took my monomania as devotion to my art. It was something to be admired, and a normal consequence of their profession.

Ben Farrell had even coined a phrase for this: 'Fake it till you make it,' he had advised. It was an amusing notion that also applied to what I was attempting to accomplish. Could I pretend normalcy well enough to fool even myself? Would that, in fact, make me normal? I fell into sync with the others and stroked the hides in counterpoint to their tune. I lost myself for a time in the pleasant blending of talents that comprised our merry band.

And there they were, the barflies. Some of the serving maids and other single ladies present gravitated toward our stage. Lacking the lofty pretensions of the noble born, such women were often attracted to a handsome man who seemed confident. I knew they wouldn't bring me the intimacy of genuine affection, but they were tempting, nonetheless.

She stood out from the others. She wasn't the comeliest lass in the place, but something about her eyes spoke of promise, discretion and longing. I knew using my insight I could take her feelings and mold them like clay until we were of a like mind. Some others were prettier, but most cast me that assessing glance I knew to avoid. At the next break, I would strike up a conversation with her. It would feed her pride to be selected over her fellows, and I could build upon that.

As we sat talking at the bar, Taylor's taunts came back to haunt me. Was I addicted? Lacking the experience of love for all those years, did I feel somehow *owed*? Instead of focusing on a mature relationship, would I settle for the quick comfort of a fling in a tavern? I think not. Not tonight. If there was one thing I understood of addiction, it was that the addict couldn't stop. I would forego her sweet warmth, thus proving my freedom to choose in such matters.

"Your pardon, milady," I said with just the proper amount of regret, "but I must return to the castle."

"Oooh, milady, is it?" she gushed. "Fancy another drink before you shove off? Perhaps up in my room then?"

And there it was.

"Well, perhaps just one more," I said, swallowing the last of my drink along with my dignity.

I set my firkin on its side and took the girl's hand in my own. My pulse pounded as she steered me toward the stairway. The boards creaked as we stepped up, seeking the solace of abandon. I shouldn't be ashamed of this perfectly normal behavior despite what others might think of me, or I of myself. I oughtn't deny myself one last hurrah. Tomorrow I could prove my abstemiousness.

***

It was late that afternoon when I made ready to depart the inne. Most women found it gratifying that I enjoyed cuddling, but Phoebe had to get back to work. I finished straightening my hair in the mirror while she stood by the door impatiently. Such details shouldn't be neglected. I embraced her briefly and passed out into the hall.

Downstairs, I found the minstrels had departed, and the staff was making ready for the dinner rush and the long night of debauchery to follow. I stepped out into the cold. Someone had done rude things in yellow to the snow angels. I exercised my gift to move some fresh snow over them to cover the coarse and unseemly vandalism. As I started along the path to the castle, a familiar jingling sound caught my attention. It came from behind me and was growing louder.

Before long, I made out a team of mules drawing a rather large sleigh filled with lumber and driven by two men of my acquaintance. It was Aaron holding the reins and his brother, Noah, seated beside him. The 'sleigh' was in fact one of the caravan's wagons to which two long runners had been affixed. These glided along the ground while the mules slogged along knee deep in the snow.

"Ho there. Royland," Aaron cried out as they approached. "Fancy a lift up the hill?"

I smiled and took care to meet their gazes. Aaron was brimming with glee, but his brother, though smiling also, was still of a most grouchy disposition. It usually pleased others if you showed an interest in their work.

"I wouldn't mind such," I answered him. "Where'd you get the bells?"

"They were the jester's. This was his wagon before he abandoned us. Noah thought of hooking them on the harnesses. Kind of festive, we thought it."

I swung up onto the buckboard when they slowed. I'd already thought of six ways to improve the design. But in truth it was a brilliant compromise. The wheels had been left on so that the skids could be easily removed when they were no longer required. The struts that held them affixed to the wagon's sides were sturdy while allowing just enough bend not to wiggle loose. The runners themselves were narrow so as to minimize drag while still being wide enough to distribute the weight evenly. Thus, they wouldn't likely dig through the snow and catch on the ground beneath. Based on the type and amount of lumber stacked in the back, it appeared the goal was to convert all the Tomcats' wagons. If this prototype was any gage, I estimated around two days would see it done.

"I guess this is the secret project you've been working on in the carriage house," I remarked.

"Oh it's no secret, Roy. I told Master Ross we could do it and be on our way before the week's end. It was Noah's idea. Hard work. That's the way to keep one's mind off the sauce."

It was evident despite his jolly banter that Aaron considered himself his brother's keeper. It was equally clear from Noah's aura of gloom and his silence that the older brother resented it. I sensed a history here, a delicate balance that had come unglued. I resolved to steer well clear of the calamity which might arise.

"I think this is my stop," I declared, hopping to the ground. "Good luck with the refits!"

The laden wagon continued up the hill toward the gates and soon came to a stop before them. Nearby, I saw my cousin and Addy Blessings fiddling with an enormous round snowball. It rested beside an even more enormous mound of the white stuff that had been shaped to resemble a squatting man.

"What are you doing?" I asked Lucas.

"We're building a snow-ogre," he replied. "Addy's girls wanted to know what an ogre looked like. They heard we had fought some back at Westarbor Keep."

Goody Blessing was handing Lucas vegetables from out of a burlap sac. I realized that the roundish ball standing waist-high at my cousin's feet had a grinning face. Two vertically placed potatoes were its eyes, and another jutted out to form its nose. A double row of radishes made a scowling mouth full of pointy teeth. As I watched, Addy handed my cousin two carrots he used to complete the picture. He set them to stick firmly up from the edges of the jaw. These carrot tusks then framed its potato nose.

"Levare," my cousin incanted.

I invoked my mage sight to observe his technique. When we had first started, Lucas would never have attempted so large an object for levitation. Even after discovering how to harness his talent to wind his vines together, such a substantial snowball would surely tax his powers near to their limit. It wasn't hard to imagine him 'rolling' these massive snowballs with his winding. Lifting them, he would soon discover, was quite a different matter. I called upon the hive to assist.

"Levare," I uttered.

With an inaudible droning, a thousand copious little points of light swept out to amass beneath Lucas' struggling vine. They helped convey the ogre head up to rest atop its massive torso. The final effect was comical. The vegetable ogre sneered down at us from its potato eyes. It more resembled a happy salad plate than a fierce denizen of the untamed western wilderness. So threatening it was that bunnies might be drawn from their dens to feast gleefully upon its face. Upon noting this inadequacy, Lucas frowned.

"Well, I didn't want it to be *too* scary anyway," he announced.

We set off to find Angie and Sera. Addy said they were off playing with the elves. We tracked them. It wasn't difficult. We just followed the tracks in the snow and sounds of girlish laughter. Rounding a bend, I was confronted by an impressive sight. The girls were halfway up the hill atop which rested a miniature fortress sculpted from the ice and snow. Icicles rimmed its battlement, jutting up to sparkle in the late afternoon sun. The turrets that graced each corner of the sublime structure had sharply pointed roofs.

Angie threw a snowball with her mitten'd hand. It fell wide and a bit short. Nonetheless, this drew a scathing rebuke from the castle's defenders. Toolhup and Benalav stood up from behind its walls and launched a decisive retaliatory strike against Angie and her sister. No quarter was offered as they rained down snowballs upon the pair. These splatted against the retreating backs of the would-be assailants and a full rout ensued. Sera failed to retreat in good order and fell, crushing the armful of ammunition she'd been cradling.

I had never been particularly competitive. I had seen the fervor it had oft aroused in others, causing them to better themselves thereby. But the need to do well at another's expense had always seemed unnecessary. Better to strive toward goals of my own making and let what others did be to their own credit. Nevertheless, it offended my sense of fair-play to see these professionals flaunt their superior tossing skills so. Even now, they mocked the girls, shouting out Elven words and juggling snowballs between them as though begging their small adversaries to take another run at it. I looked over at my cousin. He returned my regard and nodded his agreement. We walked over to the girls to strategize.

"Just keep making snowballs and toss them up in the air," my cousin was telling them a few minutes later.

"Look at 'em flickering," said Sera resentfully. "Aye, I'll be your cross bite if you think you can give them their bastings."

"Right bully beggars they are," Angie agreed. "They oughtn't to throw those beggar's bullets so hard at a bantling!"

The children's speech amused me to no end. I had caught on to it gradually after the Blessings had joined our ranks. More refined people of my acquaintance called it the vulgar tongue. This private speech of the lower classes seemed just as familiar to them as it was baffling to others. Some said it was an entirely different language, but it was really only a mish-mash of tortured similes and made-up words for nefarious activities. Still, it was colorful and achieved its purpose, masking the speaker's intent from possible nearby listeners. I resolved to become fluent in it.

Our plan having been set, we began by moving closer. The elves didn't react until we threw our first volley. As professional jugglers with decent cover and an uphill advantage, they had no trouble pelting us soundly.

"Impedimente," I muttered as my blue disc flared to life.

It was the same spell I had used at the battle for Westarbor's gates. The one the goblins called 'the accursed shield of the blue king.' Next, Sera and Angie began lofting snowballs into the air above my barrier. It was my cousin's job to guide these to their proper targets. Although he couldn't handle a very large mass, Lucas had gotten a lot better at launching smaller missiles.

"Viburnum pugna," he improvised.

Thus, the assault on *Chushapethia* Castle commenced. Lucas would strafe the Loredonians who would be forced to duck behind their battlement. This would allow me to rest my shield briefly while we advanced. In the end, the elves emerged from their fortification. I, in turn, dropped my protective barrier, and a free-for-all battle ensued. Though outnumbered, the elves were quick, dodging nimbly our amateurish efforts and returning two for every one they got. Sera surprisingly landed a good one on Benalav's face. Her mitten'd throws proved too unpredictable to dodge properly in close quarters. At last, we fell panting and laughing to the churned up ground.

After we neglected to declare a victor, I headed back toward the castle, and Addy gathered the girls to go with her and Lucas to see the snow ogre. Dinner would be served soon, and I'd best get cleaned up and dry. I supposed nineteen wasn't *really* too old to enjoy a snow day. Miss Toolhup and Benalav were in their eighties, after all.

***

Three days later, the caravan stood arranged to depart. My cousin's snow-ogre had been joined by a trio of snow-goblins who menaced the path leading down to the village. Several of the local boys had been knighted for the deed in a mock ceremony presided over by the Elven queen of Castle Chushapethia. Using Lucas' sword, Tazbeth Tulip had overseen their oaths to guard and protect the snow fortress until spring.

The radiant sky had melted clear the path leading into town, but the high roads leading in and out of Ingolnook remained buried. Thick saddle blankets covered the mules like barding over their harnesses, and the jingling bells had been removed.

The Reynolds brothers hadn't dared make alterations to the baron's coach, so Taylor, Lucas and I were assigned to ride in the wagon the jester had abandoned. Lord Leopold assured us he would see our Liege's coach was swiftly returned to him. It would also bear a full kit of the Stein's gray-banded pigeons back to Westarbor. So I sat beside Taylor on the bench of the makeshift sleigh as we awaited the signal to move out.

The lady Stein offered Cameron an escort of Leopold's knights down to their southern border. She wanted to make certain no bandits would further imperil the shipment or the Stein's honor. Master Ross accepted this offer. Thus, two full lances of mounted men were to precede the caravan down the road. This had the added advantage of trampling down the snow, so our mules might have an easier time of it. The knights selected for this mission were Sir Daniel Grant and Sir Alfredo Santiago.

Also accompanying us was the baron's chamberlain, Mason Moore. Though somewhat elderly, the man could sit a horse and fancied a bit of a jaunt through the countryside. He saw it as an opportunity to collect reports and news from municipalities and parishes along our route. He'd assert his authority to smooth our way and make certain we were afforded the hospitality due to favored guests of his liege.

I didn't miss the bumping and swaying I usually endured as the wagon glided smoothly over the beaten snow. It was in this manner we were comfortably conveyed through the southern reaches of Barony Stein. We stopped briefly at various hamlets and villages and dined at many a roadside tavern. On entering the southern highlands, I noted a change. I had heard of Leopold's agricultural innovations, but yearned to see its centerpiece for myself.

These hilly badlands had once been deemed unsuitable for farming. It wasn't level, and the climate was too arid for most crops we considered worthwhile. It was split in its middle by a deep gorge, far at the bottom of which ran an inconstant and untamed river. Prior lords had written it off as unproductive land. It was for this reason it had been named Worstershire (as opposed to Worcestershire, which I'd heard was a very lovely place indeed).

Leopold's policies, however, had transformed the place. To start with, the farmers here didn't plow a straight furrow. To better preserve what little rainfall there was supplemented by another wondrous method, they planted in great curving rows that followed the contours of the land. Each row would catch and hold the water rather than allow the runoff to be wasted, carrying along with it equally precious topsoil. Next, we saw a great mill standing atop one hill. From its side protruded four great arms. We were told the frameworks of these sported sailcloth during the harvest season and caught the wind to cause its turning. Lucas claimed it would be challenging to regulate the speed of rotation with such an inconsistent source of power. Also, one would be at the mercy of the wind for ones milling needs. We were assured they managed quite nicely.

Finally, a system of aqueducts had been constructed at great cost to bring water to the top of each hill. I could see their towering support struts rising from the snow-blanketed landscape we traversed. We turned uphill toward the highest of these. It was off the road, but Mason assured us the view from the top would be more than worth the delay, and Cameron concurred.

As we approached the highest point near the edge of Quaboshiqua Gorge, we were bidden to disembark our wagons and proceed afoot. At the top, I could make out a great arc of gleaming metal, and I marveled at its size. The pièce de résistance of Leopold's system of irrigation was the great water lifter that sat in the gorge below. It was a genuine marvel. As we came to the top, we were shepherded out upon a viewing platform that hung over the gorge's lip. A sturdy railing skirted it, but I was nonetheless struck by a sense of vertigo as I stepped forth on shaky limbs. A vista spread out beneath us, one which left me flabbergasted.

The great wheel was enormous in scope. Its reality stretched beyond the bounds of my imagination. I had heard it described, but no description could capture the sight which reached from the lip of that gorge to the river below in a gigantic array to outshine, overstep and eclipse my expectations. It was to our mill wheel back in Westarbor as a mygalom was to a spider. Unlike that wheel, affixed to its rim were swiveling buckets rather than paddles. These would dip into the rushing waters of the river below to convey their loads up to the top, whereupon an unmoving arm would cause them to tip into the aqueduct.

"*Hutejha tazbeth jibia, vanuji tinka ghajh!*" said Miss Toolhup.

"*Oho nuqua jatlah ghah,*" Benalav cracked wise.

The wheel was still at present. A locking mechanism near its center had been set. Moreover, the Quaboshiqua River was currently crusted over with ice. Here and there were clear patches that showed it still flowed, but its force imparted no movement to the wheel.

"It's quite a sight. Don't you think?" remarked Mason to Cameron.

"I do," Cameron replied at once. "Every time I see it, I am awed anew by its grandeur."

"Have you ever seen it in the summer?"

"I have. I had the good fortune one year to be passing through during your celebration of plenty."

"Ah. Then you've seen the Worstershire Rites of Bravery."

I'd heard of this but wasn't certain what all it entailed. I was prepared to ask him to explain, but my cousin beat me to it once again.

"The rites," said Mason, "are conducted each summer once the crops have all been planted. The young men of Worstershire are given the chore of sanding, waxing and greasing the aqueduct along its entire length. As a reward of sorts, they are given turns hopping into a bucket of the wheel. This lowers them to the river below where they are dunked under and lifted back to the top. When their bucket is overturned, they slide down the aqueduct all the way to its terminus. There they are deemed bravos of Worstershire and celebrated with a feast."

"I wish it was summer," said Lucas sullenly. "Hey, why hasn't it rusted?"

"A valid question, young man. I'm afraid only the dwarves can answer it, and they're keeping mum. You see, when Javier Lewis was commissioned to design the great work, he realized timbers alone would prove insufficient."

Javier built this? And I thought he was just a kook.

"Ordinary iron or even good steel would develop the problem you so astutely point out," he continued. "He knew, however, that the dwarves had devised a method using a secret mix of alloys and coatings to render iron impervious to rust. Stainless steel, they name it. Calling in all his favors with them, Javier had each piece forged in the dwarven smithies of Echo Hills to his exacting specifications. It cost Lord Leopold a small fortune and several prized works of art and historical treasures from the Stein legacy. These now reside with Lord Brax

Steelaxe in his ducal halls at Greatforge. But the end result is what you see before you. Oh, it still needs maintenance and painting from time to time, but it's stood up well to the ravages of the river over the last ten years or so."

"We know Javier," said Taylor. "He's our artillator back in Westarbor."

"We are aware," said Mason, his aura shifting to one of mild disapproval. "Leopold thought the world of Sir Vincent back in the day. He expected great things from him and wasn't disappointed. Leopold still hasn't forgiven your baron for stealing Master Lewis away from him. He recommended him for a dovecote project some years back, and the fellow never returned. The man is a genius, but also a tad rattlebrained."

"How so?" asked Cameron.

"You should have heard what he wanted to name the thing, but our lord put a quick end to that. 'Since it's made of an undisclosed alloy of iron,' he said, 'we shall call it the ferrous wheel.' Javier also termed all this 'a modest feat of civil engineering.' Now I ask you, does this look modest?"

"Add to that," said Sir Alfredo, "there was nothing civil about it."

"Speak on, man, what was the problem?" asked Cameron encouragingly.

"Well," began the knight, "Javier was from my home town in Freemark, so I know him well. Much of the time, he potters about aimlessly, working at this or that. But when an idea takes hold of him, presto! He transforms into the most stubborn of men. This was such a project."

"Sounds like the man we know," said Taylor. "Go on."

"No sooner did Javier have his great wheel assembled than there arose a problem. You see, this stretch of the Everclear River was governed by a capricious nyad named Quaboshiqua. She was proud to have carved a gorge so deep. She ran wild and free through it as all such faeries do."

This answered another question I'd had. The river below was marked as the 'Everclear' on the king's map, but the locals all referred to it by that other name.

"Like all of her kind, she despised being trapped or bound and greatly feared the touch of iron. When first Javier lowered his ferrous wheel to touch the river below, she began to rage. She splashed about angrily, overflowing her banks and undercutting the cliffs where Javier sought to anchor it. For months, Javier sought to overpower the nymph with his science as all knew she could not be calmed. He would tame her; he thought."

"Well it appears to have worked," said Lucas.

"Not exactly," Mason returned. "After months of unexpected delays while the two butted heads, our good lord appealed to the king. Now faeries acknowledge no human ruler, having their own twin hierarchies instead."

This was getting complicated, I thought.

"There are the helpful faeries of the Seelie Court. Most brownies fit into this category. They seek peaceful coexistence with humans and do small favors, asking mostly just to be left alone. In their view, our kingdom can overlap with theirs. Then there are the unseelie fey. It is they that play spiteful little tricks and steal infants from their cribs. They hold that humankind are a blight on their way of life, gobbling up their wilderness and giving them nothing in return."

"They have a point," Benalav observed.

"Be that as it may," the chamberlain continued, "we had to discover to which court Quaboshiqua belonged, Seelie or Unseelie. If it were the former, perhaps some accommodation could be reached. So the king sent to Conclave and bade his mages there to look into the matter."

I perked up at this. I wondered how I would go about carrying out such a task.

"The council of masters sent one of their number to investigate. Zaid Guthrie was a wily old wizard whose specialty was animals. On arriving at Worstershire, he tackled the problem straightaway. Whether seelie or unseelie, no faerie would ever submit to artificial constraints. But any of them would bow to the power of nature. He therefore took himself upstream a few miles and convinced a family of beavers to build a dam.

This trapped Quaboshiqua on the west side above said dam, for she considered the semi-aquatic creatures to be her children and would never do them harm. Not only did this fend off the crazed nyad, but it also calmed and regulated the river's flow, thus aiding the irrigation project immensely."

So elegant, I thought. The masters of the conclave must be truly wise. It will be a joy to study among them. I would one day learn that not all the mages were as level-headed and enlightened as good Master Guthrie.

"It is for this very reason," said Mason Moore, "that hunting beaver is now considered a high crime in Barony Stein."

"Heed the man, Royland," said Taylor.

"Bite me, Taylor," I replied.

Lucas looked confused.

We returned to the wagons and headed back down the hill to resume our trek. Mason had told us we should return sometime in the summer or spring. The highlands were lovely with all the plants growing and the ferrous wheel turning and all. There was even a petition circulating around to rename the area 'Bestershire'. But this was being strongly opposed by traditionalists who would deem the re-dubbing disrespectful to their forebears.

So on we rode with our shadows laying to the left and crawling over the snowbanks keeping pace. It would be a shame to lose our escort at the Stein's southern border. It was nice to have clear roads over which to glide and fine Innes at which to dine.

CHAPTER TWELVE

The Innekeeper

"I'm a fighter. I believe in the eye-for-an-eye
business. I'm no cheek turner. I got no respect for
a man who won't hit back. You kill my dog, you
better hide your cat."

~ Muhammad Ali ~

We had crossed the border and parted ways with our
escort. The next barony over was that of Baron Jordan Murphy.
It marked the first time I had set foot outside the Province of
Northford. Lord Murphy owed his allegiance to his grace,
Conner Deerfield, duke of Deerfield. Though we still had a long
way to travel, at least we were now in the same *province* as
Conclave. The border guards were very polite and assessed
only a modest tariff on our goods. In Deerfield, trade was highly
encouraged.

Once again, my thoughts turned to the letter from Megan.
Since the missive had flown directly from Westarbor, the news
was recent, and my lady was less restrained in her writing. The
baron planned to construct an aerie for the gryphons atop the
west tower and was urging Stein to do likewise. Thus would

begin a chain of fast messenger posts where full letters and small packages could be swiftly borne about the kingdom. Her father was most excited about this prospect. So much so, that he wanted *me* to sound out the masters of the conclave about sponsoring a hostelry for gryphon riders at Conclave. This would be the next leg of the system. My liege would send his diplomats and negotiators forthwith, but he wanted to give the masters adequate time to consider the matter.

I understood that my lord wanted to move quickly, and I was conveniently placed. But was I really suited for such a task? Although I was getting better, my ignorance of the social niceties had caused me difficulties on more than one occasion. I recalled with chagrin one of the final conversations I'd had with Megan before leaving on this journey.

"When you think you know best," she had remarked, "it has been noted that you often phrase your advice as commands: 'You must do this' and 'You cannot allow that.' I find it refreshing and somewhat endearing, but it grates upon the knights and your other social superiors. They are accustomed to a certain deference due their stations and believe you to be undermining their authority. This only gets their backs up and causes you trouble. Privately, I care not. But when in public, it would be better were you to consider your words with more care."

Thinking back, I'd had to admit that I owned this habit of speech. It would explain a lot of the mischief that had befallen me in recent months. I had wanted to thank Megan for pointing it out, but couldn't resist injecting a note of humor in my reply.

"My lady mustn't think that," I said with a spreading grin.

Noting her sustained dour expression, I took another tack.

"Point taken," I had said, shrugging with eyes downcast. "I shall strive to do better and thank her ladyship for the thoughtful and gentle rebuke."

"See that you do, my protector." She had enjoined me.

Her slightly upturned lips gave the lie to the stern glare she'd maintained. I had since tried to curb my tongue in accordance with Megan's advice, but it was a work in progress.

It's hard to break the habit of a lifetime based on a single lesson in elocution, however lovely and memorable the instructor.

When I composed my reply, I'd recounted our adventures to date. I promised to broach the matter with the mages as soon as I saw an opportunity to do so. I hadn't been as homesick as I had expected. Novel sights and my caravan mates had kept me well distracted thus far, not to mention sword battles and running for my life. But the letter had caused a shift in my way of viewing the journey. I began once again to long for the simple pleasures of home and the company of those I had left there. I still had Roy, but he seemed strange to me now. Well, he was always strange, but now he was becoming somehow distant as well. Many of his new activities didn't include me. And when they did, he seemed dismissive of my contributions and feelings.

The roads in Deerfield Duchy weren't as bad as we had feared. At the bidding of their duke, Lord Murphy and his fellow barons had already sent several mounted patrols down the full length of the king's highway. This had the effect of trampling down the snow and easing the way for travelers. We could probably remove the runners from our wagons as the remaining snow wasn't so deep. Cameron decided to wait and do this at the caravansary farther to the south. Either mode of travel would work for now, and there could yet be some additional snowfall in the days ahead. Still, we felt well protected by the frequent patrols that enforced Murphy's law.

We were hosted at several other baronies along the way. It became monotonous and began to run together after a time. That's not to say there weren't unusual and impressive sights at every turn. It's just that my mind was becoming overwhelmed by novel sights, sounds, and smells. After a while, something that would have fascinated me a fortnight ago seemed like just one more unlikely event among many.

At the first such stop, Taylor asked whether I wanted to resume my sword training.

"You did well for a first match against so fierce an opponent. Would you care to cross blades?"

"I think not," I replied.

"Chicken," he declared, looking suddenly upward and snapping his fingers. "What? I only just remembered Addy mentioning we were having chicken for dinner tonight."

"It's not that, Taylor," I said. "It's just that I've achieved what I set out to accomplish and am satisfied. I've had my fill of swordplay. I may be oh for one, but I'm content with that tally. I can now retire my father's blade and bear it with dignity should the occasion once again arise."

"That's a very mature attitude for one your age," said Taylor. "If you're certain then."

As I turned and headed for the cook wagon, I felt a sharp rap on the back of my head. Turning about, I saw Taylor nonchalantly examining his nails and spotted an acorn lying on the ground between us. This only proved Taylor lacked a mature attitude for *any* age.

***

At the junction of two key roads was the caravansary. It was a place where caravans could rest and reorganize. The Tomcats arrived in good order near the day's end. Master Ross was well pleased with the trip north, notwithstanding the harsh weather and the dangers we had endured. Lord Deerfield had granted the lands to the merchant's guild of Fairglen and cosponsored the caravansary. This was chiefly at the king's behest. Several such venues lay scattered throughout Osten to encourage and foster the trade that was the kingdom's lifeblood.

Other caravans were present here, but despite some small rivalries among them, I sensed the community spirit that pervaded these men. Tales were exchanged and goods swapped about as each prepared to set out on the next legs of their respective journeys. I once again began feeling the outsider as many of these new faces were well-known or familiar acquaintances of the other Tomcats. Amid their happy reunions and hasty introductions, I failed to retain my sense of belonging among these long-time brothers of the road.

The Reynolds brothers wasted no time in detaching and disassembling our wagons' runners. The erstwhile sleighs soon sat upon their wheels once more. Some of our mules were retired to rest here and were replaced by fresh beasts from the caravansary's extensive stables. Ollie Reed saw to this business. Most of us were at our liberty to explore the grounds while Cameron Ross met with the other caravan masters to conduct business. Although the administrative core of the Tomcats would remain intact, several of the traders and itinerant workers that comprised it would peel off here. They'd join other caravans bound for the kingdom's capital at Fairglen to the east. Likewise, we would be joined by some new wagons whose owners preferred to accompany us on our trek to Conclave to the south. These matters and many others were negotiated by Master Ross and his fellows.

Taylor had business in Fairglen, but would first see Roy and I safely to our destination before circling back to follow the eastern road.

It turned out the caravansary had an ale house. I shouldn't be surprised. What *did* surprise me when I entered was discovering Roy within, facing off against a burly man with a raised fist. The man looked unsteady, but was to my cousin as a bull was to a frightened colt.

"I'll ask you again," said the man, tottering before his overturned chair. "What was you sayin' to my Rita, you wretched bastard?"

Roy, with his hands raised defensively before him, muttered some smooth reply. The man became further enraged. Before I could think better of it, I stepped over to the man and placed a hand upon his upper arm.

"What's the trouble here, goodman?" I asked. "My cousin is quite harmless; I assure you."

The man whirled about to face me, shrugging the offending hand from his person. He glared down at me with bloodshot eyes and frowned, confused.

"You heard him," declared the man. "The skinny beggar just asked if I was 'congenitally incapable of keeping a civil tongue.' Now I ask you, was he callin' me a dog in his fancy way? Else wise what have me genitals to do with me tongue?"

Though clearly irate, the man was just as obviously drunk. I could work with the confusion this engendered, I thought to myself. Keep him talking. We don't want this to devolve into fisticuffs, after all.

"Which is it?" I shot back, "Is he fancy or a beggar? That's a bit of an oxymoron if you ask me."

"What's that you just called me boy?"

Uh-oh.

"It simply means a contradiction in terms," I hastily asserted.

"Shut your filthy mouth, or I'll shut it *for* you, shorty; there are ladies present!"

Laughingly, another man stepped over from the bar and drew the man's eye.

"You better watch your step, Joe." He said. "That's Lucas Harper you're threatening there. After wiping the floor with a goblin horde with his magic, I heard he challenged a baron's son to a duel. He fought that full blooded knight to a standstill using no magic whatsoever."

This 'Joe' was looking more confused than ever. But he re-assessed me in a glance tinged by caution.

"I didn't mean to insult you, Joe. And I apologize if my words offended any ladies."

"Ah... well then, since you took it back, perhaps I won't thump you," he finally said with false bravado.

There were all kinds of courage, but I could tell this was merely scaramouchery. The second man uprighted Joe's chair and handed him a fresh tankard. Joe seemed mollified by this. Royland, however, was glaring at me with something akin to loathing. I couldn't be sure, for I had never seen such a mood dominate his face on the few occasions he would even meet my gaze. My cousin turned and stalked off in a snit. Something was definitely going on with him.

I ordered some ale and went off to a corner to stew about it. The other patrons left me alone but glanced over at me from time to time, whispering to one another. Where did these dumb rumors about me come from? I knew that Maestro Bok's silly song was initially to blame. Now everything I did was getting blown all out of proportion. Tomorrow, no doubt, I would be credited with single-handedly defeating a dozen strong toughs at the tavern whilst singing a ballad and drinking a keg afterward.

Then I'd best get a start on that keg, I mused, raising my tankard once more.

***

A few days passed, and we were ready to set out once more. I tried making amends with my cousin, but he seemed to be avoiding me now. Cameron, too, was all bent out of shape. Since emerging from his meeting he'd been overly brusque with everyone. He even yelled at Taylor for leaving our wagon flaps undone.

"What's got his britches in a knot?" asked Taylor after the man had left.

"I think he's upset over Harold leaving us," said Ollie Reed who was seeing to our team.

"Where's Harold going?" Taylor asked.

"I'm not sure," replied the farrier. "When I went to saddle Harold's mule, he told me to leave off. He also told me there were some military horses in the stables and I was to fetch them and hitch them up to the cook wagon."

We finally got the story from the Reynolds brothers. Apparently, some muckety-muck had arrived from Deerfield and conscripted a bunch of wagons, our cook wagon among them. Some new abomination had been perpetrated by the dark druids and the duke was mustering fresh troops for the king to bolster the southern forts. On hearing of the troubles, Harold Hunt had decided to re-enlist. The raw recruits would need some experienced officers. He'd been given his old rank of lieutenant.

This left Cameron short a man. He was interviewing prospects for a new roustabout, but we all knew that Harold had been much more than just that to him. Loss of the cook wagon was a blow as well. It was to be used to supply the soldiers on their march south. Noah and Aaron were hastily converting one of our more standard wagons to serve our needs, but the various accoutrements were in short supply. Until we could acquire them, we might lack for the good hot meals to which we'd grown accustomed.

Hence it was a bleak company which set forth toward our next stop. Soon into our journey, we saw the open field on which the troops bivouacked. We saw men being drilled and put through their paces. It was with many a fond farewell that we delivered Harold into the waiting arms of his new unit. He left driving our cook wagon. I considered myself as patriotic as the next fellow. But although I'd heard an army marches on its stomach, it still kind of rankled that now they'd be marching on ours.

We didn't tarry to trade. It was known that if the commanders glimpsed something they considered needful, they might requisition it through their quartermaster. Such purchases were paid for with military scrip, which was devilishly difficult to dispose of and required a lengthy stop at the provincial capital. I was fairly certain that no government could ever survive long if they took to using paper as money.

At the caravansary, we'd been warned about a plague spreading through the lands to the south. Our caravan master had to invest more time each day plotting the safest route southward, skirting the affected areas. So we picked our way cautiously forward toward our goal of Lake Placid. The merchants among us plied their wares at each small hamlet. But we found the citizens wary and less welcoming to strangers at each succeeding stop. Eventually, Cameron threw up his hands and decided to cut his losses. He would count his blessings (all four of them) and turn back northward after our last stop at Conclave.

This final destination was drawing nearer each day, and I couldn't help but wonder about what my cousin and I might find there upon our arrival. I had, by this time, grown quite attached to the caravan and fond of the friendships that had blossomed therein. Once again, I was to be snatched from the bosom of that which was familiar and thrust into the unknown. Having gone through such once already bent my mind toward acceptance. Surely, at the conclave, I would meet new friends and find things to pique my interest in just such a manner as traveling abroad had become comfortable to me. I might even come to miss the pigeons that had been our constant companions since departing my home in Westarbor.

Taylor made shameless use of Royland's gifts to assess the newest members of the troupe, those who had joined us at the caravansary. He wouldn't put it past Lord Downham to insert another spy among our company. Master Ross had already vetted the men, but Taylor wanted to be certain. He conducted quiet interviews around the evening cook fires to assure the newcomers were who they alleged while my cousin sat nearby acting as a human truth detector. Nor was I permitted to join them in such endeavors.

"No offense, Lucas," Taylor had once rebuffed me, "but you're Ill-suited to clandestine maneuvering."

I had accepted Taylor's judgment on the matter, but the casual smirk Roy had tossed my way stung a bit.

Once again, Cameron called us to a halt. By this time, our wagon traveled at the caravan's head, preceding even that of its master. Although I didn't invoke it often, Master Ross was quite taken with my ability to smooth out the rough spots of the road ahead. It got us through the worst of the tangles on these backroads we were forced to ply. Moreover, my affinity for plants could push back the brush that encroached upon the roadways in places, but I had to step down to accomplish this latter feat.

At the crossroads ahead stood the by now familiar marker. The trail ahead led to the village of Shanningham, which was to be our stop for the night. At its center, a crude wooden sign had been staked into the ground. It was painted to depict a skull and crossbones, marking the village as being under the duke's quarantine. Apparently, the plague had spread since last we had gathered information on its progress. The signpost marked the cross trail as leading to Buntingworth, a hamlet so humble that it wasn't even marked on Cameron's map. Nonetheless, it was too late to turn back and still too bitterly cold to set up a decent camp.

With a deep sigh and an unhappy grimace, Master Ross decided to chance the detour. Whatever accommodations could be had at this 'Buntingworth,' be it even a simple barn, had to be preferable to spending the night outdoors. He would soon have cause to regret this poor decision.

And so it was that the Tomcats arrived late at night at a settlement too small to even be called a hamlet. The musicians were silent. Not only was the hour too late to properly announce our arrival, but the maestros also worried about their instruments. Though the snow had mostly melted, the frigid air wrought havoc upon their strings, causing them to fall out of tune and rendering them subject to breakage. Outdoors, they could only achieve a macabre, screechy parody of the songs they normally played.

The settlement lacked a proper mayor. Cameron met with its reeve to negotiate lodgings for the troupe. The amount he charged for the meager barns and rooms that could be let were outrageous, yet we paid them. The man had us dead to rights, and by his gloating grin, he knew it well. Roy and I were given a room at the ale-house cum inne suggestively named "The Shady Lady." To recoup at least some of his losses, Cameron had gotten a discount by promising a performance there on the following day. He also held out for meals as our new cook wagon wasn't yet fully up to snuff.

I was so tired that I headed directly up to our room, barely even noticing the lurid decor in the common room or other amenities to be had. I stepped into the room, wanting only to plop down on its rough, straw mattress and nod off. My shoulder was gripped by a restraining hand. Looking back, I saw my cousin was frowning.

"Lucas," he said, "do you still have that clay you carry about in your Bob?"

"I think I still have some," I replied.

"Fetch it out and give me a minute."

I rummaged through Bob and retrieved it. Roy was sending out his hive mites. To my mage sight, they appeared as little specs of light, like those thrown up by a fire when a log resettled. They were presently swarming over the mattresses and floorboards nearby. A half a minute later, I saw movement. A line of minuscule mites and bugs were snaking up the wall toward the single window that graced our room. A larger centipede skittered forth a moment later to join them. Another line came from the deer's head mounted on the wall. Some gnats and other flying insects joined the exodus from that source as well. After a few minutes, all of these had disappeared over the window sill and exited our room.

Roy then accepted the brick of clay and rolled it into a long ropy worm. This he pressed firmly along the crack through which his discrete little sparks had shepherded the offending pests. He took one last puzzled look at the deer head. It was a four point buck, not much of a trophy but the room's only nod to decor. Removing his cloak, he hung it over the hart's horns, then sat down on his mattress to unlace his boots. I regarded my mattress and its threadbare sheets. I could scarcely credit how many vermin had been purged from it.

"It should be safe enough now," said my cousin.

"Thanks, Roy," I returned.

"Sleep tight," he said.

Retrieving my sleeping draught, I prepared to do so.

***

When morning came, I again felt the odd lethargy that was a natural consequence of the green elixir. Rather than fighting to overcome it, I decided to lay abed. The caravan wouldn't set out early as was their habit, having promised a performance at The Shady Lady. For once, I could lounge about and enjoy a bit of rest while the sun took fully to the sky. Its first rays were just creeping over the windowsill as I groggily lay nestled in my mattress. I let my body gradually and naturally overcome the effects of the numbing draught.

Roy was absent from his cot, and the deer's head stared down unencumbered by the cloak he had hung upon its antlers.

After a time, I bestirred myself and made ready for the meal promised by the innkeeper during the prior night's negotiation. I didn't expect much, given the seedy nature of the establishment.

I considered the plague. It was the one thing that could cause a caravan not to be welcomed by a community. No one was certain exactly how sicknesses spread. One common belief was that it was carried about by small mites or animalcules too tiny to be readily seen. These would crawl all over everything they touched and infect healthy folk after they passed from someone who was ill. In this light, Royland's precautions on the prior night made sense.

You sure wouldn't want to get caught inside a quarantined area. In some villages, it got so bad that there weren't enough hale folks left to tend the sick. And those that there were had other problems. No one would come to trade, and they had trouble getting food and medicine. Whenever we encountered the skull and crossbones, we left there what supplies we could spare and bypassed the region entirely. The poor wretches would be killed outright by the duke's men should they be caught trying to flee such an area. I was soon to learn just how fleeting life could be and that any of us could be laid low by a sudden twist of fate.

Stepping down the stairs and emerging into the common room below, I was met by surprisingly delightful smells. The food being prepared seemed of a quality superior to what I would have credited. The locals stepping into the inne were the same bedraggled lot we had seen on the prior evening. Their clothes were patched and dirty. One even had a hound at his heels and no one objected. The room's appointments, on the other hand, seemed relatively recent and elegant. It was a dichotomy I couldn't fathom until I had circulated a bit.

"Hello, Mort," shouted a newcomer to the bearded barkeep.

"Hello yourself, Chester," the man replied as he garnished a plate and handed it to a barmaid.

"Word is we've got some dandy entertainment heading our way today, fit for fancy folks."

"Yup. Compliments of the house, it is."

People continued to arrive, drawn by the promise of a show. I hustled to a table where Taylor sat reserving a seat for me amid increasingly more pointed glares. The maestros and my cousin were setting up on a stage near the room's rear. The common room of the Shady Lady was larger than I had supposed based on the town's population (or lack thereof). I listened in on the chatter from a table nearby.

Apparently the proprietor was newly arrived from up north. After the prior owner had died, this Mortimer Wilkinson had arrived with ambitious plans for the Lady. He had invested a fair amount of coin into its expansion and was favorably regarded by those living nearby. He was known to be well-heeled and generous and was bringing a measure of prosperity to the small community. The citizens of Buntingworth now speculated that Goodman Wilkinson had somehow lured the Tomcats here. If things kept going their way, Mort'd be the one credited with finally putting Buntingworth on the map.

I ordered my complimentary breakfast with the serving maid when she passed by refilling drinks. When the band struck up, I could feel the joyous mood spread among the other patrons. They were being treated to a show the likes of which had rarely graced their dreary lives. Some were nearly dancing in their chairs to the lively tunes of the Tomcats' quartet. I was proud of my cousin. A year ago, I'd have never pictured him being the focus of so much cheer. As his drum set the time for the piece, I marveled anew at how much he'd changed.

"Your food will be ready soon," said the maid as she cast an intrigued glance toward the stage.

"You should talk to their drummer," Taylor casually remarked. "If you're nice, he might show you his magic."

Roy rarely showed off his magic. But that wasn't what Taylor meant, nor did she take it so. This joke had gone on long enough. Having been raised in the wholesome environment of his father's farm, I feared my cousin's new extroversion might grow into callous selfishness. Yet the archer kept egging him on. I resolved to ask Taylor to leave off when next we had a private moment.

Then the next ballad began. Why did it have to be that insipid song that had caused me so much grief? I knew Maestro Bok was proud of the piece, and it *was* catchy, but did he have to play it at every stop along our journey? When they got to the second verse, the one about how I'd run off the horde and saved the barony, there came a crash from the kitchen. Looking over, I spotted Mort sporting an angry scowl. Likely, he was only upset over the breakage, but he seemed to get over it quickly enough. Before long, he was completely relaxed and went back to garnishing the plates as a serving maid tidied up the mess.

Before long, my meal arrived. An ample sausage lay atop a pile of mashed potatoes swimming in a gravy that looked as good as it smelled. When it was set before me, I took up my cutlery and prepared to break my fast. A fly buzzed over and landed on the sausage to spoil the otherwise fine presentation. I swatted at it to shoo it away, but it lingered strangely. With a feeble hop, it landed upside down on the wooden table then began buzzing in circles thereupon. Annoyed, I squashed it with my palm and began wiping the mess upon my napkin.

As I once again took up my fork, my plate suddenly slid off the edge of the table to land face down on the floor. What the hell, Roy? I knew my cousin to be the culprit. Even now, I could make out the remnants of his little specs of magic swirling from the overturned dish and returning to him. I guess he was upset about my killing the fly, but what a spiteful way to retaliate. I glared over at Royland. He had ceased his drumming and was standing up even as the dog dashed over to snatch my sausage from under our table. My cousin looked angry as he stalked over.

I prepared to give him a good scolding, but he stepped right past me to whisper urgently into Taylor's ear. They were casting sidelong glances toward the bar where Mort stood staring at the commotion. The other musicians had by this time halted their playing, following a discordant, scratchy sound from Liam's vielle. As though to fill the void, there came a sudden whining from the dog, rising above the pall of silence that had fallen over the room. The other patrons looked on in shock as the hound violently gagged, retched and fell over to lay still.

Taylor suddenly leaped to his feet, overturning his chair as he jabbed a finger at the white-faced proprietor.

"I recognize you now, Truman Huber!" he accused. "You are wanted for questioning. That beard can't disguise your features. All in Westarbor know of your crimes. Come along quietly now."

In response, the man leaped over the bar and ran for the door. He paused only briefly to twist its handle, and in that pause had Taylor nearly upon him. Elbowing Taylor in the midriff, the wily innkeeper crossed the threshold and dashed without. But he hadn't accounted for the icy conditions of his front stoop. I watched with horror as the man's feet shot upward and he came crashing headfirst down upon its wooden planks. There was a sharp crack as his head encountered the deck. He rolled to a rest with a split skull and his neck bent unnaturally. I was certain that whoever had coined the phrase 'head over heels' had never seen the like, for it had been quite the reverse. I was equally certain that Mortimer or Truman or whoever he was now lay stone cold dead.

The stunned silence was soon broken by an angry shout.

"He killed Morty!" cried a man near our table.

Several onlookers grabbed Taylor and roughly restrained him. Royland and I were soon surrounded as well. We made no move to resist as we were borne toward the back and hedged in by the locals along with the others from our troupe. Men were hovering over the still form of Mort, shaking their heads and casting angry glares our way. It was then we saw a most curious sight. We had thought the dog dead after witnessing its convulsions prior to its collapse. However, as we watched, it suddenly sprang up to a stiff-legged and stilted stance. It then fled through the gaping doorway, shouldering past the legs of the stupefied men.

It would be a long time before I puzzled out what all had occurred. We had some time to kill as we waited in our makeshift jail while the men of Buntingworth sent for their local lord to dispense low justice. The man Taylor had accosted was wanted in Westarbor for high crimes against the baron. He was a known spy and saboteur who had posed as an equerry at the baron's stables. It was suspected he was a mage as well. In defiance of the king's law, he hadn't declared this gift. It was also suspected he'd had something to do with the attack upon my father at the mill, using poor Madam Elsa as his pawn. I expect we'll never know the full extent of his deviltry now that he was gone.

Royland had sensed the intense hatred the man directed toward me. What he had against the Harpers was anyone's guess. Moreover, being most sensitive to insects, my cousin had felt the anguish of the fly when it had alighted upon my poisoned dish. At least the dog had survived eating that poison-laced sausage. Dogs are pretty hardy; perhaps it had retched it up quickly enough. His owner was still out looking for the mutt. Murderous Morty lay out in the woodshed, his cold corpse frozen stiff.

***

I sat composing what I wanted to say to Lady Megan as the wagon bumped along. It had been a straightforward matter to prove our right to apprehend Truman Huber. When the local knight had arrived, Taylor had simply produced the warrant for his arrest and various documents proving he was acting at the baron's behest. The townspeople still mourned the loss of their late benefactor, but were happy to divide up his possessions and seemed ready enough to carry on without him.

When we stopped for the evening, I would add to the letter. I had been composing it since we left Barony Stein. I wanted to include the bit about us arriving safely at Conclave. Once there, I would entrust the letter to Taylor, who would convey it back to the caravansary. It would be spring soon enough. In time, my letter would find a northbound caravan to take it the rest of the way.

Taylor too was holding back. He wanted to note the death of Truman, but didn't want to use up an extra bird until he could report our safe delivery as well. He would only have ten pigeons for the king as it was. Four of the remaining eight would be given to the conclave along with a dozen of Stein's grey-banded birds. The final four from Westarbor he'd keep to report on the progress of his shipment to Eagle's Keep.

I'd miss Taylor. We'd been through a lot together. At least I'd still have Royland. But, though he'd saved my life, my cousin was still cold to me. When I'd go back to join him in the wagon's bed, he would leave and sit on the bench beside Taylor. We'd scarcely exchanged two words since Buntingworth. Oh, he was civil, but only just. I think he was apprehensive about what we might find at the conclave.

I could see the lake off in the distance. Although perhaps not so large as Lake Ganymede, Lake Placid was the largest in Deerfield Duchy. It was almost perfectly round and was said to have been formed by the impact of a falling star. We got that story from the elves who in turn, had heard it from the woodland fey. This threw the lake's origin again into doubt because the fey were known to value tales more for their fanciful nature than for their truth.

Lake Placid sat several leagues to the north of the province's capital itself (also called Deerfield). I had been told that Deerfield the city was an urban metropolis larger in population than all the minor boroughs I had seen combined. Despite its name, one wouldn't likely find a deer therein, much less an open field not reserved for some particular civic use. In this capital sat the duke, and from it he and his council governed.

The village of Conclave had formed around the grotto near the lake where the conclave of mages met. It was divided into quarters (of which strangely there were five). Most of it was a fairly ordinary city with smithies, bakeries, and shops and with farmlands surrounding. The unique thing about Conclave was the mage's quarter and its centerpiece, the Academy. It was to this quarter (quintile?) of Conclave that journeymen aspirants such as Royland and I went to seek our new masters.

Selection by a master was a serious matter that would affect us for years to come. I hoped we'd each find someone who could best instruct us in our gifts and guide us toward masteries of our own. Better still, wouldn't it be wonderful to find a wizard who would take us *both* as journeymen?

The wagons stopped, and the Tomcats made ready for the final mile and the ceremony of welcome. Royland didn't join the minstrels up on their wagon. This would be his final stop. Yesterday evening, Maestro Bok had told us not to fear and revealed his new protege in the art of rhythm. Last week while composing near a stream, the good maestro had stumbled upon Addy and her girls doing their laundry. The new Tomcats Quartet featured Angelica Blessings playing the washboard, a set of thimbles affixed to her fingers. It may have lacked the deep resonance of Roy's goblin drum, but she made up for it in clickety-clack.

So as we approached the gates of Conclave, I smiled. Whatever changes the future held, I was sure I could manage them. Change wasn't always bad; it was just... different.

Epilogue

"Revenge is sweet and not [at all] fattening."

~ Alfred Hitchcock ~

"L-la-l-l-lah."

I stalked down the trail.

"L-la-l-l-lah."

It was a problematic thing for a small dog to kill a man; it was. Not a sure bet.

"P-pa-p-p-pah."

Pretty easy it was to kill an unwary child, though. And a child, despite her small size, at least had hands. I paused at the sign. It was the skull and crossbones; it was. And right next to it a stack of supplies. I kicked it over and moved on. Hands could hold a knife - a knife that could slay a sleeping man.

"K-k-ka-ka-kah."

I felt the cold closing in again. Although I couldn't verbalize as yet, it wasn't strictly necessary. So I thought it real hard: 'internum calorem.' This spell of inner warmth would keep the corpse I was 'riding' from freezing up, but it was costly; it was. My private cemetery was nearly tapped out. I knew where I had to go. Shanningham was just up ahead. I could practically smell the dead and the dying from the village wracked with plague. It wouldn't be enough at the rate I was burning my magic.

A month ago I'd had it all. Basking in my revenge on Westarbor, I'd headed south. I took on a new name. As my father was once Sir Geoffrey Wilkins, I thought 'Mortimer Wilkinson' would be a dandy alias for a promising young necromancer. I found a fun little village well off the map, a place no one'd notice if a few men went missing. The Shady Lady Tavern was my new digs. After killing its owner, it was an easy matter to use my fortune to buy the place. I had respect. I had all the liquor and women I could want.

But then it all fell apart. I'd set it all up so nice. All Downham had to do was keep the cavalry from riding in to the rescue and Westarbor would've been a mere footnote in history. Then here comes a troupe of minstrels right into my place of business singing about Westarbor's salvation. Well, my revenge had a new name now; it did. And that name was Lucas Harper!

But first things first. I had to survive. I didn't know my gift could still work after my body was done in. How could I? Only now I could never rest to replenish my magic center. Only one thing would do that. Lucky for me, I'd scouted out the village ahead. I crept over the fence and entered the yard.

The man lived alone.

I pushed open the outbuilding's door, then quickly closed it behind me. On the nesting boxes sat the broody hens, them whose pecking made no nevermind to me. I started cracking necks. And as each expired, I felt a sliver of my magic return. What a ruckus they made. Good. I kept one alive, just breaking her wings.

Any minute now.

And the door flew open. Before me stood the woodcutter with his ax. He was strapping and well-muscled, just the type I was needing. His eyebrows flew up in surprise. It was no fox in his henhouse. I'll give him credit for not hesitating. As the axe bit deep into my chest, my hands sought his throat. There were faster ways to kill a man. I reckon I could've snapped his neck, but suffocation would leave me a fitter corpse. Nearly five minutes it took with him struggling all the while. But when it came, it was worth it.

As the man emerged into my private cemetery, I felt the influx of his life's energy and was wreathed by the ecstasy that accompanied it. My magic center surged as it filled near completely up. His body sagged in my clammy grasp, but I held him upright and squeezed until I was sure. Before his body could lose any of its warmth, I entered it and watched my erstwhile shell crumple to the ground. I left the broken chicken where she lay thrashing. I could come finish her off if she survived the night.

Meanwhile, I could rest toasty and warm in the woodcutter's cottage. He had a well stocked woodpile, as one might expect. This remote from the village proper, neighbors won't be an issue. If anyone *did* show up, I'd pretend to have the plague, and they'd sure keep their distance. I started pinching marks on my forearms while it'd still bruise.

Now, where was I? Ah, yes. Revenge. Since some little stripling of an apprentice mage had robbed me of my righteous revenge (and my life) it would only be fitting to return the disservice. It felt good to have a purpose again; it did. I stared into the flames. If what they said about him was true, my opponent was formidable. He could shake the earth, move large objects and the like. Too bad the poison hadn't worked out.

Moreover, he'd be at the conclave, surrounded by mages who could detect my minions with their mage sight. Hmmm. This would take some planning. I would be patient. Shanningham Village would be my haven for now. As I could only ride a corpse for four to six days, I'd have to nip out and find a fresh one now and then. Plague victims would do in a pinch if they hadn't rotted too far. I'd have to get them before they were burned, of course. Once winter passes, I'll have an easier time of it. I should make my move in the spring. Though figuratively speaking the old saying might be true, for me, 'revenge is a dish best served warm.'

I never understood why I had such difficulty making intelligible speech when riding a corpse. It was like the part of the brain that governed such was unavailable to me. It probably didn't help that most of my practice had been with animals. If I was to go on not living like this, it sure would be useful if I could verbalize. I think I have to learn to speak all over again like a baby, but I'd do it or... well... *keep* trying.

"M-ma-m-m-mah."

Afterword

Dear Reader,

Not everyone reads an author's afterword. I myself often skip them and usually only give them a read when I have thoroughly enjoyed the book and it leaves me wanting more. I thank you in advance if this is your sentiment or else for your diligence in doing so. Originally, this book was to be named "Chaos at the Conclave" and I had lofty plans for Lucas and Royland to meet and interact with the other mages there. The caravan trip was to be a few chapters to set up some plot elements and ready the reader for the main action.

In writing the journey, however, I was drawn into the exciting world of the trade caravan and its potential for excitement and mayhem. I like to keep my readers' interest through the 'boring bits', but in detailing these scenes I invested too heavily in the 'minor players' and my word count was rising too rapidly to do them proper justice in the framework I had envisioned. Like George Bernard Shaw's Pygmalion, I had become enamored of my own creation and thoroughly trapped.

I was reluctant to cut out any of the action on the road to Conclave. Rather than shorten the trip as any good editor might have advised, I extended it and made it the primary focus of the story. I therefore decided that "Chaos in the Caravan" would be a more proper title for such a novel. The adventures of Lucas and Roy at the mage academy could always be continued in future tales. Rest assured that many ideas for such are already percolating in my mind.

Sales on my first book, "Mayhem at the Mill" were lagging as was typical for most self-published titles. And COVID-19 had forced us all indoors. Since my many other activities were curtailed, I decided it was time to buckle down and complete a second novel. I became concerned when writing chapter two,

'The Minstrel.' I liked how the writing was flowing, but I felt it was missing something. The answer turned out to be simple. One couldn't properly write a chapter involving music without a more thorough understanding of the topic.

I have always been musically inclined. My senior choral group was one of those activities that had been 'harshly curtailed' by the Corona outbreak. I was sitting out on my porch one morning feeding the birds when a song came to me. I'm fairly good at 'Name that tune,' but couldn't for the life of me place it. Taking this as a basis, I composed 'A Knight's Lament.' My sister, Terry, helped me with the timing and arrangement. I went on to compose 'The Gates of Westarbor Keep', 'Fair Folk Hearken', 'The Westarbor Waltz' and some others.

You may have noticed this book is dedicated to 'The Curfiss Family.' Let me tell you a little about that. Some of this you may recognize as inspiration for my writing. My father ran a small construction crew. A fellow named Dave Curfiss came to work for him when I was a young man. Dave was (and is) a character. His stories, jokes, and antics always made the days seem shorter. He was also an older guy other than my father in whom I could confide.

The opening joke that launches this tale: 'Green Side Up,' is one first told to me by Dave. And though it was not one of his better ones, I hope I used it well in my writing. His humor helped shape my attitude and outlook on life. Sometimes, when I am writing dialog for 'Uncle Robert' in these stories, I think to myself: 'What might Dave say about that?' That's a deep impact for forty years later.

I have four sisters. Third eldest is my sister, Christa. While working for my father, Dave started dating my sister, and they were married. Christa and Dave love children and wanted a large family, but because of a rare blood mismatch could not bring new babes to term after their first son was born. Their hearts were just too big to be stymied by this, however. Through fostering and adoption, Chris and Dave extended their family and are now grandparents many times over.

Christa is a registered nurse and has for many years specialized in maternity and delivery. As to Dave, we could all do with an 'Uncle Robert' in our lives. So to Chris and Dave and all their beautiful family, I dedicate this novel.

If you would like to know more about me or my writings, please visit my website at www.thormans.org. Feel free to leave a comment or ask a question. Writers live for feedback from their readers. Make sure to check out the songs I've written and recorded which relate to the novels. I'll be embedding them into the audio versions of the books, but they're kind of fun to hear if you enjoy Mayhem and Chaos.

Till Next Time Then,

Dan

Appendix I

Fun Fact: The 'old tongue' I use for spell verbalizations is simply Latin. You can usually plug a spell name into a Google translation to find its literal meaning. Below is a fairly comprehensive listing of Spells used thus far in my books:

aqua exstinguit	Water Quenches
ambulare interitus	Withering Stride
capturam petram	Catch Rock
digitus flamma	Flame Finger
gloriabitur securis	Force Axe
iactare spheara	Spinning Toss
impedimente	Shield/Protect
inexsuperabilis	Permanent Wooden
permanens lignea	Impregnability
internum calorem	Inner Warmth
levare et colligentes	Lift and Pull
levare et conicere	Lift and Throw
manent vigilate	Remain Alert
miscere cogitata	Combine Thoughts
motis cessabit	Calm of the Grave
podagra flammae	Gout of Fire
praemium	Explode
radet ovium	Sheer Sheep
spacium girabit	Rotate
sternetur tinea munda	Maggot Cleanse
suspendium tenaci	Choking Grip
tenera pluviam	Tender Rain
terram aratro	Earth Furrow
viburnum pugna	Snowball Fight
visio tenebris	Darksight

Appendix II

Elven

When Tolkien wrote of his elves, he developed a large body of lore surrounding them, including a language and runic alphabet all their own. Rather than adopt these tropes, I decided to work out my own traits, idiosyncrasies and history for a long-lived and distinctive people living alongside humanity. Pointy ears - check. Slender of build - check. Habits and predilections? These were an open book to me.

I do confess to one slight bit of quasi-plagiarism. Rather than invent an entirely new language, I chose instead to base my 'Elven' speech on a well established fantasy language to give it a proper grammatical structure. I use an English-to-Klingon translator then massage out the glottal stops so the 'Elven' language can be more flowing and lyrical.

It seems to keep a nicely consistent vocabulary... It also forced me to think of alternate words for those that proved untranslatable. I wonder whether this would count as cultural appropriation? It wouldn't do to have a group of angry Klingons (or trekkies) after me! Here is a fairly comprehensive listing of the 'Elven' phrases presented in this novel and their meanings. They are listed in the order in which they appear.

"Benalavioshi, rothuchi ioshi!" (Benalav, hold these a moment!)

"Nuvapua watheesh" (The first people; elves)

"Najhema siqua!" (Forest bear!)

"Jhivath shohvath batlaponia noba" (You do me honor with the gift of your name)

"Beniwia jitejhenom, sovath" (You're walking too fast, sister)

"Ngengi vileah vinay, Benalavioshi" (I want to see this lake, Benalavioshi)

"Weja nitevia lothnia. Lucas vilessa" (We're not alone, brother. I see Lucas)

"Benalav batlamey Najhemaram" (the glory of the forest night)

"Benalavioshi" (Little glory)

"Toolhup vejha Sorsoos" (Whisper of the wind through the trees)

"Hop leng poH" (The time to travel far)

"Vallahimay" (Profession; Wise skills)

"Chatha tutha miqua" (they are ashamed of their bodies)

"Iway jagha poH" (Blood enemy times)

"Wova zeja bosch tazbeth" (Our bright and shining queen)

"Waheevay puachoqua"

(Sylviculturalist; One who preserves the land and its resources)

"Puhi Lorédon nagemmahia" (The beautiful, forested land of Lorédon)

"Washtojavi!" (One who deceives!)

"Chushapethia" (Ice and snow)

"Hutejha tazbeth jibia, vanuji tinka ghajh!"

(By the queen's unshaven armpit, It is so huge!)

"Oho nuqua jatlah ghah" (That's what she said)

Appendix III

The Vulgar Tongue

When writing certain characters of the lower classes, I was often tempted to deliberately use poor grammar and eye dialect. In some cases, I do. But this quickly ceased to be amusing and, I thought, came off as hokey and trite. When conceiving the skulduggery surrounding Taylor's narration of the Tyrant and the Tinker, I decided to instead make use of the more colorful language of the rogues of England from the early nineteenth century. Though not strictly from medieval times, there was likely a similar dialect in use by the lower classes in those days.

I took as my main source the "1811 Dictionary of the Vulgar Tongue" by Francis Grose. I made up a fair number of words along a similar vein and took liberties with some few others. Only a few characters make extensive use of this mode of speech. And, as always, I try not to distract the reader with these bits and to provide adequate context to allow an immersive reading experience. Royland calls them 'a mish-mash of tortured similes and made-up words for nefarious activities.' I hope you enjoy their inclusion and offer this brief appendix as fair recompense for your forbearance. They are in the order in which they occur in the book.

"What's the cackle?"
(So, what news do you have for me?)

"If you want it, you need to do me an earnest."
(I'll tell you if you do me a favor)

"The lay is getting too grand for my gullet"
(It's becoming too dangerous for me)

"If I sing, I want your guarantee you'll do that"
(Promise me this, and I'll be your informant)

"Is your cackle worth the seed corn?"
(Is your information worth it?)

"A pair of checkered wabblers "
(Two of lord Downham's soldiers)

"Bus nappers" (Constables)

"Where they were diving"
(Where the meeting was taking place)

"Rum padders - the well-equipped sort"
(Heavily armed bandits)

"Prad" (Horse)

"Bung nipper" (Pickpocket)

"A tinker's dam" (A spot weld made by tinkers)

"Some royal's rust gets nipped"
(Some nobleman's copper is stolen)

"A hole that needs plugging"
(An information leak that must be stopped)

"Crashed" (Killed)

"Drinking tea with the pigs"
(Tortured by the authorities for information)

"I squealed, now where's the cheese?"
(I told you; where's my reward?)

"Prad prancers" (Horsemen)

"Bloody-backed buggers" (Soldier's wearing red livery)

"Lage of duds" (A buck of linen)

"Dandy prat" (Fancy Ass)

"Keep yer mitts from me whiffles"
(Keep your hands off my private parts)

"I'll give your nazy neck-stamper his bastings"
(I'll beat up that drunken boy of yours)

"The batty old egg cracker" (The crazy cook)

"Piepowder" (Traveling merchant)

"Spinning us a line" (Telling us a false tale)

"Too much of a bite" (Too much of an imposition)

"Look at 'em flickering" (Look at them gloating)

"I'll be your cross bite" (I'll be your willing accomplice)

"give them their bastings" (Give them a beat down)

"Bully beggars" (Imaginary beings to frighten children)

"Beggar's bullets" (Stones; or in this case, Snowballs)

"A bantling" (A child)